"You're going to Thailand."

Langford stared blankly at the American. "Me? Go to Thailand?"

"Just listen. Shiba has pulled the skids on you. That's fine. So you disappear. I can get you and the girl out of Japan, no formalities, no problems. Boat to Hong Kong, plane to Bangkok. From there, you go on up to the monastery at Suk Chiang and collect the dirt on Shiba."

"You're out of your bloody mind. I've got enough problems."

"You'll have more if you don't do as I suggest. The U.S. can't go into Thailand officially . . ."

Langford and the girl, Yita, left that night.

BERESFORD
OSBORNE

CHARTER
NEW YORK

A DIVISION OF CHARTER COMMUNICATIONS INC.
A GROSSET & DUNLAP COMPANY

Published by arrangement with Futura Publications Limited.

First Ace Charter Printing July 1981

Manufactured in the United States of America
2 4 6 8 0 9 7 5 3 1

FOR STEPHANIE

'When the American pilot was released by the Kempei Tai torturers, a Japanese officer came forward and unsheathed his famous Osamure sword. The prisoner tried to back away but his guards used their bayonets on him. Then the officer smiled and replaced the sword in its polished leather sheath, saying "We are the Knights of Bushido, of the Order of the Rising Sun. We do not execute at sunset but at sunrise".'

Extract from evidence given before the International Military Tribunal for the Far East, 1946

Prologue

I

It was a little after dawn when the young monk walked slowly across the open space separating .he main pagoda from the monastery's outer buildings, but already the heat was intense and the humidity oppressive. The echoing throb of cicadas had given way to the chattering of birds which darted colourfully among the tall palms and bamboos ringing the perimeter of the monastery. The air was very still and the hundreds of bells hanging from the pagoda and under the eaves of the other buildings were silent. But from within the long *kyaung* beyond the pool of the sacred turtles came the resonant chanting of monks at prayer, their incantations accompanied by the rhythmic plip-plop of clapper-boards.

Reaching the shade of a papaya tree, the young monk paused, staring towards the perimeter and into the thick jungle beyond. After a few moments, he went on his way, his head bowed. It was then that a long burst of automatic fire shattered the calm. The young monk spun round, staring upwards and flinging up his arms as the bullets ripped into his flesh. He crumpled slowly into the dust, the delicate saffron robe turning deep crimson.

High in the main pagoda, Soichi Heyashi sat cross-legged and peered down into the compound, his jaw hanging open as he struggled to believe the evidence of his startled senses. Khaki-clad figures suddenly streamed from the jungle. A grenade exploded against the flimsy wall of one of the *zayats*[1] which quickly burst into flames.

---

[1] *rest-houses.*

Four monks staggered out but were shot down immediately. More detonations followed, dull thudding sounds interspersed with the sharp rattle of sub-machine guns.

Alone in his tiny cell, Heyashi became aware of a painful tightening in his chest and felt the quick, uneven throbbing of his own heart. There was a blistering dryness in his mouth and beads of sweat prickled on his lined forehead. When he realized that he was holding his breath, he drew air into his lungs and the pain slowly subsided as he gradually emerged from his state of shock.

Heyashi leaned forward, frowning as he stared through the narrow slit cut into the stonework. He saw the group of novice monks file out of the refectory, their leader, a short, bespectacled young man, holding a length of bamboo to which a strip of white cloth had been attached. Heyashi knew the boy and shut his eyes as one of the attackers levelled his gun. It was impossible to distinguish whether the young novice was hit by one or several shots but when Heyashi opened his eyes again, the boy was lying on the ground, his hands still clutching the makeshift white flag. The other novices now stood in a line, their hands clasped on their shaven heads.

More monks entered the compound and were quickly herded together and ordered to squat. A series of explosions came from the other side of the monastery and sent dull, thudding echoes rumbling away into the jungle. The fragrant morning air was now filled with smoke and the smell of cordite. The attackers roamed the precincts of the monastery, shooting at random and firing the wooden buildings. Then three wooden carts pulled by oxen lumbered into the compound and the monks looked on, helpless as their food and treasures were looted.

The abbot's dwelling, a small but ornate building, was ablaze from end to end. As Heyashi watched, a monk ran screaming across the compound, frantically tearing at his burning robes. Then the man fell and lay writhing in the dust, his piercing shrieks cutting the air as he burned to death. The attackers seemed to enjoy the spectacle, many of them pausing in their work to stare at the monk's final agony.

The ox-carts were almost full now and the captive monks were being divided into two groups, each of the holy men being questioned at gun-point. After a few minutes, a group consisting mostly of younger monks was escorted to the edge of the jungle, leaving the others, nearly sixty of them, huddled together on the ground. Then the abbot was dragged into the compound.

Heyashi began to weep, the tears welling from his dark, slanted eyes and cascading down his parchment-like cheeks so that he had to keep blinking to maintain his vision. Not that he wanted to see what was happening below him. In his fifty years of life, Heyashi had witnessed too much bloodshed and had no desire to see more, but he felt compelled to watch, as if the simple act of seeing the bloody carnage was in itself a form of ritual penance.

The abbot, a frail man whose sixty or so years in the Buddhist monastery had left him ill-prepared for the events of that day, struggled with his captors and eventually regained his feet. He stared about him, his face expressionless. The cloying odour of burning flesh had displaced the more acid smell of cordite and the old man moistened his lips and swallowed as if to stop himself from vomiting. Then, in a soft, modulated voice, he began to speak to the attackers' leader, but another explosion drowned his words. Slowly, the old abbot turned to see a fiery pillar of smoke rising from what had been the refectory. Apart from the main pagoda, only two of the monastery buildings remained undamaged: the kitchen with its storerooms, and the hospice. Even as the abbot stared blankly towards its carved roof, much of which he had helped to re-build with his own hands after the Japanese occupation, the hospice was fired.

From his hiding place, Heyashi had been able to see what the abbot had missed: the three terrorists carrying a drum of the kerosene used by the monks for their lamps.

Through the uncovered windows of the hospice, the attackers had been plainly visible as they poured the oil over the teak floor and onto the bodies of the old and sick men who had expected death to come as a gentle friend. As the flames billowed upwards, Heyashi closed his eyes, his body swaying back and forth, convulsed by hopeless, helpless grief.

Heyashi opened his eyes again when he heard the shout from below, a stab of cold fear piercing his very soul. He hugged himself in a vain attempt to remain still but as he peered anxiously through the slit, he realized that the shout had not been aimed at him. The leader of the attackers was bellowing orders and although Heyashi couldn't catch the man's words, their awful meaning was soon made clear.

The abbot was being pulled towards a carved arch supporting a heavy, gilded canopy. The image of the reclining Buddha was pushed aside and quickly reduced to tiny fragments which sparkled in the sunlight shafting through the smoke. Then two men came with a rope which they secured to the arch.

Knowing what was about to happen, Heyashi prayed only that the head monk might die quickly. But his prayers were not to be answered. All he could do was to sit in the safety of his secret cell and suffer the pain of his own impotence. He fought the urge to vomit, resisting the vicious contractions of his stomach as he watched the execution of the man he had come to love as a brother.

Soichi Heyashi had entered the Me Win monastery near the Burmese town of Thayetmyo in 1945 but he was far from being the usual kind of novice monk. Apart from being very much older – he was then nearly forty-seven – he had come to Burma as a *Tai-i*[1] with the Imperial Japanese army. In the beginning, the Japanese had been welcomed as liberators from British rule but as the war progressed and they bled the country white for their own

[1] *Captain.*

12

ends, the Burmese welcome soured into a bitter hatred.

A sensitive man and an unwilling soldier, Heyashi deserted his post as Adjutant of the Thayetmyo garrison and sought sanctuary in the Me Win monastery. *Shin Toon* was one of the few monks who had extended the hand of friendship, taking the Japanese deserter into his own care, teaching him, helping him to come to terms with himself, protecting him against potential betrayal from within the monastery and the frequent incursions of the Japanese from without. By the time war had ended, Toon had become the abbot of Me Win and as the monks settled down to re-build in peace, Soichi Heyashi was finally accepted without question.

Time passed quickly and on January 1, 1948, the British finally departed and the Union of Burma was founded. There were weeks of celebrations, colourful processions and general rejoicing but the new nation quickly received a baptism of fire. Communist-led insurgents stirred up trouble, especially among the non-Burmese tribes whose territories had been included in the Union. Faced with the real possibility of disintegration, the Burmese government reacted harshly and the country was plunged into a bloody civil war. One of the prime targets for the terrorists were the Buddhist pagodas, always undefended and invariably yielding much-needed medical supplies, food and valuables.

And so it was on that April morning in 1948 that the rebels came to Me Win. In less than an hour, the monastery had virtually ceased to exist. The sky was darkened by the smoke which had risen above the flames, a pall for the many who had been gunned down or burned alive. The few who had abdicated their vows and joined the insurgents now stood on the edge of the jungle, discarding their robes as they watched the hideous finale.

Heyashi also watched. But unlike the young monks, he understood the hurtful humiliation and the reality of pain. Toon had been stripped naked and the rope tied around his ankles. Then the terrorists hoisted him up so that his old, thin body hung upside down beneath the heavily-ornamented canopy, swaying like a pendulum. As the terrorist leader shouted abuse, some of his men spat while others urinated against the abbot's head. And when one of the older monks stood up to plead with the rebels, his body was shredded by gunfire. Then two terrorists with long, curved knives came forward and began to hack at Toon's naked, living flesh.

Crying and whimpering like a child, Heyashi watched, his own body racked by the pain which he knew Toon was suffering. The knives were razor-sharp. Each cruel stroke split open his skin, releasing streams of dark, arterial blood which ran down to drip from his head until the ground beneath became a crimson quagmire.

As he prayed for Toon's death, Heyashi heard another shout. It was the final order. The air reverberated with the stuttering clamour of machine guns as hundreds of rounds were fired into the ranks of the sixty or so who had remained loyal to their vows. And as the last echoes of the shooting died away, a grenade exploded in the kitchens. The orgy of destruction was over.

The ox-carts laden with the supplies looted from the monastery lumbered slowly away into the jungle, followed by the rebels and their new recruits.

No birds sang and the only sounds were the crackling flames and the crash of falling timbers as the last buildings collapsed, sending showers of glowing sparks into the smoke-darkened sky. Only the pagoda itself remained intact, its massive stone blocks impervious to fire and bullets, the ornate, carved pinnacle continuing to stand guard over the faith as it had for nearly three centuries.

The sun climbed relentlessly into the sky and the birds returned to the trees surrounding the pagoda. But now they included vultures which circled high in the air, drawn by the scent of death. Heyashi watched them descend, his eyes red-rimmed and dry. He had no more tears to shed, no more grief to give.

For the Buddhist, life is *Anicca, Dukkha* and *Anatta* –

Impermanence, Suffering and Soullessness; each living person is the architect of his own destiny, the creator of his own *Karma*. Only when the cycle of reincarnation has been completed can *Nirvana*, the ultimate peace, be reached. But no such teachings could enable Heyashi to accept the bestial slaughter of his friend, *Shin* Toon.

Heyashi had supposed that government troops or the militia from Thayetmyo would come to the monastery, but they did not. And when he finally decided to move, the sun was already low on the western horizon.

With a heavy heart, Heyashi started to descend the narrow, worn stone steps, pausing when he was about halfway down. After a moment's hesitation, he turned and began pulling at a seemingly immovable pillar. The pillar did move, a slab of wall swinging slowly inwards to reveal the concealed chamber which housed the monstery's archives. Heyashi stooped and entered cautiously, waiting for a moment to let his eyes adjust to the semi-darkness.

The air inside was fragrant with the scent of jasmine and the coolness washed over his aching body like fresh rain. The masons who had fashioned the pagoda had done their work well. The sickening miasma of death had not penetrated the vault and Heyashi inhaled the cool, sweet air as he walked slowly along the rows of niches, feeling rather than seeing their contents in the gloom. Then he stopped as his fingers touched cold metal. Carefully pulling the object from its recess, he left the chamber, immediately pushing at the pillar which operated the simple pivot mechanism. The stone slab swung back into place with the merest scraping sound and Heyashi resumed his descent. Not until he reached the door leading out of the pagoda did he examine what he had removed from the chamber. It was a simple tin box, rusty and battered, its lid secured with thick hemp cord which bore the Me Win seal pressed into a heavy glob of yellow wax. Clutching the tin box under one arm, Heyashi emerged cautiously into the daylight.

The first shock was the sudden noise of the startled

15

vultures as they flew up, hundreds of pairs of wings beating the heavy air. Heyashi followed the dark, predatory shapes with his eyes. Then he looked down and suffered the second jolt.

Nearly all the corpses had been torn open. The gaping wounds were discoloured and already hosts to teeming hordes of maggots. Worst of all was the stench and Heyashi felt his stomach churn as he breathed it.

The abbot was dead. Perhaps because of the canopy, the vultures had left his mutilated body alone but the blood-caked corpse was crawling with flies. For a minute or so, Heyashi stared at the black, seething mass, a living shroud. Then he turned away, dropping to his knees. Only then did he finally vomit, spewing up the meagre contents of his stomach in an evil-smelling, yellow bile.

As soon as the paroxysm had passed, Soichi Heyashi stumbled blindly into the jungle, the small, tin box pressed against his body. He had no idea where to go. He only knew that he must flee for his life, find somewhere beyond the reach of his enemies. Later, he would seek revenge. But not against the men who had sacked the monastery and killed his only friend. The vengeance which Heyashi sought belonged to the past; his greatest sorrow caused by the fact that it had taken the bloody attack on Me Win to set him on what he had always known, deep in his own heart, would be his true destiny.

II

On September 28, 1948, five months after the raid on Me Win, Heyashi, bearded and clad only in rags, arrived at the *Wat* Keo above the tiny hamlet of Suk Chiang in north-west Thailand. As the crow flies, the distance separating the Thai hamlet and Me Win is some two hundred miles. But Heyashi was a fifty year-old monk and not a bird. Moreover, he was a fugitive who had had to travel mostly by night, avoiding even the rough tracks which passed for roads, and face the necessity of having to cross the Burma-Thailand border illegally. At a conservative estimate, he had travelled more than four hundred miles, all of it on foot and much of it through some of the most difficult jungle in the world. It was also the rainy season, the time of the monsoon, and when he staggered into the *Wat* Keo, leaning heavily on a stick and clutching the battered tin box, he was almost delirious. The monks took him in as an act of charity but when they saw the remains of the Me Win seal on the tin box, they knew that the sick, bearded stranger was one of their own kind.

Heyashi lay ill for nearly a year, frequently delirious and often comatose, but in January, 1950, one of the U.N. Medical Missions to Thailand arrived at Suk Chiang and was able to provide the drugs which undoubtedly saved his life. Nursed by the Thai monks, he gradually regained his strength. Once he had passed the crisis point, he was impatient to be well again. He had an important story to tell. Perhaps if he had been able to find someone with the right connections willing to listen, many things might have been different.

Desperately disillusioned and still far from fit, Heyashi confided in the head monk. His superior urged him to forget what was past and to abandon what he termed an 'unworthy quest for revenge'. Heyashi complied and the rusty, battered tin box which he had carried out of Burma, was placed in the archives of the *Wat* Keo and forgotten.

PART ONE

ONE

1

There was a deep depression centred east of the Korean
peninsula over the Sea of Japan and moving slowly
southwards. The consequences of this phenomenon were
that the northern island of Hokkaido experienced high
winds and heavy snow falls, while Kobe, Japan's second
largest seaport some seven hundred miles south of
Hokkaido, had very little wind but a lot of rain. It was also
extremely cold.

As he drove into the Kobe dockyards at 6.45 on the
morning of Friday, November 4, 1977, Kit Bailey knew
nothing about the total meteorological situation and could
not have cared less. The windscreen wipers of his Datsun
were going full-pelt but still his visibility was limited to a
few, blurred yards. It was only just beginning to get light
and Bailey frowned as he peered through the windscreen,
carefully piloting the car through the maze of bonded
warehouses and workshops. The rain was inconvenient
and uncomfortable but the Japanese workers seemed
oblivious of the weather. During the eleven months he had
worked in Kobe, Bailey had noted that the rate of progress
on the ship known as BC-9 had remained virtually
constant. Neither the cold, wet winter nor the hot, humid
summer had made any difference. There was little
absenteeism and a seemingly constant enthusiasm for
work.

Only once during his stay had the pace slowed and that
was in the spring when the labour force had begun their
annual pay talks. It was known as the Spring Offensive, a
time when virtually the whole of Japanese industry went

21

on strike or worked to rule. As always, it had all been very orderly and polite, the disruption lasting just ten days, by which time the board of the Shimada Corporation and the workers' representatives had reached agreement. But that year, the pay talks had coincided with *sakura*, the time of the cherry blossom. Avid tourists even in their own country, the Japanese would put on their best clothes and travel many miles to see the pinky-white clouds of blossom and take hundreds of thousands of photographs. Kit Bailey had found it a curious spectacle and would have liked the opportunity to delve deeply into the mythology of *sakura*. But there had been no time. BC-9 was behind schedule.

He halted the Datsun outside the gates which separated Pier 13 from the rest of the dockyards, wound down the window and presented his pass to the security guard. All the guards knew him, knew the car and knew that he had Grade One Security clearance, but the checking ritual was always thorough. When they were satisfied, the gate was opened and Bailey pressed his foot on the accelerator. After driving a short distance along the pier, he swung the Datsun into the parking lot and switched off the engine.

Staring through the rain-streaked windscreen, he sighed as he buttoned his heavy, American-style trench coat. Then he turned and picked up the laminated safety helmet from the passenger seat and jammed it on his head. The crash-hat was white with a red band which identified the wearer as a senior executive, and over the stubby peak at the front there was a stylised *S*, the logo of the Shimada Corporation. Bailey resented having to wear the hat but the regulations were unequivocal and rigidly enforced. He sighed again and stared out at the sheeting rain which drummed rhythmically on the roof of the car. The dark hulk of BC-9, a massive tribute to Japanese shipbuilding technology, towered over the pier, dominating the yard and dwarfing men and machines alike.

Reluctantly, Bailey opened the door and left the warm interior of the car, shuddering as the icy-cold rain slashed against his face. His hands dug deep in his pockets, he walked quickly towards the group of huts which housed his office. All around him on the pier, other figures moved through the rain, their yellow-coloured safety helmets indicating that they were mostly labourers. Some were heading towards the gate at the end of their shift. Others were busy at their appointed tasks. Brightly-painted fork-lift trucks, their hooters blaring monotonously and their tyres sending up plumes of water, pushed, pulled or carried their loads with a strange kind of determination, like so many mechanical ants. The air reverberated with noise – the persistent whine of drilling punctuated by the ear-splitting crack of heavy steel rivets being driven home. But Bailey was no longer conscious of it. After nearly a year, his ears had somehow learned to filter out the metallic cacophony, leaving his brain insulated and free to concentrate on the job.

Reaching the huts, Bailey flung open the door and went inside. He threw off the safety helmet, hung his sodden coat on a hook and went straight to the coffee machine, feeding in the 100 yen coins and then waiting for the plastic cup of hot, brown liquid to appear. It didn't taste much like coffee but Bailey had adjusted to that too.

Because the huts were sited at an angle, Bailey was able to sit at his desk and see the entire length of BC-9. It was an awesome sight. When it finally sailed, BC-9 would be the world's biggest merchant ship. At one thousand, three hundred and eighteen feet, six inches, in length, BC-9 was just eighteen inches short of a quarter of a mile long. She measured two hundred and fourteen feet, eight inches, across her beam, had a deadweight of 492,000 tons and drew 102 feet, seven inches. She was also well powered by an I.H.I. turbine set rated at 51,164 shaft horse-power, giving a maximum speed of seventeen knots. But the real beauty of this mammoth sea-going giant lay in her computer-controlled simplicity. Including the captain, the total complement did not have to exceed seven men and in an emergency situation, one man could effectively control and navigate the ship, sitting at a huge console which didn't even permit a view of the sea.

BC-9 – the letters stood for Bulk Carrier, the figure signifying that she was the ninth big ship to come into the Shimada fleet – was the realization of a dream by Toshiro Shiba, the multi-millionaire boss of the Shimada Corporation. But the dream had threatened to become a nightmare. Begun in 1973 in a specially constructed dry dock at Yokohama, the ship seemed to symbolize Japan's growth and prosperity. With her keel barely laid, Toshiro Shiba was able to contemplate the world-wide interest with satisfaction. All his instincts told him that he had backed a winner; that BC-9 would eventually become the first of many such ships with operating profits running into billions of yen. Then came the 1974 oil crisis.

All over the free world, stock markets collapsed, currencies which had looked so reassuringly hard proved catastrophically soft and the price of oil, capitalism's life-blood, rocketed. Some of the biggest tanker fleets were dispersed at giveaway prices while most of the others were laid up to gather weed and barnacles in the most inexpensive anchorages their owners could find. For a brief period it looked as if Karl Marx's prediction of the demise of the capitalist system was about to come true. In boardrooms in almost every major city, the men who controlled vast industries and the lives of millions of workers, were forced to take agonising decisions. Panic was in the air. Almost everything on which they depended had suddenly become unstable.

In his lavishly appointed Tokyo office, Toshiro Shiba had to face the possibility that the result of the Shimada Corporation's immense investment in BC-9 could be nothing less than the world's biggest white elephant. But Shiba was not a man to panic. He refused to regret what was past or be intimidated by the present. Instead, Shiba looked to the future, watching and waiting. He didn't wait long. By the end of February, 1975, he saw a way out, a means of using the ship profitably. That it would require many more millions of yen was almost incidental.

The first stage was the reconstruction of the Corporation's dockyard facilities at Kobe. Working flat out, these were completed by the beginning of June, 1975, and the BC-9 was then towed around the coast from Yokohama and made fast to pier 13. The thick, steel warps had barely been secured before teams of men poured into the hull to begin work. At first, Shiba himself directed operations, making use of specialists available within the Shimada Corporation, but it soon became clear that outside help was needed. Shiba's requirement was for a very special kind of man and as progress on BC-9 slowed in the autumn of 1975, a small team of trusted people began touring the world in search of that man.

With typical Japanese thoroughness, Shiba's lieutenants drew up a short-list and then proceeded to collate complete dossiers on each of the men whose names appeared there. There were three Americans, two Germans, two Englishmen and a Frenchman. Each was subjected to discreet but searching inquiries. By March, 1976, Toshiro Shiba knew the most intimate and private details of each unwitting candidate. Bribery, interception of mail, telephone tapping and even illegal entry had been used to secure the data which Shiba required. He now knew the men, their families, their health records, their financial situations and their political affiliations. Some were married, some were single. Each had arrived at his position by a different route. One was a known Communist, another had flirted with Fascism. One was a homosexual and another was dependent on a mixture of alcohol and drugs. But they all had two things in common: all were highly qualified nuclear physicists with practical experience, and all possessed additional knowledge of heavy industrial engineering.

Toshiro Shiba spent a week going through the files and then made his selection: Christopher Edwin Bailey. A graduate of Cambridge University with post-graduate qualifications from Harvard, Bailey had worked for a time with the United Kingdom Atomic Energy Authority before returning to Cambridge to carry out a research project into the re-processing of nuclear waste. From there he had gone to work for the German Bayer Group at Leverkusen. He was single, in good health and had no political black marks against him.

On Tuesday, April 6, 1976, Bailey received a telephone call at his apartment in Schlebusch. The following day he lunched with one of Shiba's top executives in a private room at an hotel in Cologne and received an offer that amazed him.

There was no question of Kit Bailey refusing to come to Japan. At first, he had hesitated on the grounds that he already had a contract with Bayer but like a poker player sitting on four aces, Toshiro Shiba simply put more and more money on the table until the English physicist knew that he must accept.

Bailey's contract was set for one year with the option of a six month extension. All his expenses would be paid and his salary would be the equivalent of fifty thousand pounds sterling, not subject to Japanese taxation. In addition, a further sum amounting to two hundred thousand pounds would be credited in quarterly instalments to a Swiss bank account. Born of poor, working class parents in Manchester, Bailey's life had been governed by a mixture of poverty and scholarships. By accepting the contract with the Shimada Corporation, he would be able to concentrate on the research of his own choosing and never have to worry about money again. It was this security which had provided much of Bailey's initial enthusiasm for his work in Kobe, but as the months had passed, he began to experience a growing feeling of discontent.

For all his engineering experience, Bailey was a scientist, a brilliant technician who could convert abstract theory into the practical – and profitable – reality. His work on BC-9 made him unique. Scarcely a week passed without some major or minor scientific breakthrough. He wanted no commercial benefit from his work above what he was already receiving and knew that most of his discoveries were of little commercial interest. But as a scientist, he wanted to write papers, give lectures and enjoy at least some of the prestige accorded by the scientific world to men and women who contribute to Mankind's knowledge. It was not to be. His contract with the Shimada Corporation demanded total secrecy and as his time in Japan drew to its close, Bailey was becoming increasingly reluctant to remain silent.

As he stared at the looming hulk of BC-9 on that November morning, Kit Bailey was pondering another and more immediate problem. Her name was Yita Izumi, a Eurasian Japanese girl whom he had met at a party shortly after arriving in Japan, with whom he now shared a small but luxurious apartment on the Yamamoto-dori. At first, the attraction had been purely physical. But if their love-making had always left him deeply satisfied, it was the way she cared for his every need which had slowly made him realize that he loved her deeply and wanted to marry her. Yita had taken his sudden, blurted proposal with a strange, calm detachment which seemed to border on sadness. Then she had refused in such a way as to indicate that she would never consent.

Bailey sat at his desk and stared at the ship, the memory of Yita still fresh in his loins. He wanted to leave Japan, wanted to go home. But he wanted Yita to go with him as his wife. He knew – or thought he knew – that their life together would be good, that he could make her happy – as happy as she had made him during his stay in Kobe.

2

The coffee had gone cold and tasted even more brackish than usual. Bailey threw the plastic cup into the bin specially provided, rose from his seat and began pulling on the lightweight waterproof overalls he wore when aboard

BC-9. As he secured the long zip up the front of the garment, he caught a glimpse of himself in the mirror and stared for a moment, scowling slightly at the reflected image. In two day's time, he would be forty years old. The face belied his age but Bailey still scowled at the thinning hair and the pale, pasty complexion of his face. His eyes were red-rimmed and bloodshot. He needed sleep.

Jamming the safety helmet on his head, Bailey left the hut and crossed the pier to where a gangplank rose steeply against the ship's side. Nodding to the watchman, he climbed upwards, the rain spattering off his overalls. When he reached the top, he glanced briefly down at the quay and then stepped inside the hull.

The interior of BC-9 was another world. The unfinished steel decking was cluttered with tools, equipment and thick cables which curled everywhere like so many snakes. Bailey stepped over the cables with practised ease, adjusted the position of his crash-hat and began to walk for'ard, his broad shoulders slightly stooped, his eyes narrowed as he took in a mass of detail. Some of the men greeted him with a nod or a wave but no one spoke. Apart from the language difficulty, the inside of the steel hull amplified and echoed the noise so that any meaningful conversation would have been impossible, even if Bailey had had any command of Japanese. He could have had an interpreter with him but preferred to go his own way and only made use of the man for the daily progress meetings held in his office at noon.

He glanced quickly at his watch. It was still only a little after seven, leaving a good four hours before that day's meeting. It was rather special because Shiba himself would be there. Not that Bailey had any worries about that. They were ahead of schedule and over the past few weeks, problems had been few and minor. Only one part of the ship worried him.

Bailey turned off the main companionway and mounted a temporary flight of steps constructed by the carpenters. One of the men was still working on the steps as Bailey ascended but he stood aside and smiled. Bailey nodded, absently, and continued on his way, concentrating on his route. There were two more vertical ladders and some hundred yards of litter-strewn walkway to traverse before he could climb out on to the main deck.

At this stage in the ship's construction, the main deck was little more than a desolate expanse of steel plating which glistened in the rain. Bailey paused for a moment, trying to imagine what it would be like to stand on the deck once the ship had gone to sea. Then he glanced round and noted that the carpenter had followed him. There was nothing particularly odd about the man being there but something made him look again across the rainswept deck. The man had vanished.

Shrugging to himself, Bailey walked carefully along the deck until he reached a massive opening. He squatted down, shrouding his eyes with his hands as he peered into the gloomy interior.

Nearly two hundred feet below, a team of welders was at work. The men were barely discernible but Bailey could see the iridescent flashes of their acetylene torches and the showers of bright orange sparks which spewed around them in the half-light.

On a conventional cargo vessel, the interior of the hull is divided horizontally and vertically to provide a series of holds at different levels. The construction of the BC-9 was radically different and from his vantage point on the main deck, Bailey was able to peer right down to the inner lining of the hull at the very bottom of the ship. Put simply, the hull of the BC-9 was more or less completely hollow. When the vessel was commissioned, the hollow spaces would be filled with specially prepared linings, insulants and cooling systems, all of which Bailey had designed single-handed and which were at that moment being brought from Yokohama on purpose-built barges.

Bailey had hoped to be able to see rather more of the work going on below him without having to leave the main deck. Because of the layout of the ship, the only means of

29

access to where the welders were working was through the hatchway. The welding team had made the descent by rope ladder and rising to his feet, Bailey walked across to the steel bollard to which the ladder had been secured. He contemplated the ladder for a moment, glanced down at the flashing acetylene torches and then moistened his lips with the tip of his tongue. One of the problems he had come up against during his work on BC-9 was the discovery that he had no head for heights.

Kneeling down, Bailey rubbed his hands together and prepared to descend. Then he caught another glimpse of the carpenter. The man was coming towards him along the main deck, almost strolling, casually. Bailey frowned, trying to decide just what the carpenter was doing on deck and what it was that puzzled him about the Japanese. Then he became conscious of the rain drumming on his helmet and eased himself on to the rope ladder.

It was not pleasant. The ladder swayed abominably and he could feel his palms streaming sweat. Little pockets of intense heat stung at his armpits and his crotch. His legs suddenly buckled and he paused, taking slow, deep breaths. His mouth became very dry and swallowing required an immense effort. With painful slowness, he resumed his descent but after a few feet was forced to stop. He felt an almost irresistible urge to look down but knew that he must not, that if he did, he would lose what little was left of his nerve. Instead, he stared upwards at the large square of light.

His heart pounded painfully in his chest as his eyes picked out the dark silhouette of the man peering down at him. Seen against the rectangular patch of light, it was impossible for Bailey to positively identify the figure poised some fifteen feet above him, but he knew beyond any doubt that it was the same man who had followed him to the main deck. He also discovered what it was that had been puzzling him: the Japanese was not wearing a safety helmet.

It was entirely irrational for Bailey to suppose that the

30

absence of a laminated plastic helmet was incontrovertible proof that the man intended to kill him. But some sixth sense which owed nothing to any scientifically-based logic told him just that.

In the micro-second which it took these thoughts to pass through Bailey's mind, his body had already begun to react. There was no question of him continuing the descent. It was too far and would allow the Japanese too much time. He had begun climbing upwards without being wholly aware of his actions. Then the ladder jerked and as Bailey's feet lost contact with the rungs, he swung outwards, his entire weight suddenly dependent on the strength of his hands.

His knuckles glowed a creamy-white colour as the rope bit into his palms and he struggled to get his feet back on to the rungs. Then the ladder gave another sickening jerk and Bailey looked up, catching one last, whirling glimpse of the dark figure peering over the edge as he fell away.

Bailey's scream echoed dully in the vast steel cavern as he plummeted down, his hands still gripping the rope with impotent ferocity when his body smashed against the unyielding steel plating at the very bottom of the ship. His spine was snapped in three places, his legs and pelvis splintered and his skull split apart against a jagged edge of steel, like an egg against the rim of a frying pan.

The team of welders neither heard nor saw him fall and only became aware of what had happened when the end of the ladder crashed heavily around them.

TWO

1

On the morning of Monday, November 14, 1977, Richard Trelawny Langford sauntered casually from Aldgate Underground in the City of London and headed down Aldgate itself towards Leadenhall Street. Considering it was a Monday morning, he felt surprisingly contented and was even smiling to himself. The weekend, which he had spent mostly in bed, had been a great success and in spite of the time of year, it was a bright, almost warm morning. Due to an industrial dispute, the *London Times* was in short supply that day but even if Langford had seen a copy, it is doubtful if he would have noticed the tiny paragraph on the Overseas News page about the death of Doctor C.E. Bailey. And had he chanced to read the brief, almost cryptic report, it would have meant nothing.

Pausing at a kiosk, Langford bought a pack of cigarettes and then mounted the steps leading to the offices of Maxwell, Hewens & Partners. Nodding briefly to the uniformed commissionaire, Langford took the lift to the fourth floor, staring at his reflection in the polished woodwork of the lift-car. Only then did the smile begin to fade from his lips. He disliked the overheated offices and the grinding routine of the insurance business. Not that his own work or life-style owed very much to routine but Langford had come to regard the office as a kind of prison. Then the lift came to a stop and the doors slid open.

'You're late,' said his secretary, looking up from her typewriter.

'Always,' Langford replied, going into his own office. 'Any coffee?'

Peggy Ashmore followed him in and placed a cup on the desk. 'I think you'd better guzzle that and get moving. Mister Maxwell wants you.'

'Maxwell?' said Langford, his expression one of surprise as he sat down and sucked at the coffee. James Maxwell, the senior London partner, did not usually arrive at the office until noon on a Monday. And he was rarely anxious for any direct contact with Richard Langford.

'He's been wanting you since nine-thirty. They tried ringing your flat but ...'

'Ah.' Langford stared at the clock on the wall which told him that it was five to eleven. 'I was away. For the weekend.'

'Was she nice?'

Langford smiled. 'Jealous?'

Before she could reply, the telephone jangled and she raised the receiver to her ear. 'Mister Langford's office ... yes, he's on the other line ... yes, immediately he comes off.' She let the receiver drop back into its cradle and raised her eyebrows. 'If you're wise, you'll run up to the sixth floor. The Old Man sounds rather unhappy.'

'Aren't we all?' Langford abandoned his coffee and walked to the lift.

'You're to go straight in.' Grey-haired Miss Pym in the outer office regarded him with stony contempt as he did just that.

'You rang, sir?' he said, lighting a cigarette.

Maxwell fixed him with an icy glare. 'Yes.' He made a show of studying the gold Omega chronometer on his wrist. 'Ninety minutes ago. Why weren't you here?'

'I didn't know you wanted me.'

'Would it have made any difference if you had?'

Langford was silent.

Scowling, Maxwell bit back his anger. As always, he was confused by Richard Langford. Most of the time he disliked him, despising him for his middle-class background, his very minor public school and the fact that he had been cashiered by his regiment. Everything,

33

Maxwell had often thought, was wrong with him. He stared across the desk, studying Richard Langford, his expression sombre. Tall with dark, wavy hair, the man's clothes were always immaculately tailored and yet worn casually, if not carelessly. His complexion was always lightly tanned, as if he had just returned from a skiing trip, and he gave an impression of an agile, wiry kind of strength.

But James Maxwell was a sound judge of character and he could appreciate Langford's good points. In spite of the terse, insouciant manner, he was good at his job. And he had no side to him. There was no pretence. Langford was a tough, brash devil-may-care young man with a reputation for laying any woman he cared to cast his pale, intense eyes over. For his part, James Maxwell was intelligent enough to realize that the root cause of his ambivalence was pure envy. For all his wealth, his well-connected background, his scholarly achievements at Winchester and the Military Cross gained in Korea, he was a dry, brittle man. The fact that he was one of the City's most respected insurance underwriters and that he had built a business which now boasted offices in New York, Paris and Hong Kong was of little account. He would have swapped places with Richard Langford any day.

'The Shimada Corporation,' he said and gestured Langford to sit when he was already seated.

'Japanese outfit?'

'In a way. A more accurate description would be multi-billion dollar conglomerate.' The dark pouches under Maxwell's eyes gave the impression of being filled with fluid. 'They're really a New York client. We're only concerned with their shipping interests.'

'Ah.' Langford smiled, expectantly. 'A trip to New York?'

'No,' Maxwell snapped. 'Hewens is flying over.' He looked again at the gold Omega. 'I want you to meet him

34

at Heathrow. His flight's due in about eight but check with my secretary.'

'I did have a previous engagement.'

Maxwell glared across the desk. 'Put her off,' he rasped.

'It's a he, actually. And we were going to play squash. Is it important for me to meet him at the airport?'

'A damn sight more important than squash. Anyway, he's just stopping over for a few hours, on his way to Paris.'

'Okay. What's it all about?' Langford flicked the ash from his cigarette into a cut glass ashtray the size of a soup plate.

'Difficult to say because I don't have all the details but it …' He hesitated, thoughtfully. 'The boss of Shimada is a man called Toshiro Shiba. He's a very big wheel indeed, commercially and politically.'

'So?'

'I should bank on a trip to the Far East, if I were you. It seems that the Japs are getting a bit accident-prone of late, which could mean that we have to pay out a lot of money. I just want to know what's happening.'

'How does Hewens fit in?'

'They're his clients but …' Maxwell leaned forwards, still frowning. 'Look, Richard, there's something odd going on.'

Langford permitted himself a wry smile. When Maxwell used his first name it signalled that he needed help, that the firm he had established after leaving the army in 1954 was running into trouble. 'Aren't you being rather less than frank?' he said, quietly.

'I spoke to Hewens late last night. It wasn't a good line but it seems there's been a number of claims lately which add up to more than the usual run of industrial accidents. Hewens says he's worried about it and so am I. He's very pro-Jap but just between ourselves, I've always been a bit wary of our little yellow friends. Anyway, we've agreed that you should go and take a look around. Just a little gentle probing. And Richard ...' Maxwell leaned back in his chair. 'Keep me informed, won't you?'

'You mean that you're not?'

'You know what I mean. If there's anything in this ... if there's any trouble, I want to know about it. Hewens may trust the beggars but I ... well, you know.'

'No, I don't,' said Langford, stubbing out his cigarette. 'But I can guess,' he added, rising from his chair, his lips twisting into a thin smile.

'You're a smooth bastard, aren't you?'

'I am what I have to be.'

'True,' Maxwell conceded. 'But don't let it go to your head. Conceit leads to carelessness and that in its turn usually costs money.'

'Bit early in the week for aphorisms. But don't worry, if there's any trouble, I'll let you know.'

2

Back n his own office, Richard Langford made two telephone calls, the first to a stockbroker in the City, the second to a journalist working out of Fleet Street. Then he went to the reference library on the ground floor, selected four large directories and returned to his office where he remained until shortly before four-thirty, missing lunch. On his way out, he stopped by Peggy Ashmore's desk, his gaze resting on her well-rounded breasts.

'Would it be easier if I took my top off?' she said.

'Depends what you have in mind. Right now, I'm going. There are four books on my desk to be returned to the library, if you will.'

'Anything else?' she countered, acidly.

'Yes. I'd like you to telephone this number. Say I've been called to an important meeting and won't be able to make the appointment.'

Peggy Ashmore took the slip of paper which Langford proferred. 'Another broken heart?'

Langford shrugged. 'Maybe. See you.'

His secretary stared after him. 'If her heart isn't broken, then at least something else might remain intact.'

'Like I say, you're just jealous,' he said, stepping into the lift.

Forty minutes later, Langford paid off the taxi outside the Wig and Pen in Fleet Street and went inside the club. He stood for a moment at the entrance to the ground floor lounge and then walked across to a table where a thin-faced man rose to greet him.

'Is there a story in this?' he said, without preamble.

Langford smiled and signalled for drinks. 'No, just a fee.' He pulled a manilla envelope from his pocket and laid it on the table. 'What have you got?'

The journalist shrugged. 'Not much, I'm afraid.' His hawk-like eyes rested briefly on the envelope. 'There wasn't much time. Probably not worth what's in there.'

'That's for me to judge.' He paused as the waiter came with their glasses. 'Okay, fire away.'

The journalist took out a notebook. 'Shimada Corporation. Headquarters in Tokyo, offices throughout the world except London.' The man hesitated as if expecting an interruption but none came and he continued. 'Big in shipping, mostly tankers. Property — that's almost all in the Far East; electronics and road transport in the States and Canada. They've got factories in France, Germany, Belgium and Japan, of course.' He paused again, rubbing his face. 'Not much on the directors. All Japs. Just so many names, really. Toshiro Shiba, he's the boss. Then there's the deputy M.D., a guy called Norihiko Samwashima and two others, Tasaki and Komai.'

'Is that all?' said Langford.

'For God's sake, I do have a full-time job and …'

'Okay, forget it.' He slid the envelope across the table. 'Here.'

'That's all right. It's not worth it.'

'Take it. It isn't my money.'

The man smiled. 'All right. And thanks. If there's

37

anything else you want, consider it already paid for.'

'Naturally.' Langford raised his glass. 'Cheers.'

'Likewise.' The journalist sipped his drink. 'There was something else, something that came over the tape. I only saw it by chance.' He flicked through his notebook. 'There was an Englishman, a man called Bailey, who was killed last week in one of the Shimada shipyards. Does it mean anything?'

Langford's expression tightened. 'I don't know. What else?'

'Nothing. It happened in Kobe. Said he was some kind of scientist.'

'Cause of death?'

'"Accident aboard latest Shimada super-tanker." That's a direct quote from the tape. Useful?'

'Possibly. Have you got his full name?'

'No ... yes, I have. Doctor C.E. Bailey.'

'H'm.' Langford drew a long breath. 'How quickly could you fill in the details?'

'Not before tomorrow. There's the time difference between us and Japan and I have other things to look after.'

'Very well. Get me as much information as you can without arousing too much interest. Call me in the morning. Okay?'

The journalist nodded. 'Are you certain that there isn't a story in this?'

Smiling, Langford shook his head. 'If there is, you'll have it. But meanwhile, you keep your mouth shut.' He stood up. 'That's just one of the reasons you get a fat fee for so little work.'

From the Wig and Pen Club, Langford took another cab to his mews flat in Groom Place off Chapel Street, just a stone's throw from Belgrave Square. He had acquired the flat from the proceeds of a legacy and if it was a bad investment from the point of view of the high outgoings which bit deeply into his income, it provided just the right kind of *milieu* for Richard Langford's social life. The interior was starkly masculine and the decor and fittings all spelled taste and money. Or extravagance. His other major source of expenditure was parked in the garage located below the mews flat: a rally-tuned TR7.

Lying in a hot bath with a whisky on the side, Langford stared up at the ceiling and let his thoughts range over the day's events. The idea of a trip to the Far East appealed to him for no better reason that it would be a break from the stultifying routine of the Leadenhall Street office. But he was less enthusiastic about the firm's New York partner, Meyrick Hewens. Nor was the problem of Langford's own making. On the face of it, the American was simply a partner looking after the firm's interests in the States. On the face of it. Richard Langford had made it his business to find out what even the most well-informed of Maxwell's senior executives did not know: James Maxwell was on the brink of retirement and had sold out to Meyrick Hewens.

Sipping at the whisky, Langford used his toes to start the hot tap running and resumed his study of the ceiling. After the army, he had been unemployed until James Maxwell had taken him on as a claims investigator. Right from the start, it had been clear that Maxwell had created the job as a favour to Langford's father, now dead. But for all that, Richard Langford had proved his worth. He knew that although Maxwell disliked him, he also trusted him and the two men shared a curious kind of mutual respect. Quite how he would get on with Meyrick Hewens, Langford could only guess. He had met the American just twice and neither occasion had provided much opportunity for conversation. His most vivid memory was of Hewens' wife, a vivacious redhead with deep-set hazel eyes which said bed in capital letters. Had the opportunity presented itself, he might easily have thrown discretion to the winds and taken Lois Hewens at her unspoken word. In the event, nothing had happened but as he climbed from the bath and wrapped himself in a heavy robe, Langford wondered whether Hewens would be bringing his wife with him on this trip.

Sticking to the fast lane of the motorway, Langford headed towards London's Heathrow airport. He kept the TR7 at a steady seventy until he was well clear of two police patrol cars and then pressed his foot to the floor. After a short burst at 110mph., he slowed down to a more sedate ninety and arrived at the airport a few minutes after Hewens's plane had touched down.

'I think you know Lois,' said Hewens when they emerged into the arrivals lounge.

Langford nodded. 'Nice to see you again, Mrs Hewens.'

'Please, you must call me Lois. And I'll call you Richard, okay?'

'Clever of you to remember.' They shook hands.

'We've booked in at the Post House,' Hewens broke in. 'I'm flying out first thing in the morning. Paris.'

'Ah,' said Langford.

He had parked the TR7 in a No Waiting zone. They all squeezed into the car, Lois Hewens giggling as she revealed her very shapely legs in the process of climbing into the cramped space behind the two seats.

Hewens had reserved a suite and once installed, Lois went to take a bath, leaving her husband and Langford in the lounge. When he had poured two good measures of Scotch, Hewens lowered himself heavily into a chair, his tanned, lined face set in a worried expression.

'I don't know how much James has told you,' he said.

Langford's thoughts flitted quickly over what he knew. 'Not much. He said you had all the details.'

'Okay.' Hewens paused to light a cigarette. 'The Shimada Corporation are building a new oil tanker. It's going to be the biggest in the world and we're handling the insurance. At the moment, it's fairly evenly split between Tokyo, New York and London. I need hardly explain that we're talking millions of dollars.' He drew on the cigarette and leaned back in the chair. 'Over the past few months, there's been a series of accidents on the ship and each one has resulted in a claim. In relation to the total liability, the money we've had to pay out so far hasn't amounted to all that much but ...' Hewens hesitated and fixed Langford with a penetrating stare. 'How much do you understand about the insurance business?'

'Enough.'

'Okay. The word has come through that the Tokyo market doesn't want such a big share of the Shimada business. In other words, they want out. That means London, because I don't think it would be economic from the client's angle to increase the New York share. You with me?'

'Yes, I think so.' Langford stubbed out his cigarette. 'Why don't the Japanese want to handle the business?'

'That's the question. There could be a number of reasons, some to do with the advantages of dealing in sterling or some other currency, others concerning overall policy. But it is unusual. However ...'

Langford was about to speak when he caught the sound of Lois Hewens splashing in the bath and for a moment or two, his thoughts took another turn. Then Hewens' voice broke in.

'Did James Maxwell tell you about a man called Bailey?'

The question was unexpected and Langford was nearly caught off-guard. 'No,' he answered, truthfully. 'He didn't.'

'We-ell, Bailey was an Englishman, a technician employed by the Shimada Corporation. He died last week in yet another accident aboard the tanker at Kobe – that's where she's fitting out. Now we all know that accidents happen but taken together with Tokyo's decision to off-load their share of the business, I ... we, James Maxwell and I, have agreed that you should pay a visit to Kobe and ... well, just take a look-see.'

'Are you suggesting that this man, Bailey, was murdered?'

Hewens gave a non-committal shrug. 'I don't think I

can usefully suggest anything at this time, Richard.' He chewed his lower lip for a moment. 'Keep it as one of your options, if you like. What I ... we need for you to do, is find out everything you can. You have a free hand to do whatever you think necessary but try not to tread on anyone's toes. And something else ...' He paused again, staring into his glass. 'I think it might be better if you reported directly to me on this matter. There's no point in James being overly worried about it.' He smiled, uneasily. 'Besides, there may be nothing in it to worry about.'

'What exactly do you expect me to find in Kobe, Mister Hewens?'

'Please, call me Meyrick. Hopefully, Richard, nothing.' He rose, took Langford's glass, and went to the sideboard. 'The other aspect of this matter which you have to bear in mind is Toshiro Shiba himself.' He placed the topped-up glasses on the table and sat down again. 'He's a big, important man. Very important. Nothing happens in Japan that Shiba doesn't know about. It's one of the reasons why the Shimada Corporation is so powerful. So, anything we can do to help our client must be beneficial to ourselves.'

'That still doesn't tell me what I'm looking for.'

'Go to Japan, Richard. Nose around a little. Find out if there is anything to be found out about Bailey and let me know. I think it's fairly safe to assume that your course of action will be dictated by events. And if you succeed, there'll be a big bonus in it for you.'

'Thanks,' said Langford, raising his glass. 'Here's to whatever I'm supposed to find in Japan.'

'*Kampai*!' Hewens grinned, revealing a set of evenly-matched dentures. 'Roughly translated, that's Japanese for mud in your eye.'

Langford nodded. 'Very probably. Do I have a contact in Japan?'

'Sure. You're expected but as far as they are concerned, your mission is simply routine. The usual inquiry pending our acceptance of a formal claim.'

'You mean a claim covering this man Bailey?'

'That's right,' said Hewens, leaning forward in his chair. 'I've arranged for you to see Samwashima. He's the Number Two in the Shimada Corporation and quite an important guy, so take care, huh?'

'How do I do that?'

'By being discreet.'

'Will I meet Toshiro Shiba?'

Hewens smiled. 'No way. You might just get to see the Emperor of Japan but Shiba ... forget it. Anyway, he can't be expected to know about this, so ...'

'What about Tasaki and Komai?' said Langford.

The American shot him a puzzled frown and then nodded. 'I can see you've done your homework. Well done. I like a man who finds out his facts first. But no, they don't take any active part in the running of Shimada.'

'Have you ever met them?'

'No, never. They're just names, kinda sleeping partners, I guess.'

'Tell me about this Mister Samwashima. What's he like?'

'Sam,' said Hewens. 'He likes to be called Sam. He's okay. Very polished, very shrewd and very westernized. You should get on well with him and you'll find that he goes out of his way to be helpful. In fact, I like to think of Sam as a real pal, you know?'

'Good.' Then Langford rose to his feet as Lois Hewens entered the room wearing a silk robe which revealed rather more of her body than it covered.

Hewens also stood. 'I want you to leave as soon as you can but perhaps you could spare tomorrow to look after Lois while I'm in Paris? As soon as I get back from France, we have to fly straight on to New York and I did promise her some sightseeing.'

'Of course,' Langford said. 'My pleasure.' And the sparkle in Lois Hewens' dark eyes told him that it would be hers as well.

43

THREE

1

The following morning, Tuesday, November 15, Meyrick Hewens flew from London Airport to Paris. By eleven-thirty, he had checked into a small hotel, *L'Auberge du Parc*, on the Boulevard St. Marcel. It was not the kind of hotel to which Hewens normally gave his custom. Like James Maxwell, he was a wealthy man who liked using his money to buy the best. But the hotel had two advantages which suited Hewens' purpose. It was relatively unknown and totally discreet. The American's sole concession to comfort was to take one of only three rooms which had private baths. Once installed, he changed into casual slacks, a fawn roll-neck sweater and a light anorak. Then he left the hotel and walked down to the Avenue des Gobelins until he found a pay-phone. The line was busy. Hewens stared out at the thin drizzle which had begun to fall and decided to stay put and keep trying.

By the time Meyrick Hewens eventually got his call through, his wife was sitting in a bistro called Jack's on Chelsea's Kings Road.

'This is perfectly charming,' said Lois, smiling across the table at Richard Langford. He helped her to oysters and a young, very dry Muscadet.

'Jack's an old friend of mine.' He grinned. Jack was short for Jacqueline, who had had the good sense to remain anonymous.

'I love oysters,' Lois cooed. 'You're obviously a connoisseur.'

'Maybe. But I'm also rather curious, so tell me, how

44

come you didn't go to Paris with Meyrick?'

She shrugged her sloping shoulders. 'Business. You know how it is? He'll be rushing around and I don't speak the language and ... well, you're here, aren't you?'

'Not for long. The call of the Orient and all that.'

'Long enough.' She sipped her wine and stared at him over the rim of the glass. 'I've never been to Japan. Have you?'

'No.'

'Meyrick has. Last year. But he wouldn't take me. Couldn't, I guess. More business.' She smiled, ruefully. 'I'll never understand men.'

'I would have thought that you understood them very well.'

She treated him to a knowing look. 'Maybe in some ways, but not in others.'

When they had finished the oysters, Langford reached across the table and gently took hold of her hand. She didn't flinch, as he had known she wouldn't. 'We have some duck to come. It's a house special. And after that, I thought ...'

'Yes?' Their eyes met.

'Some sightseeing, perhaps?'

'Depends on the sights. Do you know anywhere ... restful?'

'As a matter of fact I do. I think I know just the place.'

After lunch, they walked to where Langford had parked the TR7. He tore off the parking ticket and thrust it into his pocket.

'Is that expensive?'

'Cheap at the price.' He swung himself behind the wheel and started the engine.

Even Richard Langford was startled at the lack of pre-liminaries once they were safely inside the mews flat at Groom Place.

'Nice,' she murmured, looking around as she peeled off her tailored jacket and then pressed herself against him.

45

Feeling his body react, she drew a sharp breath. 'Very nice, Richard.'

They kissed and went quickly into the bedroom where he undressed her with the skill of a man who knows all there is to know about women's clothing. He tried to slow the pace but Lois Hewens had other ideas and within a matter of minutes, she was pulling him on to her with all the desperate urgency of a middle-aged virgin. But what she lacked in subtlety and finesse, Lois Hewens more than compensated for by her sheer animal lust. It was over very quickly and only then was Langford able to introduce her to the kind of love-play which he usually used to begin rather than end an encounter.

Later, when they were lying on the bed smoking, she chuckled to herself.

'You must have had a lot of women,' she said.

Langford raised himself on one elbow. 'I would guess we're about even.'

'That's not very complimentary to a married woman.'

'Perhaps.' Langford drew on the cigarette. 'Doesn't Meyrick ever ... well, complain?'

She shook her head. 'How old do you think Meyrick is?'

'I don't know. Forty?'

She smiled. 'One thing about my husband, he doesn't look his age. Would you believe fifty-four?'

'If you say so, yes. Does that mean ...?'

Lois nodded. 'I love Meyrick very much. He's one hell of a nice guy but he's a lot older than me and we don't share the same appetites any more.'

'Ah, I see.'

'But he's very understanding. He knows that I have my needs and so ... well, here we are.'

'Do you mean that he knows that we're ...?'

'My, we are prudish, aren't we?' She giggled, softly. 'Of course he knows. He's lived. He knows that if you put two healthy young people together, they're gonna react.' She leaned over so that he could feel her breasts pressing against him. 'Anyway, you'll soon be gone to Japan and we'll be back in New York.' She ran her free hand across his chest and then down, over his belly. 'I've heard strange things about Japanese girls. You should have a pretty nice time.'

'Maybe.' Langford pushed his cigarette into the ashtray as he felt himself becoming hard again. 'What else have you heard about Japan?' he said, taking her cigarette away from her and caressing her nipples with the tip of his tongue.

Lois let out a long gasp of pleasure. 'Japan? Who needs Japan?' And she clutched at his shoulders as she arched her body.

'Tell me later,' said Langford, feeling her fingernails bite into his flesh.

2

While Richard Langford was making love to Lois Hewens, her husband was standing under the trees near the cemetery on the southern perimeter of the Bois de Vincennes. The skies were leaden with cloud and the air filled with a fine, persistent drizzle. He stared fitfully at his watch and his lips compressed into a scowl of irritation. Then he heard the car.

It was grey Citroen DS19, old and shabby, with a Paris registration. Hewens watched it, his eyes narrowed, his hands in the pockets of the anorak. When the Citroen had pulled up some fifty yards distant, he walked slowly towards it, peering in at the driver as he came up alongside. Then he opened the front passenger door and got in.

'You're late,' he snapped. 'I've been waiting an hour. More than a Goddamned hour. Where the hell have you been?'

The man behind the wheel regarded him with a dull, almost hurt expression. 'I am sorry,' he murmured. 'It could not be helped. There was a meeting, someone from the Ministry.'

Hewens made a grimace and wiped his face with a handkerchief. 'I thought you had quit?'

'*Mais certainment, M'sieu.* I have, as you say, quit. But there were some things which I had to clear up. Now I am finished.'

'You're sure about that?' Hewens glared at him. 'Accepting this offer is one thing but if you still have a contract with the French Government ... hell, that's a ball-game which I don't want any part of. No way.'

The Frenchman smiled, mirthlessly. 'It is as I told you. Finished. You have brought everything I shall require?'

Hewens nodded and handed over a package. 'Count it later. There won't be any written contract. You know that, don't you?' The Frenchman nodded. 'Okay, how soon can you leave?'

'As I told you on the 'phone, M'sieu, I have things to which I must attend.'

'Yes, I remember.' Then Hewens frowned. 'Why wouldn't you talk on the telephone, Picot?'

'A precaution, nothing more.'

'Are you trying to tell me that your 'phone could be tapped?'

'*Non,* I think not. But one is still careful. It is perhaps habit, yes?' He smiled and placed the package which Hewens had given him in the glove compartment. 'So, that is that, no?'

'Not quite. Are you being blackmailed, Picot?'

'What makes you think that?' The Frenchman's tone was suddenly wary. 'Why should I be blackmailed?'

Hewens laughed but there was no humour in the sound. 'Do I have to spell it out, for Christ's sake?'

Picot shrugged his narrow shoulders and stared through the rain-streaked windscreen. 'Things have changed, *M'sieu.* It is no longer the disgrace it once was to follow one's nature, you know?'

'If you say so,' said Hewens, wrinkling his nose in distaste.

'France is more....' He searched for a word. 'Liberal, yes?'

'Liberal or otherwise, you just play it cool, Picot. And keep your mouth shut. I don't want any of your pretty-boys chattering all over Paris. Or anywhere else, okay? I mean, you wouldn't want anything to happen to you, would you? Like someone might just decide to alter the structure of your pretty little face if they thought you weren't quite kosher. You know what I mean?'

Picot stared at the American with unconcealed hatred. Then his colourless lips twisted to form a sardonic grin. 'Do not imagine, *M'sieu*, that because of what I am, I have no capacity for self-defence. That would be a costly mistake.'

Hewens suddenly became aware of the strong smell of perfume in the car and opened the door. 'I don't make mistakes, Picot.' He went to move but felt the Frenchman's hand on his wrist. The grip was surprisingly firm.

'There is one more thing, *M'sieu*. You said that the Englishman, Bailey, had decided to quit, no?'

Hewens turned and let the door swing closed again. 'So what?'

'You think perhaps that France is on the moon?' Picot stared at him, his thin face taut, the dark eyes narrowed into pin-pricks. 'They killed him, didn't they?'

Hewens moistened his lips with the tip of his tongue, a rapid, involuntary movement.

'Tell your friends that Claude Picot must be handled with care, *M'sieu*. Special care. If anything happens to me, the consequences could be far-reaching. You understand me, I hope?'

'Are you trying to threaten me?'

'*Mais non, M'sieu*.' He smiled and shook his head. 'I am merely offering you advice, very sound advice.'

Hewens glared at him, his fists clenched. 'Don't you even try to advise me, you little fag bastard.'

49

Picot uttered a shrill laugh but there was a detectable measure of real hurt in his eyes. 'I can leave letters,' he muttered, softly. 'I do not know or wish to know about the Englishman. But as I say, you must make your friends understand that this is one fag bastard who can destroy them and their plans. And I could do that alive or dead. *Au revoir, M'sieu*. We shall not meet again, I hope.'

Hewens sighed. 'Picot, you don't know what you're about, do you? If I so much as hinted about these ... these letters you mentioned, you'd be finished. And not before they had made it their business to get a hold of them. Do yourself a favour and don't try setting any traps because you're about to play in a different league.'

Hewens slid out of the car and slammed the door. Then he stood for a moment as Picot started the engine and drove away, a heavy cloud of exhaust smoke belching from the old Citroen as it disappeared from view. The American glanced around hoping to find a taxi but the road was deserted. Cursing softly to himself, he began to walk through the cold drizzle, wincing as a motorbike suddenly roared past him, as if from nowhere.

3

Peggy Ashmore laid the folder on Langford's desk and waited for him to put the 'phone down. 'Everything's in there,' she said. 'Passport, cash, travellers' cheques and the photo-copy files you wanted.' She turned away and then hesitated. 'Oh yes, Mister Maxwell says to tell you that he can't see you.'

'There's no such word as can't.' He jumped up and went to the door.

'But he said ....' Peggy Ashmore shrugged and shook her head as she watched Langford bound up the stairs.

He barged straight past Miss Pym into the partner's office without knocking. James Maxwell regarded him coldly.

'I'm busy,' he snapped. 'I have an important speech to prepare and I ...'

'And I have a plane to catch,' barked Langford, slamming the door. 'I have to talk to you. Now.'

His face reddening with anger, Maxwell stood up. 'I have a speech to make and ...'

'Forget it.' Langford selected a chair and sank down.

'I beg your pardon?'

'You heard me, Maxwell. I talked to Hewens. He was very helpful. Gave me a lot of useful background information but neither he nor you seem able or willing to tell me just what it is I'm supposed to look for. However, I also talked to Hewens' wife.'

'So I gather. You should be more careful.'

'Give me time and I'll show you just how careful I am. Why didn't you tell me about Bailey?'

Maxwell frowned as he resumed his seat. 'Bailey? Who's Bailey?'

'You mean you don't know?' Langford stared across the desk at him.

'No. Who is he?'

Langford lit a cigarette. He knew Maxwell pretty well and even if he hadn't had the opportunity to study him at close-range, he was puzzled. Because his judgement told him that Maxwell was lying.

'I asked you who this man Bailey is,' said Maxwell, irritably. 'Since you want to deal in riddles, I'll —'

'Doctor C.E. Bailey was — and I stress the past tense — was a nuclear physicist. You knew that, didn't you?'

'I did not.'

'Hewens as good as suggested that Bailey was murdered.'

'Impossible.'

'Why is it impossible for someone you've never heard of to have been murdered, James? Tell me, please. I'm interested.'

He tried to cope, tried to get out of it but it was hopeless and they both knew it. Then Maxwell got to his feet and

51

walked across the room to a cabinet.

'Drink?'

Langford shook his head. 'No, thanks. Are you going to tell me about Bailey?' He watched Maxwell pour himself a large Scotch and add just a quick splash of soda, his trembling hand clinking the glass against the syphon. 'Well?'

'It's a difficult situation, Richard.' Maxwell paced the room for a moment and then returned to his desk.

'It's a bloody sight more difficult for me, not knowing what I'm supposed to be looking for when I get to Japan. Or hadn't you thought of that?'

'I ...' Maxwell stopped and shook his head. 'I can't tell you any more than Hewens has.'

'You could have told me about Bailey, couldn't you?' When Maxwell didn't reply, Langford smashed his fist down on the desk. 'Damn you, Maxwell, why can't you tell me the truth?' Then he checked himself and lowered his voice. 'All right, I'll tell you what I have found out about this man Bailey, the nuclear physicist you've never heard of.

'Fact one: he came from an appallingly poor family in Manchester. Two: miracle of miracles, he won an open scholarship to Winchester. Three: he went on to Cambridge and then to Harvard. The man is brilliant, maybe even a genius. So, fact number four: he returned to England after post-graduate work at Harvard and applied to join the United Kingdom Atomic Energy Authority, right? Yes, by God, I can see I'm right. So the powers that be go into his background. Of course, Bailey gets a first class reference from Winchester, from his housemaster. All well and good. But the security people in Whitehall probe a little deeper. They want to check up on the house-master and so who do they choose? Why, none other than James Wallace Maxwell, that respected old Wykehamist with a glowing army record, member of Lloyds, a ripe candidate for the Mansion House and an old chum of a certain senior civil servant.'

'All right, Langford, you've made your point.'

'Good. I'm glad. Now perhaps you'll fill in some of the gaps.'

Maxwell took a heavy gulp at the Scotch. 'How did you find out that much?'

'Not through Hewens. No way. I have other sources and no, I'm not going to reveal the hows and whys.' Langford slowly got to his feet and went to the drinks cabinet. 'Mind if I help myself?' he said.

'Naturally, I couldn't vouch for Bailey himself,' said Maxwell, softly.

'Naturally.' Langford, glass in hand, resumed his seat.

'But as you say, I was able to vouch for the people who had provided Bailey's references. You must remember that the Government were very wary then. And Bailey's father had been a member of the Communist party.'

'Jesus,' said Langford. 'What about his grandfather?'

'It's all very well for you to mock, Langford. You're too young to appreciate fully the difficulties faced by the authorities. There had been too many scandals with scientists. Whitehall still remembers men like Fuchs and Nunn May. Anyway, Bailey was cleared and worked at both Harwell and Aldermaston until he went back to Cambridge to carry out some research programme.' Maxwell coughed.

'You knew that he left Cambridge and joined the Bayer Group in Germany, didn't you?'

'Not at the time, no. There was no reason why I should have.'

'All right, James, when did you first hear about Bailey again?'

Maxwell hesitated for a moment and then gave a shrug. 'About three months ago. Someone came to see me, someone from Whitehall.'

'British Intelligence?'

'Perhaps. They didn't leave any visiting cards. You've served in the army. You know the form. It was then that they told me that Bailey was in Japan and working for the

Shimada Corporation. It was news to me and I had nothing to tell them about it. My name was in their file on Bailey. That was why they came and ...'

'Quite. Then someone murders him. Why?'

'There's no proof that he was murdered. It's all conjecture.' Maxwell drained his glass and banged it on the desk. 'For God's sake, you seem to think that I ...' He shook his head. 'I can't tell you any more, Richard. You know everything now.'

'More than you think,' said Langford, quietly. 'What does Meyrick Hewens expect me to do? Find Bailey's killer, is that it?' He paused and waited for Maxwell to answer but he remained silent and Langford said, 'What exactly is Hewens' interest?'

'The Shimada Corporation, of course. They're his clients.'

'And this is his firm now, isn't it?'

Maxwell eyed him with a sudden wariness. 'What do you mean?'

'That you sold out. Why?'

'Damn you,' hissed Maxwell. 'Is there nothing you don't know?'

'Quite a lot. But don't worry, I can be discreet.'

'I had to sell out. It was ... it was just a run of bad luck, I suppose. A string of heavy claims. I was in danger of going under and as we already had an arrangement with Hewens, a merger seemed logical and ...'

'It was no merger, James. You sold out, lock, stock and barrel.'

'I'm still a partner.'

Langford nodded. 'And running scared. Like Hewens. So perhaps now you'll tell me why?'

'I'm not scared, not any more. As for Meyrick ... well, you'll have to ask him.' James Maxwell went again to the drinks cabinet. 'The end of the year, Richard. That should see me out. Shan't see the Mansion House.' He poured another large measure of whisky and didn't even bother with the soda. 'Tumour.' He swung round and tapped the side of his head. 'Didn't know that, did you?'

Langford felt his mouth go dry. 'No,' he muttered. 'I didn't.'

'All those headaches. Said they could operate but as good as told me that I hadn't got a cat's chance in hell. Anyway, I didn't fancy the idea of having holes bored in my skull.' He laughed, uneasily. 'So, can you keep that under your hat as well?'

'Of course. But ...' Langford bit his lip. 'Can I trust Hewens?'

'Completely,' said Maxwell. 'He has his own methods. He's very American, which is only what you'd expect. He's rather brash but he's shrewd and he'll run this operation very well.' Maxwell stared at him for a long moment, his eyes somehow blank. 'I can't guarantee that he'll keep you on but I'll give you a recommendation, of course.'

'He doesn't trust me,' said Langford, curtly. 'If he did, he would tell me what I need to know about the Shimada Corporation.'

Maxwell pondered the statement for a time, his head nodding from side to side. 'Maybe. Personally, I am of the opinion that he only suspects something is going on and he's determined to find out what it is in case he – and the firm – get landed with a massive claim.'

Langford sighed, heavily. 'Lois Hewens told me that her husband has spent a lot of time on the 'phone recently. Talking directly with Toshiro Shiba in Tokyo. Does that make sense?'

'Very much so. Shiba is immensely powerful. There are those who say he is a major prop for the Japanese government.'

'So what was Bailey doing in Kobe? Building Shiba a private atom bomb?'

'I don't know,' said Maxwell.

'Does Meyrick Hewens know?'

'I ... I think not.'

Langford smiled. 'So, that looks about right. I have to

55

find out whether or not Bailey was murdered and just what he was doing in Kobe. Is that it?'

'Probably, yes.'

'Only probably? Come on, James. I need to know.'

'Richard, if I knew any more, I would tell you. You must believe me. And as for Hewens trusting you, I think he's waiting for you to earn that trust.'

'Earn it?' Langford grinned. 'What does he have in mind, the wages of fear? The whole thing stinks. Sorry, no deal.'

'Please, Richard.' Maxwell leaned forward, his face suddenly drawn. 'Name your price.'

'For what?'

'For finding out what is really going on. I have money and no one to leave it to when I go, so ...'

'What are you offering me, James?'

'Security. For life. All I ask is that you give your confidence to Hewens and help him. He saved me, Richard. Saved this firm. Now he's in deep with Shiba and the Shimada Corporation. I scent danger and so does he but I think my sense of smell is a bit keener than his.'

'All right. I'll do what I can.' Langford stood up. 'I'm sorry. I really mean that. Very sorry.'

'Don't be. In some ways, I have the advantage of knowing what's going to happen to me. I can be prepared.' Maxwell held out his hand which Langford took. 'I was wrong about you. You're not just a smooth bastard. You're a proper devious bastard.'

Langford smiled. 'You knew my father.'

'Yes.' Maxwell released his hand. 'Watch your step, Richard.'

'Rely on it.'

'I have to.' After the door had closed, Maxwell waited a few moments and then pressed down the switch on the intercom.

'Yes, sir?'

'Get me all the details of the account to which Langford's salary is credited.'

'Right away, sir.'

'And Miss Pym?' Maxwell frowned as he kept his hand on the switch.

'Sir?'

'Telephone Mister Dell at the Worshipful Company of Ironmongers or whatever they are and tell them I can't speak at their dinner tonight.'

'Er ... what shall I say, sir? It is rather short notice.' Miss Pym's metallic voice had a sudden edge to it.

'Tell him what you like. Say I'm dead if you want to. I don't much care. And get Dobson to bring the car round. I'm leaving early.'

4

Claude Picot's apartment occupied the top floor of a dreary looking building in the Rue Danton in the Pre St. Gervais district of Paris. He had lived there for five years, in theory alone, in practice sharing with a succession of young men. During those years, Picot had created within the apartment a world of his own, a world of colour and beauty, very different from the environment in which he worked and a dramatic contrast to the building in which the apartment was located.

The three lower floors were used as offices. The stairs and landings were dull, often dirty, always cold and uninviting. But the interior of Picot's home was very different. The hall was done out entirely in black. The carpet, the walls, ceiling and woodwork. The only relief came from a mirror with an ornate white frame below which stood a carved ebony table. Of the doors leading off the hall, one led to the sitting room which provided another dramatic contrast. The predominant colour was a subtle shade of crimson lake, perfectly matched so that walls, ceiling, carpet, curtains and woodwork were all one. The furniture was very modern and very expensive, upholstered in a creamy-white shot silk. A glass-topped table mounted on simulated ivory tusks stood behind the

57

long sofa and on the table, a tall lamp cast in bronze stood like an obelisk. The lampshade was a work of art in itself, the heavy parchment overlaid with hand-made cartridge paper on which a very talented artist friend had drawn a magnificent action-picture of young boys running naked. It was a masterpiece, every tiny detail of the lithe young bodies faithfully represented. The Frenchman loved it very much indeed.

Claude Picot was in the kitchen when the doorbell echoed softly through the flat. He was preparing a salad and quickly wiped his hands. Then, clasping the twin security locks, he peeped quickly through the spy-hole and opened the door.

'I thought you weren't coming,' said Claude, smiling at his visitor and then carefully shutting the door after him. 'Can you stay?'

The boy nodded, his hand brushing at the long hair which fell over his forehead. 'For ever,' he said, smiling as Claude kissed him gently on the lips.

Picot frowned. 'For ever? What do you mean?'

'My uncle has turned me out.' The boy giggled, softly. 'So, here I am.' And he held up the small grip he was carrying.

Turning, Picot led the way into the sitting room and poured two glasses of wine. 'It is difficult, *ma chère*. I do not know what to say.'

The boy smiled and took his wine. 'I love you, Claude. You love me. No problems now. Just like we always said ...'

Picot sipped the wine and placed his glass on the table. Then he went to the window and stared through the heavy net curtains. 'It cannot be. I am sorry, but it cannot be.' He swung round, his lips moving soundlessly. 'My job with the Ministry is finished. I have new work now. Abroad. I have to go ... the money, you understand?'

Shaking his head, the boy moved quickly across to the window. 'But ... but you'll come back? Soon, yes?'

'Not soon, no. I must go for a little time, perhaps some

months. And then, well, I do not know what will happen.'

Tears sprang from the boy's eyes. 'But you told me, you promised that we could be together ...'

'Please, listen to me, *ma petite*.' Picot went to him and led him to the sofa. 'Don't cry, uh? My love, I know what I told you but I must go because there is money to be made. Please, you must be brave. I will come back, only not for a little time.'

'But I can stay here, *non*? I mean, Claude, I have nowhere to go and I could look after everything for you.'

Picot's face creased in a frown. 'No, that would not be a good idea. You must find somewhere of your own. Then, when I return, we'll – '

'You won't come back. I know you won't come back. You no longer care for me.' The boy regarded him for a moment, his face flushed with a strange, uncomprehending anger. 'Where are you going?'

'I cannot tell you.'

'*Alors!*' rasped the boy, almost triumphantly. 'There is someone else, isn't there? You have tired of me.'

'You are too young to understand. I need money,' Picot suddenly shouted.

Jumping up from the sofa, the boy backed away. 'No, that is not true. You have lots of money. I know you have. Why don't you like me any more? Haven't I done everything that you wanted?'

Picot nodded, dumbly. 'Yes but – ' Before he could continue the boy suddenly hurled the glass of wine at the wall. Countless red stains exploded on the creamy-white silk upholstery. Picot backed away, his jaw sagging open.

'I hate you,' the boy screamed, his fists tightly clenched. 'Hate you!' Then he swung round and rushed at the heavy bronze lamp, clawing at it like an enraged animal.

Picot started towards him. 'No!'

But the boy reached it first and in a split-second orgy of destruction, tore the precious lampshade into shreds.

Picot screamed. Then the lamp itself swayed and fell heavily to the floor. There was a blue flash as the wire was torn from the socket and the room was filled with the acrid scent of burnt rubber.

'You bastard!' Picot's harsh shriek and his blazing eyes suddenly cowed the boy. He backed away, his face white with fear.

'I've given you everything, you filthy little guttersnipe.' Picot's whole body was shaking with anger. Then he bent down and picked up the lamp from which the torn shade now trailed like so much waste paper. 'Damn you! Damn you!'

'Claude –' The boy's voice was choked. 'I'll mend it … I'll … I'm sorry. I didn't mean to do it. I lost my temper. I'll clean it up. I'll do anything.'

Picot stood holding the heavy bronze in his arms as if it were a dead child. His face was red with anger but his thin lips were without colour. Then he started to move forwards crunching a segment of the broken wineglass beneath his foot. 'Damn you to hell!' Even before his shout had died away, he hurled the lamp at the cringing adolescent.

For all his carefully cultivated femininity, Claude Picot's body possessed an extraordinary strength. The force with which he threw the lamp was lethal. The boy had neither the wit nor the time to move and the base of the lamp struck him just below the right eye. He crashed backwards, cracking his skull against the corner of the window sill.

Claude stood for a long moment contemplating the devastation. Then he went to the kitchen, filled a jug with cold water which he poured over the boy's face. There was blood there and the water washed it away to reveal a deep jagged gash, but the boy didn't stir and no more blood came from the wound. Dropping the jug, Picot ran into the bathroom, knelt over the lavatory pan and began to vomit.

When he returned to the sitting room, he seemed surprised that the boy was still there and bent over him, gripping the limp wrist. But there was no pulse, as Picot

60

knew there would be none. Another wave of nausea swept over him but he fought it successfully and then went across the hall into the box room which he used for storage space. The tiny room was musty and Picot opened the window to let in some fresh air before he emptied a large, old fashioned cabin trunk of books, papers and long-since discarded clothes. Then he dragged the empty trunk into the sitting room, noting the marks it left in the deep pile of the carpets.

Putting the boy's still warm body into the cabin trunk proved surprisingly easy. The limbs were supple and folded obediently as Picot manoeuvred the corpse into a foetal position. After he had checked that the lid would close properly, he surveyed the room. Seeing the small grip by the door, Picot snatched it up and after some difficulty succeeded in jamming it into the trunk, pressing it against the boy's face. After one more thorough search, he covered the body with the remains of the lampshade, closed the lid and snapped the locks shut. The keys had long since disappeared and after a moment's hesitation, he fetched some heavy string from the kitchen and carefully bound up the trunk like an enormous parcel. Then he dragged the packaged body into the box room and surveyed the scene, his face puckered by a deep, worried frown.

After some thought, he up-ended the trunk and stood it in a corner, tidying up the books and flotsam which it had previously contained but making no obvious effort to conceal the trunk. Picot then selected two empty suitcases and carried them into his bedroom, laying them carefully on the silk coverlet before returning to the box room again. Licking his thin, colourless lips and swallowing to ease the dryness in his mouth, Picot closed the door and locked it, placing the key in his pocket. Then he began to clean up the debris in the sitting room, sighing as he examined the wine stains on the creamy-white upholstery. Any attempt at cleaning would only make them worse.

Two hours later he left, carefully double-locking the

front door before descending the shabby, echoing stairs. When he reached the front hall, he paused and tucked a small envelope in the caretaker's mail box. Then he went out into the Rue Danton, quickening his pace as he turned right into the Avenue Jean Jaures and then right again into the Rue Louis Blanc where his grey Citroen was parked. After placing the two suitcases in the boot, he climbed into the driving seat and started the engine. Glancing quickly at his watch, he noted that the time was exactly nine-thirty p.m. and that it was Friday, November 18, 1977.

5

As Claude Picot drove into the centre of Paris, British Airways flight number BA391 took off from London Airport for Tokyo. Seated uncomfortably in the economy section of the Boeing 747, Richard Langford also looked at his watch. It said eight-thirty, Greenwich Mean Time. As the plane climbed steeply, Langford sighed, remembering his all too brief encounter with Lois Hewens. But his feeling of pleasure was tempered by another memory: James Maxwell. Langford could recognize that he had always had a sneaking regard for Maxwell, a curious kind of grudging respect. But as the airliner levelled out and turned east, he realized that he actually liked him.

6

In the darkly panelled office which overlooked New York's Broad Street, Meyrick Hewens sat at his desk and stared at the row of ships' chronometers mounted on the wall opposite him. In New York, the time was three-thirty in the afternoon but in Tokyo it was five-thirty in the morning and far too early for telephone calls. Lighting a cigarette, he walked to the window and stared down at the traffic. Because it was a Friday, the evening exodus was already in full-swing and Hewens grimaced. Lois was intent on spending the weekend at her parents' house near New Bedford on Nantucket Sound. Already tired by the trip to Europe, Hewens dreaded the two hundred mile drive but because he dreaded an argument with Lois even more, he had reconciled himself to the journey. As it was, he knew she would be irritated when he plucked up enough courage to telephone and explain that he had to remain in the office at least until half-past seven to make his Tokyo call. Hewens anticipated his wife suggesting sending a cable and began formulating an answer. In theory, there was no objection but in practice, he knew it could be unwise to put anything in writing about Claude Picot. Even the mere fact that he would arrive earlier than expected. Returning to his desk, his tired brain suddenly remembered Richard Langford. Cursing aloud, he reached down to the bottom right-hand drawer and took out a bottle of Scotch he had bought in London and started to drink, having suddenly made up his mind that if Lois wanted to go to her parents', she could go alone.

7

Unknown to Meyrick Hewens, Claude Picot's movements were also being monitored by another party. His name was Jean-Jacques Rueff. He was short, bearded and had served with the French Foreign Legion in Indo China and Algeria. But with his beard, long dark hair and faded jeans, his bearing was not that of a military man, and mounted on the powerful Suzuki motorcycle, he could easily have been mistaken for a pot-smoking hell's angel. It was an image which Rueff rather liked, especially as the long hair was a wig which could be discarded at will.

Using the Suzuki to defeat the chaotic Paris traffic, Rueff had followed Picot's grey Citroen all the way from its parking place in the Rue Louis Blanc to an underground car park near the Invalides Air Terminal. From there he had followed his quarry on foot, maintaining a safe distance until Picot had checked in for Japan Airlines' flight number JL440 departing for Tokyo via Moscow at eleven-twenty p.m., Paris time. Once he had seen Picot's two suitcases roll away on the baggage conveyor, Rueff went to a pay-phone and dialled a number. The conversation was brief, lasting less than a minute. Then he replaced the receiver and walked inconspicuously from the terminal to where he had left the Suzuki. After kicking the engine into life, he donned his crash helmet and quickly disappeared into the swirling traffic in the Avenue de Tourville.

FOUR

1

From Toshiro Shiba's office on the twelth floor of the Shimada Corporation headquarters on Tokyo's Chuo-dori Avenue, it was just possible to get a distant view of the Imperial Palace. It was Shiba's habit to spend a few moments standing at the window every morning, staring meditatively at the trees surrounding the castle, begun in the seventeenth century for the Tokugawa Shogun. But on the morning of Friday, November 18, Toshiro Shiba was so pre-occupied that even the habits of many years were cast aside.

Seated at a massive table, Shiba contemplated instead a file which his secretary had placed before him. The grey folder was edged in red, signifying that only Shiba, his secretary and Norihiko Samwashima, the deputy managing director, had access to it. Carefully turning each page, Shiba's eyes scanned the rows of Japanese characters. The triple-glazed windows blocked out all the noise and bustle in the street below. Only Shiba's rhythmic breathing and the gentle rustle of paper disturbed the silence.

Closing the file, Shiba turned to a small panel set into the top of the table and pressed a red button. Then he leaned back in his chair and stared at the wall, his rounded, unlined face radiating an inner calm, his well-manicured hands resting gently in his lap. For a moment or two he closed his eyes, opening them again when the door swung open. Samwashima entered, bowed and soundlessly closed the panelled door behind him before taking one of the deeply-upholstered chairs set around the table.

Shiba leaned forwards, his grey hair catching the light. He tapped the file with his forefinger. 'There are risks. Too many risks.'

Samwashima, taller, slimmer and slightly balding, nodded gravely. 'There have always been risks.' His voice was quiet. 'We have always known that. So far, we have managed to avoid them. In the present situation, I see no problems which cannot be overcome by …' There was a momentary hesitation. 'By sensible management.'

'I am concerned about this man from the insurers,' said Shiba. 'It is not a good time to have people studying us.'

'Routine.' Samwashima shook his head. 'We have nothing to fear. I shall attend to him myself, take him to Kobe and give him every assistance. He will not remain long.'

Shiba removed his thick, horn-rimmed spectacles. 'Are you saying that there is no cause for concern?'

'There is always cause, Shiba-*san*. I am merely pointing out that, with care, we need have no fears. Bailey's accident was unfortunate, especially at this stage of the project.'

'Accident?' Shiba replaced the glasses and smiled, bleakly. 'Was his death an accident? The police in Kobe took an interest. I do not like that. The reputation of the Corporation is a precious asset. We cannot afford to jeopardize it by assumptions based on rumour. Damaging rumour which may lack evidence but which is nonetheless all too real.'

'The police inquiry was merely routine.' Samwashima's hands went automatically to his pockets in search of cigarettes. But Shiba's unremitting hatred of tobacco was too well known for even his obvious successor to consider the idea of smoking. 'That has been taken care of. They are satisfied.'

Shiba nodded. 'I have considered the current situation. It seems that we cannot reliably go ahead without outside help. Our people lack the necessary experience to complete Bailey's work. Therefore Bailey must be replaced. It will require only a short-term contract.'

'Are you certain we cannot manage?'

Toshiro Shiba eyed his deputy with almost glacial coldness. 'I have already said that Bailey must be replaced. The question is, who? The list remains. The same people, with one exception, still exist.'

'The exception?'

'One of the Germans has died.' Shiba opened the file and passed it across the table. 'My choice,' he said. 'Would you agree?'

Samwashima glanced quickly at the open file and nodded. 'If it must be, then ... yes. I have no objections. There will have to be further checks made, of course.'

'Yes.' Taking back the file, Shiba drummed his fingers on the table. 'It does not matter. We have time. And I wish the insurance inquiry to be safely completed before any further moves are made.'

'That will cause delays.'

'Certainly. But it cannot be helped. Security is all important. My negotiations with the government are reaching a very delicate stage. We dare not be seen to be taking short-cuts. Everything must be just so.'

'But with respect, Shiba-*san*, suppose you fail? Suppose the government scientists at Kyomo do not co-operate?'

'There can be no question of that. Already they are very close to, if not actually above and beyond their danger levels. The service which we alone shall be able to provide is both necessary and urgent. So ... when you have dealt with this Englishman, get Bailey's replacement to Kobe as discreetly as possible.'

Samwashima nodded. 'It shall be done,' he said, rising. Then he hesitated. 'Will you raise this subject at the next board meeting?'

'It has never been raised before.'

'But as directors, Tasaki and Komai should surely know – '

'I decide what it is they know.' Shiba's calm, benevolent expression suddenly changed and for a brief moment, the multi-millionaire head of the Shimada Corporation might have been hewn from flesh-coloured granite. Then he relaxed. 'What have you done about the girl?'

Samwashima's face glistened with perspiration. 'What girl?' he asked.

'The woman arranged for Bailey.'

'She remains at the Kobe apartment. I had thought that she might be of further service to the man from the insurers – '

'No,' said Shiba, firmly. 'He will stay at an hotel. The Oriental. We do not wish to encourage him to prolong his stay. No, pay her off and get rid of her.'

'As you wish, Shiba-*san*.'

With the barest inclination of his head, Shiba signalled that the interview was at an end.

As he descended to his own office on the floor below, Samwashima experienced a sensation of unease in the pit of his stomach. More than anything else in the world, he wanted to succeed Toshiro Shiba. He wanted to occupy the lavish penthouse suite on the top floor with its luxury office; to preside over the massive Shimada Corporation and enjoy the absolute power that went with it.

Once he had closed his door behind him, Samwashima finally lit the much-needed cigarette, inhaling the smoke with immense relief as he sat down behind his desk. There were papers to be dealt with, calls to be made. But not for the first time, Samwashima sat and stared into space, pondering his relationship with the man whose devotion to the Shimada Corporation was little short of obsessive.

The Corporation had been created by Shiba to rise like the Phoenix from the ashes of a defeated, humiliated Japan. Using capital acquired from black market dealings – a phase of the company's history to which no one ever referred – the name Shimada soon became synonymous with progress, prosperity and profits the world over. Growth was rapid, but always carefully consolidated to ensure stability and continuity. Toshiro Shiba's personal axiom was that today's success should be used to safeguard against tomorrow's failure. But there had been few significant failures and as he savoured the cigarette, Samwashima was able to smile at what he might inherit from the man to whom Fate had given no sons.

Though far from being the biggest building in the world's fastest-growing, most densely populated city, the Tokyo HQ of the Shimada Corporation was still in many ways unique. Its twelve storeys contained an apparatus of power which might have been envied by more than one of the world's leaders. Certainly the degree of control exercised by Toshiro Shiba was that of an absolute ruler accountable to no one but himself. His orders were relayed around the world by a private communications system which included a privately-owned satellite. A gigantic armada of ships sailed the seas under the Shimada flag, their masters following Shiba's orders with the unquestioning obedience of automatons. In the world's major capitals, high-ranking ministers were kept as well informed of the Shimada Corporation's dealings in the money markets as they were about the state of the dollar or the yen. Thousands of workers and their families, scattered across Western Europe and North America, depended on Toshiro Shiba's ability to take the right decisions at the right time. And his alone.

Stubbing out his cigarette, Samwashima felt a mixture of respect and fear. Shiba was the Master, the merchant prince, always one step ahead. He, Samwashima, was the pupil, always lagging a little behind, always fearful that he might somehow fail and lose the succession. It was a very real fear which sometimes robbed him of sleep, often made him nervous and unsure. It also caused him to question his own personal loyalty to the man he had served faithfully from the very beginning. In Samwashima's troubled mind, loyalty merited reward. But what if that reward should be denied?

Lighting another cigarette, Samwashima lifted the

telephone and ordered coffee. As he sat waiting, he scanned his timetable for the day and remembered that he had to attend to Yita Izumi when he went to Kobe with the Englishman. He chewed his lip, thoughtfully. In theory, he was second only to Shiba. But in practice, he realized, he had no real power whatsoever.

A secretary brought the coffee, poured it, added cream, bowed and withdrew. Samwashima had hardly noticed her. He sat immobile, his expression rigid, his eyes staring sightlessly into space. And as the coffee began to grow cold, the deputy managing director of the Shimada Corporation knew beyond any shadow of doubt that his loyalty to Toshiro Shiba had reached its zenith. He, Norihiko Samwashima, had procured a prostitute for Bailey's amusement. Now Bailey was dead and it fell to Samwashima to dismiss her like a common whore-master on the *Ginza*. It was dishonourable work.

2

Yita Izumi sat quietly in the small living room of the apartment in Kobe's Yamamoto-dori and contemplated the photograph of Kit Bailey which she had propped up against a table lamp. On the bookcase, an electric clock ticked away the seconds, then the minutes, until nearly an hour had passed. Yita slowly stood up, walked across the room and dropped into the classic kneeling position, resuming her study of Bailey's image, her lithe body gently swaying to and fro as she re-lived the morning of Friday, November 4.

Her emotions were confused, a curious mixture of gratitude, shame and dread. She was grateful that Bailey had never known the truth that she was a paid woman. She was ashamed not because of what she was but of her lack of grief. She had shed no tears for the man whom she had sincerely loved – the only man she had been able to love. If she had given her body to more men than she could remember, she had kept her soul intact — until Bailey had broken the seal, gently and unwittingly. Now Yita dreaded the future, fearing the uncertainty which she had known so well in the past.

She remembered how the manager of the shipyard had sent a clerk to the apartment to tell her of Bailey's death. The young man had stated the facts artlessly, brutally and without thought: Bailey-*san* had fallen to his death. The cardboard box containing his personal effects had been deposited at her feet. Everything was there except his clothes, the clothes which had covered his smashed and mutilated body, the clothes stained with his blood.

Opening the box, she had deposited his things around the apartment just as he would have done: the watch, wallet, pocket-knife, cigarettes and lighter and loose change, all arranged on the bedside table, just as he would have arranged them had he lived to return that evening. She hung his heavy trench coat on the hook in the tiny hall. In that way, for a few hours at least, Kit Bailey continued to live. He was there with her in the apartment, almost a physical presence. Until the night came. Then he somehow faded. The bed was empty and cold. Quite suddenly, the inanimate objects which had been a part of him and which had preserved his being for a few, brief hours, were no longer capable of sustaining the presence. Once again, Yita was alone.

The empty hours passed slowly. Then had come the funeral. Yita could picture the small, Protestant church which had seemed so alien. The young padre who had taken the service hadn't known Bailey, had even got his name wrong. But somehow it didn't matter. The funeral was a mechanical, meaningless ritual and a source of deep hurt. With two exceptions, the few who had attended were all Japanese. Kit had made few friends among the large and socially-active European population of Kobe. Apart from the young padre, the only other European was a

71

swarthy, thick-set man with dark, wavy hair. She thought she had seen him around town, maybe in a bar or club or restaurant but she didn't know his name. Later on, she thought that she should have lingered and tried to speak to him after the service. But the cold, penetrating stares of the Japanese men told her that she shouldn't have attended. She was Bailey's whore, without status, without sympathy. Without friends.

Rising to her feet, she went into the bedroom and took a suitcase from the cupboard. Very slowly, Yita gathered her few possessions and folded them into the case. They had not told her to go. Yet. They would, of course, probably sending some young clerk like the one who had brought her the news of Bailey's death. But she wouldn't be there, and they could keep their money, although she had need of it. But at that moment, her greatest need was to preserve his memory, undefiled.

She closed the lid of the suitcase and sat on the edge of the bed, her face set. There was so little for her to cling on to, just a memory, frail and brittle. Yita knew virtually nothing of Bailey's past, his home, his family – apart from the fact that both his parents were dead. His work was a closed book. She only knew that it was important. And secret. The fact that she knew so little about him had been of no account while he was alive. There would have been time to learn all she needed to know later on. For all her firm refusals, Yita had made up her mind that she would marry him – provided he still wished it – just before he returned to his home. Now there was nothing. Just the empty, soul-searing degradation of selling her body, the only commodity which she had to offer.

Then the doorbell had started to ring. Gradually, the repeated tone bored into her consciousness. She ran to the door, so muddled that for a moment she even thought that it might be Kit.

Opening the door the three inches permitted by the safety-chain, she peered on to the landing and stared at a swarthy, thick-set man with dark wavy hair.

'Miss Izumi?' He seemed to have an American accent and Yita nodded, dumbly. 'May I have a word with you, please?'

Yita pushed the door closed, released the safety chain and let the man enter, watching him nervously as he went into the living room. 'Who ... who are you?' she said, clasping her hands together.

'My name is Gunning. Timothy Gunning.'

'You are American?' said Yita, unconsciously adopting the sing-song, patronising tone of the bar-girl.

The man nodded. 'Yes. I've come to talk to you about Doctor Bailey. I saw you at the funeral.'

'Yes,' she said. 'You will sit?'

'Thank you.' Gunning lowered himself into the chair. 'Mind if I smoke?'

She shook her head and held out a table lighter which he took. 'What is it you wish to talk about?'

The American pulled on the cigarette and moistened his lips. 'Miss Izumi, did you have any notion of what Bailey was doing here?'

'He worked on the big ship.'

'Yes, I know that. But you don't know exactly what he did, why he was brought to Kobe?'

'No.' She shook her head and brushed a strand of dark hair from her forehead. 'Why do you ask?'

'Miss Izumi, did he have many friends here?'

'No.' The reply was given with no hesitation.

'Any enemies?'

'I do not think so. Why should he have enemies?'

Once again, the American moistened his lips. 'May I speak frankly? I know – or I think I know – that you were paid by the Shimada Corporation to act as Bailey's housekeeper. Is that correct?'

Yita rose slowly to her feet. 'You know what I am, Mister Gunning. Why ask?'

'I had to. I'm sorry.' He stubbed his half-smoked cigarette in the ashtray and stood up. 'I'm sorry.'

'You have not explained why you came here.'

'Do you still work for Shimada?'

She shook her head. 'No, I – ' She would have continued but there was a sudden dryness in her mouth, a constriction of her throat and a sharp, almost painful stinging behind her eyes. Tears were coming at last. 'I loved him,' she blurted, her voice choked by a violent sob. 'He ... he wanted me to be his wife.'

'Others have died working on the big ship,' Gunning said, watching her carefully. 'Did you know that?' She nodded. 'Miss Izumi, did you know any of the other men who died?'

'No.' She turned away, dabbing at her eyes with a small, white handkerchief. 'I know nothing about his work.'

'Did he keep any papers here? Like diaries or notebooks or ... anything like that?'

'No.'

After a pause, Gunning said, 'What will you do now?'

'I do not know.' She swung round and faced him. 'It does not matter. It is my own life.'

'Sure.' Gunning's eyes darted uneasily around the small living room. 'Could I see his things?'

Yita regarded him with a mixture of curiosity and suspicion. 'Who are you? Why have you come here like this?'

'Let's say I'm a friend of his.' He started towards a small cabinet. 'May I look?'

She shrugged her narrow shoulders. 'If you wish. Nothing here belongs to me.'

'Thank you.'

Within a few minutes, Gunning had virtually searched the apartment, or so it seemed to Yita. In fact, he had done no more than glance around, opening drawers at random but seldom delving inside. Then he returned to the living room and lit another cigarette.

'Have you been sent here by the Corporation?' she asked

'No, I have nothing to do with Shimada.' He studied her for a moment and then sighed. 'You must forgive me. I had to come here. It was my duty. I'm sorry.'

'I do not understand. What kind of duty?'

'Miss Izumi, would you talk to me about Kit Bailey?'

'What about?'

'Anything and everything that you remember. I just want you to talk about him. If you like, you can come to my apartment.'

She smiled a sad, knowing smile. 'I could, yes.'

'No, Miss Izumi, that's not quite what I had in mind. I live inside the American Consulate. Here, my card.'

Yita took the card and stared at it. 'I do not understand. Kit was British, no?'

'That's right. But his nationality isn't important. Not to me, anyway.'

Holding the card in her hand, she shook her head. 'What can I tell you, Mister Gunning? I know ... knew nothing about his work.'

The American sighed and then pointed to the photograph propped against the table lamp. 'Good likeness,' he said.

'I took it,' replied Yita, possessively.

'You know how he died, Miss Izumi?'

Yita nodded. 'Yes, they told me.' She turned away. 'It was an accident.'

'Was it?' Gunning's tone was sharp. 'I don't think so. I think – '

'Who are you?' She swung round, her face suddenly drawn.

'I believe that Doctor Bailey was murdered, Miss Izumi.'

'That ... .that cannot be. It was an accident. They told me ...'

'I know what they told you but I have ... well, not proof but a pretty good idea that Bailey knew something which maybe he shouldn't have known.' Gunning was watching

75

her carefully. 'I also happen to believe that Bailey wasn't the first but I guess you already know about that, don't you?'

Yita stared at him for a moment and then backed away. 'Get out,' she hissed.

'Miss Izumi, I think – '

'I don't care what you think. You get out or I telephone police.'

'What are you scared of, Miss Izumi?'

'Get out.' She ran to the door and flung it open. 'Go!' As Gunning left, he saw that the anger could not conceal the pain in her eyes.

3

When Richard Langford had finished with passport control and customs at Tokyo's International Airport, a tall, slim Japanese came towards him, bowed slightly and extended his hand.

'You are Mister Langford?' he said, pronouncing the *L* in Langford as an *R*.

'Yes,' Langford replied, taking the man's hand.

'I am Mister Samwashima.' The Japanese smiled, signalled to a uniformed chauffeur to take his luggage and pointed towards the main entrance. 'You will come, please? There is a car waiting.'

As the long, black Mercedes drew away, Samwashima offered cigarettes. 'I regret that there is more flying. The car will take us to the other side of the airport where Mister Shiba's private plane is waiting to take us both down to Osaka. From there, it is but a short journey by road to Kobe.'

'It's my lucky day.' Langford drew on the cigarette and thought that another flight was the last thing he wanted, even in Mister Shiba's private plane.

'No doubt you look forward to a bath and change, yes?' said Samwashima, conversationally. 'I find flying very exhausting. One becomes so dirty.'

'Yes.' Langford stifled a yawn. 'It's very kind of you to meet me personally.'

'Please, I am honoured. I shall come with you to Kobe.' He paused. 'Did you know Mister Bailey?'

'Doctor Bailey? No, I didn't.'

'A nice person. It was a terrible accident. A great tragedy.'

Langford glanced quickly at the Japanese. 'Not the first, I understand?'

Samwashima shook his head. 'Unfortunately, no. But we must take what I believe you would call the long view, Mister Langford. In all constructions on such a scale as this, there are always accidents. I imagine that statistically, they cannot be avoided.'

'Perhaps.' Langford peered from the car as they drew up alongside a white Caravelle.

'Mister Shiba's private plane.'

They got out of the car and walked to the steps below the tail while the baggage was taken aboard through the crew's entrance. A stewardess wearing a traditional Japanese kimono, obi and getas, bowed deeply as they entered the jet. Samwashima appeared not to notice her.

'Nice place,' said Langford, staring round at the sumptuous interior.

'Your suitcase will be unpacked for you. As soon as we have taken off, you may enjoy a bath and a change of clothes.'

'A bath?' said Langford, unable to conceal his surprise.

Samwashima smiled. 'Mister Shiba values his comfort. Meanwhile, the regulations demand that we are strapped in for take off.' He gestured to a seat.

Ten minutes later, when the Caravelle had levelled out and was heading south, Richard Langford enjoyed his first Japanese bath. The experience was startling. Guided by the smiling stewardess who had swapped her delicately patterned kimono for a plain white apron, he was seated on a small wooden stool and his naked body diligently soaped all over by the smiling girl. After rinsing off the soap, she led him to the tub and almost pushed him into the scalding-hot water.

Unable to stand being cooked for very long, Langford emerged and allowed himself to be rubbed dry by the girl, who then handed him a monogrammed *yakuta*, before taking him to a small dressing room where all his clothes had been neatly laid out.

'You must sample Japanese whisky,' said Samwashima, when Langford returned to the main cabin.

The stewardess poured a very large measure of the Japanese Suntory whisky into a tumbler filled with ice and presented it to him with another deep bow.

'Thank you,' said Langford, his pale eyes trying to probe her blank expression. Then he turned to Samwashima. '*Kampai!*'

For a brief second, Samwashima's face clouded. Then he grinned. 'You have been to Japan before, Mister Langford?' It could have been a statement or a question.

'No. Mister Hewens gave me the toast.'

'Ah so.' Samwashima seemed relieved. 'I trust Mister Hewens is well? We are old friends.'

'Yes, yes, he is. And he sends his good wishes,' said Langford, recalling that Hewens had done no such thing.

'Please convey mine.' Samwashima raised his glass. 'Rooms have been reserved for you at the Oriental hotel in Kobe. I think you will find it comfortable.' Before Langford could comment, he went on, 'As tomorrow is Sunday, I have arranged that you remain undisturbed. A car will call for you on Monday morning and bring you to the dockyards.'

'Thank you.'

There was a short pause and then Samwashima leaned forwards, his expression one of puzzlement.

'I must confess that I do not understand the exact purpose of your visit, Mister Langford. Of course, I realize that it is in some measure merely routine but perhaps if you could tell me what it is you seek, I may be able to be of more help.' He smiled, a quick blur of nicotine-stained teeth.

'It's ... it's rather difficult to define.' Langford drew a sharp breath. 'I just have to take a look round and submit a report. If I'm completely honest with you, Mister Samwashima, my department tends to insist on this kind of routine inquiry purely as a means of getting me away from the office.'

The Japanese seemed perplexed. Then he gave a loud guffaw. 'I like that. I think we shall get along well, Mister Langford.'

'I don't see why not, Mister Samwashima.'

'Please, you must call me Sam. Everyone does.'

'Thank you. My name's Richard.'

'Ah so.' Sam pondered for a moment. 'This is short for Dick, no?'

'No, it's the other way round. Dick is short for Richard.'

Once again, the Japanese seemed perplexed, even irritated. 'Ah, I see. Then I call you Dick.' And he nodded to himself. 'Time for one last drink before we land, Dick,' he said, snapping his fingers at the stewardess.

Langford released his glass, his expression concealing a sudden uneasiness. Samwashima was being just a little bit too helpful.

'I omitted to mention that a car and a driver will be available to you at all times,' said Sam. 'I hope that you will take advantage of this facility to see something of our country during your short stay.'

'That's very kind of you,' Langford replied, wondering just how short the smiling Samwashima wanted his stay to be.

'You will also discover that your connection with the Shimada Corporation has many advantages.' Sam's face broadened into a confident smile. 'The fact that you came to Osaka in Mister Shiba's private plane and have the use of a car and driver ... well, these things will be noted. The services you receive will be er ... shall we say, better than average?'

Langford contented himself with a bland smile.

The stewardess came back, bowed to Samwashima and whispered softly. Samwashima nodded, finished his whisky and rose to his feet.

'It is time to strap ourselves in again, Dick. We are making our descent.'

The landing was perfect and within a matter of minutes, the Caravelle had taxied to its parking place. Another Mercedes stood waiting to receive them, the driver holding the door open.

'This is Oki,' explained Samwashima. 'He will be looking after you during your stay here, Mister ... Dick.' And he smiled, self-consciously.

As he got into the car, Langford acknowledged Oki's bow with a curt nod. The chauffeur was far removed from his idea of the classic Japanese male. Apart from his height – well above Langford's six feet – Oki was broad and heavily built with a confident, almost brutish expression on his face. He was obviously immensely strong.

Once inside the Mercedes, they lit cigarettes as Oki drove skilfully through the traffic, accelerating once they were on the Hanshin Expressway into the centre of Kobe.

'This part of Japan is not very beautiful,' remarked Samwashima.

Langford nodded and stared out at the vista of industrial ugliness which flashed by. Langford put the speed of the Mercedes at somewhere around ninety and he remarked on it, partly out of interest but mostly to break the silence. Sam chuckled, softly.

'There are speed limits, of course. But no policeman would stop this car, Dick.' He stretched, luxuriantly.

Richard Langford felt no inclination to pursue the matter further. Either the Japanese was simply showing off or the police were really in Shiba's pocket. Langford reserved his judgement and the remainder of the journey passed in high-speed silence.

The Oriental hotel at Kobe was much like any other international hotel. The decor was modern, an unhappy blend of traditional Japanese with trans-Atlantic vulgarity, and the atmosphere impersonal. Langford had stayed in many such hotels, enjoying their comfort and convenience but disliking their commercial anonymity. Tired from his journey, he wanted nothing more than a bed and a long sleep but even in his state of fatigue, he couldn't fail to be impressed at the standard of service commanded by Samwashima.

There were no tedious formalities of registration. Led, flanked and followed by bowing staff, the walk across the main foyer to the waiting lift was reminiscent of a royal progress. Only the massive figure of Oki standing in the background spoilt the picture.

The lift was stopped on the fourth floor and the progress continued until they entered the suite which Langford would occupy.

'I trust that this will be satisfactory?'

'Splendid, thank you.'

Samwashima nodded and glanced around the sitting room, frowning at the tray of drinks. For a minute or so, there was absolute silence as he pointed towards the tray. Then he snapped out something in Japanese and one of the flunkeys darted across the room.

'Something wrong?' Langford inquired, longing to be left alone.

'A dirty jug,' explained Samwashima. He turned to one of the staff, speaking rapidly and sharply in Japanese.

As Langford watched, another tray of drinks was brought, the glasses and bottles clinking in the oppressive silence. He knew then that this was no elaborate farce. It was crystal clear that the staff were scared stiff and obviously relieved when Samwashima dismissed them.

'Please, you will enjoy your rest now.'

'Thanks for your help.'

'My pleasure.' Samwashima beamed. 'And do not forget about Oki. He has a room in the hotel and will be at your disposal at all times. You merely ask at the desk.'

The chauffeur stood by the door, his ape-like arms hanging limp at his sides. Langford tried to think of something to say but then, quite suddenly, the two men had gone.

Flinging off his jacket, Langford loosened his tie, kicked the shoes from his feet and lay down on the bed, staring up at the ceiling. He decided he disliked Samwashima intensely, mistrusting the outwardly urbane, highly-westernized Japanese. But he disliked Oki even more, and wondered just why a chauffeur employed by one of Japan's major companies should need to carry a high-calibre hand-gun to work.

4

As Richard Langford sank into a deep, dreamless sleep in Kobe, a Paris policeman was standing by a window overlooking the Rue D'Amsterdam near the Gare St. Lazare. In one hand, he held a thick, earthenware mug of black coffee; in the other, a cigarette, the smoke curling around fingers darkly stained by nicotine. Although it was just before eleven a.m., the policeman had only just got up. It was a Sunday, November 20, and by some mischance, he was off duty. Leaving the window, the policeman went into his tiny bathroom and began to shave.

His name was Henri Bouscat, he was forty-three years old and an Inspector in the Homicide Division of the Brigade Criminelle. Although still legally married, Bouscat lived alone, deserted by a wife who had been unable to stand the irregular hours which formed an integral part of his life. Because he could readily understand her feelings, Bouscat had accepted her departure phlegmatically and bore her no malice because he felt none. The problem – though he never saw it as such – was that Henri Bouscat was totally committed to his work. He enjoyed catching criminals. The more bizarre the crime and the more devious the culprit, the more Bouscat enjoyed the chase. He was a natural cop, with a rare understanding of the criminal mind. And he had many real friends in the Paris underworld. He was respected and had a reputation for fairness. But in spite of a good record for convictions, Bouscat's reputation within the Division was less to his credit. He was too unorthodox, had rather too many dubious contacts for his superiors' liking. Thus it was that Henri Bouscat knew that his chances of promotion were so slim as to be non-existent. But he didn't care. His work was sufficient reward.

He had just completed shaving and was about to run a comb through his greying hair when he heard the telephone.

'Bouscat,' he snapped, instantly alert and on duty again.

'Inspector Henri Bouscat?'

'Yes.' He lit a cigarette, frowning. 'Who is this?'

'You may not remember me,' said the vaguely familiar voice. 'My name is Rueff.'

Bouscat smiled to himself. 'Jean-Jacques? Yes, I remember you.'

'*Bon.*' Rueff gave a low chuckle. 'Memory like a bloody elephant. Can you meet me? I have something interesting for you … and worrying for me.'

'When and where?' Bouscat gripped the cigarette in his mouth, automatically reaching for pad and pencil.

'There is a bar on the Quai des Celestins, the *Canard Noir.*'

'I know it. When?'

'Today at noon. Can you make it?'

Bouscat said he could and Rueff hung up. For a minute or so, Bouscat stood holding the receiver, faintly aware of the buzzing dialling tone. Then he dropped it back in its cradle and returned to the bathroom.

As he combed his hair, the Inspector was puzzled. Rueff was a cracksman, an expert on safes. Bouscat had sent him down for four years in 1971 after a robbery at an art dealer's home in which a German-built strong room had been sprung open like a child's moneybox. Rueff had left no prints, no evidence at all, and Bouscat had had to build his case on a series of hunches and probing conversations with people who normally ran a mile at the first sign of a *poulet*. Strictly speaking, Rueff should have been put away for a seven year stretch but because Bouscat persuaded him to assist in the recovery of the stolen property, the safebreaker got off fairly lightly. When last heard of, Rueff had had a job in a garage near Senlis. Full of curiosity, Bouscat pulled on his shabby tweed suit and set off for the Quai des Celestins.

The bells of Notre Dame were still ringing when Rueff entered the bar. Bouscat recognized him immediately in spite of the beard. Rueff seemed disappointed.

'I sometimes wear a wig,' he explained.

Bouscat ordered two beers and chain lit a cigarette. 'What do you want?'

'Difficult to say. Got a problem, Guv'nor.' He peered at Bouscat for a moment, his eyes slightly narrowed. 'I was doing a job.'

'All right,' Bouscat said, sensing the man's unease. 'You can pretend you're in the Confessional.'

'Thanks, Guv'nor.' Rueff leaned forwards, almost eagerly. 'You know me. Strictly an in-and-out man. No hassle, right? Well, I've been a bit pushed lately and ... well, I've been doing a bit of what you might call industrial espionage, see?'

'I think I might call it breaking and entering. But go on.'

Rueff licked his lips. 'Well, there's this office, see. It's the design department for some firm that makes electronic equipment. Trouble is that the office is wired up like a bloody cat's cradle. Windows, doors, everything. Only got to look at it and the sodding alarm goes off. Anyway, I case the place. But carefully. Then I know how to get in. It's simple: through the ceiling. But that means a climbing job to the premises above. So I watch and wait. Once I know the coast is clear, we're away ... that's me and a chap with a camera. I get him inside. Jesus, you ever gone through a ceiling? It's no joke, I can tell you. But we did it and down we go. Open the safe. Easy. He takes his pretty pictures, I close up and we climb back through the ceiling. No problems. Well, I let him go first 'cos he's a bit jittery like, y'know? Then I wait. Now this place we've used to go in through, it's a real smooth joint. Belongs to some poove. Well, like I told you, times are hard, so I decide to have a look around and see if there's anything worth ...'

The bells of Notre Dame struck one. The streets of Paris were quiet and Bouscat and Rueff were the only customers in the tiny bar. Stubbing his cigarette into the overflowing ashtray, the Inspector leaned back, stretched and ordered two more beers.

'How long had he been dead?' He lit another cigarette, crumpling the empty packet in the palm of his hand.

'I'm no doctor, Guv'nor. But don't think it could have been long. No smell, you know?'

'Only too well.' Bouscat paused as the barman placed two more bottles on the table. 'What do you want me to do?'

'Keep me off the hook. What else? You know me. I wouldn't hurt a fly.'

'Perhaps a Judge might not take the same view. What happened to the job in the garage?'

'Didn't work out. Hell, what's the use? I'm not a nine-till-five man. I'm like you, Guv'nor. I like my work.'

'All right, let's just check a few facts. You're certain about the flight?'

'Positive. It was a JAL 'plane to Tokyo via Moscow.'

'I see. And the man's name was Claude Picot, yes?'

'That's what it said on the doorbell. I noticed that when I did a daylight recce of the place.' Rueff quaffed his beer. 'Look, Inspector, can't I just do a vanishing trick?'

'No. That's not on. Murder is – '

'Bloody hell, I didn't do it.'

'You found him. You broke in.'

Rueff nodded, glumly. 'If I go down again …'

'Twelve years,' intoned Bouscat. 'Seven if you give yourself up … if you're lucky. But what made you call me? It's not like you to leave any traces.'

'This other bloke, wasn't it? He didn't see the stiff, of course. But because he was with me, well, it was a messy business. All that plaster and dust and everything. I don't think I could face a dozen, Guv'nor.'

Bouscat merely nodded. 'When did you say the break-in will be discovered?'

'Eight-thirty tomorrow morning. That's when the caretaker lets the cleaners in. Of course, they won't know that the safe's been opened.'

'They might guess.'

'Doubt it. We lifted the petty cash, two radios and a few pocket calculators and things.' He grinned. 'I even made a few marks on the safe with the crowbar … just for appearances. Clever, eh?'

'Very. What did you do with the stuff you lifted?'

'In the bleeding river. Except the cash.'

Bouscat sighed. 'All right. Where can I get hold of you?'

'Leave a message here. I'll call in every day for a week. If you don't show by then, I'll assume …'

'You'll assume nothing.' Bouscat leaned across the table. 'And don't try running, will you?'

Rueff gave a hopeless shrug. 'What can you get me, Guv'nor?'

'With your record, not less than seven.' He saw the man's face muscles go taut. 'Maybe with three years suspended. But I can promise nothing.'

By three o'clock that afternoon, the French police had
forced their way into Claude Picot's apartment on the Rue
Danton. By five p.m., the body in the cabin trunk had
been identified as belonging to Emile Louis Malvy, a
student aged seventeen whose parents were dead and who
had been living with an uncle at Nanterre. Inspector
Bouscat made a statement which began, '*Acting on
information received* ...' It was the usual formula for coping
with an anonymous tip-off but the murder of the student
Malvy and the disappearance of a homosexual named
Claude Picot quickly became a very unusual case. At
exactly five-fifty p.m., Bouscat was about to return to his
flat when one of the younger officers in the Homicide
Division wondered if Claude Picot, the nuclear physicist,
could be the same Claude Picot who had boarded Japan
Airlines' flight number JL440 for Tokyo via Moscow.

It was nearly midnight when Bouscat was told to wait in
the bleak, shabby room on the ground floor of the house in
the Rue Jullien near the Lycee Michelet in the Vanves
district of Paris. The policeman knew that the building
belonged to the Service de Documentation Exterieure et
de Contre Espionage, better known as SDECE. What he
didn't know was that the building was the headquarters of
Section Nine, a relatively small team within the Secret
Service responsible for the security of French nuclear
installations and research. And as the head of the Section,
Colonel DuCros, remarked to his assistant, it was difficult
to know who was the more worried: the policeman or the
cracksman being interrogated in another part of the
building.

6

While Henri Bouscat was being interrogated in Paris, a
cream and grey Pontiac swung into the drive of a long, low
house overlooking the beach near Santa Barbara in

California. Getting out of the car, the driver, well-built, deeply tanned and almost completely bald, sounded the horn and then went round to the boot and removed a suitcase. The man's name was Neil Whitaker. He was sixty-three years old and retired. Unlike Henri Bouscat, Whitaker did know all about the workings of Section Nine of SDECE. He also knew a great deal about nuclear physics. Prior to his retirement, Professor Whitaker had taught at Harvard after many years as Director of Plutonium Research at the British nuclear research centre at Harwell.

Helen Whitaker greeted her husband on the verandah. 'Good trip?' she said, kissing him lightly on the cheek.

'No. The fish must have gone on strike.'

They both laughed and went inside the typically Californian-suburban house which belied their English origins. On the sofa table in the L-shaped lounge, copies of *Time* and *Newsweek* lay alongside *Country Life*, the *New Scientist* and air-mail editions of the London *Times*.

'Any mail?' Whitaker helped himself to a beer.

Helen pointed to a stack of envelopes which her husband scanned and then put aside.

'Nothing of interest,' he muttered, picking up the latest copy of the *Times*. 'This is over a week old. I'm beginning to think it isn't worth it.'

Helen smiled. 'It's nice to keep in touch,' she said.

Whitaker nodded, sitting down on the sofa and opening out the paper, the thin pages crackling. 'Strikes and more strikes. Poor old Engla ... Good God.'

'What is it?'

'It's incredible. Kit Bailey's dead.'

Helen frowned. 'Kit Bailey? I know the name but –'

'Young chap ... well, late thirties, I suppose. He was a Post-Grad at Harvard. Brilliant. A great future.'

'Was he ill?'

'No. Says here that he was killed in an accident in a shipyard in Japan.' Whitaker shook his head. 'What the devil was he doing in Japan?'

'I don't know.' Helen glanced at her watch. 'Fancy some lunch?'

'Yes.' Whitaker stared blankly at the news item for a moment, sighed, and then turned to the sports pages. 'Germany,' he murmured. 'He was in Germany.'

'Who was?' said Helen, just about to go into the kitchen.

Whitaker grinned. 'Never mind.'

7

His thin body wrapped in a heavy overcoat, the elderly man with the shock of silvery-white hair stood on the jetty and stared at the strands of mist which lay across the calm waters of the *Huichi Nada* separating the island of Shikoku from Honshu. It was just after dawn and very cold. The old man rubbed his wrinkled hands together and breathed deeply as he stamped his feet on the smooth stonework of the jetty. Then he paused, listening intently.

'I hear them.'

His companion, rather younger, nodded. 'The boom is being raised.'

Across the water and echoing in the stillness, came the steady throb of an engine. Then came another sound, a strange, almost ghostly clanking of chains. The two men stood in silence, watching and waiting until a white launch suddenly materialized out of the mist as it entered the tiny harbour.

As the engine died away, the boat approached the jetty and bumped against the row of rubber fenders. A young man wearing an oilskin jumped from the bows and secured the painter before leaning down and helping another figure on to the jetty.

The elderly Japanese stepped forwards to greet the new arrival. He bowed, a slight inclination of his head. 'Welcome to Shikoku.' His English was slow, each word handled carefully, as if it were a fragile piece of glass. 'I hope you have not had a too difficult journey, Mister Picot.'

The Frenchman smiled, bleakly, his face drawn, a blur of grey bristle showing around his chin.

'I am Muga Tasaki,' said the man with the white hair. He gestured to his companion. 'This is Mister Komai. He speaks no English.'

Komai bowed and remained silent as Claude Picot's bloodshot eyes studied the two men.

'You will be taken straight to your quarters, Mister Picot,' said Tasaki, nodding at the young man from the boat who now carried the Frenchman's two suitcases. 'When you have rested, we shall talk.' He bowed again and watched as Picot was led towards the house overlooking the harbour, its sombre grey-stone walls reflecting the creamy light of the rising sun.

'We have to hope that this man is reliable,' Komai said.

'It does not matter.' Tasaki buried his hands in his coat pockets and started to follow the Frenchman. 'When he has ceased to be useful, he will be killed.'

Komai nodded and the two men headed back towards the house as the sun burnt the layer of mist off the water.

PART TWO

FIVE

1

Sprawled in the rear of the Mercedes, Langford stared at the back of Oki's neck. The Japanese chauffeur drove the big limousine with an effortless skill so that Langford was scarcely conscious of movement as they edged through the Monday morning traffic towards Kobe's dock area.

Rested and refreshed after the long flight from London, Langford's thoughts were concentrated on the task set him by James Maxwell and Meyrick Hewens. A simple analysis posed two questions: how did Doctor C.E. Bailey die and what was the scientist doing in Kobe? But there were too many problems, too many question marks to punctuate any possible conclusions. Even if he could discover the precise nature of Bailey's work for the Shimada Corporation, and the how and why of his death, the other questions would remain unanswered.

In spite of reservations, Langford had warmed to Meyrick Hewens' friendly, outgoing personality. But the brief he had provided had been obstructively vague and any objective assessment of the American was coloured by the memory of Lois Hewens' supple, willing body which had been almost too readily available. Also, he would soon take over as Langford's boss. During the seemingly endless flight from London, it had occurred to Langford that the American was not unlike a poker player betting blind, as if too frightened to examine his own hand. But then Hewens didn't need to look at his cards because Richard Langford was playing them for him. And being forced to bet against the urbane sophisticate, Norihiko

Samwashima. It was not a game for which Langford much cared.

The analysis was further complicated by James Maxwell. He was dying – and yet, if his offer to Langford could be believed, was still very much in command, apparently determined to safeguard the firm against the Shimada Corporation. But Maxwell had lied about Bailey, and for reasons which were far from clear. On the face of it, James Maxwell and Meyrick Hewens were partners, each declaring full confidence in the other. But they were both running scared – or so it seemed to Langford. Certainly Maxwell had every reason to be so. He knew he was going to die and it showed. But Hewens had it made. The firm was in good shape and when Maxwell made his final exit, the American would gain substantially. It simply didn't make sense. Unless there was something else, another card in the hand still face-down on the table.

The Mercedes made a sharp right turn, the sudden movement jerking Langford into an awareness of the present. And Oki. Lighting a cigarette, he caught a fleeting glimpse of the chauffeur's snake-like eyes reflected in the driving mirror. It somehow forced him to consider what could be a more immediate problem.

Oki had been waiting for him in the hotel foyer although there had been no pre-arranged time. And the same thing had happened the previous day, the Sunday. Langford had come down from his suite intending to take a brisk walk around the block to get his bearings and would have done so had it not suddenly poured with rain. But Oki was there, standing in the foyer. Waiting. And when Langford had decided to try one of the hotel's bars, Oki had followed – not into the bar itself but simply shifting his position so that he had an unrestricted view. Langford had considered offering the man a drink but Oki as a companion left too much to be desired. Certainly there was nothing particularly engaging about the Japanese. He stood in the hotel foyer like a grotesque

94

statue, his arms hanging limp at his sides, his close-cropped head inclined slightly forwards, flat, stubby features emphasizing an inherently primitive brutality. Even his small, claw-like hands gave an impression of irresistible, almost mechanical power. The high-calibre bulge under Oki's left shoulder seemed somehow superfluous.

As the car entered the Kobe port complex, Langford glanced briefly at the rows of warehouses and workshops, the stacked containers, the vast parking lots filled with new cars awaiting shipment. The funnels of the ships loomed beyond the storage buildings. He realized that he should have been interested, perhaps even impressed, but it suddenly dawned on him that he had been overlooking the biggest problem of all: himself.

Richard Langford had always disliked the twin concepts of security and regularity. He had always fought against rules and regulations, seeing them as constraints rather than guidelines. His inability to go-by-the-book had resulted in his army career coming to an abrupt end. He was a loner and had come to recognize that there was no place for him in any systemized organization. Without James Maxwell, life would be far more difficult and certainly less comfortable. And Maxwell was as good as dead. It came as something of a shock to Langford that for the first time in his life, he was actually worrying about the future instead of merely enjoying the present.

The present intruded again into his self-analysis when Oki stopped the Mercedes outside the heavy gates which separated Pier 13 from the rest of the dock area. Three uniformed security guards, all wearing sidearms, inspected the car, examined the sheet of paper produced by Oki and peered suspiciously at Langford through the windows. Then the gates were swung open and the car moved forward.

Impressed by the security measures, Langford remarked on the guards' attention but Oki's only reply was an ambiguous jerking movement of his close-cropped head. Samwashima had mentioned that the chauffeur had a modest understanding of English and Langford assumed that Oki hadn't understood his comment. Then it came to him that he had never actually heard the man utter a word, in any language. Before Langford could consider this further, the car stopped and the rear door was opened by a Japanese wearing an immaculate overall and a white safety helmet.

Because of the helmet and the overall, Langford failed to recognize Samwashima. In fact, he barely noticed the man at all. As he climbed from the car, his senses were swamped by the combined effects of the noise and the sheer size of the ship known as BC-9.

In the course of his work, Richard Langford had seen many ships, but never anything like the massive structure which towered above him and stretched away into the far distance. He stared at the ship, his pale eyes narrowed, his lips slightly parted. That something so gigantic should have been designed for and, indeed, capable of movement, seemed almost absurd. Meyrick Hewens' words echoed dimly in the back of his mind: *It's going to be the biggest in the world ...*

'Christ.' Langford's exclamation was completely involuntary and finally broke the spell. Collecting himself, he turned to Samwashima.

Again the Japanese bowed. 'I trust you are now completely rested?' he said, leaning close and speaking very loud.

'Yes, thank you. I'm sorry, but I didn't recognize you ...' Langford grinned as he looked up at the BC-9. 'It's almost unbelievable. They ... Hewens told me that it would be big but ... well, I've never seen anything like it.'

A small truck laden with reels of cable drove past them, the two men sitting on the platform both nodding deferentially towards Samwashima.

'You must be very proud,' said Langford, feeling a need to say something.

Samwashima seemed curiously flattered. 'It is an

achievement with which we are all very proud to be associated.' He smiled and gestured towards the offices. 'If you will come this way, Langford-*san*, we shall provide you with clothes.' He tapped the laminated plastic safety helmet on his head. 'We all wear these. It is regulations.'

Scarcely able to take his eyes off the BC-9, Langford followed his host. High up on the ship's superstructure, ant-like teams of men worked with back-pack paint sprayers so that even as he watched, the red-lead undercoat was quickly giving way to a bright, shimmering white. Giant overhead cranes moved along the quay, their long, latticed booms hanging over the vessel, raising and lowering great baulks of steel. And the air was filled with the noise of drilling, the high-pitched scream of metal sanders and the thudding drone of dozens of separate power-units all over the ship. But once inside the specially insulated portable huts, the noise was reduced to little more than a gentle, distant hum.

'Will you try for size, please?' Samwashima handed him a light blue safety helmet. 'The colour indicates that you are a distinguished visitor.'

Langford pressed the crash-hat on to his head and nodded. 'That's fine.'

'Good. And you must have overalls. It is very dirty on board.'

When he had pulled on the nylon overall, Langford said, 'Which was Bailey's office?'

'There.' Samwashima pointed to a door. 'You wish to see?'

'Please.'

The Japanese produced a bunch of keys from his pocket, selected one and unlocked the door. 'All doors are kept locked,' he explained. 'For security.'

'Ah.' Langford stepped inside the sparsely furnished room, taking the safety helmet from his head and placing it on the desk. 'You seem very concerned about security,' he remarked, glancing at the plans and charts which were pinned to the walls.

'It is necessary.' Samwashima regarded him for a moment. 'Is it not so in your country?'

'Yes, I suppose it is.' Moving across the room to the window, Langford stared at the ship. 'Tell me, what exactly was Bailey doing here?' He swung round and faced the Japanese.

'Working on the vessel '

'But doing what?'

Samwashima seemed hesitant. 'Technical work ... scientific work.' He smiled, uneasily. 'Doctor Bailey was a scientist, as you know.'

Nodding, Langford turned away and resumed his study of the BC-9. 'Christopher Bailey was a nuclear physicist,' he said, keeping his back to Samwashima. 'By all accounts, he was a good one.' He paused and lit a cigarette before facing Samwashima again. 'What does a nuclear physicist have to do with an oil tanker?'

'That is a question which I am not competent to answer.' There was a discernible tension in Samwashima's voice and he moistened his lips.

'You could try.'

'It ... it is a technically complex matter which also involves security. I would have to obtain authority from Mister Shiba himself.' He lit a cigarette and drew on it. 'But such details ... they are surely of no interest for you?'

'According to my information, the vessel is powered by diesel engines. That being the case, it seems odd that Shimada needed to employ a man with Bailey's background and qualifications.'

'I will consult with Mister Shiba. But the information you require may take a little time – '

'I have time, Sam.'

'I was going to suggest that it could be sent to your office London.'

'The problem is my report.' Langford moved across the room and sat on the edge of the desk. 'The precise nature of Bailey's work here would have to be entered.'

'I see.' Samwashima relaxed a little. 'In that case, I suggest you give him the title of Technical Advisor, no?'

'Perhaps.' Langford turned and pulled at one of the desk drawers. It was locked.

'I will open it,' said Samwashima, obviously relieved at being able to change the emphasis of their conversation if not the subject. Another key was produced and the master lock turned.

'It's empty.' Langford tried the other drawers with the same result. 'Why lock an empty desk?'

'Security,' Samwashima explained, carefully locking it again.

Langford stared at the top of the desk which was bare except for a clean sheet of blotting paper and a china ashtray, a souvenir of Cologne. Frowning, he stubbed his cigarette between the twin spires of the German cathedral.

'There is something troubling you, Dick?'

'No,' Langford lied. Then he donned the safety helmet. 'Shall we go aboard?'

Thin skeins of grey cloud streaked the pale sky and a stiff breeze thudded around them as they walked across the vast expanse of the main deck. Pausing, Langford turned and stared back at the superstructure which towered over the stern. It was like standing in a desert and peering at a distant skyscraper.

'Do you not find it remarkable?' said Samwashima, raising his voice above the wind.

'I find it terrifying.' Langford adjusted the safety helmet on his head and looked around. 'Where was Bailey killed?'

'There.' The Japanese pointed and they walked towards the large opening in the deck.

'What happened ... exactly?' said Langford, peering into the blackness.

'It appears that Doctor Bailey attempted to descend by means of a rope ladder and that he failed to secure the ladder properly, so ...' Samwashima's face took on an expression of deferential gravity. 'I believe that he tried to secure the ladder to one of these ...'

'Bollards,' interjected Langford. 'And?'

'The ladder came away and so he fell. The drop is approximately two hundred feet. The medical report stated that death was instantaneous.'

Langford felt vaguely ill. Instantaneous. What did it mean? Not what people generally assumed, that much seemed certain. No one living could know the hellish eternity of micro-seconds before the actual finality of death. He turned to Samwashima.

'And nobody saw him fall?'

'No one.' Samwashima pulled at his nose with thumb and forefinger and then sniffed. 'He was alone.'

Kneeling down, Langford tried again to see into the interior of the hull. 'What's down there?'

'Nothing.'

'Nothing?' He got slowly to his feet. 'There must be something. Bailey must have had a reason for going down there.' Even on the windswept deck, it was possible for Langford to sense Samwashima's unease.

'But the nature of Bailey-*san's* work ...' Words seemed to fail him for a moment, then he continued. 'We shall never know just why Doctor Bailey decided to go down there.'

'Maybe.' Langford began walking around the hatchway, kicking at the bollards which had been bolted into the decking at regular intervals. When he reached the far side, he paused, staring out across the strip of water separating Pier 13 from the other docks. There was a flash of light as a tug came into view and Langford watched it for a time before completing his circuit of the hatchway and rejoining Samwashima.

'You are considering the accident?' Samwashima was watching him, his dark, slanted eyes narrowing into tiny pinpricks.

'Not exactly.' Langford started to take out a cigarette but the Japanese shook his head.

'Sorry, no smoking is permitted here. The risk of fire.'

As he returned the pack to his pocket, another flash of sunlight was reflected from the tug. 'Where is the ladder?'

'Ladder?' Samwashima seemed surprised.

'The ladder which Bailey used. I'd like to see it.'

'That can be arranged.' He hesitated, clasping his hands together. 'Mister Langford, what is it you suspect?'

'I don't know. Perhaps when I've discovered just what Bailey was doing here ... how he died ... perhaps I'll have the answer.'

'You seem to be taking this matter rather more seriously than you indicated would ·be the case.' Samwashima's tone was one of accusation, as if a trust had been betrayed.

'Not at all,' Langford replied, smoothly. 'It all boils down to a question of liabilities. It may well be that the Shimada Corporation cannot be held in any way responsible for what happened.'

'Quite so, Dick.' Samwashima seemed to relax again.

'Of course, there's always the question of Bailey's relatives. They might choose to start some kind of action.'

'As far as we know, he had none.'

'Well, we'll obviously have to make sure.' He started towards the side of the ship. 'Anyway, if I could have a look at that ladder ...'

'But the efficiency of the ladder is not in question, Mister Langford.'

'Isn't it?' Langford was immediately aware of the hostility in his own voice and hastily changed tack. 'When is the ship due to sail?'

'I cannot say, Mister Langford.'

'Please, call me Dick.'

'Dick ... These delays ... it is difficult for us to know exactly when work will be completed and ...'

'And you have to find someone to replace Bailey.'

But Samwashima refused to be drawn. 'It was anticipated that the maiden voyage would take place this month but now ...'

'Now I'd like to see that ladder,' said Langford, firmly.

101

The Japanese gave a reluctant bow. 'Very well. It will be necessary for us to go to the chief foreman's office. Please, follow me.'

As they walked back along the windswept deck, Langford looked again at the small tug which was moving steadily towards the open water, its stubby bow dipping into the swell and sending up plumes of spray. The thin strands of cloud had begun to knit together, breaking the sunlight into narrow shafts. Another flash of brightness came from the tug. Then Langford caught a glimpse of the dark figure alongside the wheelhouse. And the camera.

Sensing rather than seeing Samwashima by his side, he pointed to the tug. 'One of yours?'

'No, Kobe Port Authority. Why do you ask?'

Langford had to smile. The Japanese was clearly suspicious of anything and everything. 'No reason. I just find ships fascinating.'

'We find them profitable,' replied Samwashima, pertly. 'And this vessel will be more profitable than most.'

'I can believe it.' They walked for a while in silence. 'Bailey's death brings the total to four, right?'

'Yes, I think that is correct.' Samwashima hesitated as they reached the bulkhead. 'Mister Lang ... Dick.' He gave one of his self-conscious smiles. 'These industrial accidents are always a matter for great regret. But they are commonplace, some would even say unavoidable. But my point is that we ... the Shimada Corporation, are very proud of our safety record.'

'So?' Langford's pale eyes narrowed. For reasons which he couldn't define, he felt a sudden burning hostility towards the bland, westernized Oriental. All his kow-towing courtesy couldn't alter the fact that he was lying.

'It may be best for us not to press any claim in respect of Doctor Bailey. The publicity could be harmful. If there is an indemnity to be paid, we may decide to make the money available from reserves.'

Langford eased off. 'Hell, Sam, you and I both know

that this thing's cut and dried. But I have to write a report. You know the drill. Offices are the same the world over. They need paper to feed on and if I can't provide it, they'll assume I haven't done any work.'

Leaving the main deck, they passed through a series of bulkheads and cluttered companionways before reaching the top of the gangway which led down to the quay.

'I was discourteous,' said Samwashima. quietly. 'Please accept my apologies. Bailey-*san* was a friend. We all held him in great esteem.'

Uncertain how to reply, Langford chose to remain silent as they started down the gangplank. Then he caught sight of Oki, standing by the car.

'Your driver, Oki, is certainly a big chap,' said Langford, conversationally. 'Looks as if he could bend iron bars without too much difficulty.'

'Oki is not merely a driver, Mister Langford.

'Your bodyguard?'

'You could say that, yes.'

'Do you have the same problems in Japan as they have in Italy?' said Langford, recalling how one of their clients had been held to ransom and then murdered.

'It is our policy,' he said. 'There is very strict security throughout the Shimada Corporation. All our senior people are protected. And here, for example – ' he glanced along the quay, 'unauthorized entry is impossible.'

'Was Bailey protected?' Langford stepped off the gangplank and waited.

'Of course. He was very important to us.'

Langford wondered why such an important man had suddenly become dispensable.

If there was a typical Japanese, thought Langford as he stepped inside the cluttered office, it had to be the chief foreman. Short and wiry, the man was desperately obsequious, bowing deeply from the waist at every opportunity. Then Samwashima rapped out something in Japanese and the man scurried away.

'I have sent him to fetch the ladder,' Sam explained.

'Ah.' Langford stared at the rolls of plans piled everywhere. 'This man, Mister ...?'

'The Chief Foreman? He is Mister Yamada, a very senior employee. Much respected.'

Langford nodded. Whether or not Mister Yamada commanded much respect was arguable, but one thing Richard Langford had noticed: like the staff at the hotel, he was obviously scared stiff of Samwashima.

'It is permitted to smoke here,' said Samwashima, offering cigarettes. They lit up and smoked in silence until Yamada returned bearing a rope ladder which he placed on the table.

It had been neatly rolled up and secured with heavy twine. The design was conventional, two ropes, a mixture of hemp and nylon, into which varnished wooden rungs had been spliced at regular intervals. Langford reached out and touched the rope with the tips of his fingers.

'This is the ladder that Bailey used?' He glanced at Samwashima and then at the chief foreman. There was a rapid conversation in Japanese.

'This is the ladder,' said Samwashima.

Langford nodded and let his hands run over the outer rungs. Then he stopped.

'Something is wrong?' demanded Samwashima, leaning across and peering at the ladder.

Langford drew a long breath. He didn't need to take measurements to be certain that if Bailey had wanted to secure the ladder to one of the bollards, the distance between each of the rungs was more than adequate for the ladder to have been slipped over the top. That would have been the logical way to secure it. And it should have been totally safe.

'You seem troubled, Langford-san. Is there any way in which I can help?'

Langford shook his head and looked quickly at the chief

foreman. But Mister Yamada stood like a statue, unblinking and utterly immobile. 'No-o, I was just thinking.' Using both hands, he turned the coiled ladder over on its side. Bailey had fallen to his death. That was certain. There was no reason to doubt that a rope ladder had been involved. But equally certain was the fact that the rope ladder produced by Chief Foreman Yamada was brand new. No one had so much as placed a foot on any one of the rungs, let alone fallen from it. The ropes were clean and yellow; even the varnish was unmarked.

'If there is something else we can show you ...?' Samwashima's voice broke in.

'No, not for the moment, thank you.' He could feel their eyes boring into him. Then Samwashima spoke in Japanese to the chief foreman who quickly gathered up the ladder and left, bowing as he went.

There was an awkward pause and Langford felt like telling Samwashima that he had had enough of the charade. Then he changed his mind, deciding that there might be more to be gained by simply playing along. If they believed they had him fooled, so much the better.

'What do you wish to do next?' asked Samwashima.

Langford had the answer ready. 'Bailey's apartment,' he said. 'If I could see that and perhaps pick up his personal effects. I can take them back to the UK when I go.'

'The apartment is Corporation property.' Was Samwashima on the defensive again? Langford couldn't decide. In the event, the request was granted. 'I must first make a telephone call. To cancel a meeting.'

'Please, don't do that on my behalf. I can go alone.'

'No, of course not.' He picked up the receiver, dialled and after a short pause, spoke rapidly in Japanese. It seemed to Langford that he didn't wait for a reply, simply dropping the receiver back into its cradle. Then he opened the door and revealed Yamada who was either about to come in or had been listening. Ignoring the chief foreman, Samwashima led the way to the Mercedes where Oki was

105

given his instructions in the same staccato Japanese he had used on the telephone. Oki merely nodded, waited for them to get in and then closed the door.

'Taciturn,' remarked Langford. Then, seeing Samwashima's puzzled expression, said, 'Silent. Oki. He never speaks.'

Samwashima gave a dry, mirthless chuckle. 'He is dumb, a mute. He can hear and understand but cannot ... cannot produce any sound.'

Langford lit a cigarette and inhaled, slowly. 'An accident?'

'The war,' retorted Samwashima, a sudden edge to his voice.

'He looks too young.'

'Too young to have fought, yes. But not too young to have suffered. He is what we in Japan call a Child of the Bomb, a victim crippled while still in his mother's womb. There were many such mutations caused by the radiation. Leukaemia and various other cancers are the most common. But there are also many blind, many without limbs, reproductive organs and some ... some so horrible that they are barely human. As for Oki, he is fortunate ...'

Samwashima paused as the car passed through the main gate and Langford wondered how much of what they were saying could be heard and understood by the ape-like mute.

'Fate is sometimes kinder than we appreciate,' Samwashima continued. 'Oki has no voice, but he has great strength, as you yourself seem to have noticed.'

'You obviously regard him with some affection.'

'Of course. Oki would defend me with his life. He knows that he will be cared for until the end of his days and so he repays me with unquestioning loyalty and obedience. I regard him as a friend.'

'He isn't a man I would choose for an enemy,' Langford said.

If Colonel DuCros had not had a gastric ulcer, he would have remained on the active list and given his family connections, would have certainly become a general. As it turned out, his stomach put him in line for premature retirement but his family came to the rescue and he was given another job. It wasn't the army although he retained his rank, pay and pension rights. As far as most of his friends were concerned, it was just another desk job, a comfortable sinecure so that DuCros could bide his time waiting for retirement at the proper age. In fact, it was nothing of the kind. As Head of Section Nine of SDECE, Colonel DuCros had some very heavy responsibilities indeed.

Henri Bouscat knew nothing about DuCros' ulcer or his family. And as he faced the lean, ascetic figure across an expanse of desk, Bouscat was even puzzled about the Colonel's precise rôle. But the Inspector had been kept awake for nearly thirty hours, most of the time just waiting around. So Bouscat, the painstaking and normally even-tempered policeman, was angry.

'Do you people only work at night?' he growled, chain-lighting a cigarette. Somewhere outside in the Rue Jullien, a police car or ambulance sped past, its wailing siren piercing the Paris night.

'You know how it is, Bouscat.' The Colonel sighed. 'Police work, yours and mine, they're much the same.'

'We try to avoid torture,' said Bouscat, acidly.

'You saw Rueff?' DuCros leaned back in his chair and raised his eyebrows.

'I saw him.' Bouscat flicked the ash from his cigarette. 'Why?'

'Why? My dear man, he refused to talk. We had to ... to persuade him.'

'The poor bastard had nothing to tell you.'

'On the contrary, Bouscat, he told us a great deal.

Once, of course, he knew what we wanted.'

'I don't suppose it occurred to your cretins to ask him before they went to work? He had nothing to hide.'

'He'll recover.' DuCros bent across the desk and began leafing through some papers. 'About this man Claude Picot.' The Colonel paused to light a thin cigar with exaggerated, almost effeminate movements of his long, delicate hands. 'Did you know him?'

'Not before this business, no.'

'But you had heard of him?'

Bouscat shook his head and didn't bother to stifle a yawn. 'I deal with murderers, *M'sieu*, not nuclear physicists.'

'Well, Inspector, this time you may find yourself dealing with one man who falls into both categories. And a homosexual into the bargain.' DuCros paused, thoughtfully. 'If the authorities gave us proper powers, we could have withdrawn Picot's Top Security clearance three years ago. As it happened ... well, never mind. It's too late. The problem now is that the man has disappeared.'

'Defected?'

DuCros shrugged. 'It is a possibility, yes. But I do not think it likely. He had his opportunity when his 'plane stopped over in Moscow but Picot went no further than the transit lounge. We know he disembarked at Tokyo but where he is now ... we do not know. He has vanished and the only thing we know for certain is why.'

'You think he murdered the student?'

His head wreathed in a band of curling smoke, the Colonel regarded Bouscat for a moment. 'Don't you?'

'I'm not sure.' Bouscat stretched and uncrossed his legs. 'Maybe you're right, but over the years I've come to mistrust the obvious. Anyway, as we know he went to Tokyo, it should be a simple matter for the Japanese authorities to find him. His race and nationality will make him conspicuous.'

DuCros nodded. 'Forgive me, Inspector, but you are thinking like a policeman.'

'Hardly surprising, *mon Colonel*.'

'I, on the other hand, am forced to take a different view.' The Colonel reached below the desk and produced a bottle of Cognac. 'For you?' He filled two small glasses, carefully measuring the spirit. 'Consider all the implications.' He pushed a glass towards Bouscat. 'Picot has important knowledge, information which could have strategic implications. *Santé*.' He raised the glass to his lips. 'He just happens to be a homosexual who has a fight with his ... his lover during which the boy is killed. So, what does he do? Hides the body. Not very well, as you must agree. Then he simply flies to Japan.'

After a long pause, Bouscat shrugged. 'What are you asking me to deduce from all this?'

'Simply that the killing of the student – assuming Picot did kill him – is incidental. Did Rueff tell you about the man Picot met near the Bois de Vincennes?' Bouscat nodded and the Colonel continued. 'This other man may be the link I am seeking. You see, Inspector, it is my belief that Picot was going to Japan for other reasons, not merely to escape a murder investigation.'

'You obviously know something I don't.'

'Not much, I'm afraid. But your friend Rueff gave us a good description of this other man and so we have been able to create an artist's impression of him.' DuCros flicked a photo-copy across the desk. 'Our people think that he is either an Australian or an American.'

'Could be anything,' growled Bouscat, stubbing out his cigarette. 'But what of it?'

'I want this person found. There is little doubt in my mind that Rueff unwittingly witnessed a clandestine meeting. One party, namely Picot, has gone to Japan. I want to know about the other man.'

'Suppose you're right and the meeting was ... clandestine,' Bouscat said. 'Why shouldn't this other man simply be a queer like Picot, eh? A lovers' tryst?'

The Colonel wrinkled his nose in distaste. 'I will admit it is a possibility but until we know for sure, I am going to hang on to my hunch.'

'Very good. But how are you going to find this man?'

DuCros drained his glass. 'You are going to find him for me, Inspector. I know it won't be easy but – '

'Easy? It's bloody impossible. I have eight men in my team and two unsolved murders – three if we include the student, Malvy. I don't see how ... '

'Hear me out, Inspector.' DuCros paused, refilling his own glass and then pushing the bottle across to Bouscat. 'I have given this a lot of thought. An artist's impression is one thing but an eye-witness is quite another. We have Jean-Jacques Rueff who can certainly be charged with breaking and entering, possibly even with murder – '

'Rueff's no killer. He – '

'Kindly do not interrupt me.' The rebuke was delivered softly but with devastating authority. 'Rueff could be framed. Simple. So, we offer him a chance to make amends, to get off the hook. With your help.'

'My help?'

'Yes, Bouscat. According to our information, you have more friends in the Paris underworld than you have in the police. I think you're just the man I need.'

The Inspector helped himself to the Cognac. 'This other man, the one Picot met. Will there be a warrant for his arrest?'

'No. It is not necessary because there will be no arrest. This man must not know that inquiries are being made. That is most important. The primary task is to identify him, to give him a name. Secondly, we will try to locate him, but that comes later.'

'Colonel, do you honestly imagine that Rueff and me will be able to search Paris on our own? It's impossible.'

'I expect you to use your contacts.'

'But they work for money. Or certain favours.'

'We can pay.'

'I don't doubt it. But they deal in crime, *M'sieu le Colonel*, either before or after it is committed but crime, nonetheless. This kind of manhunt is ... alien.'

'How much money would it take to buy the assistance you need, Inspector?'

'Depends how soon you want results, how many people ... it is a difficult question to answer.'

'You may have fifty thousand francs. No questions asked. All I want is the name of the man Picot met near the Bois de Vincennes.'

'Fifty, a hundred, a million francs ... what's the difference? It's a gamble. There can be no guarantees. And there's another angle to this: if the man has no connections in Paris, you're wasting your time. But if he does have friends then someone will pass him the word.' Bouscat stood up. 'I'm sorry, what you ask is impossible.'

'Sit down.' DuCros fixed him with an icy stare. 'On the afternoon of Tuesday, November 15, Claude Picot met a man, probably an American, near the Bois de Vincennes. I need to know the identity of that man and I do not care if you have to crawl up the arse of every hotelier, bar *patron* and brothel-keeper in Paris to get the information. You will have fifty thousand francs, your friend Rueff and an added incentive: if you fail, I'll make sure you end your days directing traffic in the Place de la Republique.'

'I don't like your tone, Colonel,' said Bouscat, evenly. 'And I don't take kindly to threats. If you're so worried about Picot, all you have to do is pick up the telephone and call Tokyo.'

'Yes, I could do that. The result would be interesting. We could be faced with a scandal, Inspector. A leading physicist disappears leaving a corpse in his apartment. *Merde alors!* The security services would be dragged through the shit. Sodomy, atomic secrets at risk ... *non*, it is not going to be like that. We will find that man.' He handed Bouscat a card. 'This number will always reach me. I suggest you pick up Rueff and begin.'

'What about my office?'

'Don't go there. I have made the necessary arrangements direct with the Minister. Work from your apartment. And Bouscat, however much you dislike my threats, do not underestimate my power.'

3

The caretaker stared balefully at Samwashima, nodding as the Deputy Managing Director spoke in Japanese. Langford stood in the background, conscious of Oki studying him. Then Samwashima touched Langford's arm.

'He will take us up now.'

They mounted the stairs slowly and Langford found himself listening to the wheezy rasping of the old caretaker for whom the climb was an obvious effort. When they reached the top landing there was another exchange in Japanese. It seemed to Langford that the old caretaker was arguing but it was impossible to even guess at what was being said. Rather to Langford's relief, Oki had remained on the ground floor, presumably to stay with the car. Then there was a jangling sound as the caretaker struggled with a large key ring before opening the door into Bailey's apartment.

Samwashima stood to one side, motioned Langford to enter and then followed, slamming the door in the caretaker's face.

'Trouble?' asked Langford.

'A ... a difficult man.' Samwashima gave a little shrug. 'Well, Dick, this is where Bailey-*san* lived.'

The Yamamoto-dori apartment was small but well appointed and furnished not unlike Langford's hotel, a somewhat unhappy mixture of Japanese and western styles.

'I believe Doctor Bailey liked the apartment,' said Samwashima, looking around. 'This is the main living area, as you see. The kitchen is through there and over

112

there is the bedroom and a bathroom.' He might easily have been a house agent with a prospective client.

'Very nice,' Langford muttered.

'I can arrange for Bailey-*san's* belongings to be packed and brought to your hotel.'

'Yes, thank you.' Glancing down, Langford saw an opened newspaper lying on a chair and picked it up. 'An English paper?' he said, surprised.

Samwashima stared for a moment and then nodded. 'Yes. It is *The Mainichi Daily News*, a Japanese English-language paper.'

'Ah.' Langford carefully re-folded the newspaper so that the front page was facing outwards. 'Did Bailey share the apartment?'

'No. As you see, it is not large.'

'So the place is vacant right now?'

'That is so.' Samwashima gave him a knowing smile. 'I would like to be able to offer it to you but your stay will be so short.'

'No, I wasn't hinting at that.' Langford stared at the newspaper for a moment and then tossed it down on the chair. Someone – and presumably someone who could read English – had been looking at the paper. And it couldn't have been Bailey because the copy of the *Mainichi Daily News* lying on the chair had only come out that morning.

'You certainly know how to make use of all available space,' said Langford, walking into the tiny kitchen. He turned away from Samwashima and pressed his hand against the electric cooker. It was warm to the touch. So was the kettle. And the hot-water tap.

'The bedroom.' Samwashima was acting the estate agent again.

This room too was small and virtually filled by a double bed. 'If that's the bathroom over there, I'd quite like to use it.'

'Of course.' Samwashima seemed anxious to open the door for him.

Once inside, Langford slipped the bolt, went to the handbasin and turned on the cold tap. The sound of running water was reassuringly loud as he opened a small, mirror-fronted cabinet over the basin. The contents of the cabinet were much as he had expected: razor, shaving soap, toothbrush, toothpaste, hair oil, a bottle of indigestion tablets, a tube of patent ointment for haemorrhoids and a small metal container which held contraceptives.

Smiling to himself, Langford carefully shut the cabinet and then noticed another cupboard behind the door. It turned out to be an airing cupboard. Apart from the neatly-stacked sheets and blankets, there were also a number of colourful blouses, panties, bras and several pairs of tights. Closing the door, Langford turned off the tap, pressed the flush button above the lavatory and rejoined Samwashima.

The Japanese was standing by the window, staring down into the teeming Yamamoto-dori. 'I thought we might take lunch together,' he said, turning round.

'That sounds like a good idea.'

'Excellent. I know a special restaurant, typical Japanese. They serve the giant cold-water crab from Hokkaido. Very delicious. Very tender. We call it *wakkanai*.'

As he started towards the door, Langford noticed the telephone and stared for a moment at the number, willing himself to memorize it but Samwashima seemed suspicious and Langford said, 'You use Arabic numerals. That's interesting.'

'Always. Of course, it is necessary for business, our computers ...'·

'Of course.'

Once they had left the apartment, Langford was able to persuade Samwashima to descend first and as he followed him down the stairs, he quickly scribbled the number on the back of his cigarette packet.

The Junidanya restaurant on Nishi-machi was discreet

to the point of invisibility. It was also very small and crowded but finding a table was no problem because there were none. As Samwashima had said, it was typical Japanese, the real thing. After leaving their shoes at the door, they were led to a small space and squatted down on lengths of tatami matting. Exquisitely delicate waitresses clad in kimono and obi seemed to glide around them like so many brightly-coloured butterflies, serving the food in a series of little bowls. As forecast, the lunch was superb but spoiled firstly by Samwashima's insistence that they drink Japanese Suntory whisky with the meal, and secondly, by the awful discomfort of having to squat rather than sit. Langford eventually managed to achieve a semi-reclining position on the mat which made life a little easier. But only a little.

The restaurant was curiously noisy so that conversation was difficult. Not that Langford was in the mood for small talk. There were too many questions he wanted to ask, questions which his intuition told him would either be completely ignored or politely evaded. But as the meal progressed, Langford saw that he was going to face another problem. Norihiko Samwashima was laying into the Suntory as if there were no tomorrow.

'There are many good places in Kobe,' said Samwashima, talking through a mouthful of food. 'I show you.'

Langford merely nodded. The Japanese seemed intent on making a real session of it.

'Good entertainment. And women, too.' He grinned, lasciviously. 'I know a very good place for that in Osaka.'

'Sounds interesting,' Langford murmured, staring hopelessly as more whisky was poured into his glass.

'Bailey-*san* was good drinker. Him and me ...' Samwashima jabbed himself in the chest. 'Good friends. Good buddies.' Then he raised his brimming glass. '*Kampai!*'

Langford followed suit, but managed to spill much more whisky than he drank. Samwashima's carefully

115

cultivated western veneer was cracking under the impact of alcohol, his precise, fluent English rapidly degenerating into a coarse pidgin dialect. Langford knew that if he could succeed in appearing to keep pace and remain sober, he might get a glimpse of the real Samwashima. And perhaps a good deal more.

'Bailey-*san* ... he want to quit, you know that?' Samwashima licked his lips. 'Mister Shiba very worried but Sam fix it okay and Bailey stay. Sam fix everything.'

Langford leaned forward. 'Why did Bailey want to quit?'

The Japanese laughed. 'Izumi.'

'What's that?'

'Izumi.' Samwashima was still laughing. 'Clever man. Designer. Work with Bailey-*san* on ship. Then ...'

Langford waited for a moment before speaking. 'Then what?'

'Dead. Accident. Big piece of steel ... wham. *Sayo nara*, Izumi. Bailey very upset. Angry. But Sam fix it. Sam fix everything.' Then he shook his head. 'All for Mister Shiba ... my whole life ...' There was bitterness in his eyes.

'Tell me about it,' said Langford. But Samwashima had other ideas.

'Good clubs.' He began to stand up, staggered and sent bowls and glasses flying. No one seemed to mind. 'I show you, Dick. Real good.' Stooping with obvious difficulty, he picked up Langford's glass and raised it. '*Kampai! Kampai!*'

'Mud in your eye,' Langford replied, vaguely remembering something Meyrick Hewens had said.

4

By six o'clock, Japanese time, Samwashima and Langford were staggering from one drinking club to the next, under the eye of the ever watchful Oki. In London, nine hours behind, James Maxwell was just sitting down to breakfast in the Stanhope Gate service flat he used when he had to stay in town. Shortly after he had started eating, he experienced a sudden dizziness and went into the bedroom. The bottle of tablets stood on the bedside table. He took two and washed them down with the water left over from the previous evening, then lay on the unmade bed as his doctor had recommended. Ten minutes later, Maxwell got up and returned to his breakfast but the food was cold, so he contented himself with finishing the coffee and half a slice of buttered toast. Going across to the window, he looked down into the street and saw Dobson leathering the windscreen of the waiting Daimler.

Pulling on his British Warm, Maxwell picked up his hide attaché case and left the flat. He normally walked down the four flights of stairs but because of the attack, he decided to take the lift and pressed the call button. When the doors slid open he stepped inside, touching the sensor control for the ground floor. Keeping his eyes on the indicator panel, Maxwell was aware of the pain in his head. It seemed rather worse than usual but he didn't feel at all dizzy as the lift began its descent. He saw the figure 2 glow and then fade. But something happened and the lift was suddenly plunged into darkness. Reaching out, Maxwell's hands came into contact with the cold metal of the automatic doors. He heard his attaché case fall to the floor and then there was sudden pain, as if his head were being torn apart.

The hall porter had been down to the basement to adjust one of the boilers. When he finally returned to the main foyer, he saw what was happening. There was something hypnotically gruesome about the way the automatic doors opened and closed against James Maxwell's inert body.

It took the porter the nearly five minutes to shut off the power supply to the lift. He chose to do this by going down to the basement and pulling the main switch. Later, he would wonder why he hadn't simply stepped inside the lift and pressed the emergency stop button but the unexpected has a way of neutralizing the most elementary logic. And once he had succeeded in stopping the grotesque scissor-action of the automatic doors, he dialled 999 and demanded an ambulance.

Alerted by the porter, Dobson was at his master's side when the ambulance arrived some seven minutes later. On impulse, he decided to accompany Maxwell on the short, high-speed journey to St George's Hospital on the other side of Hyde Park Corner.

5

Claude Picot stared at the plans littering the big table which two servants had placed near the roaring log fire. Outside, the wind whistled around the house, spattering the rain against the windows and carrying the noise of the sea into the room.

Muga Tasaki ran his hand through the shock of white hair which shone in the fire light. 'I have checked with my people in Tokyo,' he said, slowly and precisely. 'All the equipment you have requested will be obtained and brought here.' He stared at the Frenchman for a moment. 'You do not foresee any problems?'

Picot shrugged. 'Technically, no. But what you propose is – '

Tasaki's expression suddenly hardened. 'It is not ... not your concern to judge. You are being well paid for your work here. You will ask no questions.'

'*M'sieu*, do you understand the consequences ... the potential dangers ...?' Picot shook his head. '*C'est une catastrophe*. It is madness.'

'I have said that it is not for you to judge. And anyway, Mister Picot, the threat will be enough.'

'Suppose there is a mistake? Suppose there is an accident? From the data you have provided, I can tell you, *M'sieu*, the Far East, Australia, New Zealand ...' Picot spread his hands in despair. 'All this would be destroyed, slowly, painfully.'

Tasaki nodded. 'I understand. The authorities will also understand. So, Mister Picot, there will be no danger. Unless you yourself are careless and make a mistake. That, I think, is the only risk, the only real danger.'

Picot went across to the fire and warmed himself. 'How long am I to be kept a prisoner here?'

Tasaki shook his head, vigorously. 'You are my guest, Mister Picot. You are free to use all the facilities of my residence as you wish. However, I do not think it wise for you to stray beyond the boundaries, so ...'

'So I am a prisoner.'

'No, you are making another wrong judgment. Besides, there is much for you to do, preparations to be made, plans to be finalized. There will be no mistakes, Picot-*san*.'

The Frenchman stared at the fire. 'If there is a mistake, it will not matter who makes it. The results will be beyond repair. I ask you to consider this carefully, *M'sieu* Tasaki. I have spent the greater part of my life researching and developing the technology of nuclear fission. And during my last years with the French Government, I was the director of a research programme on nuclear waste and ...'

'You tell me nothing I do not already know.' Tasaki took an engraved gold case from his pocket and extracted a cigarette, examining it carefully before placing it between his lips. 'You seem to forget that we Japanese were the first people to experience the effects of man's atomic discoveries. As a nation, we have had every reason to study these phenomena.'

'But I, as a scientist, I am afraid of what you propose. The technology is not yet fully developed. There are still some things about which we are not certain.'

'The concept of re-processing nuclear waste has been proved,' said Tasaki, bluntly. 'Methods of transportation have been tested.'

'Agreed. But such a quantity and such a risk ...'

119

'There is no risk ... provided those responsible concede our demands. You must ensure that we have absolute control.'

Picot bit his lip, clasping and unclasping his hands in pain. 'What will happen if they choose not to ... if they decide to call your bluff, *M'sieu*? What then?'

Tasaki paused to light his cigarette with a heavy gold lighter. 'You do not appear to comprehend, Mister Picot. We do not bluff. This is no trick, no infantile game. I cannot claim your expertise in nuclear physics but I know sufficient to understand that the authorities must be convinced of my – our – determination to go ahead if they dare to suggest we are not in earnest.' He paused, drawing smoothly on the cigarette as the room was suddenly filled with the noise of the wind billowing down the chimney. 'Many years ago, Mister Picot, I took an oath. It was a sacred vow. I mean to fulfil my obligation and if it means the massive devastation of which you and I as educated men are only too well aware ... well, so be it.'

Going to the table, Tasaki stared at the plans. Then he gave a low chuckle. 'When I consider the efforts which have been made to ensure that what we are about to do could not possibly happen, I see a gratifying humour in it. Do you not agree?'

'I have to pray that your plan works, *M'sieu*.'

'By all means do so. But in my experience, Mister Picot, prayers are so much wasted energy. I have watched many men pray ... some for life, others for death. The results were always the same. What was inevitable simply happened. There was a time when I also prayed.'

'You are a Catholic?'

Tasaki laughed. 'I was a Buddhist, but where is the difference? Buddha, Mohammed, Christ, they were all human, clever men who had the ability to see that their weaker brethren had an emotional need to believe in something outside themselves. Others who came later were cleverer still, for they saw that men who believed the unbelievable could be manipulated and controlled. No,

120

there is in reality only one God whom we have to placate. He is called Stupidity and he belongs to Mankind alone.'

'Then you are a cynic, *M'sieu*.'

'I am a man,' said Tasaki, going towards the door. 'But there is no time for this idle speculation. We both have work to do. Be sure to do yours well, Frenchman. If you fail me, I know of no power which will protect you from my anger.'

6

Richard Langford had never been a heavy drinker. Once he had made the discovery that alcohol impaired sexual prowess, he treated hard liquor with reserve and respect. But he could still hold his drink when the occasion demanded and if he had surreptitiously poured away more Japanese whisky than he had drunk, his intake had still been fairly hefty. He hadn't even begun to keep pace with Samwashima but it didn't matter. When last seen, Shiba's deputy was out cold, sprawled in a soiled heap in the back of the Mercedes. And to Langford's relief, Oki was with him, caring for his master and probably tucking him into bed. Langford didn't much care. The important thing was that for a few hours at least, he was free of Oki's mute, penetrating presence.

It was a little after ten p.m. when Langford returned to the hotel, obtained his key from the main desk and took the lift to the suite on the fourth floor. Quickly discarding his jacket, he pulled on a dark, roll-neck sweater, swapped his town shoes for a pair of rubber-soled chukka boots and selected a blue-black anorak from his wardrobe. Switching off the lights, he went cautiously into the corridor. There was no one about as he passed the lifts and started down the stairs.

On the first floor landing, he found a fire exit. The door opened easily, a simple bar mechanism, and Langford stepped out on to an ironwork fire escape which led down into a small yard filled with dustbins. Another door led directly into the street and a few minutes later, he was sitting in the back of a taxi, frowning as he lit a cigarette.

If leaving the hotel unseen had been simple, Langford knew that gaining access to the section of the Kobe docks occupied by the Shimada Corporation would be far from it. And once inside the perimeter, getting aboard the giant BC-9 could be very difficult indeed. But as the cab sped through the dark, deserted streets, Langford's most pressing problem was trying to decide just why he felt compelled to go back to the ship. Sober, Samwashima had been jittery and trotted out a series of clumsy lies. Drunk, he had quickly degenerated, revealing a host of tensions and frustrations but little else. Richard Langford had clung to his every slurred word but Samwashima had said nothing which might have provided the clue which he sought. Not that Langford had any clear idea what he was looking for. All he had was a hunch bordering on certainty that the death of Doctor C.E. Bailey, whether accidental or deliberately engineered, was far from straightforward.

Uncertain of the layout of the docks, Langford paid off the taxi as soon as he saw the dark outlines of ships and warehouses against the night sky. The driver seemed rather perplexed, if not downright suspicious and Langford stood on the pavement, waiting until the cab had disappeared round a corner before he moved.

He found himself inside the dock area almost before he realized it and felt a sudden glow of confidence as he walked soundlessly along a straight tarmac road towards the waterfront. The place seemed utterly deserted and his backward-glances became less frequent as he relaxed. Then he reached a long, deserted quay and knew he had made two serious mistakes.

The BC-9 was a fantastic sight, rising out of the water like a huge, steel island, the towering superstructure at the stern speckled with lights and long sections of the immense main deck swept by harsh arc-lamps. Langford swore. Common sense should have told him that the

Japanese would be working round-the-clock but the presence of the night-shift was only one error. The other was Langford's position in the docks.

The BC-9 lay alongside Pier 13, only about five hundred yards from where Langford stood. But it was five hundred yards of water. He had come into the docks on the wrong side.

Backing into a pool of shadow, Langford was almost convinced that his best course of action was to return to the hotel before Oki could resume his guard duty. Then he heard something and froze, an un-lit cigarette crumpling between his fingers as his muscles tensed. The sound was faintly familiar, a curious combination of thudding splashes and squeaks. Then he smiled to himself as he realized that a rowing boat was coming alongside the quay.

The dinghy bumped against the stonework and two men clambered quickly on to the quay, one of them securing the painter to a small bollard. They stood for a moment, lighting cigarettes and talking, quietly. Then one of them walked to the entrance of what looked like a warehouse, grunting as he slid the door open and leaned against it while his companion went inside.

From his hiding place in the shadows, Langford heard the sound of a car being started, the engine revving, noisily. Then the car emerged from the warehouse, the driver switching on his main beams so that the length of the quay was suddenly flooded with light. Langford pressed himself against the wall as the car swung round, the shafts of light sweeping over him. He heard rather than saw the sliding door being closed but all his senses were suddenly alerted as the Japanese walked straight towards him.

The man was tall and well-built. Like Oki. Unconsciously flexing his hands, Langford waited. It was difficult to get a good view because of the glare, but the Japanese had the same slow, lumbering walk as Oki. Then he stopped and began to relieve himself. And when the sound of water spattering against the ground had ceased, the man returned to the car.

Langford waited until the car had turned off the quay before he risked leaving the pool of shadow. As he stared down at the rowing boat which sat almost motionless on the dark, greasy water, he was still in two minds as to what he should do. Then he stooped, loosed the painter and climbed awkwardly into the boat which rocked as he settled himself on the thwart. Getting the oars into the rowlocks proved surprisingly difficult but he eventually succeeded and started to row towards the BC-9.

Because he had had little experience of boats, it took Langford some time to master the knack of keeping the dinghy on a straight course and for a time, it seemed that he was going round in circles as he pulled unevenly against the oars. Glancing over his shoulder, he saw that the current was taking him down towards the bows of the giant tanker, and he rested for a moment, trying to judge the speed of the tide. It was moving fast and he began to row again. He knew that if he were swept past the ship, it might be difficult to make another approach. But as he got closer, the water became slack and he was able to manoeuvre the boat relatively easily along the side of the BC-9 and around the exposed forepeak until he was sandwiched between the towering hull and the pier.

It was like being in a long, dark tunnel, every slight sound echoing around him as he carefully shipped the oars and used his hands to pull the rowing boat along the side of the pier until he found a vertical ladder. After securing the painter, he began to climb, like an insect against the immense side of the tanker.

Peering upwards, he could make out the edge of the quay and the narrow gap separating it from the hull. The space seemed tiny but as he ascended, Langford saw that there was about four feet clearance. He also noticed the massive fenders fixed to the quay, great slabs of rubber to cushion the ship against the stonework. He paused, turning to stare at the steel-plated hull. It only required a slight movement in the water, maybe the wash from some passing vessel, and the BC-9 would move, nearly half a million tons of inert matter pressing inexorably against the fenders over which he had to climb.

The extent of the risk was underlined as he neared the top of the ladder. One of the fenders had been lashed over the ladder itself, creating an overhang, and Langford hesitated, knowing that there was no way he could judge if and when the ship might suddenly move. He had taken a chance. If he chose the wrong moment, he would be hopelessly crushed, squashed like a fly.

Hooking his legs around the ladder, he slowly eased himself back and clawed at the fender until his fingers touched a torn section which he could grip. Then he began to pull himself up and over the slippery rubber, the persistent lapping of the water echoing below him. When he finally slid on to the quay, he caught the sound of voices. Then footsteps.

The four men who walked past him all wore safety helmets and carried what Langford assumed to be food boxes. He lay absolutely still until they were well clear before he slowly looked up and tried to work out the best way of getting aboard.

Knowing that there would be a watchman on the gangway, he decided to climb one of the thick cables securing the ship to the pier. The nearest one was at the bow. Moving cautiously along the very edge of the quay, he crouched down by one of the large bollards, staring upwards. It was a hell of a height but the cable was taut, the angle about fifty degrees, and he smiled to himself, recalling similar obstacles he had tackled on army assault courses.

After a quick check that the coast was clear, he swung himself on to the cable, hanging upside down and using his hands and legs, monkey-fashion.

The steel was icy cold and ragged and he could feel the strands cutting into his palms. But he was making good progress and even if his back and shoulder muscles burned with the exertion, he was fairly confident. Until the ship moved.

Something had caused the BC-9 to push against the quay and Langford winced as he heard the steel hull grinding against the rubber fenders. He was about to congratulate himself for not being in the wrong place at the wrong time when he quickly discovered he had other problems.

Because the ship had moved towards the quay, the cable had slackened and Langford was now hanging vertically. He started to slide down but checked himself just in time, the cable biting viciously into his flesh.

It took an immense effort to pull himself up the remaining few feet but as he neared the forecastle, the ship slowly eased away from the quay and the cable tautened again. In one jerking movement, Langford threw all his weight forward and crashed heavily on to the deck. His hands were streaked with a stinging mixture of rust, oil and blood, and his breathing reduced to shallow, frantic gasps.

Only after some minutes did it occur to Richard Langford that he might have been seen, that someone might be there. He looked up. The forecastle was deserted, as was the flat, empty expanse of the main deck. The only problem now was the floodlighting, great stretches of harsh, glaring brightness through which he would have to pass in order to reach the hatchway where Bailey had fallen to his death.

It was nearly one o'clock. More than three hours had elapsed since Oki had dropped him at the hotel. Once again, Langford hesitated. Then the thought that Oki might at that moment be checking up on him spurred him into action. Standing upright, he simply walked from the forecastle, going carefully down the steps and on to the main deck. Because of the lighting, the massive superstructure at the stern was somehow blacked-out so that Langford could barely see it. But he knew that anyone in the right position in the stern would be able to see him. There was no cover, no concealing shadow. He was in the open and moving normally seemed to be the most sensible camouflage.

Another effect of the lighting was to make the gigantic deck appear much smaller but as he headed aft, Langford realized again the distance he had to cover and began to wonder how he should react if someone, anyone, caught him. But before he could come to any firm conclusion, he experienced a bitter sinking feeling in the pit of his belly and knew that he had had a wasted journey.

For a brief moment, he thought he had come to the wrong hatch, but a quick glance around at the rows of bollards bolted into the decking convinced him that he was standing on the very spot from which he and Samwashima had peered down into the dark steel cavern. The significant difference between then and now was that a series of six-inch steel plates had been bolted over the opening.

Langford grimaced as he stared at the immovable covering. Whatever it was that Doctor Bailey had gone down to inspect was beyond reach – unless Langford could find another means of access. Then the blaring of a siren filled the air and once again he had cause to curse his carelessness. He had been lucky and gone aboard during a break. Now he could hear workmen on the quay and the sound of machinery starting up, he remembered the ear-splitting volume of noise when he had visited the ship with Samwashima. It was time to quit.

Langford needed to reach the relative safety of the forecastle before anyone came on to the main deck. He sprinted for'ard, pulling off his belt as he ran. And just as he reached the cable-port, he saw a group of men emerge into a patch of light towards the stern.

Doubling the belt over to form a loop, he was about to begin his descent to the quay when something made him pause. He stared down at the main deck. He could see something in his mind's eye but it refused to come into

127

focus. Something was wrong. But for all his concentration, Langford couldn't decide what it was. Then he became aware of the group of men who were now advancing along the deck.

Going down was a lot easier than coming up. Using the belt like a pulley and his legs as a brake, he gradually let his weight take him down the cable. Not until he was halfway did he catch sight of the hunched figure by the bollard and by then, it was too late.

Because he was concentrating on the figure below, Langford misjudged his landing. He slipped awkwardly from the cable and fell on his face. The Japanese let out a startled yelp and dropped the bottle he was holding.

As the bottle smashed against the quay, Langford rolled over, jumped to his feet and felled the man with one blow. Catching him as he sagged forwards, Langford caught the overpowering scent of whisky and grinned with relief as he leaned the unconscious workman against the bollard. It was doubtful that the Japanese would have had time to see enough to provide a description of him. And even if he had, the chances were that he would be reluctant to say anything.

Anxious to get clear, Langford didn't give a thought for any possible movement of the BC-9 as he lowered himself over the rubber fenders and used his feet to grope for the ladder. And by the time he had manoeuvred the small rowing boat away from the pier and out into the open water, he had completely forgotten the risks he had taken. He was even still smiling slightly as he rowed towards the opposite quay. Because although he hadn't got any closer to solving the mystery of Bailey's death, he suddenly knew what had been nagging at his tired brain. He had begun by thinking that his subconscious mind had registered something unusual. But the opposite was true. Something was missing. And Richard Langford believed he knew what.

By four a.m., Langford was back in the small yard at the rear of the hotel. He was tired, his hands throbbed with the cuts and he was filthy. But his fatigue, the pain of his lacerated flesh and the state of his clothes were the least of his worries. He swore aloud, holding his breath as the burst of invective echoed back to him in the confined yard. Leaving the hotel had been too simple. The fire door had opened without difficulty and it was this which had made him careless. He should have hooked up the locking bar so that he could have gone in as easily as he had come out. Now he was trapped outside the hotel.

It was still pitch dark. Leaving the yard, Langford circled round the hotel until he was standing opposite the main entrance. He couldn't be sure that the Mercedes parked just a few yards from the entrance belonged to Oki. But the car looked somehow familiar.

Langford risked going closer, walking slowly across the road at an angle and peering into the brightly-lit foyer. Two clerks stood behind the desk. And just beyond them, seated in a position which gave him a view of the entrance and the lifts, was Oki.

There was no point in hanging around and Langford headed past the main entrance, turning into a narrow side-street. Somehow he had to get back inside the hotel without being seen – either by Oki or the clerks at the desk. He had little doubt that if he were seen by anyone, the information would be passed on. Once Samwashima discovered that he had been out, it wouldn't take too much mental exertion on the part of the Japanese to work out where and why.

Engrossed in his problem, Langford almost missed the tiny alleyway that led towards the centre of the hotel block. He turned into it. Then his nose picked up the scent of cooking. It was a good smell and brought the saliva to his mouth.

There were a series of doors and the first one he tried led

into a large kitchen. Three chefs were standing with their backs to him, each concentrating on their work. Langford noticed a bank of light switches just inside the door. His hand slammed against them and the kitchen was plunged into darkness. There was a shout followed by the sound of smashing crockery. Langford darted towards a nearby swing door, through into a bleak, brightly-lit passage. Then he saw the service lift and jumped into it, hammering at the controls.

Stopping the lift on the fifth floor, Langford sprinted along the corridor and down the stairs to the fourth. He saw no one and by the time he reached the door to his suite, the key was ready in his hand.

The door swung open. Langford withdrew the key, flicked on the light and kicked the door closed in one movement. The sudden brightness made him blink. Then he stepped into the room and froze. The place was a shambles. But what jarred him into total alertness was the hunched figure by the window. And the darkly threatening muzzle of a Smith & Wesson automatic pointing towards his chest.

SIX

1

There was a dull, echoing silence as the two men faced
each other. Langford knew that if the Smith & Wesson
was a 39, it carried an eight-round magazine; if it was the
59, there could be a maximum of fourteen 9mm
Parabellum slugs. It was an ideal weapon for a
professional killer.

But then there was the click of a safety catch and the
gun was slipped into a holster behind the intruder's right
hip. Langford took a pace forward. 'Who the hell are you?'

'Hold it right there, Mister Langford.' The man's hand
hovered. 'We neither of us want trouble.' He was
American. And confident.

'What are you doing here? Who are you?'

'I'm paying a call.' Almost like a conjurer, the
American produced a card which he flicked on to the low
table in front of the sofa. 'Maybe you'd better sit down,
Mister Langford. You look as if you've had a rough time.'
And he smiled as he leaned against the wall. 'You get
knocked down by a truck or something?'

'Timothy G. Gunning, American Consulate, Kobe.'
Langford frowned as he read aloud from the card. 'Does
diplomatic immunity now extend to breaking and
entering?'

'Sometimes.' Gunning put his hand in his pocket and
drew out three small round objects which he placed on the
table. 'Sorry about the mess but I had to find these. Did
you know they'd bugged the suite?'

Staring down at the tiny microphones, Langford shook
his head. 'Who's they?'

'They could be a whole lot of people but I guess I have in mind your Japanese friend, Frankenstein. He has a room on the next floor and a trunk full of equipment, including a tape-deck which he keeps running twenty-four hours a day. It's not working too well right now.'

'Just who the hell are you?'

'A friend, Mister Langford.' The American lit a cigarette and sat in the chair opposite. 'Let's just say that I'm as interested in Kit Bailey as Maxwell, Hewens and Partners.'

'Tell me more.'

Gunning looked at his watch. 'You've had quite a night. But they dropped you back here about ten, so where have you been for the last six hours, Mister Langford? Or do you prefer *Captain*?'

'What else don't you know?'

'Probably more than you can remember in one go. Richard Trelawny Langford, one-time Captain in the Special Air Service. You hold – or to be more precise, held – a pilot's licence. You were an intelligence officer, specially trained in anti-terrorist warfare and infiltration. You did one tour of duty in Northern Ireland, took matters into your own hands ...'

'Get to the point or get out.'

'Hey there, take it easy, man.' The American got up and went to the tray of drinks. 'Scotch, no ice and a splash of water, right?' He gave a soft chuckle. 'Here, drink this. You look as if you need it. Now, about your interest in the late Doctor Bailey – '

'That's my business. Right now, I want to know why you're here – and why all this?' He gestured round the room. Timothy G. Gunning knew just how to tear a place apart.

'I came for a talk. Ever see one of these?' He produced what looked like a pocket calculator. 'It's a tracer. You press the button and you get a reading. If it goes over a certain figure, you have a pretty good bet that someone has a transceiver operating within ten metres or so.' He

132

returned the device to his pocket. 'For the moment at least, we can talk freely. My intuition tells me that you've spent the last six hours trying to get into Pier 13, right?' He paused for a moment, watching as Langford sipped the whisky. 'Okay, don't say anything if you don't want to. I'll simply mention that your firm handles the insurance for most of the Shimada fleet, that your people in London and New York are getting kinda jumpy and that Bailey's death prompted them to send you to Japan. It just happens that I could explain a few things –'

'Just explain what you're doing here. And the gun. I don't take kindly to being threatened.'

Gunning sighed. 'I've already told you that I had to make certain we wouldn't be overheard. As far as the gun is concerned ... well, I just had a sneaking suspicion you might be Oki and he's an animal I don't care to tangle with.'

'All right, you expected Oki. Then I come in. But it's my suite. So what the hell do you want?'

'Has it struck you that Doctor Bailey might have been murdered?'

'You still haven't answered my question.' Langford stood up and went to the telephone. 'Are you going to talk or am I going to call the police?'

'Relax, Langford. Go on, take the weight off your feet. This could be your last chance. Right now, your chum Oki is sitting down in the foyer because that's what he's been ordered to do. But when he eventually goes back to his room, he's going to discover that someone has cut his wires.' Gunning picked up the three microphones and rolled them in the palm of his hand. 'We think that Bailey was murdered, Mister Langford.'

'We?' Langford glared at the American. 'Who's we?'

'The people I work for, the American government.'

'I might have guessed. I knew some CIA people in Ulster, so-called under-cover agents. About as subtle as a tribe of Arabs in a synagogue.'

'I do not work for the Company, Mister Langford. Like

133

you, I'm an army man, strictly GI. But right now, I'm on loan to the United States Nuclear Regulatory Commission. Frankly, we don't much care whether Bailey's death was accident, suicide or pre-planned homicide. We just want to find out what the hell a nuclear physicist has to do with the world's biggest oil tanker.' He paused. 'I can see that the same question has occurred to you.'

'So what?'

'So I was going to propose we work together for a while. We do have a mutual interest, Mister Langford.' He stubbed out his cigarette. 'I have nothing but admiration for your attempt to get on board the *Shimada Maru* – that's what they're calling the BC-9 when she finally sails. But you mustn't let failure worry you. They've got that yard sewn up tighter than a nun's snatch. The nearest we've got is taking pictures.'

'Was it you on the tug ... yesterday?'

'You're observant. I like that. Yes, it was me. But I wasn't so concerned with the ship. I needed a good shot of you to send over the wire to Washington.'

'Why?'

'I wanted a positive identity check. There's a NATO file on certain people. You're on it. It was just a precaution before I made my approach.'

'Conscientious, aren't you?'

'We manage.' His lips formed a sardonic smile. 'If you'd been seen coming into the hotel looking like that ... hell, they'd have guessed. And all for nothing. Their security is good, Langford.'

'Obviously not good enough.' He helped himself to another drink.

'You mean you got into the yard?'

'Yes, I did.'

'How?'

'That's my business. But for what it's worth, I also got aboard the ship.'

134

Gunning regarded him with a mixture of suspicion and disbelief. 'You got aboard the *Shimada Maru*?'

'Yes.'

'What did you see? What did you find out?'

'That's my affair and nothing to do with your Regulatory Commission or whatever it is.'

'Don't try to give me the run-around, Langford. You're skating on wafer-thin ice right now. And maybe it could pay you to cultivate one or two influential contacts in Washington. It is true that Meyrick Hewens takes over your firm when Maxwell retires, isn't it?'

'When he retires, yes.' Did the American know about James Maxwell's illness? Langford decided not. 'Before I do anything, Mister Gunning, I have to call London.'

'No way. There won't be any calls to London except – '

'Really? Well, I have news for you. I work for Maxwell in London and I'll damn well do what I think best.'

'You misunderstand me,' said Gunning, quietly. 'I was going to say that anything you want to say to London can go through the Consulate's communications system. That way, you can guarantee security.' He glanced quickly at his watch. 'Look, time's running out. I need to know why Bailey was here and you're trying to find how he died. We can work together, Langford.' He hesitated, chewing his lip. 'Did you know Bailey had a woman in Kobe?'

'I guessed, yes.'

'She's still in residence at the Yamamoto-dori apartment. Maybe if you went to see her, talked to her ...'

Langford nodded. He had every intention of returning to the apartment but decided against mentioning it to Gunning. 'What's her name?'

'Yita ... Yita Izumi. She's quite a broad, too.'

Langford stared vacantly into space. 'We'll see.'

'The way I figure it, you could call on her, make out you're Bailey's brother or something ...'

'You mean you haven't tried?'

'I tried and failed. Maybe I was too hasty. Perhaps you

could find out if she knows anything.'

'Perhaps.' Langford lit a cigarette. 'What did you say her name was?'

'Yita Izumi. Why? Have you already met her?'

'No. But I seem to have heard the name somewhere.'

'It's a common enough name. And the Japs don't have too many surnames to go round.' Gunning rose. 'Have we got a deal?'

'I'll think about it.'

'You don't have the time, pal. These guys play rough.'

'So do I. And I also play alone. It's safer.'

Gunning smiled. 'You think so? You don't know what you're up against, do you?'

'And thanks to your methods, it's going to be a damn sight more difficult for me to find out.' He picked up the microphones. 'What happens when the gentle Oki finds out about these?'

'They'll be even more alert than usual. So take care, huh?'

'Ah, I see. A set-up.'

'I need your help, Langford.'

'I can imagine. And I need you like a hole in the head.' He tossed the microphones on to the table. 'Put them back. And while I take a shower, you can get on with a bit of housework.'

'Like shit. Either we have a deal or – '

Gunning seemed totally unprepared as Langford grabbed his arm, jerking him round and wrenching the Smith & Wesson from its holster before he sent the American crashing against the sofa.

'You sonafabitch.'

'Not a pretty expression, Mister Gunning. Now get to work. With luck, Oki won't know anything's been touched.'

Taking the gun, Langford showered, shaved and spent a few minutes putting sticking plaster on his hands. The cuts from the steel cable weren't deep but his palms felt as though they were on fire. By the time Langford had changed into a suit, the American had almost finished.

'Not bad.' Langford slipped the magazine from the automatic and then proceeded to empty the magazine itself. He smiled as the last of the fourteen rounds fell to the floor and threw both the gun and the magazine down. 'About that deal. If I find out anything, I may call you. But there's one condition. Just keep off my back.'

'Okay, if that's the way you want it. But I have a job to do.'

'You're not doing it very well, are you? If you had been, you would already have made one important discovery.'

'Like what?' Gunning was staring across the room, his eyes narrowed.

'The world's biggest oil tanker, wasn't that what you said? Well, I don't think that it is an oil tanker. Or if it is, I've never seen one quite like it.'

Closing the door behind him, Langford again used the fire exit and once he was on the street, walked quickly round to the main entrance of the hotel. It was still dark and the Mercedes was still parked outside. But when he peered through the plate-glass doors into the foyer, he saw that the seat which had been occupied by Oki was now empty. Langford risked going closer but he could see no sign of the Japanese chauffeur. As he walked away from the hotel in search of a cab, the blood on his hands was mixed with sweat.

It was just after five a.m., Tuesday, November 22, 1977.

2

In London it was still Monday and just after eight o'clock in the evening. For Miss Pym, it had been a particularly harrowing day. On arrival at the Leadenhall Street offices, the commissionaire had presented her with an urgent message that she should go to St George's Hospital. According to the message, Mister Maxwell had had an accident. Miss Pym organized a taxi, gathered up a note-

137

book, pencils and the leather-bound address index which listed practically everyone with whom Maxwell had ever come into contact, and set off. It was a frustrating journey. The cab jerked and crawled its way through the rush-hour traffic and it was after ten-thirty before Miss Pym reached the hospital. Dobson, the chauffeur, met her in the main waiting room. He looked grave, and not without reason.

It was almost midday when Miss Pym finally learned the truth. Her notebook and address index would not be required. James Maxwell had undergone emergency brain surgery. The surgeon explained that he was still alive but unconscious. It was not expected that he would come round much before eight o'clock that evening; that he was, by medical definition, critically ill. As his secretary and personal assistant, Miss Pym reacted with characteristic calm. Her crisp orders jerked Dobson out of his morbid torpor and he was soon driving her back to the office. Although she sat in the front passenger seat of the grey Daimler, she remained silent, her face a mask which concealed a tidal wave of grief. She had worked for Maxwell for nearly twenty years. He still called her Miss Pym and she would never have considered not prefacing his name with *mister* even in casual conversation behind his back, but throughout the years, she had grown to love him almost passionately.

Once back in the office, she telephoned Maxwell's wife. It was a difficult conversation because the couple had been legally separated for many years. Her news was received coldly and when she replaced the receiver, Miss Pym felt grateful that Maxwell had no other family. The next problem was the firm. Alone, she drafted a statement to the effect that Maxwell was ill. Then she thought better of it. Most Mondays, he never even came into the office, especially if he had spent the weekend in the country, so he put the statement to one side, picked up the telephone again and demanded to know the time in New York. When the operator informed her that New York was five hours behind London, she asked for a personal call to be

138

put through to Meyrick Hewens. He wasn't available. She sent out for some lunch and rang St George's hospital but there was no change in Maxwell's condition. And so it went on throughout the rest of the day.

Sitting at her desk, straight-backed, her white hands folded demurely in her lap, Miss Pym stared at the wall of her office. Over the doorway leading to James Maxwell's room, an electric clock jerked away the seconds. The operator abandoned the switchboard, connecting up all the lines so that any incoming call would reach one of her three telephones. And the commissionaire also went, commanding her to make sure the burglar alarm switch was in the down position when she did, finally, choose to leave.

At eight-forty, Meyrick Hewens came over the line from New York. Miss Pym told him what had happened. She had to shout and could barely hear his reply. After a time, she yelled that she would call him back, hoped he could hear her and replaced the receiver. Then, almost immediately, another of the telephones rang. She snatched at it, greedily. What little colour remained in her curiously unlined yet middle-aged face, drained away. James Maxwell had died at eight-thirty-two without regaining consciousness.

Struggling to control her trembling fingers, she dialled New York. There was a long pause before the ringing tone.

'Maxwell-Hewens-Partners.' This time, the toneless voice of the American operator was crystal clear.

'This is London. I want Mister Hewens, please.'

'I think he's engaged. Who is that please?'

'This is Mister Maxwell's sec …'

She could get no further. Her throat suddenly tightened, her eyes streamed tears and she began to sob. The wave of grief which she had been holding back throughout that long day had finally burst through her dam of resolve.

139

3

Hymie Gold was a prosperous New York art dealer. He was happily married with three daughters, which was one of the reasons Lois Hewens liked him. The others were that he was rich and gave her a great many presents – and that he had the largest penis she had ever encountered, circumcised or otherwise. Simply holding it as she guided him into her was enough to produce an orgasm. And when the telephone beside the bed jangled at precisely the wrong moment, Lois screamed her anger.

Grabbing at the telephone, Lois pushed Hymie away and clamped her other hand over the mouthpiece as she heard her husband's voice. He was coming home immediately to pack. He had to fly somewhere. Then he hung up.

Lois felt a sudden, liquid warmth against her thigh.

'Shit.' His face streaked with sweat, Gold jumped off the bed.

'Get out,' hissed Lois, snatching at a box of tissues. 'Meyrick's on his way.'

'Fuck Meyrick.'

'Please, Hymie, you've got to leave.' She followed him into the bathroom.

'Not without a wash, for Chrissakes.'

'Wash later.'

'Like hell.' He shoved her aside and stepped into the shower. 'Of all the humiliating things to happen.'

Still naked, she gathered up his clothes. 'Please, hurry.' Seeing that Gold wasn't in the least put out, she clenched her fists. 'Please, I lied to you. Meyrick doesn't know ... he'll go mad ... he ... he has a gun. He could kill you.'

Gold jumped from the shower, pulled a towel over himself and began dressing, his flesh still moist and steaming. 'You stinking whore. You told me that he didn't ... couldn't ...'

'Just get out. Please. I'll call you.'

'Don't do me no favours, lady.' Pocketing his necktie, he

struggled into his vicuna topcoat. 'And when he gets here, explain this.'

The blow to her face almost knocked Lois Hewens off her feet and she was still staggering under the impact when she heard the door slam.

By the time Meyrick arrived at the apartment, he was in a foul mood. His secretary had had immense difficulty getting him a flight to London; the New York traffic had been made worse by a burst water-main and the sight of his wife's bruised and swollen cheek prompted the kind of suspicions which he preferred not to think about.

'What in God's name have you done to your face?' he growled, rushing into the bedroom and flinging open the wardrobe.

Lois shrugged, helplessly. 'That silly bitch of a maid ... left a door open in the kitchen ...' She watched her husband thrusting clothes into a valise. 'What's happened, Meyrick?'

'James Maxwell's dead. I have to go to London.'

'Oh my God. How?'

'Brain tumour. Why the goddamn bastard couldn't warn me ...'

'Can I come?'

'No. I won't be gone more than a couple of days – '

'Please let me come, Meyrick. I'm so sick of being alone in the apartment – '

'I said no.' From the bathroom, Hewens extracted his shaving kit. 'Look at you. Anyone would think I married a prize-fighter.'

'Please, Meyrick. I want to come to London.'

'No time.' He stared at his watch. 'Okay, I'm going. I'll cable the office and tell them to let you know when I'm due back.' As he picked up his case, Hewens saw a black leather billfold lying on the floor just by the bed. He stooped and tossed it to his wife. 'He left you a tip.'

'You're an unfeeling bastard. If you didn't neglect me ...'

Very slowly, Hewens walked across the room and then

cuffed her hard across the other side of her face with the back of his hand. She let out a yelp as his graduation ring cut into her cheek.

'I've never much cared about what you do, Lois. You know that. But that's my goddamn bed and I won't have other guys ...' He shook his clenched fist at her. 'By the time I get back, I want that bed outa here and two nice singles in its place. Okay?'

The blood streaming from her face, she sank down on to the bed and heard the door slam yet again. Then she began to sob.

4

As Meyrick Hewens's PanAm 747 lifted off from New York's Kennedy airport, dawn was just breaking over Kobe. It was very cold and in spite of his heavy coat, Richard Langford felt chilled and tired as he paid off the cab and walked towards the entrance of the apartment in the Yamamoto-dori. Although it was so early, the streets were busy. Glancing up at the top windows, he saw that there were lights on in the apartment.

He stopped by the main door and peered at the row of buttons. Then he pressed the one clearly labelled *Dr C.E. Bailey* and waited. Nothing happened. He was about to press the bell again when something made him push the door. It swung open and he started up the stairs. There was a radio playing somewhere, discordant, Chinese music. When he reached the top landing, he found another bell and pressed it. Seconds later, the door inched open and he saw that it was held by a chain. He also got his first sight of Yita Izumi.

She peered through the gap, eyes narrowed, lips slightly parted. 'Please?' she said.

'Miss Izumi?'

She nodded.

'My name is Langford. I've come from England ... about Doctor Bailey.'

She looked at him anxiously. 'It is very early.'

'Yes, I'm sorry. May I come in?' Their eyes met and after a moment's hesitation, she pushed the door closed, released the chain and then admitted him.

'I ... I'm not dressed,' Yita murmured, securing the door again behind him.

Langford walked slowly into the living room. Two suitcases stood by the window, both bearing Bailey's initials. It was very warm in the apartment and he started to take his coat off.

'I will put some clothes on,' she said. 'Please wait.'

He watched her disappear into the bedroom and close the door. Sitting down, he noticed the copy of the *Mainichi Daily News* and fingered the crumpled pages. And he thought about Samwashima.

The Japanese had a lot to hide. Above all, there was the business of the rope ladder, a clumsy lie for which there seemed no plausible explanation. Langford lit a cigarette and stared sightlessly across the room as Samwashima's slurred voice echoed dimly in his mind. '*Izumi. Dead. Accident. Big piece of steel ... wham. Sayo nara, Izumi ...*'

'You knew Kit ... Doctor Bailey?'

Langford swung round and saw that Yita was standing in the doorway. She wore a simple woollen dress which accentuated her fragile body.

'You like coffee?'

Langford nodded. 'Please.' Then he realized that he had been staring. Despite his exhaustion, he could still appreciate Yita Izumi's exquisite beauty. She possessed a curious, doll-like quality and her dark liquid eyes reflected gentleness, sympathy. And something else, something which Richard Langford eventually decided was fear.

'I'm sorry to have disturbed you so early,' he said, following her into the tiny kitchen.

She shrugged her narrow, sloping shoulders as she prepared the coffee. 'It does not matter, Mister ...?' She turned, her lips framing the question.

'Langford. Richard Langford.'

'Yes.' She turned away. 'You have come for Kit's things.' It was a statement and there was an inherent sadness in her tone, as if parting with Bailey's belongings would be yet another tragedy. 'I have packed them, as Mister Samwashima instructed.'

'Thank you. I'm sorry ...'

Yita suddenly smiled. 'You are always saying sorry. You worked with Kit, no?'

'No,' said Langford. 'We were ... cousins.'

'Ah so. I understand now.' She poured the coffee with swift, delicate movements. 'You must accept my sympathy, Mister Langford.'

'Thank you.' Langford took the coffee and they returned to the living room, sitting down and facing each other. 'Can you ... can you tell me what happened?'

Yita nodded. 'Kit fell from a ladder. It was an accident.'

'Yes, I see.' The hot coffee tasted good and warming. 'Miss Izumi, I ...' He glanced at her but had to look away. Her dark eyes were fixed on him, full of apprehension.

'You wish to ask about Kit and me?' She paused and then smiled, sadly. 'He wanted to make me his wife. I refused him.'

Langford was feeling increasingly uncomfortable. He suddenly didn't want to hurt her like this, any more than she already had been hurt. But time was running against him and he tried to decide what Oki would do when he discovered that the listening devices had been tampered with and that Langford had gone from the hotel.

'You must not feel embarrassed, Mister Langford,' said Yita, quietly.

'No, of course not.' He took a deep breath. 'I want to ask you some questions. It may be difficult for you but please believe me, it is very important.'

'I have answered many questions already.' She stared into her untouched cup of coffee. 'You are going to tell me that Kit was not killed by accident.'

'I'm afraid so, Miss Izumi. All the evidence –'

'Nothing you or the American can do will bring him

144

back, Mister Langford. He is dead.'

Draining his cup, Langford stubbed out his cigarette and moistened his lips. 'There were others. One of them was also called Izumi.' He watched her carefully but there was no discernible alteration in her expression.

'Kenji Izumi was my step-father.' She might have been praying, her voice suddenly flat and lifeless. 'I did not know my real father. He was an American, a soldier.'

'Your step-father, Miss Izumi, how ... how did he die?'

'An accident,' she murmured, head bowed. 'An accident.'

'There have been a lot of accidents on the ship.'

'It is Fate,' she replied, finally looking up. 'What is written ...'

Langford had to swallow to ease the dryness in his mouth. 'Can you tell me what happened to your step-father?'

'I was told that a crane carrying something ... it hit him ...' She shook her head. 'It is no longer important.'

'Miss Izumi, I believe that both Doctor Bailey and your step-father were murdered. Maybe the others were deliberately killed, too.'

Yita turned and stared at him. 'Belief is for mortals, proof is for the Gods. That is a Shinto saying, Mister Langford. It is very ancient and very true.'

'Others may yet die, Miss Izumi. People like Bailey, like your step-father. If we ... if I could prove what I believe to be true, maybe those people could be saved.'

For a time, Yita remained silent and motionless. 'You would destroy much more than you could ever save.'

Langford felt his expression harden. Whether genuine or assumed, Yita's Eastern fatalism was beginning to make him angry. 'You obviously don't have a conscience. I'm sorry for you.'

But Yita looked on, hopelessly. 'I warned him what could happen. I tried to protect him but he refused to listen.'

'What do you mean?' Langford leaned forwards, his

145

face taut. 'What did you try to warn him about?'

'Many things of which he had no understanding, things belonging to the past. You would not understand.'

'Try me, Miss Izumi.'

'No.' She stood up. 'Like Kit, the past is dead. Let the spirits rest in peace, Mister Langford.' Yita gestured towards the two suitcases. 'Those are what you came for. Take them and go.'

'I'm not interested in Bailey's possessions. I want to know who killed him. And why.' He stared into her face. 'I think you know the answers to those questions.' Langford rose from the sofa and went towards her. 'Is Samwashima involved?' She didn't answer. 'He is, isn't he? He telephoned you. Told you to clear out while he brought me here. Why?'

Yita shook her head. 'You cannot understand. Please, take the things and leave here. I will not talk about it. Ever.'

'For God's sake, how many more people have to die?' Langford struggled to control himself. 'Look, I lied to you. I'm not Bailey's cousin or his brother or anything. I'd never even heard of him before all this. But I represent people in London who have an interest in the ship and we must know why Bailey was murdered. It's very important.'

'Important for money?' Her expression became one of contempt. 'Now Kit is dead, nothing is important. And it was an accident.'

'Was it? I don't think so. Since I arrived in Kobe, I've heard too many lies, seen too many scared people. Like you, Miss Izumi. But you may have reason. They killed your step-father and Bailey. You could be next.'

'If it is written, then ...' She spread her hands. 'Please, you must go. Return to London, Mister Langford. What happens here is ... is perhaps what should happen. I do not know.'

'You're talking in riddles, Miss Izumi.'

She stared at him for a moment, as if puzzled. Then:

'Yes, a riddle. I understand that. It is like life. There is no answer on earth, only in *Nirvana*. Then we find peace.'

'I can't wait that long.'

'If you pursue the answers now, Langford-*san*, you will not have long to wait.' She walked to the door and held it open.

'Very well.' He grabbed at the two cases. 'But I'll come back,' he said.

'And I will not be here, so your journey will be wasted. Goodbye, Mister Langford.'

He hesitated at the door. 'I'm sorry. I ...'

'Goodbye.' Yita began closing the door against him.

Langford could have resisted her with ease but he had no will to do so. She looked so small, so frail that he was afraid for her and suddenly conscious of an almost over-powering urge to protect her against whatever threatened.

He stared at the blank door and sighed. The suitcases weren't all that heavy but awkward because the landing and the stairway were narrow. He began the descent, holding one case in front of him, the other behind. At each step, they bumped noisily against the banisters, the sound echoing around him. When he reached the next landing, he paused for a moment, flexing his hands. Then he picked up the cases again and started down the second flight. Hearing the main door bang followed by heavy footfalls on the stairs, Langford grimaced. There was little enough room for two people to pass without luggage. Leaning over the banisters, Langford just caught sight of a dark figure coming up. Hurrying, he stopped on the landing and waited, Bailey's two suitcases standing one on top of the other beside him. Only when the ascending figure reached the turn of the stairs immediately below him did Langford see that it was Oki.

The massive Japanese stood at the bottom of the stairs and peered upwards, his dark, snake-like eyes narrowed into glistening pin-pricks, the close-cropped head tilted back slightly so that the brutal-looking jaw was stretched from the throat. Then his lips moved, soundlessly forming

147

a smile of malevolent anticipation.

Langford swallowed and would have backed away but he was against the wall, the two suitcases a barrier at his side. He could feel his pulse thudding in his temples and the film of moisture which had suddenly sprung beneath the dressing on his palms. Then Oki's arms moved, slowly, menacingly, his stance that of a wrestler about to grapple his opponent.

Richard Langford was fit and reasonably strong. He had also been well-trained in the art of un-armed combat. But he knew that against the muscular bulk of Oki, he had little chance. He had to retreat to the apartment, and Yita Izumi.

Oki began climbing the stairs, placing one foot before the other so that his ascent was like a slow-motion film sequence. His lips were still fixed in a reptilian grin. A curious hissing sound came from between his teeth.

Langford watched and waited, his eyes fixed on Oki's extended arms. Very slowly, his grip tightened on the handle of one of Bailey's suitcases and as Oki moved inexorably nearer, he let the suitcase pivot on the one below it and braced himself, broadening his stance for better balance. Then Oki stopped.

The hideous hissing sound issuing from Oki's lips seemed to drown out every other noise as the two men prepared to fight. Langford had one advantage: he was standing on the higher level. But Oki's massive weight would more than compensate if Langford made a mistake.

Then Oki lunged upwards, his arms wide, his grotesque hands outstretched as if to claw his opponent's life from his body.

In one fluid movement, Langford hefted the suitcase above his head. Oki's mouth opened and he laughed, silently. Langford was doing precisely what he had suspected he would do and Oki ducked his close-cropped head. Which was exactly what Langford wanted.

Using the case as a counter-weight, Richard Langford put all his strength into a powerful kick which smashed into Oki's jaw. There was a sharp gasp for breath as the Japanese lurched backwards, his hands clutching desperately at the banisters. Then Langford hurled the suitcase for all he was worth.

As the first case thudded heavily against Oki's body, Langford spun round, grabbed the second and vaulted up the next flight of stairs. From below came a throbbing crash as Oki somersaulted downwards.

Langford didn't bother to look. He knew well enough that the powerfully built Japanese would probably withstand the fall without any significant injury. By the time he had made the top landing, he knew that his assumption had been all too accurate. Oki was charging, bull-like, up the stairs. There was blood on his face, violent anger in his eyes.

Hammering on the door to Bailey's apartment, Langford felt the pain burn through his cut hands and shouted for Yita to let him in. Panting and hissing, Oki rushed towards his quarry like a primitive giant. The first time, he had miscalculated. But now he made no calculations whatsoever. Oki was motivated by pure fury. He saw Langford lift the second suitcase but didn't react until the case was poised above his head. Then he reached up like a basketball player, trying to push it away.

Langford didn't wait that long. Dropping to his knees, he let the suitcase fall to the floor and in the split-second before Oki made his final lunge, slammed the case against the man's shins.

Oki's feet were knocked from under him and he fell. Langford yelled for Yita and backed away but not before the Japanese had secured his ankle in a grip which threatened to pull him over. Desperate, he hung on to the banisters and kicked out.

Langford was now sitting at the top of the staircase with Oki hanging on to his ankle and trying to steady himself. Then the door to the apartment swung open and Yita came on to the landing.

Distracted, Oki looked back a micro-second before

Langford kicked him in the face with his free leg. Oki gasped, released his grip and started to slide, then quickly checked his fall, the muscles in his forearms knotting beneath the sleeves of his jacket.

Yita cried out and when Langford turned, he saw her holding his overcoat. He grabbed the coat, pushed Yita back into the apartment and just as Oki charged, he flung the coat over the man's head. Before Oki could pull it off, Langford had dived into the apartment and slammed the door.

Yita was standing in the centre of the living room, her head shaking from side to side in panic. 'He will kill you,' she gasped.

Langford's reply was drowned as Oki threw himself against the door. It held, but only just.

'Fire escape?'

'No ... no fire escape. No way.'

There was another crash and even the door frame itself moved, sending a shower of plaster to the floor.

'Jesus.' Langford stared round the apartment for something, anything to use as a weapon in spite of the fact that he knew he had little chance of stopping Oki.

Then came a tremendous thud followed by the sound of splintering wood. The door didn't open. It fell into the apartment, Oki charging over it like an express train.

It was an ashtray or some ornamental paperweight. Langford never knew which. He simply plucked it from the table with his left hand, tossed it into his right and hurled it at Oki's head. It was a good throw but the glass object simply shattered into a thousand fragments as it impacted against Oki's close-cropped skull.

If Oki had had a voice, the hissing sound would have been a scream as he lurched drunkenly towards Langford. Yita started shouting in Japanese and attempted to come between them but Oki brushed her aside and before Langford could make another move, he felt the vice-like grip of Oki's fingers around his neck.

Time stopped. Richard Langford punched and kicked

his assailant but he might as well have been hitting a brick wall and as Oki tightened his stranglehold, Langford felt his strength ebbing. His lungs seemed near to bursting and he could feel his heart pounding as it struggled to survive without oxygen. Then he began to feel dizzy and his hearing became distorted so that Oki's frantic, triumphant hissing became like a roaring, turbulent sea crashing against unyielding rocks. Only his sense of smell seemed to remain unimpaired and the rank stench of Oki's breath sickened him.

The room began to revolve. There was a series of rapid explosions inside Langford's brain and as he lost consciousness, the last thing he heard was a thunderous, deafening roar.

5

In Bracken House, the headquarters of London's *Financial Times* in Cannon Street, Percy Hildreth had a layout problem. An advertisement for a Middle East bank had been cancelled for reasons unknown and so Hildreth had to fill the space. He glanced quickly at the news features which surrounded the blank space and picked up his telephone. After a short conversation, he replaced the receiver and marked up a new headline to appear in upper and lower case type. Over the headline, Hildreth scrawled a note to the effect that the picture could be sized-up. He was still staring at his work when a bearded reporter entered.

Percy Hildreth glanced up at the newcomer and then tapped the page with his felt pen. 'Pad that,' he growled. 'I need at least two hundred words.'

'It's an obituary,' said the reporter.

'So what?'

'Well, it shouldn't really be there. It should be – '

'I know where it should bloody well be but there isn't room.'

'Anyway, I can't pad it out any more, not without going

through the files and there isn't time.'

Hildreth mouthed an obscenity. 'Look, it isn't my fault the ad was cancelled and we can't just leave a blank space.'

The reporter stared down at the copy. 'Suppose we put in two pictures?'

'Two?' Hildreth sucked at his teeth. 'What do you mean, two?'

'Simple. We have one of the old guy and one of his successor.'

'Have we got it on file?'

'Yes. I was going to use it but there wasn't enough space ... then.'

'Well, there is now. Too much.'

'There is another problem,' said the reporter. 'It'll mean that the piece ceases to be a straight obituary. Strictly speaking, it's a feature ...'

'God in heaven, I haven't just joined. I know it should be in the Insurance section and I know it's a cross between an obituary and a feature. We'll just have to live with it.'

The reporter heaved a sigh. 'I was hoping to go early, too.'

'Pity.' Hildreth thrust the page at him. 'Perish the thought that the paper should interfere with your social life.'

'If we sized up both pictures we could probably get away with ...' He squinted at the layout. 'Hundred words?'

'Fifty if you like,' muttered Hildreth. 'I don't care. Just so long as it makes sense. And please, tell those cretins downstairs to get the captions the right way round. There are enough dead men still working in the City without another one coming in to take over a leading insurance company.'

'They're underwriters,' said the reporter.

'If you say so. Just pad it out and then we can all go home.'

'Know something?'

Hildreth looked up, sharply. 'What now?'

'You take it all too seriously, Percy.'

'When I was your age ...' But the reporter had already gone.

6

The weight had been lifted from his body but breathing was painfully difficult and Langford couldn't think why. Voices echoed strangely around him in the darkness. Then he was falling, plummeting downwards at incredible speed. Death seemed inevitable because Langford knew about the ladder. That much was certain. Like Lois Hewens. She was certain. And easy. Then it was as if someone had been sawing at his throat with a very blunt knife. He tried to swallow, felt himself cough and finally opened his eyes.

For what seemed like a very long time, Richard Langford was seeing nothing but an expanse of white. Only when he eventually shifted his gaze did he realize that he had been staring up at a ceiling. Then his brain jerked back into gear and he started to remember.

'Are you all right?' The sound of his own voice was strange and as he sat up, he winced with pain. 'What happened?'

Yita opened her mouth to speak but no words came and she pointed.

Turning his head proved very painful, so Langford rolled over, only to come face to face with Oki. It was like an electric shock. Langford pulled himself to his feet, staggering backwards as he strove to recover his sense of balance. 'Is he dead?'

'I think ...' Yita's voice was barely more than a hoarse whisper. 'Yes, I think he is dead.'

Langford stepped carefully across the room and bent over the inert body. After feeling in vain for a pulse, he flicked the giant's eyelids. 'He's dead, all right.' Langford stood up and faced Yita. 'How?'

153

'I ... I used ...' Then she pointed again.

'Christ.' Seeing the gun lying on the floor, Langford retraced his steps and picked it up. For a moment, he thought that it was a German Lüger but closer inspection revealed that it was an 8mm Japanese self-loading Nambu. 'You used this?'

'Yes. I ... I had to.'

Langford laid the gun on the table and returned to Oki's corpse. It was lying face-up and was unmarked apart from the minor wounds which Langford had inflicted. Then he knelt down and heaved the body over. Plumb in the centre of Oki's broad back was a jagged hole which had poured dark blood. 'If you hadn't done that ...' He left the sentence unfinished and picked up the pistol again. 'Where d'you get this museum-piece, Yita?'

'It was the property of my step-father.'

'War souvenir?'

'It was his. It belonged to him.'

Langford replaced the gun on the table and took out his cigarettes. 'I should have telephoned instead,' he growled, seeing the scrawled number on the packet. After lighting up, he felt his neck and went over to the mirror on the far wall. The marks of Oki's fingers were clearly visible, livid weals of compressed flesh.

'What are you going to do?'

Yita's voice somehow jarred him.

'Have a drink. Have you any whisky here?' She nodded and went to a cupboard, handing him a bottle of Export Black Label and a tumbler.

'Kit liked that, she said, watching him slosh the amber spirit into the glass.

Langford gulped at the whisky. 'Bully for Kit.' He poured another measure and then sat down. 'Jesus.' He carefully felt his chest. 'That bastard must have trodden all over my ribs.' Shutting his eyes, he sank back, breathing slowly and deeply.

'You are hurt?' Yita came to him, her strangely

European features twisted as she frowned.

'I'll live.' He stared at her, confused. Part of him wanted to curse her, even strike her but she looked so beautiful, so frail that his first thoughts were devoted to devising ways and means of extricating her from any involvement with Oki's death. Then he sighed, knowing that he was being unrealistic.

Yita gazed down at the corpse. 'What shall we do, Mister Langford?'

'For the moment, nothing. I need to think. But you can help by answering some questions.'

'I cannot.'

It was Yita's suddenly wooden expression which roused Langford's temper again. 'You'll bloody well answer or – ' He stopped as she backed away, stark fear etched deep in her soulful eyes. 'Someone, probably Samwashima himself, for all I know, but someone's going to come looking for him. And then for you.' Langford jerked his thumb at the corpse.

'I did it to protect you. The police ...'

'Sod the police. Do you think that Samwashima's going to be worried by the police? No way, Yita. Any more than he was worried by them over Bailey's murder. Or your step-father's, come to that. So you are going to answer my questions ... even if I have to beat the answers out of you.'

Yita nodded, dumbly. Then she pointed. 'The door. Can you fix the door?'

'Christ.' Langford stared at the flattened door. 'I'll try.' Standing up, he went into the tiny hall. With some difficulty, he raised the door which was still just connected to its frame, and tried to manhandle it back into the opening. It took some minutes but he eventually succeeded. Only when he came to sit down again did he stop to consider how it might look from the other side. Then he gave up worrying.

'I do not know what I can tell you.'

'Have a think about it.' Taking Gunning's card from his

pocket, he picked up the 'phone and dialled. The call was answered almost immediately. 'I'm at Bailey's apartment,' said Langford, without preamble. 'Oki's dead.' He paused for a moment. 'Can you come round here?' Before Gunning could reply, there was a knocking at the door and Yita gave a shriek of fright. 'Hang on.' He turned to Yita. 'Find out who it is.'

Yita went to the door and called out in Japanese. A male voice answered, Yita replied and then turned to Langford. 'It is the caretaker. He says we must move the suitcases. They are in the way.'

'Tell him yes.'

'I've done that.'

'Gunning? Listen, we'll come to you ... okay, outside then.' Langford slammed down the receiver. 'We're getting out of here.'

'I am not packed.'

'Too bad.'

'No, please. Just one minute.' Yita fled into the bedroom and emerged less than a minute later clutching a small grip.

'Clean up some of the glass. I'm going to move our late friend.'

Shifting Oki's body tore Langford apart but he wanted to get it at least out of sight in case someone decided to pay a casual visit to the apartment. After some difficulty, the corpse was persuaded into the fitted wardrobe. Once he had managed to close the door and secure it, Langford picked the rug from the bedroom floor and carried it through into the living room, carefully positioning it over the bloodstain.

The door posed another problem. Getting out was easy but wedging the smashed frame from the outside proved nearly impossible. Not until Yita suggested a length of cord secured on the inside and then hung over the top, did they succeed in pulling it into place. Langford cut the cord which remained and stared at his handiwork.

'Provided no one looks too closely ...' He glanced at

Yita and half-smiled. 'Come on, let's get the hell out of here.' He started down the stairs, collecting the suitcases on the way.

As they came out into the street, Yita saw a cab and waved. It pulled over and the driver opened the rear door with his remote control lever.

'Tell him to go to the American Consulate,' snapped Langford, pushing Yita in first. But the driver didn't need a translation.

'*Amurrican Consurut*,' he echoed, smiling broadly as he accelerated into the traffic.

'Damn.' And Langford winced as he turned round.

'What is it?' Yita's tiny voice was full of fear.

'The car. Oki's Mercedes. It's parked back there.' He scowled as he massaged his neck.

'Don't worry, we're not going back.'

Langford didn't voice his thought that going anywhere might prove difficult if not impossible. 'We also forgot the gun,' he whispered.

Yita patted her handbag. 'I have it.'

Langford gave a sigh of relief. 'Well done. We'll have to get rid of it later.'

She seemed upset. 'But it belonged to my step-father,' she said.

'Then it's the kind of heirloom you can't afford.' And he winced again, wondering just how many of his ribs Oki had managed to crack.

SEVEN

1

Osaka is Japan's second-largest city and lies some thirty miles east of Kobe. Once the capital city and known as Naniwa, Osaka was the great cultural centre during the Tokugawa period which lasted from 1600 to about 1860, when it was eclipsed by Tokyo. Then it became an important hub of industry and commerce and developed a curiously European atmosphere. Every important company operating in Japan maintains offices in the city and the Shimada Corporation was no exception.

Samwashima enjoyed his visits to Osaka. The offices were spacious and pleasantly situated in the broad, tree-lined Mido-Suji Street which always reminded him of a Paris boulevarde. And there was also the attraction of the Sonezaki baths just across the bridge over the Tosabori river. After a long, hot soak, a skilful masseuse would pound and pummel his body until he could feel the first, certain stirrings of an erection. Then the woman would retreat, ushering a young girl into the warm cubicle, a girl who was always carefully schooled in the subtle art of coaxing an orgasm from tense, tired, middle-aged bodies like his own. In spite of the clinical speed and efficiency of the contrived copulation, the physical and mental relief was a thing of beauty. But the main attraction of visiting Osaka had little direct connexion with Samwashima's sexual inadequacies. Here Samwashima was free of Toshiro Shiba, conveniently overlooking the fact that the homage which was shown him owed everything to his position as Shiba's deputy. It was enough simply to enjoy the use of the sumptuous penthouse suite on the top floor of the building from which he could conduct his business fortified by the copious cigarettes which Shiba so despised.

On the morning of Tuesday, November 22, as Richard Langford and Yita sat in the taxi on their way to the American Consulate in Kobe, Samwashima scanned the latest progress reports on the BC-9. The Japanese was only half concentrating on the reports, his mind and body already anticipating the delights of the baths which he would visit later that day. Besides, the closely-typed pages dealing with construction details of winches, derricks, life-rafts, lighting and fire safety fittings were beyond his grasp. It was sufficient that Chief Foreman Yamada had stated – in writing – that work was on schedule; that the senior electrical supervisor also confirmed that the computerized navigation systems, including radar, wireless and sonar, were now fully operational and awaited only the sea trials. Another report, this time from the head of Shimada's personnel section in Tokyo, confirmed that the captain-designate, a fifty-two-year-old sailor whose many years of sea-going experience had been supplemented by a specially devised training course in Tokyo, was ready to take up his new command.

Lighting a cigarette, Samwashima sighed and leaned back in the deeply-upholstered chair. Except for the final touches to the work for which the late Doctor Bailey would have been responsible, the BC-9 was on schedule. Now they had to wait until the Englishman had left Japan.

Samwashima closed his eyes for a moment. In spite of his drinking session with Langford, he didn't feel too bad, just a faint, nagging headache which a light lunch of fresh fruit and *sake* would cure. He smiled to himself, a smile of contentment and anticipation. Then the door opened and a secretary entered.

'What is it?'

'Samwashima-*san*,' began the secretary, bowing, 'We have received a telex from Tokyo. Mister Shiba is flying to Osaka. He will arrive in one hour and asks that you meet him at the airport '

Samwashima felt his stomach twist, destroying instantly the sensation of anticipatory pleasure in the pit of his belly. He nodded and the secretary withdrew, leaving him to contemplate the reasons for Toshiro Shiba's apparently sudden decision to visit Osaka.

Drawing heavily on the cigarette, Samwashima rose and began pacing the room. He himself had checked Shiba's list of engagements. The head of the Shimada Corporation had a full schedule of meetings, lunches and dinners – in Tokyo. And yet ... he moistened his lips with the tip of his tongue as he returned to the desk. Then he snatched at the telephone and asked for a number, his fingers drumming impatiently as he held on.

The operator at the Oriental hotel in Kobe was helpful. When no reply could be obtained from the suite occupied by Richard Langford, someone was sent up to check. Samwashima waited, his mouth dry, the tightness in his stomach increasing. Then the courteously efficient operator informed him that Langford-*san* was not in the hotel and that his bed had not been used. Should she leave a message? Samwashima merely shook his head, as if the operator could see him, and replaced the receiver.

Getting to his feet again, he went to the other side of the room and picked up another telephone, a private line. From his inside pocket he took a notebook, flicking through the pages before pressing out a number. The seconds passed slowly, the ringing tone echoing in his ear. After nearly two minutes, he put the 'phone down, stubbed the cigarette into an ashtray and walked across the room to the window.

For a long time, he stared down into Mido-Suji Street. The trees were bare of leaves, the traffic was heavy and the wide pavements crowded with people. But Samwashima saw none of this. He was trying to visualize the small apartment on the Yamamoto-dori, picturing in his mind's eye the girl. And Oki. He looked at his watch. Oki should have been there, in the apartment. It was inconceivable that he had completed the task Samwashima had set him.

He should have been there and picked up the telephone, tapping the mouthpiece to identify himself.

Samwashima tried the number again, carefully making certain that he pressed the correct buttons. The result was the same. Then the secretary returned and informed him that a car was waiting to take him to the airport.

'My driver?' said Samwashima, suddenly hopeful.

The girl shook her head. 'Oki-*san* is not here. It is our driver and he says that the traffic – '

'Yes, yes.' Samwashima waved her out of the room and lit another cigarette. He had no reason to suspect that something – anything – had gone wrong. Yet he felt a powerful sense of foreboding which sharpened the ache in his head and pulled at his stomach.

Pouring some water from a crystal carafe, he swallowed two tranquillizers and began gathering together the reports on the BC-9. Pulling on his overcoat, he glanced around the lavishly appointed room and felt a surge of bitterness. Everything in it belonged to Toshiro Shiba. Everything was valuable. If the red-laquered Tensu chest was worth millions of yen, the bronze figure dating back to the Kamakura period which stood on top of the chest was priceless, irreplaceable. Yet Samwashima knew that his master had no real appreciation of art. The pieces were all simply investments, an integral part of his immense wealth, mere possessions to be bought and sold at will.

As he left the room, Samwashima wished he had the courage to destroy all the beautiful things in the apartment for no better reason than that they, like himself, belonged to Shiba. And as the high-speed lift carried him to the waiting limousine, he was filled with regret because he knew beyond any doubt that when Toshiro Shiba wished to destroy him, he would do it without a second thought.

The traffic was worse than usual and by the time the car drove into the private section of Osaka's International Airport, Samwashima was sweating profusely. Toshiro Shiba was not a man to be kept waiting but in fact their

161

timing was perfect, the car pulling up within seconds of the pilot shutting off the rear-mounted jet engines of the gleaming white Caravelle.

'Shiba-*san*,' said Samwashima, bowing. 'We did not expect ...'

Shiba merely nodded and stared at the chauffeur. 'Where is Oki?' he demanded, sliding into the back seat.

'An errand ... in Kobe.' Samwashima swallowed to ease the dryness in his mouth.

As the car moved away, Shiba closed the glass partition separating the driver from his passengers. 'Last night,' began Shiba, 'I reached agreement with the Government.' He smiled. 'The terms are very favourable to us.' Then the smile suddenly faded. 'But we must move quickly. As I suspected, the disposal problem at Kyomo has become urgent. You have the latest reports on the ship?'

Samwashima placed his attaché case on his knees and snapped the locks open. 'Everything is on schedule ... as planned ... except ...'

'Of course.' Shiba sniffed, wrinkling his nose and glancing quickly at Samwashima as if to indicate that even the residual aroma of cigarette smoke on his clothes was unacceptable. 'The Englishman ... what has happened to him?'

'He will be leaving Japan within the next day or so,' replied Samwashima. 'There are no problems.'

'Good. I have already cabled our senior representative in America. The approach will be made to the man we agreed should replace Bailey. And this time, there must be no mistakes.'

'Very well, Shiba-*san* but ...' He drew a sharp breath in a vain attempt to ease the tension in his guts. 'How much will this new man be told?'

'He shall have the use of the original plans. I know that Doctor Bailey made some alterations and there have been other, technical modifications but ...' He paused, thoughtfully, his rounded face creased by a deep frown. 'There is one problem yet to be overcome. The Minister has demanded a certification from a qualified person that the project is without unacceptable risk.'

'I see. That would mean Bailey's replacement knowing everything. He could not be expected – '

'All I expect for the moment is that the new man will supervise the completion of Bailey's work. Once this has been done, we will decide the most advantageous method of satisfying the Minister's requirements.' Leaning forward, Shiba slid open the glass partition. 'You are to take us direct to Kobe. We shall go to the shipyard,' he said, and shut the partition again as he turned to face Samwashima. 'You have no engagements in Osaka, I trust?'

Samwashima licked his lips. 'None,' he said.

'Good.' Shiba grinned, almost mischievously. 'Have you been to the Sonezaki baths already?'

Feeling distinctly uneasy, Samwashima shrugged. 'No, I ... how did you know?'

'How? That is unimportant, my friend. What matters is that I know. And that you are aware of my knowledge.' He clasped his hands together and peered from the car window. 'I also understand your concern about the future. I share that concern.'

After a long pause, Samwashima said, 'I ... people within the Corporation are beginning to speculate that when you retire, Shiba-*san*, the choice of your successor ...' He faltered.

'Let them speculate. I have no immediate plans to retire. But you, Samwashima-*san*, are to go abroad. When this project has been successfully completed, it is my intention to expand our business in the United States. You will become Executive Vice-President of a new American holding company.'

Samwashima slowly nodded his head. He muttered his gratitude as he felt his body relaxing and the tension slowly subsiding. But in its place came bitterness and resentment. From his office in Tokyo, Toshiro Shiba's authoritarian rule extended all over the world. However grandiose their titles, his overseas executives had little real power. And as the car sped towards Kobe, Samwashima recalled the ancient Japanese proverb: *he who throws a fleshless bone to the starving dog only increases its hunger.*

Shiba was staring at him, the pupils of his eyes distorted by the thick, horn-rimmed spectacles. 'I have every confidence that you will fulfil your task more than adequately,' he said.

Forcing a smile, Samwashima nodded. 'Thank you, Shiba-*san.*' He craved for a cigarette but hardly dared even to think about it. And gripping the attaché case resting in his lap, he stared fixedly at his own image reflected in the glass partition which divided the car. The death of Doctor Bailey, he decided, had been a kind of watershed. Whatever Shiba's plans, Samwashima knew he must now begin to lay the foundations for a takeover. He had served his master with unquestioning loyalty and refused to accept any lesser reward than one upon which he had long set his heart. But he needed help, allies who would rally to him when the moment came to topple the merchant prince who had created the massive Shimada Corporation. And Norihiko Samwashima knew exactly how and with whom his new alliance must be made.

2

Gunning was already waiting outside the American Consulate in an anonymous grey Mazda when the taxi came up. Thrusting a note into the driver's hand, Langford started to get out but the man gesticulated angrily at him. Yita said something in Japanese, took the change and handed it to Langford.

'Never give tip in Japan,' she said. 'Not custom.'

Langford stared for a moment at the departing taxi and then pocketed the coins.

'Get in,' snapped Gunning. 'We haven't got all day.'

Langford pushed Yita into the back of the car and then

walked round to the front passenger seat. He had barely closed the door when Gunning let in the clutch and the Mazda jerked into motion.

'What's the hurry?' growled Langford.

'You said you killed Oki and now you ask what the hurry is? Jesus.' Gunning gave him a deprecating grin. 'What happened?'

'It's a long story,' replied Langford, cautiously.

Gunning swung the car round in a tight u-turn and headed up Flower-dori Street. 'I'm listening.'

'I killed him.' Yita's voice from the back of the car was cold and toneless.

'You?' Gunning almost looked round but stopped himself. 'How?'

Langford filled in the details.

'You were lucky,' muttered Gunning, slowing down as they approached a red light. 'In some ways.'

'Where are we going now?'

'Suma.' As the lights changed to green, Gunning accelerated. 'It's Kobe's answer to Coney Island, like it's a dump. But we ... the Consulate, have a house there. It's secluded and comes in useful from time to time.' He paused to light a cigarette, letting the car slow as they approached the access to the Hanshin expressway. 'Where did you get the gun, Miss Izumi?'

'It was the property of my step-father.'

'And he was killed on the ship, too,' said Langford, looking at Yita.

Gunning nodded. 'Okay, now I want you two people to listen to what I'm going to say because I don't intend repeating myself. One, you've killed Samwashima's favourite pet gorilla. He isn't going to like that and when he finds out, I should plan on not being around. Two, and this really applies to you, Miss Izumi, I have a whole lot of questions needing answers. You're going to supply them.'

'I will say nothing,' Yita replied, forcefully.

'Lady, you don't have any choice in the matter. Whether you like it or not, you're in one hell of a spot.'

'I had to do what I did. He would have killed ...'

'No kidding? What was Oki doing at the apartment?'

Yita shook her head. 'I do not know why he came.'

'I'll give you two possible reasons: either he simply followed Langford, which seems unlikely in the circumstances. Or ... and this is just my theory, he came for you, Miss Izumi.'

'Me? But why?'

'Why did they kill Bailey?' Gunning paused, his eyes flickering upwards as he watched her reactions through the driving mirror. 'Why did they kill your step-father?'

'It ... I ...' She bit her lip and shook her head.

Gunning sighed. 'Perhaps I should say one more thing, Miss Izumi. If you won't answer my questions of your own free will, there are other methods that can be used.'

'I don't like the sound of that,' rasped Langford. 'If you think that you can – '

'You have no inkling of what's at stake here, Langford,' Gunning half-whispered. 'What's it to be, Miss Izumi?' He glanced in the mirror again. 'All sweetness and light or electrodes strapped to your tits? I can see you know what that might feel like. Good.'

'There is nothing I can tell you,' said Yita, her voice soft. 'I know nothing.

'We'll see about that.' He sensed rather than saw the movement of her hands against the car door. 'If you look carefully, you'll see I took off the door handles. Yours, too, Langford. And if you still feel like trying anything heroic, take a look behind. See that green sedan with four guys in it? They're my people.'

Langford faced forward again, regretting the sudden movement and massaging his neck. 'This place, Suma. Is there a doctor there?'

'Why, you got problems?'

'Nothing serious. Just a few dents left by Oki, that's all.' He pressed his hands against his chest. 'Whatever's at stake, Gunning, Yita saved my life. I won't forget that.'

'Maybe Samwashima won't let you. And the way these guys play their games, you could end up regretting that Madam Butterfly here ever did come to your rescue.' He shot Langford a sideways glance. 'Ribs?'

'Yes.'

'We'll get someone to take a look ... but later.' Gunning wound down the window and flicked his cigarette from the car. As he closed the window, he settled himself at a slight angle in the seat, his hands resting casually on the steering wheel.

'What will they do about Oki?' said Langford.

'Depends who finds him first.' Gunning pursed his lips and then shrugged. 'If an outsider, someone without any tie-up with Samwashima, finds Oki and sends for the police ... we-ell, that could prove difficult. But right now I'm not too worried because the last thing they want at this time is trouble with the authorities, not the public variety, anyway. My guess is that Shiba will just want everything buried nice and quiet.'

'That suits me.'

'Not if you're one of the things they want buried it won't.'

They drove in silence for a while, Gunning meticulously observing the speed restrictions as the expressway swung towards the coast and Suma.

Then Langford spoke. 'What protection can you offer, Gunning?'

'Enough. But she has to co-operate. And so do you. By the way, I've had your things picked up from the hotel. They're in the trunk.'

'So ... Samwashima will assume I've done a bunk.'

'Uh-uh.' Gunning flicked the trafficator as he prepared to turn off the expressway. 'All taken care of. We're highly efficient when we have to be.'

'What do you mean, all taken care of?'

'Just that. With luck, Samwashima will think you've returned to London. I got one of the girls at the Consulate to telephone the Shimada office at Osaka, a polite thank-you message. Hopefully, he'll assume you're on your way home.'

'What happens if he decides to call the London office?'

'You could have problems,' retorted Gunning, sounding the car horn as he turned into a driveway barred by heavy, wired gates.

3

Helen Whitaker answered the front door and stared at the well-dressed man who carried a raincoat over his arm.

'Mrs Whitaker? My name is Robins. I have an appointment with your husband.'

She nodded and stepped away from the door. 'You telephoned ...?'

'Last night.'

'Yes, I remember. Neil's expecting you.' She led the man through the hall and pushed open the door of her husband's study. 'Darling, it's Mister Robins.'

'Come in. You're very punctual. Excuse the mess.'

'I'll bring some coffee for you,' said Helen, and closed the door.

Whitaker shifted a pile of papers off a chair. 'Sit down, please.'

Robins hesitated, staring at the clutter of wood, glue and paint which littered the desk. 'That's some model,' he said. 'The USS Enterprise?'

Whitaker shook his head and gave an almost sheepish smile. 'No, I'm afraid it's the Ark Royal, the last British aircraft carrier.'

'I'm impressed. As an ex-Navy man, I never saw models that good before.'

'You're very kind. It's a new hobby, since I retired. I rather enjoy it, like being a sort of armchair-sailor.' When his visitor had sat, Whitaker lowered himself into his own chair and rubbed a hand across his bald head. 'What exactly can I do for you, Mister Robins?'

'Well, sir, it's a rather delicate matter ...' He paused, looking up as Helen Whitaker came in with two cups of coffee on a tray. 'Very kind. Thank you.'

After an awkward moment, she withdrew, her eyes darting over the stranger and then stealing a last, inquiring glance at her husband.

'You were saying?' said Whitaker, pushing the tray towards Robins.

'A delicate problem, sir. Have you ever heard of the Shimada Corporation?'

Whitaker considered the question. 'No, I don't think I have.'

'A Japanese organization. I work for them in the States, in New York. They have been engaged on a rather special programme of nuclear research for some time now. I'm afraid I can't tell you much about it because I'm no expert but they're faced with a problem which they can't solve on their own.'

'I see.' Whitaker blew on his coffee. 'Do you have any idea what the problem is?'

'It concerns plutonium, Professor Whitaker, and we know you're one of the foremost authorities – '

'I'm rather out of it now. Been retired for nearly three years.'

'We know that, Professor.' Robins cleared his throat, nervously. 'Look, sir, may I speak frankly and in confidence? My people in Tokyo have been in touch with the U.S. State Department and the United Kingdom Atomic Energy Authority. Both organisations raise no objections to your going to Japan – '

'I haven't said I'm going anywhere,' Whitaker remarked, sharply.

Robins pulled an envelope from his pocket, opened the flap and extracted some papers. 'You may care to inspect their letters.' He handed the two sheets of headed notepaper to the Professor. 'As I told you, sir, I'm no

169

expert and I'm not in a position to give you any details but – '

'Don't know either of those people,' said Whitaker, returning the letters. 'That's one of the problems of the age we live in. Everything gets so big that one doesn't know people any more, just titles or reference numbers. But you were saying, Mister Robins ... a problem?'

'The Shimada Corporation are building a carrier for nuclear waste. This is top-secret, of course. There was another physicist working on the ship, a man called – '

'Kit Bailey,' interjected Whitaker. 'So that's what he was doing. Well, well. I gather from the newspapers that he was killed in an accident. A great tragedy.'

'Yessir.' Robins hesitated. 'Unfortunately, the personal tragedy could be overshadowed by another much greater. Bailey's work was incomplete. Because of the accident, he left a lot of details to be tidied up.'

'And you want me to go to Japan and finish the project?'

'Exactly so, Professor. Of course, the Shimada Corporation would pay you well and pick up the tab for all your expenses.'

'It's a nice thought but ...' Whitaker gently fingered the half-finished model of the aircraft carrier. 'You need a younger man. I don't know who to suggest but no doubt you have other contacts.'

Robins looked disconsolate. 'When I talked to Tokyo on the 'phone, Professor, I spoke to Mister Shiba himself. He explained that your name was on their original list of potential people to work on the project.'

'I'm very flattered, Mister Robins, but no, I'm too old to go gallivanting about shipyards on the other side of the world.'

'For about four weeks?' said Robins. 'That's all the time it will take. And as far as money is concerned, Mister Shiba suggested a payment of fifty thousand US dollars.' Lowering his voice, Robins added, 'That can be cash paid anywhere in the world, Professor.'

'You amaze me.' Whitaker's eyes narrowed as he studied the clean-cut young man. 'That's rather a lot of money for so short a time, isn't it?'

'When you have a problem, sir, you have to pay to get it solved. And the way I hear it, plutonium is kind of dangerous stuff.'

Whitaker nodded. 'Yes, kind of ... but are they handling the plutonium now?'

'They wouldn't tell me, Professor. It's rather odd, when you come to look at it. Here am I, offering you a highly-paid assignment and yet I barely know anything about it. All I do know is that it's urgent. The line from Tokyo wasn't too good but Mister Shiba sounded worried.'

'If they're handling plutonium, they may have every reason to be worried. I assume that this is some form of nuclear waste from a power plant?'

'Yessir. But we ... the Shimada Corporation, are only concerned with the transportation of the waste.'

'Re-processing,' muttered Whitaker. 'Yes, I suppose ...' He sighed and scratched his bald head. 'Perhaps I could telephone you? I'd like to discuss it with my wife and ...' He smiled as he caught the startled look on Robins' face. 'Don't worry, Mister Robins. I was being discreet about atomic secrets when you were still playing with pop-guns.' Then he shook his head. 'I'm sorry, that wasn't meant to be rude.'

'That's quite all right, sir.' Robins handed over a card. 'I have to fly back to New York right now. If you could call me there – and please call collect – say tomorrow about midday your time?'

'Very well but I must warn you that even the money you offer – '

Robins stood up. 'Forgive me, Professor, but I think this could be a sort of emergency. Mister Shiba is a very important man and for him to call me personally ...'

'I'll telephone you tomorrow,' said Whitaker, showing

171

Robins to the door. 'Thank you for coming.'

Robins pumped Whitaker's hand. 'No, I have to thank you. It's been a privilege.'

'What a funny little chap,' said Helen as her husband closed the front door again. 'Are you going to do it?'

'Eavesdropping?'

'Well …' Helen grinned. 'You were talking very loudly.'

'And you were listening very quietly.' Whitaker strode into the kitchen and helped himself to a beer from the ice-box. 'What do you think?'

'If it isn't dangerous, think of the money. After all these years, Neil, you could afford your boat.'

'Yes.' He nodded and pulled the ring-opener so that the beer began to froth out of the can as he put it to his mouth.

'Is it dangerous?'

'I would doubt it. But the transportation of radio-active waste can be tricky.'

'Do you want to go?' Helen stood in the kitchen doorway, her head cocked to one side. 'I don't mind.'

'It's not the money, though God knows fifty thousand dollars would be very nice.'

'And paid anywhere in the world,' said Helen. 'Greece and a yacht … Oh yes, Neil, that could be nice. But not if it's dangerous.'

Whitaker sucked at the beer can and shook his head. 'If it is dangerous – and I can't see how at this stage – but if they do have a problem which they can't solve without help, one is almost ethically obliged as a scientist to do what one can.'

'You are going to do it, aren't you?'

Whitaker shrugged. 'We'll see. I'll ring them tomorrow. But meanwhile, we'll sleep on it.'

Helen Whitaker went into the lounge and stood for a moment in front of the bookcase before selecting a worn, cloth-bound volume. After leafing through the pages, she snapped the book shut and stared at her husband. 'It says that Japan is very cold in the winter. I'll go and sort through your wardrobe.'

The house was obviously close to a railway because the oppressive silence in the sparsely-furnished room was broken at regular intervals by the quick, rhythmic drumming of passing trains. Langford was barely conscious of the sound. At that moment he was almost wholly obsessed by Yita Izumi who sat facing the window, her face taut, her dark eyes reflecting her fear. She scarcely looked at Langford at all. Or at the American. It was as if she were in a hypnotic trance, physically present and very beautiful but mentally and perhaps even spiritually absent, as if all her inner strength was pitted against some invisibly powerful force which threatened her very soul.

The spell was broken for Langford when a particularly noisy train rumbled past the house, and he shifted his gaze to the American, seated with his back to the window, a dark, featureless shape. Langford lit a cigarette. Then Gunning cleared his throat.

'We don't have that much time, Miss Izumi.' His voice was quiet, his tone one of regret. 'You're safe here. But only if you co-operate with us. Do you understand?'

Yita nodded and for a moment it seemed to Langford that she was about to speak. Her lips parted slightly, but no words came.

'Miss Izumi, unless you're prepared to talk ...' Gunning's eyes narrowed. 'I don't want to have to use force.'

'Can't you see she's scared rigid?'

'Knock it off, Langford.' Gunning glared at him, turning his head so that his profile became silhouetted against the window. 'What's it to be, Miss Izumi?' he said, slowly looking back at Yita. 'What say we start with your step-father?'

'He was a draughtsman.'

Gunning nodded. 'And he worked with Bailey, right?'

'No, not really. He designed things ... cranes, machines for winding cables and ... and things like that.'

'You're doing fine, Miss Izumi,' said Gunning, gently. 'But he was doing work for the big ship, the *Shimada Maru*, wasn't he?' She nodded. 'And he knew Doctor Bailey?'

'Yes, he knew him.'

'And did he know about your association with Bailey?'

'Yes.'

'But he didn't approve?'

Yita slumped forwards and stared sightlessly at the floor. 'He … he said …'

After a long silence, Gunning prompted her. 'What did he say?'

'That it was dishonourable and …' She looked up. 'My step-father wished me to leave Japan, to go to America.'

'Why?'

'Because … because my real father was an American. In Japan, I cannot make a good marriage. I am half European. There are many like me. We work in the bars and the clubs. I think you know that.'

'Sure.' Gunning nodded and shifted his position. 'You got on well with your step-father?'

'Not at first, no. There was another child but she died. After that it was different. He seemed to need me. Then my mother became very ill. We thought she would die but she lived. And afterwards, my step-father was much kinder. He cared for me.'

'Okay, that's fine. You want a cigarette?' Yita shook her head. 'When your step-father died, Miss Izumi, you were shocked, weren't you?' Gunning lit a cigarette for himself and his dark outline against the window was wreathed in bands of smoke which caught the sunlight. Yita hadn't replied. 'Did your step-father know they were going to kill him?'

Yita ran a hand through her hair. 'I should like that cigarette, please.'

Before Gunning could react, Langford was at her side. 'Here.'

As she took the cigarette, she looked at him and attempted a smile. Then she bent over the lighter which

174

Langford held for her. 'Thank you,' she murmured, a faint trace of the smile still lingering in her face.

'Did he know, Miss Izumi?' Gunning's question seemed to echo around the room.

'Yes, he knew.'

Gunning let out a sigh. 'Why did Samwashima want to kill him?'

'Not Sam.'

'Then who?'

She hesitated for a moment. 'I do not know,' she said, peering intently at the American, sensing his suspicion. 'It is the truth. I do not know, but I think – '

'What do you think, Miss Izumi?' There was a sudden edge in Gunning's tone.

Yita puffed at the cigarette, exhaling the smoke through her nostrils and gently feeling her lips with her tongue. 'When my mother became ill, I was in Tokyo. I came back to Kobe as soon as I heard that they had taken her into the hospital. I went there with my step-father ... they did not expect her to live and he was very upset.' She paused, pressing the cigarette to her mouth. 'That evening, we returned to the apartment and my step-father drank very much. He started to shout at me but when he saw that I was afraid, he became calm and made me promise to leave Japan if anything happened to him. I did not understand. Then he said that there would be much trouble and that he had brought dishonour on himself and Japan.' She lapsed into silence and the room throbbed as another train passed.

'What did he mean by dishonour?' asked Gunning.

'In the war ...' She stared vacantly at some ash which had fallen in her lap and then brushed it off with swift, jerky movements of her hand. 'My father worked for the Shimada Corporation because ...' She shook her head and began to cry.

'But the Shimada Corporation wasn't started until after the war, Miss Izumi,' said Gunning. 'Start again. What did your step-father mean by dishonour?'

'After the surrender ... you cannot know what it was like. I was not born but sometimes now I have the feeling that I was there. Your soldiers came and took Japan. Everything was very difficult. There was little food, no work ... many were without homes. When my step-father was released by the British, he came back to Japan but he had no home and no work. It was then that he approached Toshiro Shiba and ... and forced him to give him money, to give him work.'

Gunning stood up and walked across the room. 'So Izumi was blackmailing Shiba, right?'

'Yes, but ...' She looked round for an ashtray. Langford supplied it and she stubbed the half-smoked cigarette out.

'And was that what he meant by dishonour?'

'No, you do not understand.' Yita wiped away the tears which glistened on her cheeks. 'My step-father was really a good man. What he did ... what he tried to do was a good thing. It is Toshiro Shiba who carries our guilt. My step-father did not mean to blackmail him for ever. But he needed work and money and Shiba was starting his business. He had a great fortune, even then. And my step-father was loyal to him and worked hard for the Shimada Corporation but there were things which he knew ... about the war, about Shiba ...'

Returning to his seat in front of the window, Gunning blew a long plume of smoke into the air and sighed. 'What sort of things?'

'Bad things.' She shook her head. 'Very bad things. In the time when my mother was in hospital, my step-father was very upset. And afraid. It was then he told me about the photographs.'

'What photographs?'

'I am not sure ... they took the pictures in the war ... in Burma ... they used them for ...' Yita frowned and said something in Japanese.

'Propaganda ... war publicity,' said Gunning. 'Go on.'

Yita stared at him. 'You speak Japanese?'

176

'Some. But never mind that. Have you seen these pictures?'

She shook her head again. 'No ... there were two photographs which my step-father had but I do not know where they are now. Maybe ... maybe Shiba took them after my step-father – '

'So there are other pictures which your step-father knew about, is that right?'

'Yes.'

'Where are these other photographs, Miss Izumi?'

She thought for a moment before answering. 'My step-father said that it was better for them to be left ... forgotten, that the past is finished, dead.'

'Where are the other pictures?' demanded Gunning.

'Kit ...' She stopped, abruptly, and looked up, her hands clasped anxiously in her lap.

'What about him? Was he involved with your step-father in blackmailing Shiba?'

'No. He never knew until ...'

'Until what, Miss Izumi?'

'Please, I do not know ... I am confused ... I ...'

Gunning jumped up. 'The only thing that's confusing you right now are the lies you're trying to concoct, Miss Izumi. Now we'll have one more try but if you can't tell me the truth, I'm gonna run out of patience. What was the connection between Doctor Bailey and your step-father?'

'There was no connection until ... until my step-father was dead.' Yita seemed to sag, exhausted. 'At the time my mother became ill, I was working in Tokyo. I had worked there for a long time in many different clubs. Then I discovered that it would be better to work in one club, to have a contract. I did this but it was not until many months later that I discovered the club was owned by one of Toshiro Shiba's companies. It did not seem to matter. Then my mother became ill and I returned to Kobe. My employers were very kind to me and gave me another job in one of their clubs here, in the Motomachi. It was at this club that I met Samwashima. He was kind to me.'

'And Sam set you up for Bailey, right?' There was a discernible measure of scorn in Gunning's tone but Yita raised her head and looked straight at him.

'I am not ashamed,' she retorted. 'I have never begged and never owed money. However it began, Kit and I had something beautiful. Even my step-father began to understand; then he was killed.'

'By Shiba?' Gunning waited. 'Was he trying his blackmail stunt again?'

'I think ...' She had folded her arms under her breasts and hugged herself as she swayed in the chair. 'I think Shiba ordered his death. But I had no proof.'

'So you talked to Bailey?'

'Yes. I needed to talk about it. My mother ... she is so old now and cannot understand. I was upset and said things which should have remained hidden. Kit loved me, Mister Gunning. He wanted to help me but he did not understand ... I tried to warn him ... tried to protect him but he refused to listen to me. He said the big ship ... the *Shimada Maru*, was evil and that because of what I had told him, he had to do something. I begged him and pleaded with him but he would not listen.'

Gunning was pacing the room now, his shoes squeaking. A train rumbled by, more slowly than the others so that the clanking of the wheels and the couplings reverberated through the building. 'What was Bailey intending to do, Miss Izumi?'

'I am not sure. He said he wanted to talk to someone, someone from the Americ ...' Although her lips continued to move, no sound came as she gazed at Gunning, wide-eyed. 'You?'

Gunning nodded. 'We'd arranged to meet the day he was killed. But you knew that, didn't you?'

'No. I did not know of you then.'

'And you'd told Bailey where these other photographs could be found.' It was an accusation and Gunning stood over her, threatening. 'Now you can tell me, can't you?'

'I do not know.'

'That's a lie.'

She looked up at him, meeting his penetrating gaze with a sudden firmness. 'No. They are better to be forgotten. Too many have died.'

'Sure, that's great.' Gunning turned away. 'And I suppose the killing will stop if you don't tell?' Then he swung round. 'For Christ's sake, Yita, don't be ridiculous.' His sudden shout cracked the air like a whip and Yita jumped. 'Where are the other pictures?'

'In a monastery ... a Buddhist monastery ... there's a monk ... maybe he's dead now, I don't know.' She was shaking, her frail, delicate body trembling.

'What monastery? Where? What's the monk's name?' Each of the questions was like a bullet and ricocheted around the room. 'Come on, lady, I need to know.'

'You're not the bloody Gestapo,' snarled Langford, coming between them.

'Stay out of this, Langford, or I'll have the guys outside finish what Oki started. Now, Miss Izumi, I am going to count just five. One. Two – '

'The monk is ... was called Heyashi. He was Japanese.'

'And where's the monastery?'

'It is near a place called Suk Chiang, somewhere close to the Burmese border.'

'You mean it's in Burma?'

'No, in Thailand.'

'Thank God for that.' Gunning sat down, breathing heavily. 'Okay, we're almost through, Miss Izumi. But there's one more question: who else did you tell besides Bailey?'

'I have told no one,' said Yita, firmly.

'Who else did you tell?'

'No one.' She shook her head, vehemently. 'I told no one.'

'You're a Goddamned lying Nip whore.'

'That's enough.' Langford advanced into the centre of the room. 'She's all in, Gunning.'

179

The American ignored him. 'You talked, lady. You told someone exactly what you told Bailey, exactly what you've just told me. Right?'

'No, I ...'

Gunning came towards her, menacingly. 'The photographs ... your step-father ... this place in Thailand ... Bailey ... come on, Yita, save yourself the hassle. We both know that you told someone else.'

'Please, I –' Then she gave a shriek as Gunning grabbed her by the hair, jerking her head back as he cuffed her across the face before letting her fall to the floor. 'Who did you tell?'

Yita was sobbing at his feet, but Gunning reacted swiftly as Langford came at him. Using his left forearm to parry Langford's punch, he drove his right fist hard into the Englishman's chest. The blow lacked weight but coming on top of the punishment inflicted by Oki, it was enough to send Langford staggering back against the wall, gasping for breath as his body was pierced by needle-like shafts of pain.

'Who did you tell?' intoned Gunning, one foot poised as if to kick the girl.

She coughed, a harsh choking noise as she fought to control herself. 'Sam ... I told Samwashima.'

Gunning sighed and bent down to help her up but she shrank away from him, fear and hatred in her eyes.

'You bastard.' Langford leaned heavily against the wall, his face ashen.

'I'm sorry.' Gunning said. 'I'm sorry, but I was right.' He glanced down at Yita. 'Why did you tell Samwashima?'

She was kneeling now, one arm resting on the back of the up-turned chair. 'Sam has been kind to me. He has helped me and always been a friend.'

'Samwashima is Toshiro Shiba's right-hand, lady. The moment you told him, you sealed Bailey's fate as sure as if you'd pushed him off that ladder with your own hands.'

'No.' Yita slumped forwards, covering her face with her

180

hands. 'No, I do not believe you.'

'Too bad.' Gunning stared at Langford. 'Okay, let's have a drink. We'll have someone take a look at your ribs.'

'Thanks for nothing. I prefer to make my own arrangements.' Langford eased himself away from the wall, wincing with pain. 'I'm going and I'm taking her with me.'

'No way.' Gunning shook his head. 'God-in-Jesus, do you think I enjoy behaving like Attila the Hun? Besides, by killing Oki, you've put Samwashima on the spot. He's going to want you out of the game. I have some calls to make right now and I'll arrange for a Medic to check you out. Then we'll talk some. Whether you like it or not, Langford, we're going to have to work together.'

'I don't like it.'

'Too bad.' He paused. 'If it's any comfort, you didn't tell me anything about the *Shimada Maru* I didn't already know.'

Langford stared at the American for a moment. 'And Bailey?'

'We'll talk later.' He turned to Yita. 'I'm sorry, I really am. But I had no option, Miss Izumi. I had to know the truth.'

She looked up at him, hatred and contempt radiating from her eyes. 'Why can't you leave the past to die?'

'Because it's still very much alive, lady. And dangerous. Think about your step-father and Doctor Bailey. And if Langford hadn't paid you a visit when he did, you'd be in the same situation – very dead.'

5

Chief Foreman Yamada sat in the small cubicle which passed for an office and stared blankly at his own image reflected in the window. Glancing at his watch, he considered yet again the pros and cons of going home. It was nearly seven o'clock, some two hours after his official departure time, but he felt obliged to remain. Squinting, he peered through his reflection into the darkness. The silhouette of the *Shimada Maru* stood out massively against the night sky and further along the quay, a pool of harsh, yellow light indicated the spot where a team of men were working. Yamada tried to remember what it was they were doing but he was tired, his brain seemed to have seized up and he wanted nothing more than to climb into his Toyota and drive back to the tiny house he shared with his wife in Yabe-cho in downtown Kobe. Then he heard the raised voices from along the corridor and knew that he must stay put. With both Shiba and Samwashima on the premises, the chief foreman felt uneasy, knowing that they might send for him. He hoped they wouldn't. Shiba was plainly in a bad humour and Yamada felt too fatigued to cope with the man whose ruthless power dominated so many lives. Sighing to himself, Yamada picked up the telephone and dialled his home. His wife would have to expect him when she saw him.

Inside the office which had been occupied by Doctor Bailey, Toshiro Shiba sat behind the desk and fingered the china ashtray, the souvenir of Cologne which Bailey had brought with him from Germany. The Venetian blinds had been lowered and Samwashima was in the process of adjusting the slats so that no passer-by could see inside the office.

'You have been clumsy and stupid,' Shiba stated. He removed his heavy horn-rimmed glasses and rubbed his eyes. 'Had you sought my advice, this fiasco could have been avoided.'

Samwashima left the window. 'Shiba-*san*, I could not know – '

'You could have taken the trouble to find out that the woman possessed a weapon.' He paused as he replaced the glasses. 'You could also have remained sober.'

'But we know that Langford has – '

Shiba's hand suddenly swept the china ashtray from the desk so that it crashed to the floor and shattered. 'We know nothing except that the Englishman has disappeared. I have checked with my contacts in Tokyo and Osaka. He has not left Japan. The message was a trick. And we have also lost the girl.'

Samwashima turned away, biting his lip. He wanted to smoke. 'Shiba-*san*, perhaps if we called London …'

'London will know nothing yet. And I have already made what arrangements I can. You,' he pointed at Samwashima, his finger stabbing the air accusingly, 'You have made a serious misjudgement which I shall not forget.'

'What can I say?'

'Nothing. But you can listen and mark well what I say. Bailey's replacement, Whitaker, has agreed to come here. You will remain with him at all times. You will act as his interpreter, his assistant, his body servant, even. You will both live on board the ship for the duration of his stay.'

'What if this Whitaker discovers the truth?'

'He must not.' And Shiba shook his head so that his silvery hair glistened brightly in the harsh, fluorescent lights. 'The Minister has now stated that absolute secrecy as to our intentions must be maintained. Whitaker will complete Bailey's work but he must not know more than we have already had to tell him. We cannot risk another accident.'

'But you know that Bailey –'

'I know nothing,' snapped Shiba. 'Nothing. There must be no more mistakes.'

'When does this man arrive?' asked Samwashima, his face streaked with perspiration.

'Thursday morning. My secretary will provide you with the necessary details. You will meet his plane, escort him here and stay with him until you take him back to the aeroplane. Not one minute must pass without you knowing precisely where he is and why.'

'Such behaviour might make him suspicious, Shiba-*san*.'

'That I do not mind. He may suspect what he chooses. It is what he can prove which will matter to us.'

Nodding, Samwashima finally sat down. 'What if the ship has to sail before he is finished?'

'That does not matter. In fact, it might aid our security precautions. You and Whitaker can sail with the ship and the voyage from here to Kyomo will provide the time needed for sea-trials. Once you berth at Kyomo, everything may be left in the hands of Captain Umezu and the technicians.'

'But what about Langford and the girl?'

'Leave them to me.' Shiba rose from the chair and stepped over the broken fragments of the ashtray. 'I can manipulate the authorities. We will not be seen to be involved in what will appear to have been a fight between a visitor and a whore's pimp.' The idea appealed to him. 'You will reserve all your resources, such as they are, for the *Shimada Maru* and Whitaker.' Then he turned to Samwashima, his face set hard. 'This morning, Norihiko, we discussed your future. I expressed confidence in you for the appointment in the United States. You must now consider that confidence forfeited. We shall examine the matter again, after the *Shimada Maru* has sailed.'

Samwashima bowed his head. 'Shiba-*san*, you have my word of honour that when the ship sails, the Shimada Corporation will have safely passed an historic turning-point.'

'Words,' growled Shiba, scornfully. 'You have always been very clever with words. Now let us see how clever you can be with deeds.' He started towards the door. 'You will return to Osaka with me?'

Samwashima declined. 'Yamada is still here. I wish to speak with him and will return later.'

'Very well.' Shiba opened the door and called for Yamada.

'Shiba-*san*,' panted the chief foreman, bowing deeply.

'Samwashima-*san* has some instructions for you. Our timing is becoming critical. We must make more effort.'

Yamada nodded, bowed again and then spoke, his voice betraying his nerves. 'Shiba-*san*, I have tried ...'

184

'Of course, but you misunderstand me. I am very satisfied with your work. You have every reason to be proud. But I am forced by circumstances beyond my control to crave your help in completing everything possible ahead of schedule.' As Yamada bowed yet again, the head of the Shimada Corporation smiled. 'When the ship leaves Kobe, I shall see to it that you are specially rewarded for your great contribution, my friend.'

Chief Foreman Yamada was in a very special seventh heaven as he ushered the great man to his car, bowing copiously. And when the car had sped away, he returned to the offices and confronted Samwashima.

'You wished to see me, Samwashima-*san*?'

'No, go home. We will talk in the morning.'

'But Mister Shiba said – '

'Go,' commanded Samwashima, his hands shaking as he lit the much-needed cigarette and went into Bailey's old office, slamming the door behind him.

Perplexed, Yamada stood for a moment until he heard the telephone pinging as Samwashima dialled out. Then he smiled to himself, silently consigning Shiba's deputy to hell as he snatched his coat and left the office. He could hardly wait to get home, to tell his wife how Toshiro Shiba had called him his friend and promised him a personal reward for his work. That it was almost eight p.m. no longer mattered. The chief foreman's tiredness had simply melted away and at that moment, he would have cheerfully committed murder for the great man.

6

Miss Pym had not intended to listen in to the call which came from Japan on that Tuesday morning just after eleven a.m., London time. And the fact that she heard every word was due entirely to Meyrick Hewens. The intercom system in James Maxwell's office was unfamiliar and simply by pressing the wrong switch when he took the call, he virtually obliged Miss Pym to hear every word. Later, she would realize that she could have made use of a master switch so that the equipment in her own room was by-passed but at the time she was flustered. It never occurred to her that she was still in a state of shock, that it was simply the office routine which kept her from breaking down completely. But there was nothing routine about the telephone conversation.

'Your man Langford has disappeared,' said the Japanese voice.

'James Maxwell's dead,' replied Hewens. Either he simply didn't hear the opening remark or his brain failed to grasp the caller's message.

'I said Langford, Richard Langford, has vanished. He is wanted by the Japanese police in connection with a murder.'

'Jesus wept,' said Hewens. 'What happened?'

'A man, one of the chauffeurs, was murdered. It seems that Langford was visiting a prostitute.'

'That's all we need,' snapped Hewens, irritably.

'There is no danger,' insisted the Japanese. 'Everything is under proper control.'

'If it isn't, I want to know. Unless we're careful, the whole pan of shit could come straight back in our faces.'

'There is a replacement arranged for Bailey,' said the Japanese. 'It would seem that everything is going ahead as planned but if Langford arrives back in London ...'

'I'll handle it. Did you hear what I said about Maxwell?'

'Yes. I am sorry.'

Hewens grunted. 'So am I. Of all the inconvenient times. Jesus, I just hope you can keep your end going. If not ...'

'I will keep you informed of further developments,' said the voice.

'Okay. And let me know if the police get Langford because I have a feeling in my bones that could be very embarrassing.'

The Japanese seemed to chuckle. 'Once he is found, there will be no problems.'

Miss Pym stared woodenly at the intercom. She heard Hewens say something about *a final pay-off, whatever happens*. Then the caller hung up and when the sound of the amplified dialling tone flooded into the room, she was at last able to switch it off, her hand trembling slightly as she flicked up the lever.

Very slowly, she rose to her feet and went into the office where Meyrick Hewens sat hunched behind Maxwell's desk. She handed him some letters which had arrived earlier and surreptitiously re-set his intercom. Like her grief, her natural discretion had been pushed beyond reasonable limits. And, as she explained to Peggy Ashmore over lunch, she disliked the American and had no wish to hear any more of his conversations. Peggy Ashmore, that much younger but infinitely more worldly, suggested that Miss Pym might take a holiday and that she could fill in for her.

Meyrick Hewens as good as told Miss Pym she could go for good. He liked his secretaries to be decorative as well as efficient and Peggy Ashmore was both. What Hewens did not know was that she was also desperately concerned about Richard Langford and would make it her business to monitor all his conversations.

7

'And in case you disbelieve me,' said Gunning. 'The news has already been broadcast and it's bound to be in all the papers by tomorrow.'

Carefully pulling on his shirt, Langford winced with pain and shook his head. 'But Shiba can't – '

'There's no such word where Toshiro Shiba's concerned.' The American pulled two cigarettes from his pack and handed one to Langford.

'What about the girl?' Langford asked as they lit up.

'She's fine. And the Doc tells me you have nothing broken, so you'll be okay in a couple of days.'

'If I have that long.'

'You will.' Gunning sat down, pursing his lips so that he let out a harsh, whistling sound. 'I've been talking to our people in Tokyo, at the Embassy. It seems that there has always been a suspicion about Shiba's wartime activities. So, we're going to try to get a hold of those pictures. Then we can throw the book at him.'

'And the best of British luck,' muttered Langford, distantly.

'That's just what you're going to need. And lots of it.'

'I'll want you as a witness.' Langford frowned. 'I don't know how the Japs work but ...'

'You don't understand. You and Yita Izumi are going to disappear without trace. Like you're gonna take a little trip.'

'Go on the run? You must be joking. I wouldn't have a cat's chance in hell.'

'You're going to Thailand.'

Langford stared blankly at the American. 'Me? Go to Thailand?'

'Just listen. Shiba has pulled the skids on you. That's fine. So you disappear. I can get you and the girl out of Japan, no formalities, no problems. You go by boat to Hong Kong and then you take a 'plane down to Bangkok. From there, you go on up to this monastery at Suk Chiang and collect the dirt on Shiba.'

'You're out of your bloody mind. I've got enough problems.'

'You'll have more if you don't do as I suggest. The U.S. can't go into Thailand officially and even if there was time to set up a covert operation, Washington would never sanction it. So, you and Yita go as tourists. It's that simple. And when you get back, we nail Shiba and everything'll be just fine.'

Langford gave the American a sardonic smile. 'No way, Gunning. I'm not going to be used. Besides, no Japanese

188

court could possibly convict me, or Yita, come to that. The evidence would be so – '

'For an intelligent man, you're acting simple. Maybe Oki hit you on the head or something but you don't have any worries about Japanese courts. They're fair and dispense justice. Your problem is that Toshiro Shiba would make it his business to see that you never got anywhere near a court. You might make a cell at Police Headquarters. Then they'd release you on some technicality and ...' He shook his head. 'You'd be the late Richard Langford.'

After another pause, Langford said, 'And the *Shimada Maru*?'

'The ship was conceived as an oil tanker,' said Gunning, settling himself in a chair. 'But as you discovered, there's no way that vessel could carry oil.'

'I begin to get the picture,' said Langford, drawing heavily on the cigarette. 'They hire Bailey ... do a conversion job and you have a bulk carrier for nuclear weapons. Very neat.'

'You're on the right track but wrong,' said Gunning. 'As I told you, I'm on loan to the United States Nuclear Regulatory Commission. In theory, we're only concerned with internal matters relating to atomic energy but in practice ... well, we like to keep a weather-eye on things here and there. We first became interested in Shimada when we learned that Doctor Bailey had left Germany to come here. I've been in Japan for nearly six months now and in that time, I ... and others ... have uncovered something potentially very nasty. But let me start at the beginning.

'In the late fifties, early sixties, it was becoming clear that nuclear power was going to be important if the world was to keep pace with the demand for electricity. Your country, Great Britain, had a lead in those early days and Japan didn't want to know. Then the Tokyo government decided to buy a British nuclear reactor. They chose – not that there was much choice at the time – a thing called a

189

Magnox gas-cooled reactor. You still have them working in Britain and they're fairly effective. Anyway, the Japs sited their imported Magnox reactor at a place called Tokai Mura and it went critical – that's nuclear jargon meaning that it started to work – in 1965. The Magnox design was far from perfect but it gave the Japs the opportunity to exercise their national genius: copying and improving.

'Using the British reactor as a working model, they started to develop their own ideas. Of necessity, they were broadly based on the British design but eventually they came up with a whole new concept which made use of sea-water not only to produce the steam for driving the turbine generator but also as a coolant for the reactor core itself. These were both fairly revolutionary concepts, not least because they meant that the Japanese had successfully developed an economic de-salination unit and that they had overcome the problem of de-contaminating the sea water used as a coolant. They built the new plant on a small island called Kyomo, little more than a barren rock some fifty miles south-east of the Osumi peninsula. That's near the bottom of Honshu, the main island. Officially, the area is designated as an artillery testing range which gives the authorities a legitimate excuse to keep it off limits. And that's just as well because for some time now, the technicians at Kyomo have been facing a major problem.'

Gunning paused and chain-lit another cigarette before continuing.

'Like most conventional nuclear reactors, Kyomo uses a form of enriched uranium oxide as its fuel. The uranium comes in rods clad in stainless steel and these are inserted into the core of the reactor. Our information is that the Kyomo reactor has not been using the uranium with the maximum efficiency, so the fuel rods have had to be replaced with greater frequency than was originally envisaged.

'The uranium oxide fuel rods get burned up in the

reactor and become caked with what nuclear engineers term *crud*. The rods are then classified as irradiated and once they're pulled out of the reactor, they have to be very carefully stored in cooling ponds, literally concrete and lead tanks filled with water which has to be kept circulating. After maybe a hundred or so days, the irradiated rods are ready to be re-processed. So what began as a technically simple construction has now become infinitely complex. The uranium oxide fuel rod is caked with this *crud* which consists of different fission products, including krypton-85, strontium-90, iodine, caesium, the remains of the uranium itself in a changed molecular structure and ... this is the nasty one, plutonium. In case you'd forgotten, plutonium is the key ingredient for nuclear weapons.

'What's happened at Kyomo is that the plant has made and is continuing to make a mountain of nuclear waste. And that's bad news.'

'But I thought that the re-processing of nuclear waste was fairly staightforward,' said Langford. 'In Britain—'

'Sure, in Britain, the U.S., France, Germany and even, just recently, South Africa, the re-processing of nuclear fuel has become just another industry. But not in Japan. They don't have the facilities and they don't want to develop them. Politically, the whole nuclear scene has become a white-hot potato. After Hiroshima and Nagasaki, the slightest whisper of nuclear problems causes a kind of fulminating national neurosis to break out.'

'Understandable,' murmured Langford.

'Maybe so, but on Kyomo, they're getting desperate. Our information is they have even used up their emergency storage tanks. So if they have a radio-activity alert, they could be virtually powerless to take remedial action.'

'The ship.' Langford shook his head. 'Bailey was working on converting the oil tanker ...'

'You've got it. Somehow, the stock of irradiated fuel rods has got to be transported to whichever country agrees to carry out the re-processing. We know that the Japanese government have been trying to arrange various deals but nothing has been firmed-up yet. The most likely country is – '

'But that could mean thousands of tons of – '

'That's what worries us.' Gunning frowned. 'But without having plans of the ship, it's almost impossible to quantify its carrying capacity in terms of nuclear waste. The bulk of the *Shimada Maru*'s tonnage will have to consist of shielding, a fairly hefty mixture of concrete, lead and a ceramic lining. Added to that, you need a very sophisticated cooling system which would probably be triplicated so that it was entirely fail-safe. Then there's a whole range of instruments to monitor the state of the cargo during the voyage.'

'I see. How dangerous is it?'

Gunning shrugged and pursed his lips, thoughtfully. 'Dangerous isn't the right word. In not too many weeks time, the *Shimada Maru* could leave Japan carrying the most lethal cargo in the history of the world. If something were to go wrong, we're not talking so much about a danger as a lethal certainty. If you have an oil spill at sea, you can clean up – eventually. But with nuclear waste – and remember that the major item on the agenda is plutonium which remains active for nearly twenty-five thousand years – there is no conceivable action we could take which wouldn't be utterly futile.'

After a long silence, Langford said, 'What would happen?'

'Depends. If the *Shimada Maru* were to be badly holed or sunk off the coast of Japan, you could probably write off Japan, Korea, much of the coast of mainland China, the Philippines, New Guinea ... maybe the north coast of Australia. That's just for starters. All marine life would die and it is just possible that Malaysia and maybe even India could be affected. At best, you must think in terms of hundreds of thousands of lives lost. At worst, the figure could run into millions.'

192

'A kind of Doomsday,' said Langford.

'Yes, in a way. And there are other equally horrific possibilities. If there was some kind of failure within the ship and a chain reaction began – '

'An atomic explosion?'

'Not of the kind you're thinking of but, yes, an explosion of sorts. The difficulty is that with plutonium waste, you don't need much more than a fire-cracker in the wrong place at the right time.'

'But if the Japanese are so anti-nuclear energy, why ... how has this come about?'

'Commercial greed is one explanation,' said Gunning. 'But perhaps a fairer one is that they simply sailed into uncharted waters and lost their way. Then along comes the Shimada Corporation. Someone – probably Toshiro Shiba himself, seeing as how he almost runs Japan – someone had a hell of a good idea on how to use a damn great white elephant.'

'I'll have to pass this information on to London,' said Langford. 'Without insurance – '

'No way. The Jap government will simply underwrite the deal. No, we – and I mean Washington – want to keep this nice and quiet. That way, the situation can be controlled and no one need know. You see, Mister Langford, there is another angle to this: the political side.' Gunning leaned forwards, his face taut. 'There's a proliferation of political groups in Japan, some Right wing, people like the guys who pushed the Emperor into the last war, and some on the Left. If there were an atomic scandal here, a kind of nuclear Watergate if you like, the present government would fall and we could end up with one of the two extremes in power. No one wants that.'

'You could have told me all this before,' said Langford, bitterly.

'There wasn't time. Anyway, you would have run a mile.'

'What makes you think I won't? I've got no reason to hang around.'

'Try leaving Japan and see what happens. I did warn you not to tangle with Oki. Remember?'

Langford nodded. 'You also knew all about Bailey, didn't you?'

'No, by no means. He was the clue. But let me fill you in on the late Doctor Bailey. In Kobe, there's a thriving little community of ex-patriot Americans and Europeans. There's usually a party somewhere and it's a pretty good life ... except that Bailey wanted no part of it. He had his woman, his apartment on the Yamamoto-dori and his work. He stayed aloof and I knew that I had to make contact with him or I'd get nowhere. It wasn't easy. Then, about eight weeks back, there was a reception at the British Consulate in Osaka. I had to go and it was pure luck that Bailey is there, complete with Yita Izumi.

'So we get talking but I can sense that he's uneasy. He wasn't afraid, at least, I don't think so. He just seemed ... I don't know.' Gunning scowled. 'But the important thing was that I'd made contact. After that, we met twice, once by accident in the street and then by arrangement a few days later. I had suggested going to a show and we made up a party. I was anxious to talk about his work but I only had to hint at the subject for him to clam up, so I just played him along. Then something happened. It was the day before he died, about nine in the evening, I guess. The telephone rings and it's Bailey. He said, "I understand that you're with the U.S. N.R.C." I was caught because there was no way I knew he could have got that information in Japan unless he had made inquiries through London. I hedged a bit and he seemed to understand. He asked me if I could meet him the following evening. I said, sure, so we arrange a time and place, a small drinking club used by tourists and Europeans here. Then I asked him why? He said, "I have something important to discuss". Then he hung up. Less than twelve hours later, he was dead.'

'Fell off a rope ladder,' muttered Langford, his face dour

'My guess is that he wanted to see me to blow the whistle on Shiba. And he knew about the photographs, of course.'

'Of course. And so did you.'

'We ... I knew about the suspicion, no more than that. It's fairly common knowledge that the Far Eastern Sub-Commission of the UNCWC only knocked the tip off the iceberg.'

'The what?'

'The United Nations Commission for the Investigation of War Crimes,' explained Gunning. 'Look, I'm sorry. It was no part of the plan to involve you this deep.'

'Whose plan?'

'Wrong word. You might say that we've been overtaken by events.'

'I might say a lot of things, like No, for instance. Or it's not my ball-game, to coin a phrase.'

'Guys like Shiba put the lid on quite a lot of British soldiers,' said Gunning. 'You might consider that. Maybe even think of it as a chance to get even.'

'It's history. Ancient history, at that.'

The American seemed undeterred. 'You have your passport but Miss Izumi didn't have hers, so we've fixed her up with the American variety. In the name of Langford. I take it you're not already married?'

'Does it matter? This boat you mentioned, the one going to Hong Kong?'

'Just a boat. You'll see it in an hour or so. But don't get any ideas. I know that Maxwell, Hewens and Partners have a Hong Kong office. As a precaution, one of our people will meet the boat and see you safely on to the flight for Bangkok.' He tossed a wad of American dollars into Langford's lap. 'Your expenses.'

'You think of everything, don't you?'

'I try to. Once you're in Thailand, you're on your own. I have to trust you. Just get the pictures and go back to Hong Kong. After that, my people will take care of things.'

Langford toyed with the bundle of money and then

195

shrugged. 'Who put you on to me?'

'What do you mean?'

'What I say. Who pointed the finger at me? Come on, for God's sake. I wasn't born yesterday. I've been pushed into this and we both know it. My only mistake was not seeing it earlier. So who was it?'

'Does it matter?'

'Yes.'

Gunning nodded. 'Okay, you were recommended, I'll admit that.'

'Recommended? What as? The year's prize fall guy? God Almighty, you're cool, I'll say that for you.' Langford suddenly threw the money at Gunning's feet. 'I know I'm trapped but I'm buggered if I'm going to dance without knowing just whose fingers are pulling the strings.'

'My authority doesn't extend to passing on that kind of information. Anyway, I would have thought that someone like you could have guessed.'

Langford shook his head. 'Maxwell,' he growled, clenching his fists. 'James-bloody-Maxwell. I should have known. He knew about Shiba, knew about Bailey and about the ship. Him and Hewens. And your people, whatever they're called.'

'It was never intended —'

'Bullshit. I was set up.'

'No one pushed you into switching off Oki's lights.'

'Didn't have much bloody option, did I?'

'If we're talking options, you don't have that many right now.'

'When I get back to London, I'm going to tell Maxwell and Hewens exactly what they can —'

'If you get back.' Gunning looked at him. 'Are you going to pick up that roll? Take it or leave it, Langford. I don't give a shit how or why you got involved. But now you are – right up to your neck – and I'm the only one who can get you out. It's up to you.' He started towards the door. 'But don't forget the broad, Sir Galahad. Samwashima won't.'

'You're an unprincipled bastard.'

'I guess we're two of a kind.' And he grinned slightly as he watched Langford pick up the roll of dollars. 'That's better. By the way, there's something you ought to know.'

'There are a lot of things I ought to have known.'

'No, this is different. James Maxwell died on Monday. I'm sorry.' He glanced at his watch. 'We'll be leaving in about an hour,' he said, closing the door after him.

Richard Langford stared at the roll of banknotes in his hand. Another train rumbled in the distance and he suddenly realized that his anger and bitterness had been overcome by a feeling of sadness. Maxwell had lied and tricked him but the deception no longer seemed important.

EIGHT

1

A faint breeze ruffled the dark, oily sea and a cold, thin drizzle misted the air, coating everything so that as the car slowed to a halt by the small jetty, the cobbled surface glistened in the shafts of brightness cast by the headlights.

'Now what?' demanded Langford as the American switched off the lights and sat motionless in the driving seat.

Gunning glanced at his watch and then lit a cigarette. 'We're a bit early so we wait. The boat is a Taiwanese freighter. Not exactly a Cunard liner but it'll get you to Hong Kong okay.' He paused, pulling something from his inside pocket. 'While you were being bandaged, I went through Bailey's things. These were found in his wallet – inside the lining. Look at them later.'

'What are they?' said Langford, taking the envelope and staring at it in the darkness for a moment before pushing it into his pocket.

'Two photographs.' Gunning glanced round at Yita. 'The ones her step-father had. She says he must have given them to Bailey but I don't know so much.'

'It is the truth,' said Yita.

Gunning shrugged. 'Maybe.' He looked again at his watch. 'We'll have another try,' he muttered, flicking the headlights on and off. 'See anything?'

Langford stared through the rain-mottled windscreen. 'No, nothing.'

Gunning flashed the lights again. After a few seconds, two answering flashes came back across the water. 'We're in business.' He swung round and faced Langford, his features lit by the glow of the cigarette. 'One last warning. Don't try to cross me, Langford. I never intended for you to get caught up like this but ... hell, what's done is done. Just play it dead straight and you'll be okay. You come back with the mud and we'll do the slinging.'

'Don't threaten me, Gunning. I've told you before that I don't like it. If I can get the photographs, well and good. You can have them – with my compliments But don't expect any heroics because I'm not in that line of business. For you or anybody else.'

'Let's go.' Gunning swung open the door and got out.

It was very cold and dank as they made their way along the jetty and down the worn, slippery steps. From across the water, the muffled throb of an engine was clearly audible. Then a small launch appeared, the engine noise dying away as the dark shape bumped against the steps. Gunning spoke rapidly in Japanese, someone replied, the two suitcases were hefted aboard and then Yita and Langford followed.

'Bon voyage,' said Gunning, quietly.

'Sure.' Langford settled himself in the stern and watched one of the crew pole the launch away from the jetty. Then the engine started and the launch headed out into the bay.

'I am afraid,' said Yita and Langford felt her shivering.

'I know.'

'Do you have fear, Langford-*san*?'

'Some, yes.'

'I do not like the American. He is not honest, I think.'

Langford grinned to himself in the darkness. 'Maybe.' He peered ahead, screwing up his eyes in an attempt to see where they were going. There were a number of ships lying at their moorings, some brightly lit and surrounded by barges as loading and unloading went on into the night, while others showed only riding lights at their mastheads and the occasional glow from portholes or cabin windows. After a time, the shore-line was hidden by the

199

misty drizzle. Then Langford picked out the Taiwanese freighter. Apart from its riding lights, the vessel was in total darkness. It seemed low in the water and looked cold and forbidding.

As the launch slowed and bumped alongside, someone shouted and a rope ladder uncoiled towards them.

'You go first,' said Langford, steadying the ladder and helping Yita on to it. 'I'll be right behind you.'

She took hold of the ladder and began to climb. Her apparent lack of fear surprised Langford, whose thoughts suddenly turned to Bailey and the unused ladder produced by Samwashima. By the time they reached the deck, Richard Langford was shaking but Yita seemed strangely unconcerned, as if she were once again in some kind of trance.

Three or four crewmen eyed them with curious expressions which, if they weren't exactly hostile, weren't that friendly. Then the two suitcases were pulled aboard and when he looked round, Langford saw another group of men standing at the davits waiting to haul in the launch.

'You come this way.'

Turning, Langford came face to face with a short, thick-set Chinese dressed in a US Army surplus parka. 'Are you the Master?' he asked.

'You come this way,' said the man and began walking towards the stern.

Langford picked up their cases and they followed the Chinese along the deck and into a doorway which led on to a metal staircase. A blast of warm air hit them, a warmth Langford might have welcomed had it not contained the rank, stale stench of men living at close quarters, a thick, greasy smell of cooking overlaid with the sharp, acid tang of sweat and urine.

Even in the murky light of what Langford assumed to be the result of emergency battery-power, the filthy state of the ship was all too obvious. The companionway was littered with rubbish, the steel partitioning and the bulkheads streaming condensation which trickled down rusty tracks in the peeling paintwork. And as they moved aft, they passed a series of open doors leading into cabins all seemingly crammed with people. Glancing in, Langford saw that they were mostly Chinese who stared back at him, curiosity and fear written in their faces.

'Here. Your place.' The man had stopped by another open door. 'Not big but ... you alone.' He shrugged. 'Better, yes?'

Langford peered into the tiny cabin. 'Yes,' he said, deciding that even in the dull light, it looked cleaner than the other parts of the ship they had seen. He stepped inside.

'You stay here all time. No move. Okay? Food come. Regular. Good food. But you stay.'

Langford frowned. 'No windows ... no porthole,' he said.

The Chinese smiled, revealing just four black and broken teeth which seemed as if they might fall from his gums at any moment. 'Under water. Okay?' And he made a weaving motion with his hands. 'Sail now. You stay.' Then he pulled the door shut and left them alone.

'As the man said, it isn't exactly a Cunarder.'

Yita regarded him for a moment, her eyes narrowed. 'You think maybe we will sink?'

Langford forced a smile. 'I hope not,' he said, grimacing as he caught sight of the two narrow bunks, one above the other. Suddenly conscious of the sticky heat, he pulled off his coat. And as he lowered himself into a chair, the ship came alive, vibrating as the engines started. Then came the distant rumbling of the anchor being weighed.

Yita had begun to take off her top-coat. 'We're going?'

'Sounds like it.' Langford was about to comment on the dull, yellow glow of the cabin lights when they suddenly flickered, died and then came on again, very bright. 'That's better. I think.' He produced cigarettes and they lit up. Then he remembered the envelope which Gunning had given him and pulled it from his coat pocket.

There were two photographs, both snapshot size and both yellowed and dog-eared with age. Langford studied them. 'Are these the pictures your step-father had?'

'Yes, I think so.' She peered over his shoulder and pointed to a blurred face. 'That is him, my step-father.'

'We could do with a magnifying glass,' Langford muttered as he examined the photographs under the light. 'How did Bailey get hold of these?'

'I can only think that my step-father gave them to him. Or … or maybe Kit took them.'

He turned and faced her, looking into her eyes. 'You didn't give them to him?'

'No.' She shook her head. 'Please, it is the truth. I have no need to lie now. I told Kit many things but I did not know he had the photographs.'

'Okay.' Langford gazed at the blurred images, for some reason recalling his last meeting with James Maxwell, whose death still seemed unreal.

The first of the photographs was clearly a posed shot, a dozen or so Japanese officers, some sitting, some standing but all with their elegantly curved swords. Four of the officers wore what looked like pith helmets but the other heads were covered with the more familiar Japanese field caps. The second picture was entirely different and more of a casual snapshot: ordinary soldiers, some lounging. But even the cracked, blurred sepia-toned surface could not fail to hide the emaciated condition of the men or their bleak, somehow defeated expressions.

Langford and Yita looked at each other when the ship gave a sudden lurch. Then the engine note changed from a rather ragged drumming into a steady confident throb as the freighter went ahead. Langford was about to say something when the cabin door was kicked open and two men appeared.

Yita gave a tiny shriek and Langford, sensing danger, jumped to his feet.

'Food,' said the man with the four teeth as he held open

202

the door for his companion who placed a large tray on the table. 'You eat now.'

Langford stared at the selection of bowls. Whatever other smells had assaulted his senses since boarding the ship, the Chinese food filled the tiny cabin with an aroma which reminded Langford that it was many hours since he had last eaten. Left alone, they quickly discovered that the food was delicious, as was the Japanese *Sapporo* beer served with it.

Pleasantly full, Langford lit a cigarette and settled back, smiling at Yita. 'I'm sorry,' he said, gently.

'Why?' She seemed surprised.

'Your step-father ... Bailey ... everything that's happened, I suppose.'

'You cannot be blamed.' She sat hunched in the chair, her hands clasped tightly in her lap. 'Many would say that I deserve ...'

Langford waited for a moment. 'What do you deserve?'

'This.' She made a small, helpless gesture with her hands. 'What has happened ... what will happen. It is all written.'

'Yita, we've been through this before. I'm afraid I just can't buy your idea of Fate. It's – '

'You Europeans will never understand life the way we do because you refuse to see what is there to be seen. It is as if you are all blind.'

Langford sighed. 'Okay, explain it to me.'

She shook her head. 'It cannot easily be explained. Life is like ... like so many circles, so many rings which are all twined together. Each circle or ring is a life, a *karma*, and the Lord Buddha tells us that when we die, we leave one life and pass into another ... another ring, another circle. For most people, it is endless, each life being the reward or the punishment for what they do in the previous life.'

'Reincarnation,' said Langford, distantly.

'Yes. But then, for those who can achieve the perfection

taught by Buddha, for those who can become enlightened, the cycle ends. They die and achieve peace, oblivion. That is *Nirvana*.'

'And you believe all this?'

Yita hesitated, as if considering the question. 'I cannot disbelieve because I cannot prove otherwise, so perhaps ... yes, I think I do honestly believe it. It gives me comfort. And without this faith, I could not make this journey.'

'What do you mean?'

She looked away, smiling slightly. 'I must be punished.'

'Why?'

'Because of what is past. My mother ...' She glanced at him for a moment and then turned away again, as if to hide her face. 'My mother went with many men, American soldiers as well as Japanese. It was a bad thing but hunger is also bad and she did not have the strength to bear her suffering.'

'Yita, you can't spend the rest of your life torturing yourself because of what happened before you were even born.'

'You are wrong, Langford-*san*. It is because of what happened that I must seek forgiveness. Buddha taught us that it is wrong to take life and yet in the war, many lives were taken, many bad things happened.'

'For God's sake,' snapped Langford, suddenly irritated. 'You'll go mad if you even think like that.'

'Please, Langford-*san*, let me explain.' She looked at him, her dark eyes filled with a strange compassionate understanding, as if she could see into his very soul. 'When Kenji Izumi first wished my mother to marry him, she refused. He did not know that she was with child. And after I was born, my mother continued to refuse him. He thought that she was ashamed but when she told him that she was betrothed before the war to a man who had not returned, he explained why they must marry.

'My mother came from a good and prosperous family and a marriage had been arranged. But it was not to be, because of the war. He was sent away. But he was an honourable man and when he knew he would not return, he asked Kenji Izumi to search for my mother and to care for her as his wife. It was a sacred promise because the man had saved my step-father's life, and so my mother finally agreed to the marriage. But my step-father had done many bad things and when his life became linked with mine, his dishonour also became mine.'

'You're talking nonsense,' said Langford but even as the words left his mouth, he knew that he had hurt her, and she turned away, her eyes brimming with tears.

'I was born to dishonour my mother.'

Langford got up and tried to comfort her but she drew away from him. 'Please, Yita, you can't go on ...'

'You do not understand. Why do you think I am here with you? The American is right. The past is not dead. It is alive and threatens those who live. Ever since I found out the truth about my step-father, I have known in my heart that I would make this journey. And when he died ... when he was killed, I knew what would happen.'

'You knew? About the photographs? About Shiba?' But she shook her head, her lips forming a slow, sad smile.

'No. What are photographs? And what do I care about Toshiro Shiba? No, I must seek purification – '

Langford's temper finally broke. 'For Christ's sake, forget it. You're dead tired and you're talking nonsense.' He stood up and started to turn down the sheets on the lower bunk. 'Go on, get some sleep.'

'The man ...' She stared at him. 'The man who was going to marry my mother before the war.'

'What about him?'

'His name was Heyashi, Soichi Heyashi.'

'Of course.' Langford slowly sank down into the chair again. 'The monk. I should have guessed.'

She nodded. 'I need to see him, to talk with him, to seek his blessing and his forgiveness. Do you understand now, Langford-*san*?'

'I think ...' But he gave up, not knowing what to think.

'And I do not know whether this man is still alive.'

'How old is he? Do you know that?'

She shrugged. 'A little older than my mother ... he must be ... eighty?'

Langford lit another cigarette. 'I suppose even if he's dead, there are still the pictures.'

'If he has died, they will not let us see the pictures.'

'Do you know when he was last heard of?'

'Many years ago ... my step-father received a letter. He told me about it. But a long time. I was still a baby.' The tears ran down her face. 'If he is dead, I shall feel lost.'

Langford nodded. 'You're not the only one.'

2

When he had replaced the receiver, Muga Tasaki returned to the fire and lowered his thin body into the chair as a servant came with tea, bowed and withdrew.

'I have decided to exchange queens,' said Komai from the chair opposite.

Tasaki shrugged and contemplated the chess board for a moment. 'Forget the game, my friend.'

'The telephone call?'

Tasaki nodded as he sipped the tea. 'It was Samwashima. He is in Kobe.'

'What did he want?'

Tasaki smiled, slowly. 'The future. He wants the future and now he seems to understand that only we can provide it. He says he is ready to desert Toshiro Shiba and that he has information which will be of use to us.'

Komai shifted his position and leaned against the arm of the chair. 'His terms?'

'What you would expect.' Tasaki shrugged. 'He wants the Shimada Corporation.'

'That would be within our power,' said Komai, laughing. 'What did you tell him?'

'Nothing. He is coming here. Tonight.'

'How?'

Even as Komai spoke, the resonant thudding of a helicopter engine filled the air around the house, drowning the rush of the sea and the wind. Komai glanced upwards as the machine took off and passed directly over them. Then the noise faded as it headed out across the water.

'He will be with us inside an hour. We must be ready. Where is the Frenchman?'

'In his quarters,' replied Komai. 'There is a guard.'

'Good. They must not meet.'

'Tasaki-san, I do not think we should trust Samwashima. He has always been loyal to Shiba. From the very beginning ...'

'We have no need to trust him,' said Tasaki, finishing his tea. 'But he must trust us. Therefore, we will make him welcome and offer him that which he craves. As you say, it will be within our gift. But ...' And he smiled. 'What we can give, we can also take away. I do not like traitors. They are dishonourable men who do not deserve trust.'

'Could it be a trap?' suggested Komai. 'Shiba has the cunning of the fox. He has many friends. Samwashima may be the means by which he intends to lure us into the open.'

'Possibly. But Shiba has no real friends, merely people who are too scared to do anything other than his bidding. We do have friends, Komai-san, loyal friends who will fight with us because they believe as we do. This Samwashima thinks that he will use us for his own ends. Let him continue to think that. Let him have every confidence. It does not matter. Once the *Shimada Maru* has left Kyomo and is under our control ...'

Komai held up his hand. 'I have been talking with the Frenchman. It was difficult because the interpreter could not always ... but Picot is worried, is he not?'

'He is a scientist. They always worry.'

'But he has little sympathy for our aims.'

'That is understandable and why we take the precautions we do take. He is afraid. And that is good because just as the Frenchman is afraid, so the authorities.

in Tokyo will be afraid. And he could be useful to us beyond what we had envisaged. He could become an emissary on our behalf. After all, who better qualified to explain what could happen unless …?'

'I do not care for that. The Frenchman is a mercenary.'

'So is Samwashima,' said Tasaki. 'At least the Frenchman is not a hypocrite as well.'

Komai stood up and stared balefully at the abandoned chessboard for a moment. Then he walked to the window, parting the heavy curtain and peering into the darkness. 'What we have always intended,' he said, his voice very soft, 'could go wrong if the authorities in Tokyo chose to make our ultimatum public. If they did that, we should become politically unacceptable.'

'No, you are mistaken,' said Tasaki softly, brushing back a lock of hair. 'There is no one in Tokyo who would dare to reveal the threat. To do so would be a tacit admission that they had lied to the people. And what would be the point? Once the information was leaked, they would lose control. The mobs would be on the streets, chanting their slogans, throwing stones and … no, they will not dare.'

'But if they do?' insisted Komai, returning to the fire and warming himself.

'Very well, let us assume they do. The result will be panic. Then the government will fall, martial law must be declared and so … either way, my friend, we shall win. But have no fears. Our demands will be given in secret and accepted in secret because there is no other way. Then, Komai-*san*, we shall see a new beginning, a new sunrise.'

3

It was just after three in the afternoon when Henri Bouscat sagged wearily on to the mock-leather bench seat and contemplated the crowds milling around the main departure lounge at Charles de Gaulle airport. He was hungry, tired and irritable. Somewhere in the building, Jean-Jacques Rueff was talking to friends, contacts whose jobs at the airport provided the means to make a little on the side by aiding and abetting the contraband merchants. Bouscat pondered this for a moment. Rueff would be asking a favour on behalf of *someone* – Bouscat – who could one day be called upon to return the service. It might involve drugs, diamonds, explosives ... the range was infinite, the possibilities frightening even for a man whose success as a policeman had depended on many such deals over a long period of years.

Sitting next to him on the bench were two British businessmen. They were talking loudly and had obviously been drinking. Bouscat found himself listening to their conversation but apart from odd phrases – *bloody French* seemed to occur all too frequently – he could understand little of what they said. Had he not been so utterly fatigued, he might have moved to another seat. In the event, they moved first, jumping up when a British Airways flight to London was announced over the public address system.

Bouscat lit a cigarette and spread himself on the seat. Rueff had been gone for over an hour. Thus far, they had worked separately, each checking on their own contacts in hotels, cafés, bars and brothels. But at the airport, both men knew others who, if they weren't entirely beyond the law, did not operate entirely within it, so they had gone to Charles de Gaulle together. Bouscat's list of contacts had clearly been much shorter than Rueff's. Or maybe the cracksman was simply taking time to spend DuCros' money in one of the bars. Henri Bouscat grinned to himself and then noticed that the Englishmen had left their newspapers behind them on the seat. He stared blankly at the pages. The Inspector had learned English in school but for all that he could understand or read, he knew he might as well not have bothered. Then Jean-

209

Jacques Rueff appeared and almost threw himself on to the seat.

'Useless,' he growled. 'Bloody useless.'

'Took you long enough.'

'People need to be coaxed. I thought I had someone who may have seen him but it was the wrong day.'

'Before or after?' demanded Bouscat, immediately alert.

'Before. Anyway, the guy was so uncertain ...' He sniffed and scratched at his beard. 'What now?'

Looking at his watch, Bouscat shrugged. 'Lunch. I think better on a full stomach.'

'You and me both. You know something? We're wasting our time. It's hopeless. Worse than the proverbial needle.'

'You should worry. You're not paying for anything.'

'Not yet, but I do worry. People may get around to thinking that Rueff has become a grass. And that could cost me more than money.'

Bouscat nodded, almost sympathetic. 'Like myself, *mon ami*, you have no choice.' He pulled himself to his feet. 'Come on, let Colonel DuCros buy us a ...'

'*Merde alors!*'

'What is it?'

'Him,' whispered Rueff, shaking his head in disbelief.

Bouscat dug his hands in his pockets and started to look around as casually as he could. 'Which direction?'

'No direction.' Rueff touched his arm. 'He is here.' And he tapped one of a pair of photographs on the page of the *Financial Times* which Bouscat had been staring at. 'That is the man.'

Henri Bouscat grabbed at the discarded newspaper as if it might suddenly sprout wings and fly. 'Are you sure?'

'Positive.' Rueff produced the crumpled artist's impression from his pocket. 'There, not a bad match, eh?'

'There's a similarity but ...' Bouscat was sceptical.

'Peas in a pod. Anyway, that's the man I saw and you can disbelieve me if you like.'

'I'm just being cautious.' The Inspector folded the paper and stared at the photograph. 'Meyrick C. Hewens,' he murmured, reading aloud. 'An American, too. So DuCros' people were right.'

'Can we go and eat now?'

'No.' Bouscat sat down. 'Maybe we should go to my office ... my apartment. I could call someone in London and find out if –'

'Sod that,' snarled Rueff. 'Let the bastard do it himself. Besides, you told me that we only had to locate him. Well, there he is, in London.'

'DuCros won't take your word.'

'Who cares?'

'I care,' hissed Bouscat, rising again. 'Come on, we'll take a cab to the Rue Jullien. God help you if you're wrong.'

'I'm not,' Rueff replied.

4

'Meyrick, it isn't eight o'clock yet.'

'I thought I should call you. Something's come up here. I may have to stay over for a bit.'

'Then I'll come to London. Maybe we should talk some.'

'Lois, there's no point.'

'Oh yes there is. I've had enough. I want out.'

'What d'you mean?'

'Meyrick, I want a divorce.'

'Oh Jesus ...'

'I'll send you a wire when I've booked a flight.'

'Lois, you listen ... Lois? Lois?'

Alone in her office, Peggy Ashmore reached out and flicked off the switch as the dialling tone throbbed from the speaker. Then she resumed eating her cheese sandwich, her face creased by a deep frown.

Norihiko Samwashima knew that Tasaki had a mansion on the island of Shikoku and that he ran his own private helicopter. What he did not know – among many other things – was that the mansion more closely resembled a fortress, and that the non-executive director of the Shimada Corporation possessed a fleet of six helicopters. As he descended from the machine which had whirled him from Kobe, over Awaji Island and across the Naruto Straits to the rain-soaked tarmac apron, he stared open-mouthed at the other machines. Some were covered by heavy tarpaulins, others just stood waiting and all around there seemed to be movement – men in dark, high-necked uniforms, men carrying guns.

'This way,' commanded the young Japanese who had accompanied him on his flight.

Turning up his collar against the wet, Samwashima followed the young man towards the house. As they approached, they passed other men with dogs, fine examples of the famous *Tosa Inu* breed, sturdy, bellicose animals bred for fighting. Or as guard dogs. And as he caught a fleeting glimpse of the high perimeter fencing in the distance, Samwashima had little doubt that the sumo dogs which belonged to Muga Tasaki were not bred for sport.

As they reached the main entrance, the heavy wooden door swung open and Samwashima entered. A servant took his coat and waited while he slipped off his shoes and put on the heel-less slippers provided for guests. Then the servant bowed, opened another door and ushered Samwashima into the main hall.

Tasaki was waiting and bowed, deeply. 'Welcome to my humble dwelling,' he said, bowing again. Samwashima returned the compliment.

'I am greatly honoured to be admitted here, Tasaki-*san*.'

'It is I who am honoured,' said Tasaki, bowing for the third time

'Then I am doubly honoured, Tasaki-*san*.' And when Samwashima had made his third bow, the classic ritual greeting of an older Japanese society was completed and the two men faced each other.

'Come,' said Tasaki. 'There is a fire. The helicopter is a cold thing for old men such as we.'

'I expected Komai to be here,' said Samwashima, looking around as he entered.

'He has retired. And I felt that our conversation would best be conducted alone. You will take some whisky?' Samwashima nodded and Tasaki waved the servant to bring the bottle. 'Leave it,' he snapped. 'We shall help ourselves.'

They sat down. After a pause, Tasaki spoke. 'What is it you have come to propose, Samwashima-*san*?'

'An alliance. Toshiro Shiba must retire soon. As much as we venerate his age and his wisdom, his immense genius, his – '

'Go on.' Tasaki waved his hand. 'I know Shiba better than you.'

'Yes, of course. It seems that Shiba means to deprive me of my rightful inheritance.'

'Rightful inheritance?' queried Tasaki, the ghost of a smile lighting his old face.

Samwashima nodded. 'Just so. I have earned the succession, I think. Now I must act alone. For the good of all.'

'But mostly for your own,' remarked Tasaki, sipping his drink.

'Perhaps. The ship ... the *Shimada Maru*. You know the use for which it is intended?'

'The transportation of nuclear waste? Yes, we ... I know.'

'And you assume that the ship will sail from Japan to Europe with this cargo, yes?'

'Yes, it is what I had assumed.'

'Then you are wrong,' said Samwashima.

Tasaki smiled. 'So, Toshiro has come to an agreement

213

with the Russians? Or is it the Chinese?'

'No. The age of miracles is not yet upon us. The *Shimada Maru* will make only one voyage. It will be very short and very profitable '

'How so?'

Perspiring slightly, Samwashima gulped at his wisky. 'I want your word that you will help me. I want ... I want Shiba's place.'

'Then explain yourself, hissed Tasaki, the courteous cordiality of his greeting suddenly evaporating.

'When we made the decision to convert the vessel for its intended use, there was no agreement between Japan and any other country for the re-processing of the nuclear waste. Moreover, the agreements reached between Tokyo and the British and French since that time, do not allow for the transportation of the material in such massive quantities.'

'That I knew,' said Tasaki.

'Nor does any such agreement now exist. The extent to which the Kyomo reactor has failed is a closely-guarded secret known only to a few.'

'You have yet to tell me anything which I did not already know, Samwashima-*san*. It is obvious that the agreement to re-process the excess of waste material from Kyomo has been concluded in secrecy. One would not have expected it have been otherwise. But it is of no importance who has agreed to carry out the re-processing.'

'You are missing my point,' said Samwashima, his knuckles glowing as he gripped the tumbler of whisky. 'No other power has agreed to re-process the waste. I said that the *Shimada Maru* would make just one voyage. She will sail from Kyomo and simply disappear. She is to be scuttled in the Marianas Trench. The depth is believed to be in excess of forty thousand fathoms. That is more than six miles deep, the deepest sea known to man.'

Tasaki had dropped his casual, inattentive pose. 'It is

madness,' he said. 'The pressure of the water ... no, it is insane.'

'Whether or not the project is sane is no longer important.' He drained his glass and paused to mop his perspiring face. 'The vessel has been so constructed that as it sinks and the water pressure increases, so the hull collapses but in an ordered, pre-destined manner. I am not a scientist but I am now familiar with the principles. It is like a box with a series of lids. As the pressure is increased on the outer lid, so the innermost lid is secured even more firmly. And Shiba will reap great profit from this. Apart from a massive payment from the government for getting rid of their embarrassing problem, he will also receive many billions of yen from the *Shimada Maru*'s insurers. He has even spoken of building another such vessel.'

There was no way Muga Tasaki could conceal his surprise. 'How long have you known this?'

'Nearly two years now. Always I have been doubtful of the feasibility but – '

'But you now see an opportunity of making capital out of Shiba's mistake,' Tasaki interjected.

'If it is a mistake. Toshiro Shiba has yet to be proved wrong. The men in power in Tokyo look to him for support and leadership.'

'Ha!' Tasaki stood up and began pacing the room, his head bowed, his wrinkled hands clasped behind his back. 'It is madness. What happens if there is an explosion aboard the ship?'

'Impossible. The waste will be protected by cooling systems and other equipment. The state of the material will be controlled until the pressure of the water breaks the equipment, by which time the control mechanisms are no longer necessary.'

Tasaki paused and stared at his guest. 'What is the state of the ship?'

'It is anticipated that it will sail to Kyomo within the next few days, assuming that there are no problems.'

'I see.' Tasaki resumed his seat and gestured for Samwashima to refill his glass. 'You came here to seek my help in displacing Shiba. You shall have it. You have brought me good news, better than you can possibly know.' He raised his glass. '*Kampai*,' he said, quietly.

Samwashima took a slug of whisky, coughed and then shook his head. 'I bring other news,' he said, coughing again to clear his windpipe. 'I fear that it will not make such pleasant hearing.'

'Go on.'

Very slowly, Samwashima explained about Oki's death, about Langford and the girl, his face streaming sweat as he talked. 'In the war, we fought for the Emperor, for Bushido. We believed ...'

'We were betrayed,' Tasaki muttered, bitterly.

'Just so.' Samwashima seemed to regain his confidence. 'Izumi would have betrayed you as well as Shiba. And the English scientist, Bailey, was ready to give information to the Americans. Now there is this other man, Langford. And the girl. I fear danger, Tasaki-*san*.'

'And you say you have no idea where this Englishman is now?'

'No. But I am looking. Discreet inquiries are being made. And Shiba himself is also – '

'So you said.' Muga Tasaki stared at the fire. 'The paradox is almost poetic. We are about to destroy Shiba and the fabric of this dismal echo of Japan and yet ...' He shook his head, sighing. 'And yet we once again face a common enemy, just as we did when we were comrades-in-arms. And if they produce their evidence ...'

'But after so long, Tasaki-*san*, surely ...?'

'You are a simpleton,' snapped Tasaki. 'Had you bided your time and let Izumi live – '

'Shiba ordered his death.'

'So? That does not make the action any more sensible. You cut down the tree but left the roots. Now you are surprised that the tree grows afresh.'

'Perhaps I have been foolish,' admitted Samwashima.

'But when the English scientist died, I thought – '

'You did not think, my friend. You acted out of self-interest. But now we must make a common cause. You have proposed an alliance which will serve both our purposes well. But it will be necessary to form another. And this time there must be no mistakes.'

'You are suggesting an alliance with Komai?'

Tasaki smiled, ingenuously. 'Komai-*san* is my dearest friend and my most trusted confidant. No, we must combine with Toshiro Shiba.'

'Shiba? But this is madness.' Samwashima trembled, his head shaking from side to side. 'How can you suggest such a thing?'

'It is very simple. You say that you have no idea where this Englishman has gone. It is obvious, my friend. Either he, or the girl, or both of them, will be following the trail mapped by Izumi and the late Doctor Bailey.'

'Impossible. Shiba says that they have not left Japan. He says – '

'Toshiro Shiba is a powerful man but even he has his blind-spots. This man Bailey was in touch with the Americans, yes? So, it cannot be too far-fetched to imagine that they still have an interest. I will make it my business to see Shiba.'

'You will not mention that I have come here?'

'Of course not,' Tasaki snapped, irritably.

'He will be suspicious of you.'

'No more than I shall be suspicious of him. Let us face facts, Samwashima-*san*, suspicion is one of the bonds which shall bind us together. We are all worldly men who know only too well that each of us has his price. Toshiro now wants to survive. He has everything else. Your price is Shiba's removal so that you may take his place.' Tasaki laughed, savouring the joke. 'The Shimada Corporation is little enough to ask.'

After a moment, Samwashima nodded. 'What is your price, Tasaki-*san*?'

'Japan, my friend. I want Japan.'

Colonel DuCros pressed his fists against his burning stomach and breathed deeply in a vain attempt to ease the pain of his ulcer.

'I doubt if the Cognac helps, *M'sieu*,' observed Bouscat, quietly. 'Perhaps some warm milk – '

'Bollocks.' DuCros stared upwards, his lean, ascetic face pinched and drawn. 'You have posed me a difficult problem, Inspector.'

'I've done my bit,' Bouscat replied, chain-lighting another cigarette. 'I can't help it if the man is in London. At least you know – '

'We know nothing. We have the word of a thief, no more than that.'

'You have my word, *M'sieu le Colonel*. I have confidence in Rueff. Besides, why should he lie? He could have gone on, spending your money until kingdom come.'

DuCros nodded, dismally. 'I could go to the Minister and put the whole thing before him. Or I could make an unofficial request to London.' He paused. 'Or I could simply do nothing. What would you do, eh? What would the policeman do, Bouscat?'

'Type out a report in triplicate and stuff it into the nearest arsehole.'

'Crude,' DuCros muttered. 'Typically crude.'

'What else can I say? It isn't my problem. This man has committed no crime of which we are aware. In fact, as far as we can tell, he is a highly-respected international businessman.'

'And a homosexual.'

Bouscat shrugged. 'Maybe. Who knows?'

'I need to know,' shouted DuCros, angrily.

Bouscat rose. 'If you'll excuse me, *mon Colonel*, I am very tired.'

'Sit down. Here, have a drink.' He pushed the bottle of Cognac across the desk. 'Before I do anything, I think we must check with London. The question is, at what level?'

The British have their Special Branch.'

'Yes, true. And they also have SIS and the various branches of Military Intelligence. But according to the rules, I should go through the Minister's *Chef de Bureau*. You appreciate my problem?'

'Not entirely, no. Forgive me if I appear unsympathetic, Colonel, but if there exists a danger to France as a result of the disappearance of this Claude Picot ... and if this American, Hewens, is the key, then you have no decision to make.'

DuCros shook his head. 'You are a simple policeman, Bouscat. You do not appreciate the political implications.'

The Inspector got slowly to his feet and stabbed his cigarette into the already overflowing ashtray. 'That being the case, *M'sieu*, I am going home to sleep.'

'Wait,' barked DuCros.

But Bouscat shook his head. '*Non, M'sieu*. This simple policeman is too tired to care any more.'

As the door slammed, DuCros banged the desk with his clenched fists, mouthing every obscenity and blasphemy he could remember. When he had calmed down, he gave himself another shot of Cognac. But it was like pouring slow-acting petrol over the fire of his gastric ulcer and his face became distorted by the pain which suffused his body. Then he snatched at the telephone.

'This is DuCros. I must see the Minister ... yes, tonight.' He paused, licking his lips. 'Jesus-Mary. In that case, I shall have no option but to see him then.' And slamming down the receiver, he tried to ease the pain by putting his head between his knees.

NINE

1

Rather to his surprise, Richard Langford had slept well on his first night aboard the freighter. Even the close proximity of a barely clothed Yita Izumi had failed to arouse any more than a passing sensation of desire. Once he had climbed into the top bunk, sheer tiredness had combined with the steady throbbing of the engines to pull him into a deep, dreamless sleep.

Langford woke violently when the cabin lights were switched on. As he jerked himself into a sitting position and blinked against the harsh glare, he felt a stab of pain in his chest and swore, loudly. Then he stared down and saw that Yita was already dressed. The cabin door was open and the Chinese with the four teeth was standing with a tray.

'Breakfast,' he sang and passed the tray to Yita. Then he hawked, leaning out into the corridor to eject the gob of phlegm from his mouth. 'I come back. Ten minutes. You see Captain then.' And he hawked again as he closed the door.

'Charming,' said Langford, carefully lowering himself from the bunk and pulling on his clothes. He smiled as Yita poured coffee for him. 'Sleep well?'

She nodded. 'Many dreams.'

Langford shuddered as he sampled the black, oily coffee. Then he lit a cigarette and rubbed his eyes. 'I'm sorry ... about last night. I was a bit harsh.'

'You always say sorry, Langford-*san*?'

'No, only when ... well, I am sorry.' He drank some more of the oily coffee and surveyed the brittle-looking toast but decided that he wasn't hungry.

'Are you unhappy, Langford-*san*?'

'No, not in the way you mean. I'm just worried, that's all. If Heyashi is dead ...'

'There is no purpose in worry,' she said, taking a cigarette and lighting it. 'There is nothing you can do.' She pursed her lips, exhaling the smoke and then watching as it was drawn towards the air-conditioning extractor.

'Penny for your thoughts,' said Langford and she smiled.

'Kit used to say that. He used to ...' She shook her head.

'I want to hear about you.'

'There is little to tell which you do not already know.'

'You could tell me what your name means. I remember reading somewhere that all Japanese names have meanings.'

'Yita is not my real name. It was the name they gave me in my first bar. It is done so that Western customers can more easily remember.'

'Then what's your real name?'

'Kimiko,' she replied. 'It means Little Dear.'

'So. I'll call you Kimiko.'

'No.' She was staring at him, eyes wide. 'No, Langford-*san*. You will call me Yita. Please?'

Langford was puzzled.

'If that's what you want. But let's cut out the Langford-*san*. Call me Richard.'

'If it will please you.'

'For Christ's sake forget about pleasing me. What I want is for you to trust me.'

She nodded and was about to say something when the Chinese who Langford had mentally christened Four-Teeth, opened the door and beckoned them.

'You come now. Captain see you.'

'Why do they want us?' Yita asked as they went into the evil-smelling corridor.

'Who cares? At least we'll get some air. I hope.'

221

Langford got his wish when they finally stepped out on to the main deck. It was surprisingly cold and a sharp wind tugged at their clothing. Pausing, he stared out across the grey expanse of sea. In the far distance, a large container ship was heading north, the rectangular stacks giving the vessel an incongruous, ungainly silhouette.

'You come.'

Looking up, Langford saw that Four-Teeth was agitated and realized that he had been day-dreaming.

'You come,' shouted Four-Teeth.

'Sod off,' growled Langford but the Chinese merely grinned.

'Thank you,' he said, and led the way up to the bridge.

The captain of the freighter turned out to be a tall, spiky man of indeterminate race. He might have been half-Japanese, half-Chinese or half-anything and he spoke English with a curious, lilting accent.

'Welcome aboard the *Hai Shan*, Mister Langford.'

'Thanks.' Langford stared round the bridge, noting that all the equipment looked modern and that unlike the cabins, everything was scrupulously clean.

'I am sorry that you do not have better accommodation. We're not really equipped to carry passengers.'

'No?' Langford raised an eyebrow as he remembered the cabins crowded with Chinese. 'You seem to have a very big crew.'

The Captain smiled. 'Cargo, Mister Langford. At least, part of my cargo. Tell me, how is Gunning?'

'He's fine,' replied Langford, wondering what nefarious activities linked the two men.

'Nice guy. We do a lot of business together.' He began to pick at his nose with his little finger. 'Next time you come on deck, bring your passports to me.'

'Why?'

He seemed surprised. 'I have to put in the chops. You need exit visas from Japan and arrival chops for Hong Kong. It's all part of the service.'

'Then we can come on deck?' said Langford. 'Your man –'

The Captain laughed. 'Don't take any notice of Wong. You can come and go as you like while we're out here. The danger time is just before and after sailing, and then when we come into port. That's when the Immigos are waiting. Sometimes it's the narcotics people as well but they're just a nuisance. We never touch junk.'

'How very noble.' Langford lit a cigarette and offered one to the Captain but it was refused. 'I take it that your main cargo consists of illegal immigrants?'

'Take what you like.' The Captain made further incursions into his nostrils with his little finger. 'I haven't asked you any questions and I don't expect any back.'

Langford didn't pursue the subject. 'When do we reach Hong Kong?'

'In a hurry?'

Langford smiled. 'Maybe.'

'All being well, Sunday, just before dawn. But if we're held up by the weather or mechanical failure, we stand off until the Wednesday.'

'Why?'

'Because those are the only two days when the people I rely on are on duty.'

After a few more minutes of desultory conversation, they left the bridge and went aft until they found a sheltered spot in the stern.

'What is it that you are thinking, Richard?'

He shrugged and flicked his cigarette butt over the side. 'A jumble of thoughts. I've never really thanked you for saving my life.'

'You should not speak of it.'

He stared at her upturned face. 'Maybe ... never mind.'

'You are worrying about the delays?'

'Yes. Three days could mean a lot to us.'

'But you do not know.'

'We won't know anything until we get there, Yita. And I

223

want to get there quickly, just in case.'

'You must not worry, Langford-*san*. If it is written ...'
Then she stopped and smiled. 'I am sorry. I almost made
you angry again.'

'No.' He grinned back at her. 'You've just given me an
idea.'

2

Claude Picot felt little love for a world which had largely
rejected him but as he worked in the underground bunkers
below Tasaki's fortress home on Shikoku, the Frenchman
experienced grave misgivings. Not that there was anything
altruistic about Picot. He was motivated solely by
personal fear. Although there was no mention of Emile
Malvy's death in any of the French newspapers which had
been obtained for him, he knew only too well that the
boy's body could easily have been found. As an ex-
government employee, the authorities might easily have
decided to throw a security blanket over the case –
assuming that Emile had been discovered. But the
primary cause of Claude Picot's fear was Muga Tasaki.

If the Japanese had occasionally been terse or even
threatening in his attitude, he had more often shown Picot
consideration and some kindness. He had even sent
someone to fetch French-language newspapers and
magazines from Osaka and obtained a case of the *Entre
Deux Mers* he enjoyed. So there was no firm proof that
Tasaki had any intentions other than honouring the
unwritten contract and it was pure intuition which made
Picot believe that Tasaki would not pay him one *sou* for his
work. It was the same kind of intuitive feeling which drove
him to the conviction that once they had no further use for
his expertise, they would simply kill him.

The sudden noise of the heavy iron door being opened
made Picot jump and he swung round, his lips moving
soundlessly as he faced Tasaki.

'I did not mean to startle you,' said the Japanese,

carefully pushing the heavy door closed behind him. 'I understand that you are almost finished?'

Picot nodded. 'That is correct, *M'sieu.*'

'Good. Have you found our facilities adequate?'

'More than adequate, thank you.'

'Excellent.' Tasaki gazed at the rectangular metal container. 'You have carried out all the tests?'

'Yes. There were no failures.'

'But you appear unhappy. Why?'

Picot turned away and clasped his hands together. '*M'sieu*, this device – once it is set in motion, only a person knowing the combination can stop it. There is no ...' He hesitated, biting his lips as he struggled to find the words in English. 'There is no margin for error. That frightens me.'

'I find it reassuring,' said Tasaki, sitting on one of the laboratory stools. 'But you are certain?'

Picot glowered. 'Of course. I am a scientist, *M'sieu*, a technician. Not that a competent garage mechanic couldn't have built this.'

'You under-rate your capabilities. The explosives are not yet in place?'

'Of course not,' Picot snapped. 'Would you like to be blown to bits?'

'Very well, take me through the procedure. Let me see if I cannot find a fault, eh?'

Claude Picot took a key from the bench and handed it to the Japanese. 'You insert that in the lock, turn it and then pull it out.' He watched Tasaki slide the key into the lock. 'As you turn it, you may hear the mechanism work.'

Tasaki leaned forwards as he turned the key. There was a faint click followed by a barely perceptible buzzing and he nodded.

'*Bien.* The timing mechanism runs for twelve hours on a quartz clock. It is accurate to within one hundredth of a second and will trigger the detonator when 43,200 seconds have elapsed.' Picot lifted a small metal flap just below the lock, revealing a key-board and a small display panel.

'There is no way that the mechanism can be stopped without causing the device to explode other than by pressing out the correct number.'

Tasaki stared thoughtfully at the keyboard. 'We shall consider a hypothesis, Frenchman. Let us assume that someone decides to cut into the metal casing – '

'Barely possible. To begin with, you will see that there are special lugs on each of the four sides. These will be used to secure the device in position.' Picot went to the bench and returned with a metal bracket like the handle from a giant suitcase. 'This and the lugs are made from tungsten-steel alloy. Once in position, it will be immensely difficult to move.'

Again Tasaki nodded. 'Very well, I will accept that the device cannot be moved but for the sake of my hypothesis, someone has succeeded in opening the casing.'

Picot gave a deprecatory shrug. 'If you insist but remember that once the explosives have been placed inside, the case will be secured with bolts and rivets.'

'Both can be undone,' said Tasaki.

'Yes. The rivets can be prized out but one turn on any of the bolts and ... bang. You see, *M'sieu*, they are wired into the circuit.' Picot bent over the bomb and lifted off the top section of the casing. '*Voila*. You see where the bolts fit?'

'I see.' Tasaki peered in and then laughed. 'What happens if someone were to succeed in cutting a hole ... say, here.' He pointed to a section of the casing just above the timing mechanism.

'Two possibilities. Firstly, the heat of the acetylene torch which they should have to use could cause a distortion in the time mechanism. That would precipitate instant detonation. The second possibility is that nothing happens and they have gained access.'

Tasaki stared at him, inquiringly. 'In which case ...?'

'There is nothing ... not one single part of the mechanism which can be touched without detonating the device. You will observe that there are very few wires exposed. Mostly, I have relied on printed circuits. But for

226

your benefit, *M'sieu*, let us suppose that they have got into the bomb. Only a fool would touch the mechanism. That leaves the explosive. So, they try to lift it out, very gently.' And Picot made a lifting movement with his hands in the empty space which would contain the charges. 'What happens? Bang. *Fini*.'

'How?' demanded Tasaki.

'These metal rods are not simply designed to hold the explosive in position. Each one contains a magnetic electrode. You can see that there are five, one at each corner and one in the centre. Once the timing mechanism has begun to run, there is a tiny current passing through the electrodes. This creates a magnetic field, a kind of invisible circuit. Wrapped within the explosive will be a series of metal discs. These discs will reduce the energy between the magnets to the level at which I have set them to operate. Remove the explosive and you remove the discs, thus increasing the power of the current which causes a short in the circuit and ...' Picot snapped his fingers.

'You have done well, Frenchman. I congratulate you.'

Picot shook his head. 'Your own people did most of the work. I merely added a few refinements.'

'What form does the explosive take?'

'The primary charge is porous nitrocellulose. It is basically a propellant and used in mortar shells. But the main explosive force comes from fifty kilos of Japanese nitro-plastic. It is very stable and can even be dropped from a great height or baked to temperature of 50° Centigrade without danger.'

'That is good. But the device is more cumbersome than I had envisaged. What does it weigh?'

'Altogether, a little over seventy-five kilos.'

'It is very heavy.'

Picot nodded. 'Sixty per cent of the weight is in the explosives. Your own engineers had already calculated the force required. It is not like blowing a hole through a piece of paper.'

'Show me where you would place the bomb,' said Tasaki, standing up and going to the plans table.

Picot came to his side and drew a long breath. 'I had considered a number of possibilities but the thickness and strength of the shielding is such that –'

'Well, where then?' demanded Tasaki, impatiently.

Picot tapped the plan of the *Shimada Maru*. 'Here. It is the only certain point. On three sides you have these six-inch steel struts. They will act as baffles so that virtually all the explosive force is concentrated ... so.' And Picot drew a heavy arrow on the paper. 'The effect of the blast should be to rupture the main storage tank and split open the hull. It will also destroy the monitoring equipment located here.' He tapped the plan again.

'And the effect of all this?'

Picot sighed. '*M'sieu*, sometimes I think you do not understand the consequences of what you are about.'

'If so, you would be very wrong,' hissed Tasaki. Then he seemed to relax. 'But please, purely as a matter of academic interest, what would happen?'

'The explosion would immediately permit hundreds of thousands, maybe millions of curies of radioactive emission into the atmosphere. Simultaneously, the nuclear waste will begin to heat-up, we call it decay heat; sea-water will pour into the main storage area and once the pressure has equalized, liquid from the cooling systems, all of it contaminated in varying degrees, will run from the ship into the sea. After that point has been passed, there is no way that total catastrophe can be avoided.' Picot moistened his lips and swallowed. 'It is also extremely likely that the explosion would start a small fire. Exactly how long this might last would depend on weather conditions. In a rough sea, probably not long enough to cause any additional heat hazard but ... well, it would not really matter either way.'

'Would there be an atomic explosion?'

Picot shook his head. 'Not of the type associated with a nuclear weapon. But using the data I have seen as a basis for calculation, I believe that there would be an explosion caused by the chain reaction. I cannot estimate the force of this blast but it would certainly be sufficient to blow the *Shimada Maru* to tiny pieces.'

'You must not look so worried, Frenchman. It will not happen.'

Picot stared at the Japanese. 'I can only hope you are right, *M'sieu*. Because if not, you could possibly be the man responsible for the beginning of the end of the world.'

'There are already many statesmen on this earth who have had that kind of power for some years.'

'But how do they use it?'

Tasaki smiled. 'Now you have hit on the crux of the matter, Mister Picot. They don't use it. The threat is enough. But whereas they deal in bluff and counter-bluff, my threat will be a solemn promise.' He moved back to the time-bomb and stared at it. 'What remains to be done?'

'Only two things,' replied Picot. 'The combination must be programmed in and the explosive charge fitted. If you will give me the combination, the device can be made ready.'

'Very well, Frenchman. We shall set the combination together.' He reached out and touched the lock with the tips of his fingers. 'Suppose – '

'I know what you are about to say, *M'sieu*. The answer is no, the lock cannot be picked. And even if you had a key, to turn the lock back would simply cause the bomb to detonate immediately.'

'I should have known,' said Tasaki, nodding.

'You are paying me to make the foolproof machine. *Alors*, it is done. All that remains ...'

'The combination,' said Tasaki. 'I will call out the numbers.'

'As you wish, *M'sieu*.'

'One.'

After a short pause, Picot nodded. 'Next?'

'Four.'

He turned and smiled at the Japanese. 'I imagine you

229

will be able to remember the digits and the sequence?'

'Eight,' said Tasaki, ignoring the question.

It took another fifteen minutes to complete the settings. Then Picot switched on the timing mechanism and tapped out the combination on the keyboard, the digits lighting up on the display panel. 'It is a date, no?'

'You are right.' Tasaki hesitated. 'What happens now?'

'This is the only moment when it is possible to turn the lock back, so.' And as he turned the key, the display faded into darkness. '14.8.1945. I suppose I should realize its significance?'

'Perhaps,' said Tasaki. 'But you asked if I could remember it and I will tell you that I can never forget it. On August 14, 1945, the Japanese Emperor was forced to surrender to your Western Alliance.'

'I should have guessed,' said Picot. 'An artistic touch.'

'More a symbolic one.' He walked slowly to the door. 'You have served me well, Mister Picot. I am grateful. Finish your labours and then you may rest.'

Claude Picot watched the heavy iron door close after Tasaki. He knew that there were no steps he could take which would affect the outcome of Tasaki's plans. The Japanese had his own technicians and Picot was in no doubt that his work would be checked. His real value to Tasaki was his specialist knowledge, his ability to put the bomb in the right place. Now Tasaki had that information and Picot suddenly realized that he might have served him too well.

3

Colonel DuCros' relationship with the Minister was one of strained cordiality. If they had anything in common it was mutual dislike. The Minister was nearly ten years DuCros' junior, a young man with political ambition and ruthless determination. He would have preferred his own appointee to run Section Nine but getting rid of DuCros could alienate the influential people whose confidence and friendship the young politician knew he must cultivate. The Minister also knew that the Colonel was very much aware of this aspect of their relationship and that although DuCros was always scrupulously correct, showing his superior the formal deference which was his due, there was something in Colonel DuCros' manner which left the Minister in no doubt of the true position.

Having listened to the Colonel for the best part of an hour and having scanned the tersely-written report which DuCros had brought him, the Minister lit his pipe and stared thoughtfully up at the high, ornate ceiling.

'The murdered student,' he said, glancing at DuCros. 'Am I right in assuming that the police will take no action?'

'For the present, no.'

The Minister nodded. 'Good.' He paused, gently puffing at the pipe. 'But you intimate the possibility of a scandal. Why?'

DuCros shrugged. 'There is no evidence but ... a vanished nuclear physicist who is also a practising homosexual ... I have to fear the worst. The newspapers would make a meal of it.'

'Yes.' Another match was struck and the Minister drew on the pipe, his brows wrinkling. 'But this man, Picot, he could not have the latest information, surely?'

'Who knows? We ... I think not, but where scientists are concerned, it is always difficult for the layman to evaluate their usefulness.'

'Surely that is precisely your function, Colonel?'

'With respect, Minister, I am responsible for the security of nuclear installations – '

'And for the security of personnel,' said the Minister, sharply. 'However, we must consider what action to take. Picot is missing, believed to be in Japan. Therefore, we must pursue the matter carefully. Our position in Asia is delicate. We do not have many friends.'

'If I may make a suggestion,' said DuCros, slowly, 'I feel we should work through London. I would like to make an unofficial request to the British Special Branch. They can interview this man, Hewens, and then we should know more.'

The Minister considered the proposition for a moment and then nodded. 'Very well. But it is totally unofficial.' He flicked the pages of DuCros' report. 'The man who witnessed the meeting ...?'

'Rueff?'

'Yes. What have you done with him?'

'He was released. But I have men watching him.'

'Pick him up,' said the Minister. 'It may be necessary for your people to take him to London.'

DuCros frowned. 'May I ask why?'

'Certainly. If it proves necessary to make a positive identification of Hewens, I should rather it happened in London than here. As far as Picot's disappearance is concerned, there must be no leaks until we know exactly what has become of him. In the meantime, I will speak to someone at the Quai D'Orsay. There may well be a contact we can use in Tokyo.'

'What about Washington?' said DuCros.

The Minister raised his eyebrows. 'What about them?'

'The Americans have a vested interest in Japan. I would have considered it useful to let the U.S. State Department know that we have a problem.'

'You would? I find that incredible. Government policy has always been to maintain a suitable distance between France and the United States. To make such an approach – '

'Would be merely routine,' said DuCros, quietly. 'In the same way that we make routine use of the Interpol facilities.'

'No.' The Minister shook his head. 'An unofficial inquiry to London, yes. That I will sanction. But no more than that ... yet.' He glanced at his watch. 'Keep me informed of developments.'

The interview was at an end but Colonel DuCros wanted the last word. 'I must inform you that I am fearful of moving too slowly. Picot could cause us some embarrassment.'

'And I fear moving too fast, Colonel. Kindly do as I ask.'

4

'Bailey seems to have done a wonderful job,' said Whitaker

''You see no problems?' It was Toshiro Shiba who spoke, his rounded, unlined face tilted and catching the last rays of sunlight which filled the Captain's day-room aboard the *Shimada Maru*.

Whitaker shrugged. 'No-o, not yet. But I've only had a few hours here, just a preliminary look.'

'You expect to find problems?' said Shiba, the faintest trace of concern in his tone.

'No, I don't. My impression is that every possible safeguard has been included. If anything, the precautions seem almost too good.'

Samwashima stifled a grin as Shiba reacted with sudden sharpness. 'What do you mean by that?'

'Difficult to say.' Whitaker scratched his bald head and smiled. 'Given the data on the waste which I've seen, I would estimate that the shielding could have been reduced by as much as forty per cent and still provide a safety margin well in excess of international requirements.'

'We prefer that there should be no risks,' said Shiba.

'I'll go along with that but ...' Whitaker hesitated. 'The total weight ... the volume of the shielding could present problems ... the power to weight ratio, stability in a heavy sea. Whoever runs this ship is going to bear a heavy responsibility.'

'You know about shipbuilding?' asked Shiba.

233

Whitaker grinned. 'A little, yes. But I'm no naval architect. Boats have always been an interest of mine, a hobby.'

'Ah so.' Shiba nodded. 'There is so little time, Professor Whitaker. I feel confident that such matters can be left to us. Your energies must be concentrated on the security of the cargo, I think.'

'I shall do a full report when I've completed my survey,' said Whitaker, faintly aware of Shiba's implied rebuke.

'How long will that take, Professor?' It was Samwashima who posed the question.

'Not long. Perhaps a week, maybe ten days. I'll also need to examine Doctor Bailey's notes to make certain that all the pre-installation tests have been carried out on the shielding. That will probably take two or three days. If I remember correctly, Doctor Bailey was a very methodical man, so his notes should present few problems.'

Shiba said something in Japanese but Samwashima made no reply. Then he turned to Whitaker. 'Mister Samwashima will see that you have everything you need, Professor. I trust that you will be comfortable living aboard. We thought it would be more suitable than an hotel.'

'Couldn't be better. I like anything to do with boats, even when they're as big as this.'

Shiba beamed like a child suddenly given unexpected praise. 'That is excellent. And Mister Samwashima will remain on board with you.' He rose to his feet, adjusting the heavy, horn-rimmed spectacles. 'I hope you will not find our security arrangements too irksome, Professor.'

'I'm used to security, Mister Shiba.'

'Good.' The head of the Shimada Corporation smiled, bowed and went to leave the day-room.

'Presumably someone will get me a pass so that I can get in and out of the dockyard?'

'That will not be necessary,' replied Samwashima,

quickly. 'Everything you require will be brought here.'

'I assume I can leave the yard occasionally? It's my first visit to Japan and I would have liked to – '

'Of course, Professor,' said Shiba, his eyes darting towards his deputy. 'A pass will be made up and Mister Samwashima will be only too happy to act as your guide and chauffeur.'

Leaving Whitaker to unpack, Shiba went out on to the flying bridge and beckoned Samwashima to follow. 'You will be required to exercise great care and tact,' he said speaking softly in Japanese.

Samwashima nodded. 'You need have no fears, Shiba-san.'

'If that were true, I should have none, Norihiko.'

'If he carries out a complete survey of the ship, he will – '

'I know that.' Shiba stared towards the bows of the *Shimada Maru*, just visible in the fading light. 'You must speak to Yamada. Ask his advice as to what this man must not see if he is to remain ignorant of the true purpose of the shielding.' He shook his head, his face set in a grim, determined expression. 'When I return to Osaka, I will telephone Captain Umezu and warn him about Whitaker. The sooner the ship can sail, the better. And if anything goes amiss, Samwashima-*san*, I shall not be as understanding as I have been in the past.'

5

'...and there's a cable from your wife,' said Peggy Ashmore, handing the slip of paper across the desk. 'She's arriving this evening. I've told Dobson that you'll probably want him to drive you to the airport.'

Hewens glared at the cable and nodded. 'Thank you,' he muttered, hoping that James Maxwell was burning in hell and wishing that Lois could join him there.

Claude Picot had planned his escape with meticulous care. He knew that once beyond the perimeter of Tasaki's fortress-home, he would have to move quickly. He would travel across country to Takamatsu and then take one of the ferry services to Kobe. From there, the Frenchman intended to go by train to the big port of Yokohama and find a ship – any ship, which would take him far from Japan.

He pulled on the dark-blue overalls which he wore for his work, and stretched his arms. Movement was difficult because of the clothes he was wearing beneath the overalls but he knew he would have to manage as best he could. Then he took the long screwdriver from inside his sock and ran his fingers along it. The flat, wedge-shaped head had been ground away to form a needle-like point and Picot almost fondled the weapon. Then he switched out the light and went to the door, slowly pressing the latch down and inching the door open.

The young Japanese was sitting on a low stool halfway along the corridor. He was engrossed in what looked like a comic book, his lips moving silently as he read. Picot watched him for a few seconds, tightening his grip on the screwdriver which he held at his side, concealed from view. Then he opened the door wide.

The guard didn't look up until Picot had closed the door behind him. Then he rose, stuffed the comic book into his pocket and smiled. The Japanese had no orders to stop Picot-*san*. His job was to accompany him and as the Frenchman often went to the underground bunker late at night he wasn't surprised by Picot's sudden appearance.

'*Kon banwa*,' said the Japanese, bowing.

Picot nodded, took two paces past the young man and then stopped in his tracks, pointing down at the floor.

The guard reacted by coming forward, peering down anxiously. Seeing nothing, he turned and shook his head.

'*Regardez*,' snapped Picot, pointing again. And as the

young Japanese turned for another look, Claude Picot raised the pointed screwdriver and drove it deep into the man's back.

The Japanese gasped and would have yelled but Picot's left hand was clamped over his mouth. There was no pain, only a strangely warm, moist feeling somewhere between his shoulder blades. His arms flailing, he tried to bite on Picot's hand but the Frenchman had a powerful grip.

Stumbling backwards along the corridor, Picot struggled to pull the screwdriver from the guard's body. When it finally came free, he swung his captive round and stabbed him in the stomach. It was a clumsy blow and the Frenchman was sickened as he felt the blood and body liquids running through his fingers.

The man was still breathing as Picot opened the door and pushed him into the room. Kicking the door shut behind him, he released his grip so that his victim crumpled to the floor, the handle of the screwdriver protruding obscenely from his stomach. Picot flicked on the light and stared down at him.

But the Japanese refused to die and lay writhing on the floor, blood welling from his mouth. By a tremendous effort of will, Picot forced himself to retrieve the screwdriver. It came out easily this time, the bright metal streaked with blood. Bending over him, Picot felt for the guard's heartbeat with his fingers and then pressed the screwdriver into the spot where he hoped the heart lay. He heard one of the man's ribs crack. There was a sudden gasp for air, a choking cough and then silence.

Picot had anticipated some blood but nothing like the amount which had poured from the man's wounds. And as he lifted the body on to the bed, covering it with the heavy quilt, his nose caught the cloying aroma of excreta.

The sweat pouring from his face, he wanted to throw up but knew that he must not. He stared around the room. There was blood on the carpet, on the bed and even on the door. Worst of all was the fact that Picot's own hands were covered in it, as well as the front of the dark-blue overall

But there was no time to clean up.

Switching off the light, he went once again into the corridor, holding his breath as he listened for the slightest sound. All he could hear was his own frantic heartbeat and the distant hiss and swish of the sea. He started down the corridor, pausing again as he emerged on to the landing. There was no one about. Moving quickly, he descended the stairs into the back hallway and went out into the night.

The air was cold and Picot sucked it gratefully into his lungs as he walked towards the entrance to the underground bunker, carefully keeping to the grass verge so that no one should hear his footsteps. Then a dog barked and Picot felt his heart miss a beat. The animal barked again but this time was obviously far away and he continued towards the bunker.

Once inside, his hand was shaking as he reached out and pulled the iron lever on the door to the generator room. It moved with a slight squeaking sound and Picot heaved a sigh as the door swung open. Stepping over the threshold, he felt for the light switch and once he had found it, pushed the door to, blinking against the glare of the overhead lamps.

The main switchboard beckoned him, tantalizingly. He had only to pull three levers and all the power would be off – power which surged through the perimeter fencing, power for the floodlights. He glanced around, suddenly conscious of the throbbing from the generator itself. His brow furrowed, he walked quickly past the main switchboard and into the annex which housed the engine and a bank of emergency batteries. Then he saw what he wanted.

The can of water used for the generator's cooling system was only half full. Picot looked round for a tap but couldn't see one and decided to take a chance. Time was running against him and he muttered a prayer as he went back to the switchboard. Looking out into the passage, he checked that the coast was clear before wedging the door wide open. Then he picked up the can of water and hurled it at the switchboard.

For a second nothing happened and he was conscious of the noise of the empty can clattering around him. Then there was a vivid blue flash followed by a shower of sparks as the water reached the switch terminals and shorted the circuits.

Picot ran along the passageway as the lights died around him. When he emerged into the air, he could hear shouting and he hesitated for a moment as he struggled to get his bearings. Then he ran, his feet pounding the ground as he raced towards the perimeter fence. Tripping on something in the darkness, he fell headlong but was quickly up again and too frightened to worry about the pain in his leg.

In theory, the perimeter fencing which surrounded Tasaki's property was impregnable. Even without the high voltage current which surged through its wire, it was a hideous obstacle for anyone trying to get in. Or out. Some nine feet in height, the fence was topped by a tangled roll of barbed wire supported on horizontal struts fixed to the reinforced concrete posts. But at the point selected by Picot, something – probably a bough from one of the trees on the other side, had flattened the rolled wire creating a kind of platform.

His lungs almost bursting, Picot saw the section of fencing and headed towards it, slowing his pace as he pulled at the zip of the overalls. Panting for breath, he sank down and struggled out of the garment. He was sweating profusely now and shaking as he heard the dogs baying in the distance, the Sumo dogs which Tasaki always kept on the edge of hunger. Standing up, Picot folded the overall into a large pad and tucked it securely into his jacket. Then he put on the gloves he had brought with him from Paris. They were thin, tailor-made in the finest calf and he knew that they would afford little protection against the barbed wire but they were better than nothing.

After a moment's hesitation, he reached out and grasped the wire. There was no current and he started to climb. It seemed easy enough to begin with but after the first three feet or so, he felt one of the barbs rip through his trousers and bite into his flesh. Holding his breath, he eased his leg downwards, taking more weight on his hands. When he felt the barb come out, he pulled his leg up again. There was a sharp tearing sound and glancing down, Picot saw that one leg of his trousers was almost ripped in half. But by looking down, he nearly lost his balance. His hand slipped and as he struggled to heave himself upright, he felt his glove tear.

Claude Picot was on the verge of panic. He could hear the dogs and the shouting; the sound of running feet, of cars being started. One glove had gone completely but he no longer cared. He was reconciled to having his hands, arms and legs cut to ribbons by the wire. And he was almost at the top of the fence. Then the wire on which he stood suddenly snapped.

Picot fell just eight inches but he screamed with all the agony of a man falling to his death as the barbed wire tore at his legs and he felt the skin shredded from his right hand. Then another barb sliced into his left arm. But it was the strand of wire at his throat which caused him the most intense pain, a vicious, paralysing agony against which he had no defence. Physically and emotionally exhausted, even his frantic screams for help soon died away into a tearful, pathetic whimpering.

Scenting blood, the dogs had come quickly. Picot never knew just how many. They barked at him, leaping up so that one impaled itself on the wire and filled the air with a high-pitched yelping until it eventually tore itself free. It seemed like an eternity before the guards came. But the Frenchman never saw them. He was trapped, incapable of movement. Then he heard Muga Tasaki's voice.

'You disappoint me, Frenchman. I was seriously considering that afterwards, when everything was done,

240

you could go away, and with your money. South America, was it not?'

Tears of pain, anguish and frustration poured from Picot's eyes as he listened to Tasaki's slow, stilted English.

'I am sorry, Picot-*san*. It is such a pity.' Then he said something in Japanese and walked away, his feet scuffing against the gravel

Claude Picot waited for death. He imagined that it would come quickly but it did not. He had no sense of time but could somehow visualize the Japanese working to replace the burned-out fuses with a kind of desperate speed. Then he imagined Tasaki ordering someone to throw the switch so that the high-voltage current would surge through the fence and into his torn body. But the Frenchman was only half right. Tasaki did give the order but long before the generator was running at maximum révs.

It began as a slow, almost sensual tingling. Then it gradually intensified, Picot's muscles reacting as if in spasm. He screamed as each involuntary movement caused him to tear his already mutilated flesh to a point beyond which the pain no longer mattered. And when the generator finally reached full-power, he jerked his head away from the wire, ripping a chunk of skin from his throat. Looking up, Claude Picot caught a last, fleeting glimpse of the waxing moon in the moment before he died.

7

About the time of Claude Picot's death on the Japanese island of Shikoku, Inspector Henri Bouscat was standing thoughtfully in the crimson lake living-room which the French physicist had planned with such infinite care. Bouscat heard the front door open but didn't pay too much attention, knowing that there was a plain-clothesman outside the building and a uniformed constable on the landing. When he did finally look up, he saw Colonel DuCros staring at the spot where Jean-Jacques Rueff had hacked a hole through the floor.

'They told me I'd find you here.' He stepped across the path of new, clean floorboards. 'I understood that you were taking no action about the student?'

'I'm not,' replied Bouscat, tonelessly. 'The Minister sent me a memo. I'm simply looking, storing away facts for future reference.'

'I regret that I need your help once again.'

'Oh?' Bouscat stared at the Colonel for a moment. 'Now what?'

DuCros licked his lips and then shrugged. 'I released Rueff on your recommendation, Inspector.'

'That's nonsense. You did a deal with him: co-operate and we forget his break-in job here. You had to release him.'

The Colonel scowled. 'As you will, but I now want him picked up again.'

Bouscat stared at the smoking cigarette butt in his nicotine-stained fingers and chuckled. 'You mean that he gave your people the run-away?'

'They lost him, yes.'

'And so I have to dash around like a scalded cat and find him. Why?'

DuCros glared at him, his expression one of ice-cold hatred. 'Because, Inspector, I am ordering you to do so. If you wish, I can give you some more men.'

'SDECE thugs? No, thank you.' Bouscat sighed and chain-lit another cigarette. 'All right, I'll have a nose around.'

'You will search diligently and urgently,' growled DuCros. 'I want him where I can keep an eye on him.'

Bouscat shook his head. '*M'sieu le Colonel*, I am always diligent. But whether or not I can be as urgent as you would like ...'

'Find him and find him quickly '

'I'll be in touch,' said Bousca.

TEN

1

At four-thirty a.m. on Sunday, November 27, the *Hai Shan* entered the territorial waters of the British Crown Colony of Hong Kong. Visibility was bad, reduced to less than a hundred yards by thick fog which lay in great slabs on the slack, oily water. The freighter moved with agonizing slowness, long blasts of her fog horn thudding against the air. It was very cold and standing on the main deck, Langford and Yita soon found that their clothes were ringing wet.

'Richard, what will happen?'

'According to the Captain, there's a boat coming out to take us ashore.' He lit a cigarette and peered into the fog. 'Assuming that they can find us.'

'I have to thank you,' she said, her voice soft.

'What for?'

'You did not try to use me. Other men …'

'Forget it,' snapped Langford, suddenly irritated. 'This is hardly a pleasure trip.'

She turned to look over the side of the ship. Langford watched the swell of her breasts rising and falling quickly as she breathed. Then she took the Nambu pistol from her handbag and held it for a moment. Langford was still watching, but before he could react she had tossed the weapon away, staring down as it vanished without trace in the black, swirling water.

'Does that make you feel better?'

She shrugged, hunching her narrow shoulders against the cold. 'I did not want to keep it.'

'Maybe that's just as well. Someone at the airport might

have taken exception.' He pulled at the cigarette. 'What will you do if Heyashi is dead?'

'Go back to Japan. There is nothing else for me.' She spoke in a flat, toneless voice. 'You?'

'London, I suppose.'

'You have family?'

'No.'

'That is sad. Everyone should have a family, their own people. Kit never had any family. Did you know that?'

'Yes,' said Langford. 'If you go back to Japan and Shiba –'

'He will not harm me. There is no reason. If Heyashi is dead, his knowledge will have died with him.'

'And the photographs? You're wrong, Yita. The truth never dies.' Droplets of water ran from his fingers on to the cigarette and he tossed it away. 'Gunning said that the past was alive and you eventually agreed with him. Remember?'

Yita didn't reply. She turned away, staring vacantly into the foggy darkness. Not for the first time, Langford found himself a prey to conflicting emotions. He was angry with her, irritated by the wooden kind of fatalism which seemed to dominate her every thought. Her beauty, a happy blend of East and West, contrasting oddly with her personality. She was exciting but somehow dull; exquisitely delicate and yet there was an inherent strength in her character, almost an ugliness. But Langford still wanted to protect her, to shield her from the harm which men like Shiba and Samwashima so obviously intended. His problem was that Yita neither sought his protection nor seemed to need it.

'Why wouldn't you marry Bailey?' he asked.

She turned and peered into Langford's face. 'I would have married him. But I needed to wait. I needed to be sure.'

Langford nodded. The cold, moist fog swirled around them and from somewhere in the darkness, another fog-horn echoed, a dull, plaintive sound. 'Yita, you and I ...'

But the look in her eyes stopped him, as if she could see into his mind, reading his thoughts before ever he could translate them into spoken words. Langford swung round, intending to walk away but Four-Teeth appeared on the deck like some demonic spirit, his U.S. Army parka dripping wet.

'You come bridge,' he said.

When they got to the bridge, the Captain welcomed them uneasily. 'The boat's on its way,' he said. 'Someone's pretty keen to get you ashore, Mister Langford.' He stared for a moment at Yita. 'When you see your contact, tell him from me that I don't run a radio-taxi service.'

'What do you mean?'

'Just that some crazy gook called me up on the R/T. Jesus, I'll be glad to see the back of you.'

'Thanks very much.' Langford had a sudden thought. 'Your transmitter,' he said. 'Can it be linked into the Hong Kong telephone system?'

'Yes. But if you want to make any calls, Mister, you go find yourself a pay-phone. Radio silence is my motto. Okay, you go down now.' He followed them out and yelled down to Four-Teeth. 'Port side, Wong. Use ladder. Chop-chop.'

'See you,' said Langford, starting down the companionway.

'Not if I can help it.

The walla-walla appeared out of the mist, the watery chugging of its engine echoing around them as their two suitcases were lowered over the side on a rope. Langford swung himself on to the ladder and began to descend, feeling his feet slipping on the narrow wooden rungs. A wizened Chinese helped him into the cramped, malodorous cabin of the sampan. Then Yita was beside him, her face mask-like, her eyes glazed and expressionless.

The engine accelerated and the boat began groping its way through the fog, the two Chinese in the stern talking in low-pitched voices, a strangely discordant yet rhythmic duet. Langford tried to see out of the cabin but one of the Chinese shooed him back and pulled down a heavy canvas flap which reeked of stale fish and diesel oil.

The trip seemed endless, the engine chugging away, the sampan rising and falling in the oily swell. Langford kept staring at his watch. Then he glanced at Yita. 'I'm beginning to wish that we could have hung on to that gun.'

'To kill more?'

'Hopefully not. I'm just feeling a bit vulnerable.'

'You are not a coward.'

'I'm no hero, either.' He tried to see through a split in the canvas flap but the darkness was total. 'God alone knows where we're going.'

'Do you believe in your God?'

He shrugged. 'What sort of question is that?'

'Just a question.' She fell silent.

Hearing the engine slow, Langford raised the flap but came face to face with one of the crew who pressed his finger against his lips and firmly pulled the flap down again. Then someone shouted in Chinese, probably using a megaphone although Langford couldn't be sure. One of the pair in the sampan yelled back a sing-song reply. There was a pause and Langford held his breath until the engine picked up again and the sampan continued its slow progress.

Nearly an hour after they had left the *Hai Shan*, the sampan slowed and the engine sputtered before dying away, only the gentle gurgling swish of the water disturbing the quiet. Then the bows bumped against something and the canvas flap was pulled back, one of the Chinese beckoning them to come out.

Cold and cramped, Langford climbed awkwardly on to a low, stone quay. Yita came after him and their two cases were dumped beside them without ceremony by the two Chinese who quickly scuttled back into the sampan and cast off.

'Now what?' growled Langford as the walla-walla chugged away and quickly disappeared into the fog.

Yita stood beside him and shuddered. 'Richard?'

'Quiet.' He looked round, cautiously. 'There's a car coming.' Taking her arm, he pulled her to one side as a car swung on to the jetty, its lights dying away instantly, and he heard rather than saw the door open and the dark figure whose footsteps echoed around them.

'Mister Langford?'

'Yes.'

'Bring your baggage.' The owner of the voice stood by the car and held the rear passenger door open. 'Get in,' he drawled, making no attempt to help them.

Once they were in the car, their contact got in alongside the driver. 'Okay, move it,' he snapped and turned round, holding something in his hand. 'Two economy class return tickets for Bangkok.'

Langford took the tickets. 'When do we leave?'

'We have about two hours, so you'll get to Kai Tak just as they call the flight. Good trip?'

'Depends,' replied Langford. 'They seemed to be upset about the radio message.'

'Too bad,' said the man. 'But you're lucky we moved. As soon as the *Hai Shan* drops anchor, the Hong Kong police are going aboard in force.'

'Because of us?'

'No. That ship's been unloading stateless Chinese into Hong Kong for nearly two years. Seems as if they've had enough. Did Gunning brief you about Bangkok?'

'No.'

The man handed over a slip of paper. 'When you arrive at Bangkok airport, take a cab and ask for that address. Ask for Lim Mok and tell him that Gunning sent you and that you want a car, a Number One car. He'll probably try to screw you for three hundred bucks. Offer him a hundred and fifty and when he says no, start to walk out.'

'Who is this man?'

247

'Like I say, his name's Lim Mok. That's all you need to know. Once you get the car, go to this monastery, get a hold of those pictures and then fly straight back to Hong Kong.'

'How will I get in touch with you?' said Langford.

The man chuckled. 'You don't. You simply land at Kai Tak and we'll be waiting.'

The car swerved to avoid a truck and then accelerated along a broad, well-lit road overlooking the harbour.

'Then what happens?'

'You go back to London, Mister Langford. And you forget it ever happened.'

'And her?' demanded Langford, lighting a cigarette.

'Take her with you, marry her, leave her in Bangkok. I should care.'

Langford leaned forwards, resting his arm on the back of the seat. 'I care,' he said. 'The Japanese police want – '

'You listen to me, Langford. Our only concern is getting those pictures. What happens to the broad isn't my business.'

'But I'm making it mine,' rasped Langford. 'Before we get back, you have a cosy little chat with Gunning and tell him that unless he arranges a fair deal for her, no photographs. Okay?'

The man shrugged, glancing up as the car entered the tunnel linking Hong Kong island with Kowloon. 'Someone had better put you straight about the facts of life, man. To begin with, I'm not mixing it with friend Gunning. Second, we've been to a lot of trouble on your account.'

'Then get the bloody photographs yourselves,' snapped Langford.

'How do you fancy a few years in a Jap stockade, pal? Because I can arrange it.' He paused as the car slowed for the toll booths at the end of the tunnel.

'What will happen to the pictures?' asked Yita as they headed into the brightly-lit streets of Tsim Sha Tsui.

'That's not for you to worry about, lady.' He turned to

Langford. Are you going to make trouble?'

'No trouble,' said Langford. 'Not yet, anyway.'

'Great. And one more thing I'll mention. The United States may not operate officially in Thailand but don't get the idea that we haven't got friends down there.'

'Like this Lim Mok?'

'He's just a hustler. But even he knows where the bread comes from so ... yeah, maybe he'll pass the word if you try anything cute.'

The car was nudging its way through the streets which were already crowded although dawn was only just beginning to break.

'Leave your coats in the car. It's kinda stuffy down in Bangkok just now.' He watched Langford empty his pockets and then remove his top-coat. 'That's fine. Now you're just a nice, married couple, a pair of tourists going to take a few days vacation in sunny Thailand. Did they do your passports on the boat?'

'Yes. According to the stamps, we arrived in Hong Kong three days ago.'

'Okay. When we get to the airport, I'll see you through the check-in and passport control. But one false move – even when you're in the air, Langford – and you'll sign both your death warrants.' The man chuckled, softly. 'We're a little like the Mafia. We have long memories and even longer arms.'

'I can imagine,' said Langford.

'Good. That should save us all a lot of trouble.'

They were sitting in the departure lounge, Langford staring around him, his pale eyes narrowed.

'What is it, Richard?'

'I'm just looking for something.' He stood up, put a cigarette in his mouth and lit it. 'Wait here. I'll be right back.' He walked slowly across the lounge, stretching his legs. Then he saw a man in uniform and stopped him. 'Are you coming or going?' he asked.

'Going, mate. To bed. Why?'

'Could you do me a favour?' Langford took an envelope from his pocket, 'I forgot to post a letter ...'

The pilot grinned and shook his head. 'I don't take things off the airport,' he said. 'Anyway, there's a mail box over there, by those 'phones.'

'Thanks,' said Langford, starting towards the row of telephone booths as the flight to Bangkok was called. Slipping the unstamped letter into the box, he stood for a few moments, staring at the telephones Then he felt someone behind him.

'We go now?' said Yita.

'It's Sunday,' muttered Langford. 'Bloody Sunday.'

'I do not understand, Langford-*san*.'

'Never mind.' They joined the queue of passengers at the gate

2

'Had you taken me into your confidence, I could have saved you much trouble,' said Tasaki, staring round the room. 'You are a worried man, Toshiro. I can tell.'

'Why have you come here? Our agreement – '

'Is null and void. You have attempted to deceive me.'

'Not true,' snapped Shiba. 'There has been no deception. And you have been well-paid.'

'I have been used,' Tasaki retorted. 'But all that is past. A greater peril now faces us, Shiba-*san*. We must bury our personal differences. If not – '

'Do you threaten me?' Shiba removed his horn-rimmed glasses and carefully polished the thick lenses on a silk handkerchief. 'You of all people should know better than to attempt such a thing.'

'I will not presume on your hospitality, Shiba-*san*. Just hear me. You are in grave danger, as am I. This Englishman, Langford, has gone to Siam ... to Thailand. You know what that could mean?'

'Of course I know. What of it?'

'I have reason to believe that he is in league with the Americans.'

'Do you?' Shiba replaced his spectacles and nodded. 'You are being outrun by events, Muga. I have taken all the steps which are necessary.' And he stared at Tasaki, searchingly. 'I suppose you have come for money?'

'No.' The Japanese uttered a shrill laugh. 'You have caught the Western disease, Toshiro. Money, you think, can buy everything, yes?'

'Most things, yes.'

'Shiba-san, I know about the *Shimada Maru.*'

He shrugged. 'So you know. I am not surprised. I have been aware for some time now that you have well-placed contacts in Tokyo. But you are powerless, my friend. The ship will sail with its cargo and the world will not know.'

There was a long silence before Tasaki chuckled, softly. 'Which nation has agreed to carry out the re-processing?' he asked.

'If you do not already know that, I am not at liberty to tell you.' Shiba made a show of studying his watch. 'I have a meeting to attend. We have covered the trifling matter of the Englishman and what you know about the *Shimada Maru* will do you no good. If you tried to use the information, it would only harm you.'

'To sink the *Shimada Maru* in the Marianas Trench would seem to be the height of insanity.'

The colour drained from Shiba's face. 'How?' he hissed. 'How did you know that?'

'You are powerful, Shiba-san. You have great wealth and everything any man could wish. Now you stand on the edge of a precipice and should you fall, you will lose all that you treasure.'

Toshiro Shiba leaned back in his chair and fixed Tasaki with a penetrating glare. 'I have only to press a button to have you eliminated within minutes.'

'Of course. That is the risk I take by coming to Osaka. I could vanish without trace. Such is your power. But now ask yourself, why should I take such a risk? I will explain.

251

We must work together or we shall both perish. The photographs taken at Mogok – '

'I doubt their existence,' snapped Shiba.

'But I do not. Nor am I so foolish as to trust third-rate thugs to remove any who may know of these things. What happened at Mogok is history. It need never be known. But if the Englishman – '

'I have told you that the matter is being taken care of.'

'So you say. But did you imagine that when Izumi died, his secret would die with him? That when the English scientist perished, no one would ask why? I shall obtain those photographs, Toshiro. Then – '

'You will do nothing. Nothing. I have taken steps. Within a few days now, the pictures will have been destroyed.'

'And you said that you doubted their existence.' Tasaki's face creased in a sardonic grin. 'Anyway, perhaps we should discuss the Marianas Trench?'

Shiba bit his lip. 'I have to know who gave you that information, Muga. I would pay you well.'

'Maybe. But I have no need of money, Shiba-*san*. The price which I shall demand from you will involve … commitment. Like me, you took a sacred oath. I am now going to hold you to your word.'

Shiba shook his head. 'Will you never forget? Will you never give up? When we were young men, we believed what we were told. We thought we could conquer Asia. But we were misled and all but destroyed. Now you and the people who follow you are ready to begin all over again. And to what end? This is a different world, Muga.'

'If you sink the *Shimada Maru* in the Marianas Trench, my friend, it could indeed be a very different world.'

'There is no risk. Years of patient research and experimentation have gone into this project. It is quite safe.

I don't doubt that. If it weren't, you would not be so foolish as to attempt it. However, public opinion might be inclined towards another view of such an enterprise.'

'The public will never know.'

Tasaki smiled, bleakly. 'Then I must assume that I shall have your support. Silence is an expensive commodity.'

'That depends on your motives, Muga.'

'Power,' said Tasaki, lightly. 'And in return for your ... your cooperation, you would be permitted to prosper. Is that not a fair exchange?'

Shiba cupped his hands together and leaned forward. 'You are a political theorist, but you do not truly understand the delicate structure with which you are tampering.'

'Rubbish,' snapped Tasaki. 'We have become like so much small change in the pockets of the world. Our society, our ancient customs, our sacred laws have been trampled underfoot. Japan is nothing. We have power and wealth but where is the will to use that power, to manipulate that wealth? We are no longer masters of our own destiny. Like you, Shiba-*san*, Japan has been betrayed. I warn you, unless you give us your support, you are lost. Only I can offer you a guarantee of survival.'

'How so?'

'I believe that there is photographic proof of what took place at Mogok. I believe this because I have evidence that certain people are taking great trouble to procure that proof. My position is that if the photographs fell into the wrong hands, I should suffer harm but the damage to me would mean little. I would merely be forced to remain in the background while younger, untainted men acted on my behalf. But you, Toshiro, you would be destroyed. And there is one who would have it so, the one who gave me the information about the *Shimada Maru*.'

Shiba regarded the other man for a time and then nodded. 'If I were to agree to support you ... when you are in power ...?'

'That is all I ask,' said Tasaki. 'But go back on your word and I will destroy you utterly.'

'So be it.' Shiba sighed. 'Samwashima?'

Tasaki gave a light chuckle. 'You know, Toshiro, I think

you really are a man of genius. Yes, your precious Samwashima has sold himself to me.'

'Then why do you go back on your bargain with him?'

'Because I do not make bargains with traitors. Such men can never be trusted.'

Shiba smiled. 'No, Muga, you are lying. What you mean is that a bargain with Norihiko Samwashima is worthless because he has no power. Samwashima is a fool but a dangerous fool because he is ambitious.'

Tasaki rose slowly from the chair. 'Will you support me, Toshiro?'

'No, not until you are in power. Then ... Meanwhile, we are at deadlock, my friend. If you expose me, I shall expose you. So it pays us both to remain silent. Go back to your island, Muga. Dream your dreams of a new, Imperial Japan. Plan your coup and carry it out. But do not interfere with me.'

'Very well. I shall be satisfied with your reply. For the moment. But rest assured, Shiba-*san*, we shall prevail. The ideals of Bushido will once again govern the life of our nation. And then – '

'Then I will support you, Muga.'

Tasaki smiled and bowed. 'Very good, my friend. When we meet again, we shall be making history.'

'We made history at Mogok,' remarked Shiba. 'Now it must be re-written. Let us hope that this time, you will be more successful.'

'I shall.' Tasaki went to the door. 'I will leave you to take care of Samwashima in your own way.'

Shiba nodded as Tasaki left the office. Then he reached below the table and removed a small tape recorder from a drawer, smiling to himself as he re-wound the tape.

3

1977 was the year that the weather in Thailand went wrong. The rainy season should have ended in October but it started late so that as November drew to a close, it was still raining, the heat and humidity pressing down on Bangkok like a sodden blanket.

The journey by taxi from the airport into the centre of the Thai capital took an agonizing ninety minutes, the battered, clattering Datsun alternating between jarring bursts at high speed and a slow, jerking crawl through floodwater so deep that it came in under the doors. Throughout the trip, the driver sat nonchalantly behind the wheel, chattering loudly in a strange pidgin English which for the most part was utterly incomprehensible.

Seated in the back of the taxi, Yita and Langford said little. Mostly it was a case of hanging on for grim death or peering anxiously from the windows and waiting for the car to become marooned in the floods. And once they reached the city, the driver hurled the taxi into the swirling, chaotic traffic as if bent on suicide. Knowing that he would soon have to drive himself, Langford tried to work out the rule of the road but quickly decided there was none. Cars, lorries, precarious-looking motorized tri-shaws, bicycles and pedestrians competed for passage with an apparently total disregard for man or machine.

When the taxi juddered to a halt for the last time, Langford heaved a sigh. 'Where the hell are we?' he demanded.

The driver was smiling. 'You go there,' he said, pointing to a row of low, shabby buildings surrounded by water. 'Two hundred *baht*.'

Langford counted out the notes, knowing that he was being cheated but too hot and tired to care. And taking their cases, they stepped from the taxi only to find themselves ankle-deep in the green, muddy water. The taxi pulled away, its wheels creating a small tidal wave as they started towards the buildings.

A young Thai was watching them with a mixture of curiosity and anticipation before he eventually waded towards them, his colourful *pakama* flapping wetly around his knees.

'You want room?' he said, beaming.

'No,' rasped Langford. 'Lim Mok. You know Lim Mok?'

The Thai nodded, clasping his hands together and bowing his head as he made the *wai*, the traditional greeting. 'You want Lim Mok? Me take you.' Then he held out his hand. 'One hundred *baht*.'

'Fifty,' snapped Langford. 'And Lim Mok first. Then money.'

The young Thai blew his nose into his fingers and then wiped them on his *pakama*. 'Difficult. Much flood.'

'Fifty *baht*,' said Langford. 'When we see Lim Mok.'

'Okay.' And the young Thai snatched at their cases before wading away through the water.

Yita took hold of Langford's arm. 'You are worried again?'

He shrugged. 'I was just thinking that it could pay us to hire a boat.' It was a half-hearted attempt at humour but Yita took him literally.

'You think maybe Lim Mok has boat?'

Langford smiled and squeezed her hand. 'We'll see.'

'This way,' called the young Thai and promptly disappeared between two of the buildings.

'Come on.' Langford dragged Yita quickly through the water, turned into the alleyway and then stopped. 'Damn.' The ground sloped upwards so that it was above the water level. It was also completely deserted. 'We've been had,' he said, feeling for his cigarettes and leaning against the wall as he lit up.

Somewhere in the distance, a bell was tolling and dogs barked.

'What are we going to do, Langford-*san*?'

He sighed and wiped the perspiration from his face. 'Go on looking for Lim Mok, I suppose.' He stared at the rows of doors and narrow openings off the alleyway. 'There's not much point in worrying about the cases.'

Before Yita could comment, a short, squat figure appeared and was grinning, broadly. 'Hi there, man.'

Then he stared at Yita. 'Lady?'

Langford grimaced. 'We're looking for someone called Lim Mok.'

'Yeah.' The man continued to grin.

'Lim Mok,' said Langford, raising his voice.

'Yeah.' The man made a sort of bow. 'I'm Lim Mok. Boy come. Your luggage ... my house.'

'Ah.' Langford sighed. 'Where ...?'

'Please, you come in now?' And he led them through a low doorway into a wood-panelled room which smelt strongly of joss. Their two suitcases were in the corner, the young Thai sitting on them and smiling, possessively.

'Fifty *baht*,' said the boy.

Lim Mok threw his hands in the air. 'No way,' he said. 'No way. Give twenty-five.'

The boy scowled but took the money and left without argument.

'Thanks,' said Langford.

'My son,' Lim Mok explained, grinning. 'Many sons. And daughters.' He peered into Langford's face 'American?'

'English,' said Langford.

'Oh ... jolly good, no?' Lim Mok frowned as if trying to remember something. 'Yeah,' he said. 'How do you do?'

'Gunning sent me.'

The grin slowly faded and Lim Mok's eyes narrowed. 'What you want?' he asked, warily.

'A car. A Number One car.'

'Great problem. Very difficult. You got American dollars?'

'Yes.'

Lim Mok nodded, chewing at his bottom lip. 'Where you go?'

'That's my business,' said Langford but Lim Mok laughed.

'Floods very bad. Roads no good now. Number One car get messed up. Cost money.' He pointed to a row of chairs. 'You sit.'

They sat and faced each other. 'Number One car,' said Langford. 'Okay?'

'Depends where you go. You trust me, yeah? Gunning trust me.'

Richard Langford stared into Mok's round, fleshy face. He certainly wasn't a pure-bred Thai and looked rather more Chinese in his spotless white shirt and flared blue jeans supported by a heavy leather belt which was almost obscured by his bulging stomach. Langford tried to decide how little he should tell him.

'I Vietnamese,' said Lim Mok, as if he had been able to read Langford's mind. 'Meet Gunning in Saigon. Good times then. Much work. But war end and Americans go. I come here but still work for Gunning.'

'Have you got a car for hire?'

'Maybe, but roads ...' He shook his head. 'People say that floods will end on King's birthday.' He laughed, merrily. 'I say crap.'

'Okay.' Langford pressed his cigarette stub into a dented Coca-Cola ashtray. 'I want to get to Suk Chiang. You know it?'

Lim Mok frowned. 'Sure. Nothing there. Just primitive place ... few people, old monastery. Why you want to go?'

'Never mind. Can we drive there?'

The Vietnamese hawked and made accurate use of an ornate spittoon in the corner of the room. 'Maybe. You could use road up to Tak. Small town about three hundred kilometres from Bangkok. After that, road not so good.'

'But you do have a car?' insisted Langford. 'A reliable car?'

Lim Mok nodded, thoughtfully. 'Suk Chiang in hills. Not like Bangkok.'

'So what?'

'I drive you there. Good car. Very comfortable. And because you sent by Gunning, I give you special price Only five hundred American dollars.'

'Too much,' said Langford, suddenly wondering why he

258

should worry about spending Gunning's money. 'And I'd rather drive myself.'

The Vietnamese seemed perplexed. 'Difficult,' he muttered, hawking again as he walked across the room to the spittoon. 'Bad roads. You lose way. Maybe wreck car.'

'It could be better for him to drive us,' whispered Yita.

Langford shrugged. 'All right, I'll give you a hundred for the car and fifty for your driving.'

'No way, man.' And Lim Mok shook his head, vehemently. 'More than three hundred kilometres from here to Tak. Then maybe another hundred to Suk Chiang. Eight hundred kilometres there and back. Petrol very expensive now. Four hundred dollars lowest possible price.'

There was a long silence before Langford got to his feet. 'Three hundred. Take it or leave it.' And he went to pick up the suitcases.

'Okay, we make deal.' Lim Mok held out his hand which Langford took.

'And we'll start now,' he said, quickly letting go of Mok's hot, moist paw but the Vietnamese laughed.

'Morning. Take maybe seven hours to go Suk Chiang. No good in dark. We leave early. First light.'

'I want to leave now,' said Langford. 'We're in a hurry.'

Mok continued to laugh. 'You people always in hurry. Even we leave now, you no get there until tomorrow. Roads bad. No good for night driving. You have room here. All in, one price. And good dinner.' As if to reinforce his argument, he went to a cupboard and produced a large-scale map which he spread on the table. 'See?' he said, tracing the red line of a road with his finger. 'Only three hours light left now. We go in morning.'

Langford glanced helplessly at Yita and nodded. 'Okay, but first thing. Where's this room?'

'You pay me now,' said Mok.

'Half now. The rest when we get to Suk Chiang.' He counted out the notes which the Vietnamese examined with extreme care.

259

'Okay, you come,' he said, picking up their cases and taking them through an opening into a small, dark room filled by an obviously much used double bed. 'You have good night here.' And he grinned, broadly.

4

DuCros seemed surprised as Inspector Bouscat entered. 'My call was not urgent,' he said, looking up.

'Your call?' Bouscat sat down. 'But I asked to see you, Colonel.'

'You did?' He shuffled through a pile of papers. 'Doesn't matter. I just thought you should see a report which has come from the British Special Branch. You read English?'

'No,' said Bouscat, lighting a cigarette.

'Then I shall read it to you.' The Colonel cleared his throat and leaned back in his chair. 'It has just come through on the telex and is a transcription of the interview with this man Hewens.

'*As requested, we questioned Mister Meyrick C. Hewens, an American citizen currently residing at the Westbury Hotel, London, where this interview took place on Sunday, November 27, 1977, at 11 a.m. On being asked when he last visited Paris, the respondent confirmed that he had gone there on Tuesday, November 15 of this year, and stayed one night at L'Auberge du Parc on the Boulevarde St Marcel. When asked the purpose of his trip, Mister Hewens said, "It is none of your damned business." The respondent was then cautioned that the questions were being asked on behalf of the French authorities and that he would be wise to answer. Hewens then said, "What is it you want to know?" He was asked who he saw in Paris and replied, "A friend." When asked the name of this friend, Hewens said, "His name is Picot, Claude Picot."*'

'So Rueff was right,' said Bouscat, gruffly.

'There is more.' DuCros scanned the long sheet. 'Yes, here it is.

' "Why did you see Picot? Why did you meet him secretly?" Hewens replied, "There was nothing secret. We met in a public place. As to why, it is a private matter." The respondent was then informed that the French police wished to know and could order his arrest and extradition. Hewens laughed and said, "Picot is a homosexual. So am I. It was our intention to take a holiday together but he said he had other plans." In reply to the other questions you wished asked, the respondent said that he did not know why Picot should leave Paris and that he could not think of any reason why he should visit Japan. The respondent did not seem surprised at the questions. As the interview was concluded, Hewens said, "I hope that this will remain confidential." He was told that it would be up to the French authorities. The interview ended at ...' DuCros shrugged and tossed the paper down. 'So, it would seem that the meeting was as I suspected, a lovers' tryst.' And the Colonel smirked.

'Doesn't make sense,' murmured Bouscat. 'A man like Hewens picks up a telephone and ... *voila*, he talks. Why come all the way to Paris, stay a night, arrange a meeting in the rain? *C'est bizarre, n'est ce pas?*'

'What are you getting at?'

'I'm not sure, Colonel. I just think ... I don't know.'

'Then perhaps it is better not to think, *mon ami*. And about the student, Malvy. Forget him.'

'Why?'

'Because his only next of kin is an uncle who hated the kid's guts. He was a pansy. So, no one's going to stir that little pot. But I suppose having an unsolved murder on your books will irritate you, no?'

'I daresay I can live with it.'

'Then you may return to your office, Inspector. Oh yes, I have spoken to the Minister about you. Your co-operation will not go un-noticed. And when you next see your friend, Rueff, you may tell him that if I need a safe opened, I know where to come.'

'He won't be interested.'

DuCros raised his eyebrows. 'My department ... and

others in the Service, sometimes need a little assistance. We pay well and a man of Rueff's talents ... we-ell, there is scope, no?'

'Not for Rueff, no. That's why I asked to see you. You asked me to find him and I succeeded. He's dead.'

'Dead?' DuCros leaned forwards. 'How?'

'Murdered, a two-car job in the Rue Alibert by the St Louis Hospital. That's where he is now ... what's left of him.'

'You are sure it was murder, Inspector?'

'Positive. Besides, there was a witness, an old woman who just happened to be looking out of her bedroom window at one o'clock this morning. She saw Rueff standing on the corner, as if he was waiting for someone. He must have been set up. One car hit him, closely followed by another which swerved to run over the body.'

'This woman ... can she give a description of the cars?'

'Both black and one with a Paris registration. Even that's not bad for a seventy year-old.' Bouscat smiled, bleakly.

'The British Special Branch interview Hewens ...' DuCros paused to light one of his thin cigars. 'Then the man who saw Hewens and Picot is murdered. Interesting.' He glanced speculatively at Bouscat. 'Your case?'

'My department has been notified, yes.'

'I see.' DuCros swung round in his chair and frowned. 'You have any ideas?'

'Nothing firm, but ...' Bouscat stubbed out his cigarette. 'One question for you, Colonel. Was it a SDECE contract?'

DuCros gave him a wintry smile. 'If it were, my friend, you would know nothing about it. We do have some clumsy thugs in the Service but they're not that clumsy. Besides, why should we wish to eliminate this man?'

'That is what I have been asking myself, Colonel.' Bouscat stood up. 'May I have a copy of the report on Hewens' interview?'

'Help yourself.' DuCros also stood and then perched on

the corner of the desk, carefully flicking specks of ash from his lap. 'Inspector, it is obviously your duty to investigate the death of this man and I do assure you that we ... the Service, had nothing to do with it. However, I cannot help feeling that the murder of one criminal by another is almost a kind of justice in itself. Would you not agree?'

'Not entirely, no, *M'sieu*.' Bouscat folded the telex from London and slipped it into his pocket. 'It may be revenge, someone settling an old score. On the other hand, there may be a link with your American. Perhaps even with Claude Picot. All I know for certain is that it has the hallmarks of a gangland job and I want to know why.'

DuCros nodded. 'If you find anything, Inspector, you will let me know?'

'I'll follow all the correct procedures, *M'sieu le Colonel*.'

'I am less than concerned about procedures, Bouscat. If you find anything which ties this killing in with Hewens or Picot, you inform me ... immediately. You understand that?'

Bouscat nodded as he walked to the door. 'Perfectly.'

5

Langford woke with the dawn, his mouth dry, his body pouring sweat as he levered himself off the hard floor. His ribs and palms still hurt but he had already discarded the bandages and took several deep breaths in an attempt to ease the stiffness in his muscles. Then he gazed at Yita for a moment. She was lying on the bed, her body covered by a thin sheet.

'Time to get up,' he said, touching her shoulder.

She opened her eyes, staring at him as if he were a complete stranger. Then she sat up, pulling the sheet around her as she slipped out of the bed and started to dress.

Langford watched her for a time, studying her bare back and catching a fleeting glimpse of her small, firm breasts. Then he turned away, scowling to himself as he thought about the previous evening.

The dinner provided by Lim Mok had been a very curious meal, a mixture of Thai and Vietnamese food with a tin of Spam thrown in for good measure. After *tom yum kang*, a highly-spiced shrimp soup, there were various curried meats, all of which seared Langford's palate so that he drank too much *Singha* beer. Mok's tin of American spam was served dressed with a sweet and sour sauce and the meal was rounded off with large portions of *Songaya*, a baked coconut dish, very sweet and unspeakably rich. But the food had sharpened Langford's desire for Yita and as soon as they were alone, he had taken her into his arms and kissed her gently on the lips. At first, she had responded and as her body pressed against his, he felt the pleasant flutter of anticipation in the pit of his belly.

Richard Langford wanted her badly, his body suddenly demanding physical relief. But when they began to embrace, her responses were coldly mechanical and somehow distant. Then something happened to him which he had never experienced before and he turned away from her, humiliated and angry.

Lying alone on the hard, wooden floor, Langford had stayed awake for a long time, listening to the throb of insects, the distant hum of traffic and Yita Izumi's slow, even breathing. He recalled his feelings when Gunning had called her a Nip whore and then forced himself to accept that the description was apt. She was a bar-girl who had sold herself for money. Langford knew that he could have enjoyed her for nothing, using her as he had used so many women in his life. But something had neutralized his manhood and as he drifted into an uneasy sleep, he came to understand that Yita's love for Bailey was only an excuse for his sudden impotence. He wanted her, not only physically but emotionally. For the first time in Langford's adult life, he needed a woman, wholly and completely.

After they had packed and eaten a light breakfast of papaya and coffee, they followed Lim Mok from the house. The sky was grey, the opaque cloud like a kind of lid holding down the thick humidity. Within a matter of minutes, Langford's shirt was drenched with perspiration as they walked through the narrow passage. Then they came to a flooded area.

'How far?' rasped Langford, raising the two cases clear of the water which came nearly up to his knees.

Lim Mok, who had swapped his flared jeans for a blue *pakama*, turned and grinned. 'Just there.' He pointed at an apartment building. 'Keep cars there. Good road on other side.'

Langford nodded. Glancing round, he caught sight of the gilded *chedis* of the *Wat* Saket. Lim Mok saw him staring at the temple and laughed.

'Big tourist place,' he said. 'Very old. Many relics of Bhudda.'

Langford plodded through the water. 'Have you been to Suk Chiang before?'

'No,' said Lim Mok. 'But to Tak many times. Take Americans. Soldiers on furlough from Vietnam. But now no more war, so no GIs, no dollars.'

'Shame,' said Langford, stopping to drain the water from his shoes as they stepped up on to dry ground.

The whole of the ground floor of the apartment block was an open-sided car park and faced on to a busy main road. The hot, heavy air, permeated with the scent of carbon monoxide, caught in the throat. There was no wind and even the passing traffic seemed to leave the treacle-like atmosphere undisturbed. Most of the cars in the parking lot were old and battered and the one to which Lim Mok led them was no exception.

'Christ,' exclaimed Langford, staring at the ancient Volkswagen. 'Is this what you call a Number One car?'

The Vietnamese beamed. 'Number One. Top hole. Very good motor.' And he kicked one of the wheels.

'I hate to think what the Number Two models are like,'

265

he said, stowing their cases in the front luggage compartment.

After several tries, the Beetle was eventually persuaded to start, its engine knocking and clattering as Lim Mok revved it with genial ferocity. Langford listened, his practised ear picking out worn big-ends, slack pistons and a set of valves which were probably corroded beyond recognition.

'If this bloody thing breaks down ...'

'No break down,' rejoined Mok, confidently. 'I have car long time. Make many trips. Many dollars.'

As he sat in the front, Langford felt the seat give. 'I should think someone presented it to Adolf Hitler as a leaving present. Come on, let's get moving.' He turned and stared at Yita who was sitting in the back. 'You okay?'

She nodded. 'Sure, Richard. Okay.' Her voice was soft, apologetic, like the expression in her dark, liquid eyes.

It took over two hours to clear Bangkok. Many of the roads were flooded, some impassable so that Mok had to make lengthy detours, often driving at breakneck speed through narrow streets which had once been metalled but were now pitted with deep holes over which the Volkswagen crashed with bone-jarring disdain. But once out of the city, the road improved although they were frequently forced to slow to a crawl because of flooding. And after about another hour, they came to Ayudhya, one of the ancient capitals of Siam.

'Used to come here lots,' shouted Mok, gesturing towards the ruins which reminded Langford of a bombed city. 'Bring Americans.' He swerved to avoid a convoy of elephants lumbering through the town. 'Americans like search ruins. Many treasures. Even gold and silver. The GIs like take souvenirs but government don't like and police come. Very difficult. But all past now. When war stop and Americans go home, so ...'

Langford lit a cigarette, trying to collect his thoughts as the Vietnamese chattered on but the noisy bumping of the

266

car, the heat and the close proximity of Yita all seemed to combine to fog his brain.

Looking out of the car window, Langford suddenly became aware that they had left the ruins far behind. The road was deserted now, a grey, curving strip walled in on both sides by thick, matted jungle which looked dark and threatening. He remembered the Nambu pistol and as he flicked his cigarette stub from the car, Langford wished they could have kept the gun.

It was shortly after midday when they drove into Tak, a ramshackle sort of town, the few modern buildings standing out as brash, incongruous examples of European influence against a backdrop of pervasive decay and poverty. Lim Mok swung the car into a primitive-looking filling station and they all got out to stretch their legs, Langford noting that the Thai pump attendant poured almost as much oil as petrol into the engine. They bought some fruit, grapefruit-like pomelos and mangosteens. Then Langford noticed the Buddhist monks for the first time. He stared at the thin, orange-robed figures for a moment and then made his way back to the car.

'We stop for rest?' said Mok, hopefully.

'No. How much further?'

The Vietnamese shrugged. 'Maybe hundred kilometres. But road not so good. Not like main road.'

Langford frowned, thinking that even another sixty or so miles over a road worse than the one they were already on would probably finish Lim Mok's Number One car for good.

'Better rest for a while,' said Mok. 'Good to rest.'

'You rest,' snapped Langford. 'I'll drive.'

The Vietnamese stared at him, his expression one of abject horror. 'You no drive,' he squeaked, as if driving were a sacred science known only to himself.

'I'm driving,' said Langford, firmly. 'Get in.'

Mok obeyed with reluctance and sat in the front passenger seat, his fleshy face sullen and downcast.

The Volkswagen proved rather more difficult to handle

267

than Langford had imagined. The main problem was the steering gear which was obviously so worn that the wheel had to be spun round and round to achieve any real manoeuvrability, but he soon mastered the car's eccentricities and after another hour, they were speeding along the deserted road.

'Turn soon,' muttered Lim Mok, his hands clasped over his bulging stomach.

'Okay, you tell me when.'

Mok grunted. 'How long you stay Suk Chiang?'

'Depends,' replied Langford. 'Why?'

'No place ... no hotel there.'

'Doesn't matter. Anyway, what I want is outside Suk Chiang. It's the monastery, the *Wat* Keo.' There seemed to be no harm in admitting this fact which Lim Mok considered in silence. Then he pointed.

'You turn there. See?'

Langford saw and stamped on the brakes. 'Thanks for the warning,' he growled, spinning the steering wheel.

The Volkswagen eventually nosed its way off the main road on to what was little better than a rough track. The surface was appalling, the car bucking and jumping as the wheels slipped in and out of the deep ruts.

'Like I say, bad road,' grumbled Mok. 'No good for car. Maybe break springs.'

'If there are any to be broken.'

Mok sniffed and clutched at the dashboard for support. 'Why you want to go to the *Wat* Keo?' he asked, his tone one of mistrust.

'Why not?'

'Europeans not go such temples. Only tourist places. *Wat* Keo not for tourists.'

'I have my reasons,' said Langford. 'Is this river marked on the map?'

Mok nodded. 'Mei Ping. Bridge further on.'

The bridge turned out to be a crude, wooden construction which creaked and clattered as Langford eased the car on to it. Looking down, he saw that the Mei

Ping was a rushing torrent of muddy-green water swollen by the heavy rains. He grimaced as he felt the bridge sway.

Once they were safely across, Langford sighed and fumbled for a cigarette. Then the road began to climb, winding its way out of the valley into the rounded hills.

'This is beautiful,' said Langford, suddenly conscious of the unspoiled landscape and the luxuriant vegetation.

'Nothing here.' Lim Mok hawked, noisily, and spat from the car window. 'Only jungle. Americans hate jungle.' And he hawked again.

The road was climbing steeply now and Langford was forced to go down into second gear, the engine shrieking in protest. Then a flash of light made him look in the driving mirror.

'We seem to have company.'

Mok swung round and stared past Yita through the rear window at the red and green truck. He made a kind of clucking noise. 'New lorry,' he said. 'You let pass?'

Langford was about to ask why – and how – when the driver of the truck laid on his horn.

The Volkswagen was making heavy weather of the climb and Langford was on the point of slamming it into first gear as they rounded another bend and the road widened out. Pulling over, he let the lorry overtake, engine roaring.

'How much further?'

'I not know. Maybe thirty ... forty kilometre. Difficult to say.'

'Let's hope this heap can make it.' Langford swore as he smashed through the gears but the Volkswagen seemed incapable of going much faster than fifteen miles an hour up the steep gradient. Then the road narrowed again but it also levelled out and Langford pressed his foot to the floor.

As they rounded the next bend, the needle of the speedometer touched forty and Langford was about to go into top when he saw the truck ahead of him. It was stationary.

269

His immediate reaction was to stamp on the brake but the pedal went almost to the floor and he started to curse the worn-out brake shoes as the truck loomed closer. Then the canvas flap at the rear was pulled back and he saw the small, dark figure with the sub-machine gun.

In the micro-second which it took the information to pass from his eyes to his brain, Richard Langford's army training took over, just as his instructors had known from long experience that it would. He became an automaton, his reflexes governed by the very events to which his training had been geared.

'Down!'

His shout seemed to echo and then merge with the high-pitched shriek of the engine, the squealing, jolting skid of bald tyres on the rutted surface and a staccato clatter as the sub-machine gun spewed fire.

The Volkswagen plunged off the road into the jungle. He heard Yita scream and saw the front of the car split open by a continuous stream of bullets. Then Lim Mok slumped against him, blood pouring from his head.

Another burst of gunfire smashed into the rear-mounted engine but in spite of the loss of power, there was no lack of momentum. The ground sloped away from the road and the car simply rolled downhill, out of control. It no longer mattered what Langford did with the steering wheel. Or the brakes. Then the Beetle sliced into a tree with a juddering crash, the front end rising crazily towards the sky.

'We're going over,' he yelled, bracing himself against the steering wheel as the Volkswagen lurched on to its side.

There was silence. Then someone shouted, the call echoing through the jungle as Langford pushed Lim Mok's inert body to one side and used his feet to force open the passenger door. As he scrambled out on to the side of the car, he heard the sound of men coming through the trees.

270

Yita was covered in blood and Langford almost prayed aloud as he lifted her from the car, pulling her by the arms over Lim Mok who was slumped with his face pressed grotesquely against the cracked windscreen. Because of the angle, Yita was unable to see that half of Lim Mok's head had been shot away and she pointed at him, her lips moving soundlessly. Langford took no notice as he gathered her into his arms and dropped quickly to the ground.

Moving as silently as he knew how, Langford carried Yita away from the wrecked car and laid her in a hollow by a fallen tree. Then he retraced his steps, carefully closed the passenger door again and took the cigarette lighter from his pocket. He could smell the petrol but it took an eternity to find the source of the leak.

Another series of sing-song calls echoed through the jungle. Time was running out. He backed away from the car, searching his pockets for something ... anything to use as a fuse. In the end, he pulled a ten dollar bill from his wallet, flicked the lighter and held the note over the flame. Once it was well and truly alight, he tossed it towards the car and dived for cover as the first of the men from the truck came into view.

Langford lay as still as death, hardly daring to breathe as he watched the ten dollar bill slowly burning to ashes. The Thai was approaching the wreck with extreme caution, the sub-machine gun held at the ready. He came from the far side, trying to peer into the car as he walked round it but his problem was lack of height. He hoisted himself up and had just begun to open the passenger door when the petrol tank exploded.

The heat of the blast seared Langford's face as the ball of swirling fire shot upwards and a roar echoed away through the trees. The inquisitive Thai now lay writhing and screaming on the ground, his head and shoulders covered in burning petrol. Two more men came but were forced back by the heat of the flames. They seemed

271

curiously unconcerned about their comrade as his screaming gradually died away.

There were two thoughts running through Richard Langford's mind. One was Yita. He was confident that he could find her again provided she stayed put. The second concerned the sub-machine gun discarded by the Thai whose charred body lay just a few feet away from him. The weapon was just out of reach, lying muzzle-up against a clump of ferns, and inching his way forwards, Langford noted that the other Thais, three of them now, were standing well away from the far side of the burning car. One carried a rifle, holding it in his folded arms like a baby. The other two appeared to be unarmed.

Moving with painful slowness, Langford reached out until he felt his finger tips touch the metal stock of the gun. Then something else exploded in the car, showering the surrounding area with red-hot metal and burning rubber. Langford didn't wait to see the Thais back even further away but simply grabbed the sub-machine gun, rolled over and sprayed them with a burst of fire which emptied the magazine.

Even as the Thais crumpled to the ground, Langford was on his feet and rushing towards them. But they were all dead and stooping down, he picked up the rifle, trying to decide whether to check out the road or pick up Yita first. He chose the road and glancing at the burning car, tossed the empty sub-machine gun away and worked the bolt of the rifle as he started along the path made by the Thais.

Almost all of Richard Langford's military career had been devoted to urban anti-terrorist tactics. He knew little of fieldcraft and nothing about jungle warfare. But he possessed an instinct for survival and when that instinct told him that someone or something was behind him, he froze, tightening his grip on the rifle.

Carefully raising the gun as the soft footfalls came nearer, he waited until he caught sight of the dark shape and then eased the butt of the rifle against his shoulder, his left eye closing as he took aim.

'No!'

Langford felt a cold shudder pass through his body and lowered the gun as Yita sagged to the ground. Then he ran forward and took her in his arms.

She gave a sharp, choking sob. 'Langford ...'

'All right, it's safe.' But he couldn't resist a quick glance over his shoulder. 'Come on, we must get back to the road.'

'You killed them,' she muttered, accusingly.

He stared at her for a moment. 'For God's sake, Yita, pull yourself together.' He was surprised at the harshness in his voice but the rebuke was effective.

'What shall we do now?'

'You just stay right behind me. We're going back to the road. I want that truck – ' He stopped abruptly. 'Just keep behind me, okay?'

It took them about ten minutes to reach the edge of the road. The truck was still there and the Thais had left one of their number with it.

'You will kill him?' breathed Yita.

'If I have to.' Langford stared at the small figure in the white shirt and red *pakama* who squatted by the truck.

'He moves.'

Langford nodded, raising the rifle. The man stood up and went to the driver's door, swung it open and pulled out another sub-machine gun. Then he started towards them, gun at the ready.

The single shot echoed through the trees and the Thai spun round falling heavily to the ground, his finger tightening on the trigger. The air was split by a seemingly endless burst of automatic fire.

When they passed the Thai's corpse, Yita shook her head.

'You are a violent man.'

'I didn't start this,' Langford snapped, kicking the body

so that it rolled into a bush, out of sight.

'It is wickedness.' She looked up at him, her face pale. 'The Lord Buddha – '

'Can go screw himself.' And he strode across to the truck.

Once he had established that there were no spare magazines, he took the sub-machine gun and smashed it against a rock by the side of the road. Then they climbed into the cabin, Langford sitting behind the wheel with the rifle resting across his lap.

'Probably more comfortable than Mok's Number One car,' he muttered, twisting the key in the starter. Nothing happened. He tried again with the same result.

'What is wrong, Richard?'

He opened the door and jumped out, standing with his hands on his hips as he stared at the pattern of bullet holes in the engine cowling. 'Shit!'

'Why did they do that?' said Yita, coming to his side.

'The man back there did it.' He shrugged and mopped the sweat from his face. 'It's known as Sod's Law.' Then he pulled the rifle from the cabin and released the handbrake. 'Come on, let's see if we can push it off the road. It should roll.'

He could feel his strength ebbing as he put all his weight against the back of the truck, and he was just about to give up when it finally began to move, the wheels turning slowly, crunching across the rough road surface. Langford sank on to his knees and watched the truck gather speed, veer to the edge and then topple over into the jungle.

'They won't be able to find that in a hurry,' he said, as the heavy foliage crashed back like a curtain.

'Shiba?'

'Maybe. But whoever sent them, from now on ...' He held up the rifle. 'We're not taking any more chances.'

'Please, Richard.' Yita was watching him, pain in her eyes. 'What can we do now?'

He loosened the sling and shouldered the rifle. 'Walk,' he said.

Henri Bouscat perched on the corner of the table and lit a cigarette as the last of his department filed into the already smoke-filled room, the casual chatter slowly dying away as Bouscat began to speak.

'I know you're busy.' There was a murmur of agreement. 'But you all know what happened to Jean-Jacques Rueff and I hope you've all read my report.' He glanced around as the men nodded. 'Well, who's got any ideas?' He waited, scowling at the silence. 'All right, I'll start.' Standing up, he went across to a blackboard. 'This all began with Rueff seeing the American meet Claude Picot in the Bois de Vincennes.' Bouscat picked up a piece of chalk. 'Rueff, Picot and Hewens,' he intoned, the chalk scraping harshly as he wrote out the names. 'Then we have the student, Malvy. What else?' Bouscat wrote 'Japan' on the board, followed by the letters SDECE. 'The problem, gentlemen, is to find something ... anything, which links each of these elements.' And he tapped the board. 'I believe that we can disregard the student, Malvy. But these others ... I want complete dossiers on them. Rueff, Picot and the American, Hewens. I also want the statement made by *M'sieu* Hewens to the British Special Branch checked out. In short, I want to know everything there is to be known.' He peered at his men. 'Any questions?'

'We need a common factor.'

'Exactly so. Use everything, your contacts with Interpol, the Central Computer Register ... clairvoyants, if you like.'

'Are we looking for Rueff's murderers?'

Henri Bouscat glanced towards the detective and shrugged. 'Partly, yes. But I have a theory that there is something here ... something more complex than just a killing. It is a riddle, *mes amis*. And I want it solved.'

There was a short silence before a detective at the back of the room said, 'Inspector, do we have authority to go outside France?'

'The Department will not pay for you to have a Japanese holiday, if that's what you mean.' Bouscat smiled as a ripple of subdued laughter went round the room. 'But yes, use your contacts … preferably unofficially if for no better reason than it cuts down the paperwork. And one more thing: if any of you find yourself tangling with DuCros' men, back off and report to me.'

'Is it possible that SDECE knocked off Rueff?'

'I am keeping an open mind. But if there's any in-fighting with the Service, I'll be the one to do it. Unless anyone hits the jackpot before, we'll assemble here the day after tomorrow, same time. That's all.' There was a scraping of chairs and muttered farewells as they all filed out and left Bouscat to frown at the blackboard as he scratched at his lank, greying hair.

7

The darkness came quickly, a thick, impenetrable cloak thrown over the landscape. To begin with, Yita and Langford had to grope their way cautiously along the narrow road, the jungle pressing in on them. The humid air was filled with the incessant throbbing of cicadas, the vibrant croaking of the frogs and, from the depths of the tangled darkness, the echoing, high-pitched shrieks of monkeys and birds disturbed by some night-prowler. Then the moon came, bathing the jungle in a cool, pale light.

Once he had settled into his stride, Langford found the going easy. He was concerned about Yita but she showed no sign of fatigue nor made any complaint. She simply followed in silence, her face drawn and expressionless in the moonlight. Once or twice, he tried to get her talking but she seemed determined not to speak, just nodding or even ignoring him altogether.

They walked through the night, even when the moon

dropped away for the long hour just before daybreak and the purple darkness smothered everything. Then the dawn finally came, silken strands of creamy light slowly brightening the eastern horizon until the sky was fired with a livid orange glow. And with the dawn came the birds – rollers, mountain mynahs and swarms of little green parrots, all chorusing their welcome to the new day. Hundreds of tiny monkeys chattered noisily as they swung high in the trees overhanging the road. Staring up at them as he walked, Langford unconsciously took the rifle from his shoulder, carrying it at the trail.

He had been totally unprepared for the ambush and it was only as the sun came up over the jungle that he realized how close he had come to death. He moistened his lips, remembering Lim Mok, his skull blown apart; the Thai screaming as he burned to death, the four other men. Not that Langford had any regrets. He had reacted in the only way possible. What depressed him most was the fact that he considered his reflexes quite natural. But another source of worry was the realization that he had been careless. He should have searched the bodies of the men he had killed. If the odds had been against his finding anything useful it was no excuse. He sighed, suddenly tired and uncertain. Then Yita called to him.

The map had been left in the Volkswagen to be consumed, like Lim Mok's body, by the flames, and there was no road-sign to confirm that the cluster of buildings below them was Suk Chiang. But Langford had little doubt. There was no other village within a twenty mile radius.

He stared down at the primitive buildings, some of stone but most just flimsy constructions of bamboo and palm. There were a few people moving around, women and children herding what looked like goats, and the place radiated a pastoral calm. Above the village stood the monastery, the *Wat* Keo, its gilded, bell-shaped *chedi* glistening in the morning sun.

As Langford watched the monastery, he could see

277

monks forming up in the compound, their saffron robes brilliant in the sunlight.

'We seem to have arrived.'

'The gun?' asked Yita.

'Yes.' Langford frowned. He knew he could hardly walk into a Buddhist monastery carrying a rifle but he was reluctant to give it up.

'You will hide it, Richard?'

Leaving the road at a point marked by a small shrine, Langford walked among the trees until he found one with a hollow trunk. It was far from ideal but there seemed to be no alternative. When he had wrapped the gun in dry leaves secured with lengths of vine, he carefully lowered it into the hollow. Then he stood for a moment to make certain of his bearings before returning to the road where Yita had squatted down, waiting for him.

It took them about half an hour to reach the edge of the village where the road forked, one of the tracks leading up to the *Wat*. A group of Thais stood at the junction as if waiting for something. They smiled and waved, chattering gaily. Langford waved back and was about to continue up the road when the sound of chanting filled the air. It was a strangely haunting sound, resonant and ululating, and accompanied by the sonorous clashing of gongs and cymbals.

More people were coming up from the village and before Langford could move any further, a procession came into view. There seemed to be dozens of monks, obviously the men they had seen forming up in front of the temple. It was a vivid, colourful sight. They moved along in the ragged column, three and four abreast, their orange robes shimmering, their shaven heads bobbing and glistening in the sun. And in the centre of the column was an ornate palanquin draped with garlands of flowers.

'What's going on?' said Langford as they stepped back off the road to get out of the way.

Yita stared and shook her head. 'I think ... I think it is a funeral.'

Langford felt a sudden dryness in his mouth and swallowed as the palanquin passed within a few feet of them.

Some of the monks turned and gazed curiously at the two strangers, grinning and nodding. Others made the *wai*, clasping their hands together and bowing without actually stopping. Most ignored them.

The procession slowly wound its way past and at the tail-end came a group of monks wearing dull brown robes. Acting on impulse, Langford started towards them.

'Soichi Heyashi,' he said, as if the name of the man they had come so far to see was a kind of greeting.

One of the monks smiled and nodded. 'Yes,' he said, the tone of his voice strangely European.

'Is he here?' Langford was walking alongside the monk now. 'Soichi Heyashi? Here?'

The monk frowned. 'Yes,' he said. 'He is there.' And he pointed to the ornate, garlanded palanquin which Langford now saw contained a rectangular coffin.

PART THREE

ELEVEN

1

It was nearly ten p.m. when the Mercedes turned into Kobe's Sakaemachi Street. The rainswept road surface glistened in the chill glow of the street light as the car slowed to a crawl, stopping a few yards past the Daiwa Bank. When a dark, raincoated figure emerged from the shadows, the rear nearside door swung open. Moving quickly, the man got in, slamming the door as the Mercedes accelerated away.

Settling himself in the back seat, Gunning loosened his raincoat and took a pack of cigarettes from the pocket. 'You're punctual,' he said.

'I would prefer that you did not smoke.'

Gunning smiled. 'Terrible habit but I can't seem to kick it. Sorry.' The flame from his lighter filled the interior of the car with an eerie glow.

'Why did you request this meeting? You could have telephoned. You should know by now that I do not care for risks.'

'Nor do I, Mister Shiba. Which is why I needed to see you. We could have problems.'

'Well?'

Gunning glanced out of the side window. 'Where are we going?'

'He will simply drive us around Kobe,' said Shiba. 'What are these problems?'

'My people in Tokyo are worried. They've been getting some funny readings lately. According to their sources, the situation is – '

'Under control,' snapped Shiba. 'It is more than a pity that you cannot say the same.'

'As far as I know, everything's going according to plan.'

'Then your knowledge is clearly too limited to be of value. Your man was ambushed.'

'Ambushed?' Gunning started. 'Tasaki?'

'Of course – unless there is another interested party of whom we are not aware.'

'Is he dead?'

'No, I gather he survived. Of course, whether they will try again is another matter entirely and one to which you might give some attention.'

Gunning sucked thoughtfully at the cigarette. 'How do you know this?'

'I know many things, Mister Gunning.'

'Okay, here's something else you should know. Tokyo have decided that it's time the Japanese authorities were brought in – officially.'

'Who in Tokyo, pray?'

'The Ambassador, of course. Who else?'

'I was about to ask that very question.' Leaning forward, Shiba pressed a button so that the window opened a fraction to admit a stream of cold air. 'Important though your ambassador may be, he does not give me orders.'

'But Tasaki – '

'Can be safely left alone. You have only one function and you have yet to carry it out. Or perhaps the great United States has become impotent?'

'We're far from that,' rasped Gunning.

'Indeed? Then perhaps you will explain why it is that we are forced to depend on the resources of this Englishman?'

'Because your people loused it up, that's why. If you had kept Samwashima under control – '

'Enough.' Shiba held up his hand. 'I do not have time to waste arguing about the past.'

'Then let's argue about the future. The Ambassador has

laid it on the line: the time has come to call in the authorities. There's got to be official action, a properly co-ordinated operation.'

'Ah so, like your Watergate. Is that what he has in mind?'

'Listen, Mister Shiba, we've been falling over ourselves to do you a favour – '

'No, you listen to me.' He swung round, his expression bleak. 'It is I, Toshiro Shiba, who gives favours. The Japanese government depends on my goodwill and your country depends on the Tokyo administration. It is a carefully balanced structure. If too much pressure is exerted at a certain point, the structure collapses. Tasaki must be permitted to make the first move.'

'Then all hell could break loose.' Gunning drew on the cigarette. 'We have our contacts ... sources of information in Tokyo. Our people believe that Tasaki is going for a bloodless coup. There's a feeling that he'll have some kind of hold over the government, some kind of lever. We've no way of knowing just what it will be, but ...'

'Then you cannot act upon a mere assumption. Tell your Ambassador that he must leave this matter in my hands.'

'He may not choose to do that.'

'I suggest you inform him that he has no choice. Our dealings concern one objective and not until that has been realized can we develop the relationship. I trust I make myself clear, Mister Gunning?'

'It's gotten more complicated. Tasaki ...'

'Forget him.'

'I wish to Christ I could.' He stubbed out the cigarette and tried to decide whether to light another just for the hell of it.

'You can. Politically, Tasaki has no hope – unless the government move first. He has no ... no power-base, no real support.'

'I hope you're right.'

'Just leave him alone and he will burn himself out.

Shiba chuckled, softly. 'Of course, your Ambassador is quite right to be concerned. If Muga Tasaki were ever to achieve power, the American position in the Far East would be untenable.'

'I was beginning to think you didn't understand that.'

'You are foolish. What you do not understand is that if this Englishman is successful, Tasaki can be destroyed easily.'

'The same goes for you, Shiba. In fact, your position could look quite shaky, to say the least.'

'There you are wrong, my friend. I should take certain steps ...'

'You'd do a deal with Tasaki?'

'Of course. I should treat with the Devil himself if it suited my purposes. You should have realized that by now.'

'Maybe I should at that.' Gunning sighed and decided to light the cigarette. 'The other matter I have to discuss is the *Shimada Maru*.'

'I was under the impression that we had come to an understanding?'

'We did, yes. But I'm going to have to put in a report soon. I need an assurance that the ship won't be used until – '

'Do not concern yourself about it. The vessel is still fitting-out here in Kobe.'

'Still fitting-out? Your people have been busting a gut to get that boat ready and you know it. I've got to be able to tell my people that nothing will be done without inter-national agreement. Goddammit, the *Shimada Maru* filled with radioactive waste ... sailing across the world ...'

'Tell your people they need not worry.'

'I have to give an assurance.'

'Then give it.'

'Just like that? You expect me to put my neck on the block?'

'Why should I not expect that?' Shiba leaned forwards

286

and pressed the window button again. 'You are being well paid for your trouble. Or perhaps you feel that more is owed you?'

'It's small change by your standards, Shiba. But get this: if it ever comes to a straight choice between you and the United States ...'

Shiba began to laugh. 'Is the traitor about to oecome the heroic patriot? Have a care, Mister Gunning. Others have tried to betray me and failed.'

'Maybe the others weren't as well prepared as I could be.' Gunning stared out of the window for a moment. 'Okay, tell your man to stop. I'll get out here.'

'Before we part, I must know that we are agreed.'

'For the moment, yes.'

'Good. You may leave Tasaki to me. But you must keep your part of the bargain.'

'And the *Shimada Maru*?'

'Tell your people that nothing will happen. The ship has yet to undergo sea trials, so there is no problem. You have my word on that.'

'I wish I could trust it.'

'You, Mister Gunning, cannot afford to doubt the word of Toshiro Shiba. You have too much to lose ... too much to gain by trusting me.'

'Maybe.'

'No, certainly. Which brings me to my final point. When ... if, the Englishman returns – '

'He won't. He'll go to Hong Kong.'

'And then?'

Gunning shrugged. 'My people meet him and he gets paid off. He can't come near Japan. You know that.'

'But after Hong Kong, what happens to him ... and the girl?'

'How the hell should I ... Uh-uh, I get you. Sorry, no way.'

'But if he succeeds and returns with the evidence, he will know too much.'

287

'We're not even certain the photographs still exist.'

'I am certain,' said Shiba. 'And if this man finds them, he must be silenced.'

'In Hong Kong?'

'Why not? The location is immaterial.'

'I'll think about it.' Gunning rapped on the glass partition which separated them from the chauffeur and the Mercedes slowed, pulling into the kerb. 'Personally, I doubt that Langford will pose a problem.' He went to open the door but Shiba sat forward and stopped him.

'If the Englishman succeeds, I want him silenced, him and the girl. Then there can be no doubts.'

'Hong Kong is British territory. They're kinda stuffy – '

'The sum we agreed ...' Shiba leaned back in the seat. 'We shall double it.'

Gunning moistened his lips. 'It ... it could be difficult. I might not be able to do it myself.'

'You have people in Hong Kong. Issue an order. They will not question it. A man and a woman will simply vanish. No one will be interested.'

'I'll think about it.' Gunning opened the door. 'But after Langford ... we're through.'

Shiba nodded. 'I would not have it otherwise.'

2

The young monk in the brown robe came to the *sala*[1] and placed the earthenware dish of fruit on a low table. There was also a tall pitcher which Langford found contained crystal clear water, almost ice-cold.

'You have come a long way?' asked the monk, squatting cross-legged and staring at them, searchingly.

'Japan,' replied Langford, helping himself to the fruit.

'Yes.' The young monk nodded, thoughtfully. 'It is a long way.'

[1] *guesthouse.*

'About Soichi Heyashi,' began Langford. 'If I could – '
But the monk suddenly stood up, making the *wai* before
leaving.

'You must have patience,' said Yita, looking at him.
'They need time.'

'Don't we all.' Langford drank from the pitcher, wiping
his mouth on the back of his arm. 'What do you suppose
will happen?'

She shook her head. 'I do not know.'

'I thought you were supposed to be a Buddhist?'

'It is not the same here. The customs here are different.'

'But why won't they speak to us?' She didn't reply and
Langford lit a cigarette. It was nearly noon, curiously
silent and very hot when the group of monks in orange
robes walked slowly past the *sala* and peered in at them,
whispering among themselves.

Standing up, Langford watched the monks disappear
into one of the other buildings. The monastery certainly
possessed a dull, sepulchral atmosphere but the brightly-
coloured roof-tiles, the ornate gables, pointed peaks and
grotesque carvings all combined to give the *Wat* Keo an
extraordinary garishness which he disliked.

'You are not at peace,' said Yita, her voice very soft.
'You must calm yourself, Richard.'

'Just a few hours back, we very nearly entered your
precious *Nirvana*. I don't want them to have another
chance.'

'Those men cannot harm us now.'

'There may be others.' Langford stared into the trees
and grimaced as he caught sight of the monk in the brown
habit walking back towards the *sala*. 'Here comes Friar
Tuck again.'

Yita frowned. 'What is that?'

'Never mind.' Throwing away his cigarette, Langford
went to meet him. 'Look, we can't wait around here
forever,' he said, unable to conceal his irritation. The
young monk smiled.

'You come now. But she must stay here. Women are not

allowed within the precincts of the *bot*.' He looked at Langford, frowning. 'You have a jacket?'

'No. Why?'

The monk seemed puzzled. 'Why have you no luggage?'

'It was burnt.'

'I see. In that case ... perhaps it will not matter. Come.'

'I shall wait,' said Yita, seeing him glance round. 'It will be good for me to relax here.'

Langford opened his mouth to speak but thought better of it and followed the brown-robed monk into the sunlight. 'You're not a Thai,' he said, coming alongside him.

'No. I am what you would call an Anglo-Indian. But nationality, race, these things are not important to us. People come from all over the world to the *Wat* Keo to study. For Buddhists, it is a respected seat of learning.' He paused, looking down at Langford's feet. 'You will remove your shoes, please? You may take a pair of those sandals.' He watched him for a moment. 'You are about to enter the *bot*, the most sacred part of the monastery. We are at the boundary, you see?' And he pointed towards a number of carved stone obelisks. 'It is called the *baisema*. No woman must ever come inside it.'

They walked slowly across a paved courtyard and into a high, pillared hall which was cool, the air smelling strongly of joss sticks. Langford was reminded of Lim Mok's house, now suddenly filled with orphans. Then he became aware of the enormous, pot-bellied Buddha at the far end of the *bot* and stared up at it.

'The famous Green Buddha of Keo,' explained the monk. 'It is quite remarkable because it is carved from just one piece of obsidian.'

Langford nodded. 'Is it valuable?'

The monk smiled. 'One piece of obsidian nearly eight metres in height and so beautifully worked ... no, not valuable. Priceless. But come, we must go on.'

Langford followed the monk from the *bot* into another enclosed yard where a dozen or so orange-robed monks sat in a circle, their hands held out, palms upward.

290

'They are meditating,' explained his guide. 'And that building behind them is the *mondop* ... you would say library.'

Four more saffron-clad figures passed them in mute, unseeing silence, their bare feet making no sound on the warm stone.

'Why do you wear brown?' inquired Langford, as they approached a heavily gilded doorway.

'Because I am not a proper *bikku*, a proper monk. I am here only to study.' He watched Langford looking up at the gable with its curved points. 'Those are the *Nagas*. The Thais believe them to be the demi-gods of rain.'

'But you don't?'

'I am not a Thai. You wait here, please.' And he gestured towards a carved stone bench supported by two bronze lion-dogs.

Sitting in the shade, Langford was about to light a cigarette when the monk returned.

'The abbot will see you now,' he said, leading the way into a long, gloomy corridor in which the walls and ceilings were decorated with inlaid gold and silver. Then they came to a heavy, studded door which the monk pushed open, gesturing Langford to enter.

The door closed behind him with a sharp, metallic snap and Langford stared round the room, his lips forming a slow smile

'You are surprised?'

'Yes.' And Langford nodded at the small, wizened figure standing by the window, the sun shining through his delicate saffron robes.

The room in which he found himself was starkly modern, a sudden and unexpected contrast with everything Langford had seen at the monastery. The highly-polished teak floor was like the mirror-surface of a mill-pond, reflecting a very superior executive-type desk, a bank of modern filing cabinets and a range of bookshelves.

'You will be seated?' The abbot pointed to a black leather chair in front of the desk. Then he smiled, his walnut-like face strangely animated so that it was at once calm and yet full of vitality. 'You have brought death with you,' he said. 'I am sorry.'

Langford frowned. 'I have?'

The old man nodded and lowered himself into the chair behind the desk. 'There is talk in the village of terrorists, of gunfire and a burnt-out motor car. Yours?'

'In a way, yes.' Langford had pulled the packet of cigarettes from his pocket and was hesitating, awkwardly.

'Please, do smoke. I do not but others here do and there is no prohibition. We are very liberal in most things.'

'You're the abbot?'

'I am the head of the *wat*, yes. Abbot is really a Christian term.' He paused, rubbing his eyes before taking a pair of thin, steel-framed spectacles from the desk and carefully putting them on, his gnarled and twisted fingers trembling slightly. 'I believe I know the purpose of your visit, Mister ...?'

'Langford, Richard Langford. I've come from England ... from Japan.'

'Yes, I know.'

'It seems I arrived just too late.'

The old monk stared at him for a time. 'Who is the woman?'

'She's Japanese. Her name's Yit ... Kimiko Izumi.'

'Yes.' He continued to stare, the sun glinting on the round lenses of the steel spectacles. 'Buddhists believe that in order to achieve *Nirvana*, one must follow the Eightfold Path.' He paused, meditatively. 'One of the precepts ... one of the stepping-stones of that path is Truth, Mister Langford. You seek the truth by coming here, yes?'

'So Heyashi told you about the photographs?'

Ignoring the question, the head monk continued, his voice low. 'The problem about the truth which you seek is the purpose for which it will be used. The truth, Mister Langford, is not unlike a picture. It may be concealed, hidden from view. Or it can be revealed, put on display for

292

all to see in order that it may be judged. Do you understand me?'

'Yes, I think so. The whole point of my coming here is to expose what happened.'

'What did happen?' said the monk, gently fingering his saffron robe as if he were feeling the material for the first time.

Langford shook his head. 'I don't know. Heyashi knew. And there are the photographs, of course.'

'Yes.'

'You have got the photographs?' said Langford.

'They are here, yes. But tell me, the people who attacked you on your way to Suk Chiang ... they are all dead?'

'Yes.'

'And by your hand?'

'I had no option.' But the old man merely smiled.

'We always have options, Mister Langford. What you are saying is that you refused the option of death.' He smiled slightly. 'But I think you misunderstand me. I know only too well that the will to live is powerful. Were it not so, man would perhaps not have survived as a species. However, to return to the purpose of your visit. The photographs are in the *mondop*. They could be released ...'

'You want money?'

The old man chuckled. 'Please, hear me out. I was going to say that they could be destroyed.'

'I want to take them back to Japan,' said Langford, suddenly aware that the ash from his cigarette now littered the highly-polished floor. 'They will be used as evidence of war crimes. I believe that some of the people in the pictures are still alive. They can be identified and punished.'

The old man raised his eyebrows and rubbed his hands together as if moulding a piece of soft clay. 'Punished?' he demanded, sharply. 'What for?'

'War crimes.'

293

'But war itself is a crime, Mister Langford. Are all who participated in the crime to be punished? Soldiers and statesmen? The workers and civilians who may have only supported the war by condoning it, but supported it nonetheless, are they all to be punished?'

Langford drew a sharp breath, stubbing the cigarette against the pack before pocketing it. 'It wasn't my war. Nor yours. But Heyashi kept those pictures for a purpose. We ... *I* believe that he intended them to be published so that the truth would come out. Even wars have rules and the Japanese broke the rules. I think it's a reasonable assumption that if Heyashi were alive, he would have approved.'

'We believe that all life is sacred, Mister Langford. You yourself have killed ... very recently.'

'It was self-defence.'

'That does not matter. If I shoot at you and miss, and you then shoot, killing me, you are the one who is responsible for my death. Your reasons for killing me are immaterial, as is your method. You have taken life and that is wrong.'

Langford sighed, wearily. 'Look, I can't argue the point because we see things quite differently. Besides, there isn't the time.'

'The photographs have existed for over thirty years, Mister Langford. And as for your reasonable assumption about Heyashi's attitude ... Who can tell? The man who brought those photographs out of Burma died many years ago.'

Langford sank back in the chair. 'I see.'

'I doubt that,' said the old man, shaking his head and smiling, wistfully. 'The man who walked from Burma arrived here spiritually and physically exhausted. Only one thing sustained him: a desire for vengeance, a burning hatred. I do not normally see casual visitors to the *wat*, Mister Langford. But I felt compelled to see you, so that I could explain. Now I find myself faced with a decision. Should I release the photographs so that they may be used

294

to punish men for crimes committed so many years ago?'

'I think you have a moral obligation to hand over those pictures,' said Langford.

'You do?' The head monk regarded him for a moment, the pupils of his eyes like little black discs stuck to the lenses of the steel-framed spectacles. 'I also have other obligations. Am I to be responsible for adding fuel to the fires of revenge which you seek to re-kindle?'

'Justice is a better word,' said Langford.

'Now you play at semantics. But I do not blame you.' He rose from his seat. 'You are only the messenger. You have nothing to fear.'

Langford also stood. 'It's very important that I get those pictures back to Japan as quickly as possible.'

'We shall see. You will return to the *sala*, Mister Langford, and I will send word of my decision.'

'I don't want to be difficult but I've come a long way to get those pictures. And many people have died because of them. You spoke about me re-kindling the fire of revenge but that's not true. The fire never went out. It's been smouldering for years.'

The monk nodded, gravely. 'Wise words, Mister Langford. And that being so, I have even more reason to fear the heat of the flames.'

'But nothing will happen here. It won't affect you, the monastery won't be involved. Please, can't you see …?'

'You will return to the *sala*,' commanded the monk. 'I need time to decide.'

Langford sighed. 'I seem to have no choice.'

'None,' he agreed. 'Now go.'

Langford went to the door and then turned. 'You seem to set great store by the truth. But if you keep those photographs, you'll not only help to perpetuate a massive cover-up. You could be responsible for many more people dying. And why? You have nothing to fear, nothing to lose.'

'On the contrary, Mister Langford, I have everything to lose. And as for fear … yes, I confess to being afraid. But not in the way you mean. I am too old to fear death. It is the consequences which I fear.' The old man walked slowly across the room, the sandals on his feet making a faint plopping sound against the floor. Then he stopped and stared into Langford's face. 'I told you that the man who came out of Burma is dead. But that is only true in the Buddhist sense. Soichi Heyashi was re-born. It was his desire for vengeance, his bitter hatred which died when the man became truly enlightened. Or so I believed. Now … now I think I may have been proved wrong.'

Langford frowned. 'Heyashi is still alive, isn't he?'

'Yes, Mister Langford. And he stands before you now, a condemned man.'

3

'I told you never to come here.'

'And I don't care any more, Meyrick. I want a divorce.'

'Okay, so you want a divorce. You can have one. But when we get back to New York. Then I'll see the lawyers.'

'Meyrick, are you in some kind of trouble?'

'It's none of your Goddamn business.'

'But you are my husband.'

'Jesus, that's rich.'

'What did those two cops want?'

'Nothing. It was just routine.'

'Then why did you tell them that you're a – ?'

'Will you shut your mouth, Lois?'

'Please, Meyrick, just tell me what's going on.'

'You should care. Now get out, will you? This just happens to be my office.'

'Oh my God, why won't you confide in me? What happened to you, Meyrick, happened to lots of other guys.'

'I don't want to talk about it, Lois.'

'And something happened in Paris, didn't it?'

'Nothing happened in Paris.'

'You're scared, Meyrick. I can tell.'

'Okay, so you can tell. Now just go back to the hotel and we'll talk about it this evening.'

'You mean that? Really talk, Meyrick?'

'Sure, this evening. Now I have work, so ... please, Lois?'

When the door swung open, Peggy Ashmore flicked the switch of the intercom and smiled as Lois Hewens swept unseeingly past her.

4

The bell began to toll as night came and the monk in the brown robes arrived with a tray of food. Langford spoke to him but the man didn't reply.

'Have they taken vows of silence?' Langford growled as the Anglo-Indian disappeared into the darkness.

'Something is wrong,' said Yita.

The bell continued its tolling, a steady, rhythmic sound, somehow muted but penetrating still.

Some people came up from the village, standing just outside the *baisema* until a group of monks went out to them and seemed to send them away. Then the monks went quickly into the *bot*, closing the heavy doors behind them.

The sound of the great bell of the *Wat* Keo continued to echo in the darkness, drowning even the insistent throbbing of the cicadas with its melancholy. Studying his watch, Langford noted that the bell sounded every ten seconds, each ear-splitting vibration scarcely dying away before it struck again.

Richard Langford finished his last cigarette, nursing the butt in his fingers until there was nothing left to smoke. Then he swore aloud, Yita staring at him, her face expressionless in the yellow glow of the oil lamps which hung from the roof of the *sala*.

'Do you think he's finally died?' said Langford, sighing.

297

'I cannot know. If it is written ...'

'There's no one about.'

'They are all in the temple. I saw them go in.'

'Well, something's happened but I'm damned if I know what.' He began pacing the small pavilion, unconsciously nodding in time with the ringing of the bell.

The rain came suddenly, a jarring deluge which pounded on the roof of the *sala*, pouring from the gutters and rushing in torrents along channels cut into the ground by the stone paths. And throughout the downpour, the great bell continued to toll, a sombre counterpoint to rhythm of the rain drumming on the gaudy tiles. Visibility was reduced almost to nothing. Standing in the *sala* and staring out at the wall of water, Langford had a feeling of almost complete isolation.

The cloudburst died away as swiftly as it had come. The skies cleared and the *Wat* Keo was bathed in the silvery-pale moonlight. Peering towards the main buildings, Langford tried to decide where the bell was located but it was impossible to tell. There was no sign of life anywhere, not even the tiniest flicker of lamplight. It was then he realized that he was still wearing the sandals given him by the Anglo-Indian monk.

'I'm going to get my shoes back,' he told Yita, and strode out towards the *baisema*, the discordant resonance of the bell pounding in his ears.

He was rather surprised to find that his shoes were still there, even if they were full of rainwater. Picking them up, he let the water drain out. Not until the last drop had spattered onto the paving did Langford become aware that the bell had stopped.

The silence was almost tangible. Even the cicadas seemed to take time to reassert their mordant throbbing as he walked back to the *sala*. Yita was waiting, her face still expressionless.

'Now what?' said Langford, doing up his shoes. But she didn't reply and after two more attempts at conversation, he gave up, sitting on the steps of the pavilion and staring

298

into the night. He needed a cigarette.

'You will come now.' The monk in the brown habit had suddenly appeared. Seeing Langford reach for the sandals, he shook his head. 'You will not need those. And the woman is to accompany you.'

There was hostility and bitterness in the man's voice and Langford peered at him, inquiringly. 'Why was the bell ringing?' But the monk didn't reply as he led them from the *sala* and away from the main buildings. 'Where are we going?'

'You will follow me,' said the monk, without looking round.

They walked for about ten minutes. By keeping his eye on the gilded *chedi* which glowed in the moonlight, Langford knew they were walking around the perimeter of the *wat*. Then they came to another building, almost a ruin, but there was a light glowing inside and the monk stopped a few feet from the doorway.

'You are to go in,' he said, immediately turning on his heel and retracing his steps.

Langford entered cautiously. Then he saw Heyashi.

The old man was seated cross-legged on a small, crumbling stone dais, two oil lamps suspended almost immediately above him so that his face was in shadow until Yita and Langford went closer.

'This is the old *viharn* of the *Wat* Keo,' said Heyashi, distantly. 'It is no longer used and I thought it the right place for us to speak together.' He peered at them through his steel-framed spectacles, the shadowy glow of the oil lamps making his wizened face look even older. 'When I arrived here, I was possessed by evil, a prisoner of my ambition for revenge. It took many years of study and meditation for me to overcome that hatred. But I succeeded and so it was that I became head of the *wat*, the man you call an abbot. I did not seek charge of the *Wat* Keo because I never considered myself worthy but the elders thought otherwise. Now you have come here and given life to all that I believed was dead. The great bell is

299

sounded only when the head of the *wat* dies. Or when he asks to be released, as I have now done. It continues to toll until a successor has been chosen.' He paused, swaying slightly. 'I now rank with the lowest monks in the *wat* ... by choice, of course. I could have continued but my conscience forbade it. It would have been a denial of the teachings of the Lord Buddha, a negation of the truth.'

Yita said something in Japanese but he merely smiled.

'Forgive me, child, but I have forgotten my mother tongue. You said something about the truth, I think?'

'I said that we have come for the truth, Heyashi-*san*.'

'Yes, that I understand.' He turned and from behind the stone dais produced a battered tin box which he placed in front of them.

'The photographs?' said Langford, quietly.

'Yes. I have taken them unto myself again. They are now my possession and I may do with them as I choose. But there is one exception: I may not keep them. Our sacred laws permit only the barest essentials but the new head monk has given me special dispensation so that these images of the past may be disposed of once and for all.'

There was a long silence before Langford spoke. 'Are you going to let me take them back to Japan?'

Heyashi shrugged and removing his spectacles, peered at Yita. 'You are Kenji Izumi's daughter?'

'He was my step-father, Heyashi-*san*.'

He nodded, knowingly. 'Your mother ... is she still alive?'

'Yes.'

'Good.' Heyashi replaced his spectacles again and looked at Langford. 'What makes you so concerned with the photographs?'

'It's a long story.'

'We have time,' said Heyashi, lightly, but Langford shook his head.

'No, I'm afraid that's the one thing we don't have.'

'Then you must explain to me.'

300

'I'm not sure that you would be able to understand it,' Langford said. 'There's a lot of it that I don't.'

'First you must tell me your story, Mister Langford. Then perhaps I shall tell you about the photographs.'

5

'There are two aspects of the operation which concern me,' said Whitaker, leafing through his notes. 'The first is the loading of the waste.'

Toshiro Shiba extracted a red-edged folder from his attaché case and began turning the pages, his forehead creasing as he frowned. 'What is it that concerns you?'

'The data supplied by the people at Kyomo leads me to believe that a high proportion of the irradiated fuel being stored there could be in an unstable condition. While it remains in the cooling ponds, it's relatively safe. But when it's transferred into the flasks designed by Bailey ...'

'There is a design fault with the flasks?' said Shiba, looking up.

'Not as far as I can tell. They're bigger than I would have liked, eight metres by three metres, but that's not the problem. The moment the waste leaves the cooling ponds, it will begin to heat up – decay heat. Bailey has made allowance for this by fitting exterior vanes to the flasks which will allow some of the heat to dissipate until they can be coupled into the ship's cooling circuitry. My concern is that Bailey's calculations give you just eight hours in which the flasks can remain safely independent of any external cooling mechanism. If there's a hold up of any sort, some difficulty with the transportation to the ship ... a breakdown on one of the cranes ... eight hours isn't very long, Mister Shiba. There are thirteen flasks in all and if just one were to over-heat and explode ...'

Shiba nodded. 'The flasks are already at Kyomo and will not be filled until the ship is ready to receive them. As each one goes aboard, so the next will leave the power station and another will be filled. At no time will there be more than one flask in transit.'

'You've already grasped the problem.' Whitaker smiled. 'In that case, I can see no reason for delaying the sea trials.'

'The trials will be incorporated in the voyage to Kyomo,' said Shiba. 'Captain Umezu informs me that the vessel can be ready to sail within twenty-four hours. There will still be people working on board, painters, engineers and so on, but ...' Shiba stroked his chin, thoughtfully. 'I propose that you sail with the ship, Professor. Then there will remain only the matter of the certification which the government require.'

'That was my second point,' replied Whitaker.

'Ah so. What is the difficulty?'

Whitaker cleared his throat. 'Mister Shiba, I could certify that the measures taken for the protection of the irradiated fuel are more than adequate. If they were land-based, I would have no hesitation in signing the clearance certificate required by your government. What worries me is the extent to which Doctor Bailey's ultra-protective methods may have affected the stability of the ship.'

Shiba's expression hardened. 'While I have great respect for your expertise as a nuclear physicist, Professor, you are not a naval architect and are not ... cannot be expected to be competent in these matters.'

'Sir, boats have been an interest of mine for – '

'Boats?' Shiba spat the word out with almost vicious contempt. 'The *Shimada Maru* is not a boat, Professor Whitaker. It is the biggest merchant ship the world has ever seen.' The Japanese glared across the cabin.

'Mister Shiba, I believe that the *Shimada Maru* would be unstable in a heavy sea. What is more, I have talked with Captain Umezu and he at least agrees that the handling of the vessel in a beam-sea, for example, could be extremely difficult.'

302

Toshiro Shiba removed his horn-rimmed glasses and leaned forwards, his round face suddenly drawn. 'Are you now saying that you will not sign the certificate required by the government?'

'Not until I have seen an independent survey of the *Shimada Maru*.'

'You are exceeding your brief,' snapped Shiba, replacing his glasses. 'Who do you wish to carry out this survey?'

'I don't know,' said Whitaker. 'There must be firms in Japan … here in Kobe, who are competent. You probably know them already.'

Shiba seemed to relax. 'You would be happy to accept any firm provided it is not part of the Shimada Corporation, is that so?'

'Please, Mister Shiba, don't misunderstand me. I don't doubt your integrity for one moment. Any independent survey …'

Shiba stood up and nodded. 'Then it will be arranged, Professor. And you need have no fears. The *Shimada Maru* has been very carefully designed. There is no danger. I do assure you of that.' He walked across the cabin and picked up the telephone.

'It doesn't work,' said Whitaker. 'And while you're here, Mister Shiba, I may as well tell you that I don't take kindly to being held incommunicado aboard this ship. I want to telephone my wife in Santa Barbara. And I want to do some shopping.'

'I am sorry.' Shiba replaced the receiver and appeared upset. 'I shall instruct Mister Samwashima to –'

'No, just tell him to mind his own business. I'm a little old for chaperones.'

Toshiro Shiba moistened his lips. 'Our security arrangements –'

'Are ridiculous. I have security clearance from the British and American authorities. If you think I'm a risk …'

'No, of course not, Professor.' He drew a sharp breath. 'I can see that we have been inconsiderate. I am sorry. But you will accept a car and a driver? We are some distance from the centre here.'

'Yes, thank you.'

'Good.' And Shiba nodded, smiling affably.

6

'It happened at Mogok,' said Heyashi.

TWELVE

1

On Thursday, August 3, 1944, the youngest Major-General in the Japanese army arrived at Mandalay, the ancient capital of Burma. When he stepped out of the aircraft from Rangoon into the dusty, suffocating heat, he was met by the small group of officers who were to make up his staff. They all bowed deeply and one of their number, *Tai-i* Soichi Heyashi, delivered a short address, congratulating *Shosho* Muga Tasaki on his recent promotion and on his fortieth birthday which coincided with his arrival.

As the small convoy of cars drove from the grass airstrip to the Japanese HQ buildings on the outskirts of the city, Heyashi and the other staff officers speculated as to the purpose of Tasaki's visit to Burma. The newly-promoted Major-General had been sent up from Malaya where he had played a significant part in the defeat of the Allied forces and an air of mystery surrounded his transfer. It was anticipated that Tasaki would brief them once they arrived at Headquarters but there was no briefing and they were excluded from meetings which the Major-General held with the local commander. When Heyashi ventured to request orders, he was told to wait and see.

The period of waiting lasted four days until the Monday, August 7, when they were ordered to pack their kit and prepare for a journey by train up to Shwebo, some eighty miles north of Mandalay. The train, consisting of two engines and seven closed cattle trucks filled with Allied prisoners of war, arrived the following morning. A

305

proper passenger carriage was hitched up to the rear and the train pulled out. The journey took nearly five hours. They were frequently pushed on to sidings so that south-bound trains could pass and could never exceed fifteen m.p.h. so the guards sitting on the front engine could scan the track for mines. It seemed to Heyashi and the others an ideal opportunity for Tasaki to give them their orders. But he remained silent and no one felt confident enough to ask what was going on.

The train pulled into Shwebo shortly after four o'clock in the afternoon and was met by a detachment of infantry under the command of a young *Shoi-i*[1] named Kenji Izumi. In response to Tasaki's orders, the Allied prisoners were taken from the train, formed into ranks and counted. There were three hundred and twelve in all, a mixed bag of British, Australians, New Zealanders, Canadians and Americans. Using Heyashi as an interpreter, Tasaki told the prisoners that they would be marched across country to their new home. It would not, he explained, be an easy march but once they had reached the camp, there would be ample food and opportunity to rest. He concluded by saying that for every one prisoner who left the column — there was no pretence that they could be adequately guarded during the march — ten would be executed on arrival at the new camp. It was then that the senior PoW officer, an Australian Colonel, stepped from the ranks, saluted Tasaki and speaking through Heyashi, said that it was the duty of every prisoner of war to attempt escape and that the counter-measures proposed would be a flagrant breach of the Geneva Conventions. At first, Tasaki seemed amused. Then he ordered the Australian officer to be beaten with the wooden staves carried by the guards. Six of them came forward and within a matter of minutes, the Colonel was lying on the ground, his head and face severely lascerated. The column marched out of Shwebo half an hour later and when the first brief halt was

[1] *Second Lieutenant.*

called, the Australian had already died.

The march through the jungle proved arduous for captors and captives alike but in spite of the death of the Australian, a strange kind of comradeship seemed to spring up, the guards sometimes even helping men who had fallen. Tasaki's staff were still in ignorance of their final destination and some, including Heyashi, were displeased at the prospect of being attached to a PoW camp. All they knew for certain was that the column was headed for the Irrawaddy river, a fact which most of the prisoners had already grasped. What would happen next was still a matter for conjecture.

Although it was the rainy season, there was comparatively little rain and ground conditions were reasonably firm, but it still took nearly five days to reach the Irrawaddy and the encampment where a number of motor launches were waiting to ferry them across the river. The crossing took some eight hours to accomplish. By the time all the Allied prisoners and the Japanese were on the eastern bank, it was pitch dark. But there was to be no respite and the column moved off almost immediately. There was some grumbling among the prisoners but it was soon clear that the going would be easier. They were on a rough road now, the jungle on either side slowly thinning as they climbed into the hills.

When dawn came, Tasaki informed his staff that they would reach their destination by nightfall, a small town called Mogok. Captain Heyashi then inquired the purpose of the expedition but the Major-General merely smiled.

The column arrived at Mogok as darkness fell. It was teeming with rain and there was no shelter for the prisoners, many of whom were utterly exhausted. Tasaki and his staff comandeered a number of flimsy huts, sending out guards to scour the town for food. There was precious little to be had but the Japanese officers contrived to eat a reasonable meal and none showed any concern that both their own men and the Allied prisoners were without proper shelter or sustenance.

307

The column marched out of Mogok at first light, heading south-west along a well-used track which led down into a valley so that they all saw the prison compound long before they reached it. There was a high, barbed wire perimeter fence surrounding clusters of crude huts. On the far side of the fence was a small complex of buildings, some of stone but most constructed from timber and corrugated iron sheeting. Beyond them was what appeared to be a limestone quarry.

As soon as they entered the camp, it became obvious that it was already overcrowded with prisoners who were being used as forced labour. Conditions were appalling. The ground was inches deep in thick, viscous mud, there was no adequate drainage and sanitation was virtually non-existent. Tasaki immediately ordered a full parade at which the prisoners brought from Shwebo were counted. There were three hundred and eleven, of whom forty-eight were unable to stand. True to his promise, the Major-General selected ten of the weakest men who were immediately shot as punishment for the death of the Australian Colonel. The Allied prisoners were then ordered to construct huts and told that they would begin work the following morning.

At a meeting held in the command post, Tasaki and his staff met the Japanese officer in charge of the camp. Only then did they learn that it was not a limestone quarry. The place to which they had come was the Ba Wan mine, one of the most important mines in an area of Burma world famous for rubies. And the man responsible for the day-to-day working of the mine was a full colonel in the dreaded *Kempei Tai*, the Japanese equivalent of the German *Geheime Staatspolizei* or Gestapo. His name was Toshiro Shiba.

The Ba Wan Mining Company had been sequestrated in 1942 but was largely left to run itself until late in 1943 when the Japanese grasped the commercial possibilities of the mine. A semi-retired officer had been put in charge and he brought in the first PoW labour, mostly British captured in Singapore. Conditions during this initial period were tolerable and work proceeded at an almost gentle pace. Then, in May 1944, Colonel Shiba took over command. More prisoners were shipped in and working hours increased. Conditions steadily worsened. Rations were cut to the bare minimum. There were virtually no medical facilities to treat an average of two hundred men suffering from malaria, dysentery, leptospirosis and festering ulcers.

The arrival of Major-General Tasaki's column brought the number of Allied prisoners to about seven hundred, crammed into a camp originally designed to accommodate two hundred. The senior PoW officer, an American Air Force Colonel named Jensen, and a British Royal Army Medical Corps doctor, Major Stallard, drew up a long list of requirements ranging from proper accommodation to medical supplies and a substantial increase in daily rations. The list was duly presented to Colonel Shiba whose response was to order a full parade of all Allied prisoners, including the sick and dying. Jensen and Stallard were then told to kneel in front of Shiba who delivered a long harangue before taking his sword and decapitating the American Air Force officer with one stroke.

In spite of his medical training, Major Stallard fainted on the spot, a reaction which so enraged Shiba that four *Kempei Tai* guards were detailed to bring the British doctor round and then bayonet him to death. The orders were carried out with some enthusiasm, the guards using their weapons with skill. Stallard took a long time to die and suffered horribly. Shiba then commanded that the bodies were to be left where they lay as a reminder not to ask for the impossible.

As the weeks went by, Shiba's reign of terror continued unabated. Rations were further reduced to a daily quota of three hundred grams of rice per man but as the sacks were invariably pilfered by the guards, the actual weight issued was seldom more than two hundred. It would have been grossly insufficient for men simply doing nothing and the inmates of Ba Wan were being worked for twelve hours a day. The resulting malnutrition and disease caused hideous suffering and by the middle of October, 1944, an average of fifteen prisoners were dying every day. A portion of the camp had been set aside for the sick but it was in no sense a hospital because there was no equipment, no drugs and not even the most basic field dressings. It was known to the prisoners as Death Row.

After Jensen's execution, the position of senior PoW officer was taken by an Australian, Lieutenant-Colonel Clarke. In civilian life, he had been a university lecturer in oriental studies and had the advantage of speaking fluent Japanese. By dint of crafty persuasion, Clarke managed to obtain some medical supplies and an issue of clothing – many of the prisoners were now either in rags or almost naked. Thanks to Clarke's efforts, conditions showed a slight improvement because the Australian had struck a bargain: more efficient working of the mine in exchange for the so-called concessions of essential medical supplies.

Acting on a warning by the four doctors in the camp, Clarke went direct to Major-General Tasaki and demanded the time and the equipment for the construction of proper latrines. A small stream ran past the site and some Royal Engineers had drawn up a plan showing how the water might be diverted through a series of ditches to provide reasonably hygienic sanitation. Tasaki merely laughed. But Colonel Shiba, incensed that the Australian had gone over his head, ordered Clarke to be placed in the *boiler*, a box constructed from sheets of corrugated iron, just three feet square.

Clarke was already a sick man when he was put into the *boiler* and by the time he was released, seven days later, he was unable to walk and lived just long enough to learn that what he told Tasaki was about to come true. There was an outbreak of cholera in the camp.

The epidemic raged for nearly four weeks. More than two hundred Allied prisoners died, work on the Ba Wan ruby mine came to a virtual standstill and the courier who arrived every week to collect the haul of gems went away empty-handed. Both Tasaki and Shiba ranted and raged at the few prisoners just about capable of work but not until a number of *Kempei Tai* guards went down with the disease did they take remedial action. Medical supplies were brought up to the camp, bodies were systematically cremated, infected huts burnt and sanitary conditions improved. The number of prisoners had now dwindled to a mere two hundred – some five hundred officers and men having either died from overwork, malnutrition and disease, or been executed. It was time to renew the labour force and in response to Tasaki's request, a batch of four hundred Allied prisoners arrived at Ba Wan on Christmas Eve, 1944.

The camp had been enlarged beyond the original perimeter fence and the latest senior PoW officer, Brigadier Walter Stuggard, a New Zealander, remarked that conditions didn't seem too bad. He had a lot to learn.

Christmas Day was spent organizing the camp and Stuggard carried out a thorough inspection. Then Colonel Shiba ordered him to draw up a list of prisoners who should be taken from Ba Wan and put into the hospital in nearby Mogok. By the time Stuggard had found out that there was no hospital in Mogok, it was too late. He had already supplied the list of names and in response to his questions, was told that he had misunderstood. The sick men, said Shiba, would be taken to Mandalay. Brigadier Stuggard was more than sceptical about the ability of many of them to withstand such an arduous journey but he was powerless to intervene and two hundred and eight Allied prisoners, half of them carried on crude stretchers, left Ba Wan the day after Boxing Day.

The column was escorted by a company of *Kempei Tai* guards under the command of Lieutenant Izumi. Acting on the written orders of Colonel Shiba – orders which had been countersigned by Tasaki – they marched away from the camp, through Mogok and headed towards the Irrawaddy, halting about an hour before sunset in a large clearing. Sentries armed with light machine guns were posted around the clearing and Izumi carried out an inspection which revealed that two men had died. He then ordered those prisoners capable of lifting a shovel to go some distance from the clearing and dig a grave in order that the dead might be buried decently. Twelve men volunteered and were marched away. In their absence, the *Kempei Tai* guards went among the remainder, one hundred and ninety-four in all, and systematically bayoneted each man to death. The grave-diggers were similarly dealt with on their return to the clearing. Lieutenant Izumi and his men marched back to Ba Wan the following day.

Puzzled by the quick return of the Japanese and rumours brought into Ba Wan by some of the Burmese labourers employed in the mine, Brigadier Stuggard saw Shiba and demanded an explanation. He was informed that an escort had come to meet the column and that the sick prisoners would be well on their way to Mandalay. Throughout this interview, which Heyashi attended, Shiba was so polite, even cordial, that Stuggard became suspicious and when he returned to his quarters, asked for a volunteer to carry out a search along the road leading from the camp.

Perimeter security was now virutally non-existent. The camp had sprawled outwards and, as the Japanese had soon realized, the jungle was an efficient deterrent in itself. But for someone wanting to leave and intending to return, there was no great problem.

There were several volunteers and Stuggard chose two men, a Scot named Robertson and a Canadian called Hoskiss. The two left Ba Wan just after sunset, keeping close to the rough road until they reached Mogok which they skirted because it was known that the Japanese made use of the small town as a brothel. Then they continued and would have missed the clearing in which the massacre had taken place but for the noise of the wild dogs gorging themselves on the corpses.

Both men were stunned at what they saw, the whole ghastly scene of carnage bathed in the moonlight. Robertson screamed and ran into the jungle. Hoskiss started to go after him but gave up when he could no longer hear the man's demented cries. Robertson was never seen again but Hoskiss walked slowly back to Ba Wan, arriving a good hour after sun-rise by which time the working parties were already at the mine. Incredibly, none of the Japanese guards stopped him as he walked through the camp, eyes glazed. From the compound, he stumbled slowly along the worn track leading to the mine. Still none of the guards appeared to notice the late arrival but the other prisoners did and attempted to stop him. It was no use. The man was in deep shock, probably even clinically insane. He picked up one of the long-handled shovels used by the prisoners and rushed at a Japanese *Gunso*.[1]

Before anyone – fellow-prisoners or the Japanese – could react, Hoskiss had felled the man with one blow and then killed him by smashing the blade of the shovel into his face again and again before he was restrained.

Retribution was swift. The working parties were marched back to the camp where Hoskiss was bound with rope and hung over a fire in front of all the prisoners. Guards were posted everywhere, their machine-guns trained on the Allied ranks while men of the *Kempei Tai* goaded the trussed and screaming Canadian with the tips of their bayonets. When he lost consciousness, buckets of water were used to bring him round so that the torture could begin again, and continue throughout that night. All the prisoners were kept standing at attention and those who collapsed from sheer exhaustion were subjected to merciless beatings with wooden staves or rifle butts.

At sunrise, Tasaki and Shiba appeared, both officers immaculately turned out in their olive-green service dress, complete with swords. Hoskiss was cut down, the ropes untied and his blood-caked body laid on the ground. He

---

[1] *Sergeant.*

was still alive and after several buckets of water had been thrown over him, was eventually persuaded to kneel. Then Tasaki came forward, unsheathed his sword and attempted to sever the man's head.

The first blow missed and Hoskiss let out a high-pitched scream as the razor-sharp blade sliced into his shoulder. As he slumped forwards, Tasaki struck again but it took two more swipes before the Canadian's head finally rolled from his body. The corpse was then disembowelled and subjected to the most bestial mutilation.

The murder of Hoskiss was a watershed. There was no longer any pretence on either side and throughout the first two months of 1945, there were executions every day, usually of men too sick to work but sometimes as punishment for the most trivial offences. The executions invariably took place at sunrise and were usually watched by both Shiba and Tasaki. In a number of cases, prisoners hurled themselves into the latrines to drown. Others simply lay down and died or collapsed, to be beaten to death by the *Kempei Tai*.

Towards the end of February, the camp was struck by malaria. The disease did not affect the Japanese who had ample supplies of quinine but the prisoners fell sick in droves and Brigadier Stuggard begged Shiba for medical supplies. The Japanese refused and immediately ordered a general parade of the prisoners at which Stuggard was flogged until he became unconscious. In order to further humiliate the senior PoW officer, a number of Japanese guards defecated and urinated on the Brigadier's body.

For the only surviving doctor among the prisoners, Pik Heergren, a regular officer in the Dutch army, the outrageous treatment of Brigadier Stuggard was the last straw. Throwing caution to the winds, Heergren broke into the Japanese medical stores and looted everything he and two volunteers could carry. Knowing what the consequences of this action were likely to be, Heergren and his helpers buried most of the stolen medical supplies, retaining just enough quinine to dose those most in need.

But however vivid the Dutchman's imagination, he could never have foreseen the events of the next twenty-four hours.

Brigadier Stuggard had recovered consciousness to find himself dressed in strange clothes. Although extremely weak, he questioned Heergren and learned what had taken place, including the details of the Dutchman's raid on the medical stores. Before this conversation could be concluded, Japanese guards came and dragged Stuggard across the compound to Shiba's office. The Brigadier had reconciled himself to torture, perhaps even summary execution and was amazed when Shiba not only asked him to sit but even gave him whisky. He was all smiles as he explained that in view of the theft of Imperial Japanese supplies, he would be forced to take special measures to ensure that sick prisoners-of-war would be spared suffering. Stuggard was perplexed and worried. Leaving the whisky untouched, he returned to the compound to discover that Shiba's idea of sparing suffering was to have the guards bayonet all those too sick to stand to attention. And those who did manage to stand were ordered back to work. The so-called hospital section was closed and Shiba rounded off the day by ordering Heergren's execution – not at sunrise, as had been usual, but immediately.

Another general parade was called and Shiba, dressed in sweat-stained shirt and breeches, waited for the two guards who had been sent to fetch Heergren. The minutes ticked by but there was no sign of either the guards or their victim and Shiba began shouting orders. Before anyone could react, the Dutchman finally appeared, alone.

There was a gasp of surprise from the Allied ranks and even the Japanese were clearly amazed as the Dutch doctor, immaculately dressed in a uniform which he had somehow managed to preserve intact, marched across the parade ground, a red bundle gripped tightly in his left hand.

When he reached Brigadier Stuggard, he halted,

315

executed a smart left-turn and saluted. He then turned about and saluted Shiba whose only reaction was to stare, open-mouthed.

All eyes were on the Dutchman now as he took the red bundle from his left hand, kissed it and then opened it out. It was the Dutch flag. When he had wrapped the ensign around his body, he knelt at Shiba's feet, his head forward, ready for the sword. From the ranks of the Allied prisoners, someone shouted hip-hip-hip and three resounding cheers echoed around Ba Wan.

Startled by the noise, Tasaki emerged from his quarters at the same time as the two Japanese guards sent to fetch the Dutchman came running up. One had a black eye, the other was bleeding profusely from the nose and the whole affair now took on an element of tragic farce.

Leaving the parade standing at attention and Heergren kneeling in the dirt, Tasaki and Shiba returned to their quarters. They reappeared some twenty minutes later in full service dress. Colonel Shiba then informed the assembled gathering that the execution would take place in the morning, at sunrise, in accordance, as he carefully explained, with the compassionate sentiments of Bushido.

The parade was dismissed but a few minutes after dawn the following day, the sombre farce was repeated with one difference: Heergren was decapitated by a single stroke of Toshiro Shiba's sword.

The work of extracting the rubies from the limestone deposits at Ba Wan continued. Men still died, either from disease or by execution but no one reported sick in the official sense because to do so meant instant death. To cope with this, Brigadier Stuggard ordered pits to be dug inside many of the huts. It was hard, back-breaking work, especially for men always hungry and already exhausted by their toil in the mine, but there was no shortage of volunteers. The pits, christened *Stuggard's Graves*, were some seven feet long, four feet wide and three feet deep. Lined with leaves and scraps of cloth, they were covered with matting laid over bamboo poles and usually held two men who needed a forty-eight hour break from the gruelling routine.

Hot and airless, the pits were far from pleasant but as they were the only alternative to execution, there were no complaints. Since the Japanese never bothered with roll-calls and seldom searched the huts, the inmates of *Stuggard's Graves* could enjoy their subterranean respite with reasonable confidence. Until the beginning of April, 1945, when one of the guards went into a hut and fell through the floor. The results were horrendous.

Working at the mine, the prisoners were surprised and relieved when they were ordered to return to the camp some two hours earlier than usual. But their relief was short-lived. As they marched into the compound, they saw that the men who had been left in the pits – twenty-eight in all – were now lying out in the open, surrounded by Japanese guards.

After ranting at the assembled prisoners for some minutes, Shiba ordered the sick men to be returned to the pits and for their comrades to bury them – alive. Stuggard marched forwards and refused point-blank. A *Kempei Tai* guard struck the senior PoW officer with a wooden stave and kicked him as he fell to the ground. Shiba then repeated his order and when Brigadier Stuggard told him to *go to hell*, he was shot in the stomach, the guards kicking and beating him until he became unconscious.

Toshiro Shiba rapidly lost his temper. A young New Zealander was plucked from the ranks, told to get on with the burial and was bayoneted when he echoed Stuggard's refusal. Four more prisoners were killed before Shiba decided to change his tactics.

An American airman was selected, knocked to the ground and stripped naked. Two Japanese officers then set to work, hacking at the man's testicles with small pocket-knives. The airman's high-pitched screaming seemed endless before he passed out and a shocked silence hung over the entire camp.

Once again, Shiba ordered the burials to take place but

no one moved or uttered a sound. And when he yelled that unless his order was obeyed they would all be shot, his words were greeted by whistles and catcalls, the noise rising to an angry crescendo which gradually died away as all the prisoners squatted on the ground.

Shiba was beside himself with fury when a soldier wearing nothing but a ragged loin-cloth stood up and walked unsteadily towards him, stopping a few feet away. He then bowed and told him in faultless Japanese that no one would bury the sick men alive and that he could do as he pleased.

After a long pause, Shiba turned on his heel and strode from the compound. For some minutes following his exit, it seemed likely that the guards would open fire without any orders being given but they simply withdrew, leaving the prisoners to pick up their sick and wounded comrades and return to their huts.

That night, Walter Stuggard died of his wounds but he had not died in vain. By his example, he had humiliated the Japanese and his successor as senior PoW, an American naval officer, Captain Becker, was determined to build on the moral victory. Nor did he waste any time.

The following morning, Brigadier Stuggard and the five other men who had died were buried, the Japanese guards looking on. Incredibly, the guards behaved as if nothing unusual had happened and positioned themselves to escort the working parties to the mine in the normal way. But the Allied prisoners remained in their quarters, refusing to move as Becker went alone to the command post and demanded to see Colonel Shiba. Once inside the office, Becker was confronted by all the Japanese officers, including Major-General Tasaki.

In a firm, clear voice, the American read out a list of demands which had been written in pencil on the fly-leaf torn from a bible. He wanted proper medical supplies, reasonable rations, an end to intimidation, beatings, torture and executions, and an issue of adequate clothing. Shiba then asked whether the Allied prisoners would be prepared to work the mine if the demands were met. Becker said yes, provided working hours were reduced from twelve to six hours a day with no work at all on Saturdays and Sundays. After a hurried conference, Tasaki said that they would accept the terms and Becker then got him to sign the scrap of paper.

Although there was an immediate issue of medical supplies and an increase in the daily quota of rice, it soon became clear that the Japanese would not and could not keep to their bargain. From the Burmese labourers employed at the mine came rumours of Allied victories and Japanese withdrawals. These rumours were given substance by the failure of the weekly courier to collect the haul of gems culled from the mine. There was a discernible tension in the air and the Japanese seemed to lose much of their jaunty self-confidence.

On April 11, 1945, Major-General Tasaki and his staff, including Heyashi, suddenly left Ba Wan, taking about twenty *Kempei Tai* soldiers with them as an escort. They didn't return and Captain Becker, a shrewd judge of men and situations, decided that it was time for the Allied prisoners to escape. There were now two hundred and sixty-three officers and men in captivity at Ba Wan, of whom twenty-seven were incapable of walking. When told of the plan, all of the sick men begged to be left behind, knowing that they would only slow the pace. Becker refused and ordered stretchers to be constructed.

The date set for the escape was Monday, April 16. The plan was to leave the compound after sunset, moving in small groups along the road leading to the mine. They would then assemble at the entrance to the mine and set off into the jungle, heading west towards the Irrawaddy. Captain Becker was relying on the fact that the Japanese had grown complacent. The few guards who remained on duty at night were seldom alert and often fast asleep. He had also noted that the road to the mine was left completely unguarded, the Japanese obviously assuming that any prisoner prepared to take his chance in the jungle

319

would go in the opposite direction, towards Mogok.

The day of the escape passed normally. Working parties went to the mine and returned at the usual time. Among the Allied prisoners there was an air of expectancy, a feeling of quiet optimism which was shared by Captain Becker. As sunset approached, specially placed lookouts noted that Colonel Shiba, accompanied by a number of other officers including Lieutenant Izumi, were following their normal practise of sitting on the verandah of the command post, drinking.

2

Twenty minutes after sunset, Captain Becker gave the order to move. He had organized his men with care, dividing them into small groups. It seemed to Becker and his officers that the most dangerous part of the escape would be the first stage – leaving the compound and getting on to the road leading to the mine. Because of this, it was decided that the group carrying the twenty-seven men on stretchers would come last so that by the time they left the compound, the others would have at least established that the road was clear.

Timing the operation was out of the question. As with everything else of any value like signet rings, pens, key-chains and crucifixes, all watches had either been stolen by the guards or extorted in exchange for some small favour. Becker solved the problem by devising a system of link-men. When one group had reached a certain position, one man would return and bring on the next. It was clumsy, slow and increased the risk of detection. But there was a greater risk of a whole group straying in the darkness and blundering into an unsuspecting guard.

Conditions were perfect. There was no moon and the deep purple sky was speckled with stars as Captain Becker led the first group of men across the compound and past the unoccupied guard-post which marked the beginning of the road to the mine. It seemed so quiet that the men became jittery and Becker waited in the shadows for ten precious minutes before sending back the first of the link-men.

The road ran almost dead straight for about eight hundred yards before curving round and dropping quite steeply into the mine. The straight section was fenced with barbed wire some seven feet high, fencing which had been erected before the war by the mining company. It was in poor repair but in spite of the fact that there were many gaps, Becker had chosen to leave the road at a point just around the bend. For some reason, the fencing had stopped short and there was a well-trodden path leading away into the jungle.

Everything seemed to go according to plan until the advance party were within a hundred yards of the bend. It was then that Becker became aware of the noise.

Although split into small groups, there was still a total of two hundred and sixty-three men moving along the road. Some noise was clearly inevitable but in the silence of the night, it sounded as if they were all moving simultaneously and even marching in step.

Halting, Becker sent two of his officers back at the double with orders to keep it quiet and break up what had obviously become a column. For all its clumsiness, Becker's system of link-men had worked too well. All the escaping prisoners were bunching together on the road and the problem was soon further complicated.

Unaware that Becker's leading group had stopped, the men at the rear had continued moving forward, including the stretcher bearers. The situation was made worse when a group in the centre of the column misunderstood Becker's relayed orders. Instead of staying put, they turned back and the ensuing confusion caused more noise.

Reluctant to leave the head of what was now a column of marching men, Becker gave the word to move forward in the hope that some measure of order would be restored. It seemed to work and apart from the noise of scuffling feet, the prisoners were silent again. A few minutes later,

Becker reached the point at which he had intended leaving the road and discovered a new problem: the Japanese had extended the fencing.

Becker's most urgent task was to calm the men who were with him, many of whom wanted to turn back. Captain Becker had no intention of abandoning the escape – in spite of any silent fears. He knew he had to make a quick decision because if he stayed put, the column would simply concertina as it so nearly had before, with a repeat of the noise and confusion.

Once again, the column moved forward, rounding the bend and starting down towards the mine. The system of link-men had broken down completely and it was simply a case of each man following whoever was in front. Then the men at the head of the column became aware of a commotion behind them.

Cursing, Becker was about to go back himself when he was confronted by two men who had used what little strength they possessed to run the length of the column. They were so weak that the effort had all but crippled them, but in between frantic gasps for breath, they tried to explain that the Japanese were also on the road. Captain Becker reacted with characteristic calm, issuing orders in a clear voice. What the American naval officer had failed to grasp was the fact that it wasn't simply a patrol coming up behind the column. The Japanese guards were actually driving the prisoners-of-war at bayonet-point.

Knowing that there were a number of paths leading from the mine, Becker believed that it was still possible to make good the escape – even if some of them were recaptured. But as they stumbled towards the mine, the hopelessness of the situation gradually became apparent. Panic took over and none of the officers was able to maintain order. Some men were shouting, their pathetic cries echoing away into the jungle. Others attempted to climb the barbed wire fencing but none succeeded.

That the Japanese had had advance knowledge of the escape plan didn't occur to anyone, least of all Becker, until the air was suddenly filled with the stuttering throb of the diesel generator inside a stone building at the entrance to the horseshoe-shaped mine. Then the lights came on and they all knew that they had been betrayed.

There were Japanese everywhere, many of them armed with 8mm light machine guns. Resistance would have been futile and the Allied prisoners were driven towards the sheer cliff of the mine. Then Shiba appeared.

Using a megaphone, he ordered his captives back against the rock-face. The guards made it impossible to refuse, using their bayonets on anyone who even looked like faltering.

Knowing all too well what was about to happen, Becker forced his way to the front and began to plead for mercy, telling Shiba that the escape had been his idea and that he alone was responsible. Kneeling down, he begged for his men to be spared.

When Becker made another attempt, two of the guards used their bayonets on him, one of them driving his blade into the American's face with such ferocity that the tip poked through the back of his head. Incredibly, Becker didn't die but lay on the ground, writhing and screaming incoherently until Lieutenant Izumi came and shot him with a revolver at point-blank range.

The murder of Captain Becker inflamed the prisoners and those in the front tried to rush the guards. It was a useless gesture. Most were bayoneted, others either clubbed or shot down. Then one of the machine guns opened up, scything down almost the entire front rank. As the echoes died away, a sudden silence descended and only the steady throb of the generator could be heard. Everyone seemed to be waiting.

Speaking through the megaphone again, Shiba told the prisoners to remain where they were. The war, he told them, was almost over; the armies of Japan were beaten and must face the inevitable consequences. He paused, spoke briefly in Japanese and then went on in English to the effect that he wanted no more bloodshed. As his words echoed around the mine, the guards began to withdraw and the prisoners watched, amazed. Because of the glare of the lights, most of the men had to shield their eyes and many could not see Shiba. Then some of the lights went out as bulbs and wiring failed.

As the last of the guards left the mine, Shiba explained that the Japanese were withdrawing from Burma, that his orders were to evacuate Ba Wan and that the prisoners should stay in the mine until the morning, by which time he and his men would have gone.

At first, this message was greeted by a stunned silence. Then a few men began to cheer, their cries echoing back off the rock-face, but most of the Allied prisoners remained quiet. Some had begun to weep.

Throwing down the megaphone, Shiba started to walk away but paused for a moment, staring down at the sea of emaciated faces of the men over whom he had had the power of life and death. Then he began to laugh, the guards joining in so that a different sound echoed around the mine.

The laughter was still echoing back to them when he issued his final order. It was delivered softly but the results were audible for many miles as a Japanese soldier depressed the plunger.

The charges – nearly a hundred of them – had been skilfully placed high in the face of the cliff. Thousands of tons of rock crashed down on to the bodies of men who believed that they had escaped death by the skin of their teeth.

The lucky ones died quickly, their bodies smashed to pulp by massive boulders, but the majority were less fortunate. Because they had been driven close in to the cliff-face, they were largely sheltered from the falling rocks and were buried alive.

At dawn the following morning, an inspection of the Ba Wan mine was carried-out by Lieutenant Izumi. When he reported back to Shiba, he confirmed that there was no visible trace of the events of the previous night. Izumi also confirmed that both he and his men had heard faint cries coming from beneath the debris.

Two days later, Colonel Toshiro Shiba and Lieutenant Kenji Izumi left Ba Wan for the last time. With them as they passed through the nearby town of Mogok were sixteen *Kempei Tai* soldiers, one man on a stretcher and an immense fortune in un-cut rubies.

3

On April 20, 1945, Soichi Heyashi discarded his uniform and deserted his new post in the Japanese garrison at Thayetmyo. The following day, he presented himself to the head monk at the Me Win monastery and begged admission. His request was granted and Heyashi entered his new life as a Buddhist monk. But the war continued.

Allied forces under the command of General Slim re-took Rangoon on Thursday, May 3. Suddenly, the Japanese were in full retreat and Burma was plunged into chaos. Many Japanese units surrendered at the first opportunity. Others held out, fighting until the last man fell. The roads were choked with traffic of every description, liberated Allied prisoners of war marching in one direction, passing Japanese troops heading the other way and neither group seeming to care about the other. One Japanese garrison of more than three thousand men with ample ammunition, food and medical supplies, surrendered by accident to a twelve-man reconnaissance patrol led by a nineteen year-old subaltern. Such was the confusion.

In Europe, Hitler was dead and the Germans laid down their arms on May 7 but Japan fought on until the Americans devastated Hiroshima and Nagasaki with atomic bombs during the first two weeks of August. Then, on Wednesday, August 14, 1945, Emperor Hirohito surrendered unconditionally. The Empire of the Rising Sun lay in ruins and the spirit of Bushido had been exorcized. Or so it was believed.

There was a long, oppressive silence and even the throbbing of the cicadas seemed to fade so that the most conspicuous sound in the ruined *viharn* was the soft sputtering of the oil lamps.

'After the formal surrender,' said Heyashi, 'the Allied troops set up clearing stations for the captured Japanese. Thayetmyo was one of many such places. It will be difficult for you to understand how it was at that time. Strangely, there was little bitterness, or so it seemed to me.' He paused and looked away, his eyes half closed. 'Together with other monks from Me Win, I went into the town to buy oil but we were stopped by some soldiers and questioned. I was desperately afraid. It was of no interest to the Allies that I had deserted and at that time the photographs ... my thoughts ... I did not know what I should do. But the soldiers let us pass and we were able to obtain some oil. Two days later, some British officers came to Me Win. I remember seeing them walking across the compound. One was very tall and wore glasses. He had a kind face. Then, after a while, the head monk sent for me and I was prepared for the worst. I would have confessed my true identity had not the head monk warned me that the officer only sought help. They needed interpreters.

'Four of us were chosen and we went to the British camp and translated many interviews. We carried on this work for nearly three months, I think. It was clearly a violation of our sacred code but the British didn't care about that and in exchange for our services, the monastery received supplies. While I was doing this, I began making inquiries about the men I had known but they had vanished. I talked with one officer who believed that Tasaki had returned to Japan but that was all. No one had even heard of Toshiro Shiba and not until the last few days, just before the clearing station was closed, did I learn that Kenji Izumi was being held at a town called

Prome, about a hundred miles south of Thayetmyo. I shall never know what made me go there but I told the head of the monastery that there was a friend I must see and he gave me permission.

'The journey took nearly three days. And when I got to Prome, it was teeming with British soldiers. And Americans, of course. I spent nearly a week going from place to place asking for news of Izumi. And it was during those days that I realized I needed him ... someone, to tell my people in Japan ... if they were still alive, that I would never return. But when I did eventually find Izumi, he was very ill and not expected to live. There was a big hospital, full of Japanese. I remember being shocked by the conditions and then I remembered Ba Wan. It was a kind of justice, I suppose. A kind of retribution.

'Izumi didn't recognize me, of course. But I succeeded in getting him released from the hospital and we travelled back to Me Win on a cart. Kenji Izumi was suffering very badly from malaria and lack of nourishment. I remember praying that he should live and my prayers were answered. Later, he recognized me and we talked a great deal. I told him about the photographs I had taken and how I still had them. By that time, he had already spoken of the final days at Ba Wan and begged me to destroy the pictures. But I could not bring myself to do it, in spite of his promises to me.'

'Then it was true that you saved his life,' said Yita.

'Perhaps.' And Heyashi smiled, wistfully. 'Who knows? I recall that there were only two pictures which showed him and I gave them to him.'

Langford took out his wallet and produced the yellowed photographs which Gunning had removed from Bailey's things. 'These?'

Heyashi glanced at them. 'Yes, those are the two I gave him. Perhaps I should have destroyed the others then. Certainly no one was interested in them. Once Kenji Izumi had regained his health, he left the monastery and returned to Japan. I tried to find someone who would hear

327

my story and take the pictures from me but although I made use of every contact I had and even went down to Rangoon, the British authorities seemed disinterested. Then we discovered that Burma would soon become independent and I knew there was no point in going on. There was also the question of my studies at Me Win. The head monk was urging me to forget and so I did, for a little.'

'It would take some forgetting,' said Langford.

'Yes.' Heyashi nodded, slowly. 'I think it was in 1947 when I received the letter from Kenji Izumi. It spoke of many things but mostly it was about what had happened at Ba Wan. It was the letter which made me determined that Shiba and Tasaki must pay for their crimes. I realized, of course, that I would be implicated. I was there, Mister Langford. I could have protested but I did not. There were many like me, men too drunk with power or too afraid to speak out. But before I could act, the terrorists attacked Me Win …'

'Can I see the photographs?' Langford's voice was quiet.

Heyashi nodded and began to undo the thick cord but it was rotten with age and simply disintegrated in his fingers. And when the old man tried to open the lid of the battered tin box, the rusted hinge broke with a sharp, squeaking sound.

Peering into the box, Langford saw a stained khaki bundle secured with tape. Heyashi removed the bundle and gently unwrapped it as if it contained some sacred object.

'Part of my function was to take photographs of victorious, happy soldiers; of Allied prisoners of war enjoying every comfort. But as others took casual snapshots of the torture and executions, so I decided to use my skill as a photographer to create a …' He hesitated, 'A dossier, a pictorial record of the evil.' And he glanced warily at Yita. 'These images are not pleasant, child.'

'I am not afraid, Heyashi-*san*.'

328

The monk smiled, sadly. 'Nor were we when these events took place but ...' He stared down as the sepia-toned pictures slid into his lap from the square of khaki cloth. 'Mister Langford, do you think that a man ... any man, should be held responsible for crimes committed more than thirty years previously?'

Langford replied without hesitation. 'Yes,' he said, moistening his lips with the tip of his tongue as he caught sight of the first picture.

'You are still young. Hopefully, Providence will not so interfere with your destiny that the past will return to haunt you.' And Heyashi sighed as he took hold of the pictures. 'Here,' he said, handing them to Langford. 'See for yourself the fruits of our labours, the glory of the knights of Bushido.'

5

'Jesus Christ,' said Langford.

THIRTEEN

1

'It'll be dawn soon.' Langford stared out of the *sala* into the inky darkness. Then he turned and looked at Yita. 'You're crying.' She didn't answer and he went to her. 'Why?'

'So many cruel things.' She shook her head. 'I could not believe what he told us but the photographs ...'

'It's history now. Nothing to do with you.' He smiled at her, gently brushing away the tears which glistened on her cheeks. 'You weren't even born.'

'But I am Japanese,' she murmured. 'You must hate us all. It could not be otherwise. I am ashamed. When my step-father spoke of bad things, I could not know just how ...' She sighed. 'So much suffering ... so much guilt. Why? Why did they do those things?'

'Does it matter? The important thing is that Shiba and the rest will be punished, even if it is a bit late in the day.'

'Toshiro Shiba will not be punished. He is too powerful. He has too many important friends.'

'By the time these photographs have done the rounds, he may not find himself quite so popular. Besides, he won't have any friends in London or Washington and that's what'll count.'

For a long time, she sat in silence, her head bowed. Then she looked up at him. 'What must it have been like at that place ... for your people?'

'Hell, I should imagine. But there's no point in dwelling on it.'

'Hell is where bad Christians go when they die. Is that not so?'

'So they say. But I have a feeling that hell's right here on earth.'

'Richard – why would you like people to think you a hard, violent man? You are not. You are gentle, kind.' She moved closer and took his hand in hers, staring at the lines on his palm in the flickering glow of the oil lamp. 'You are a good man.'

'You don't know anything about me.'

'No, but I know you as you really are.'

'Yita …'

She gazed at him, her dark eyes full of the strange, compassionate understanding he had seen during that first evening aboard the *Hai Shan*. 'What troubles you?'

'No trouble.' He leaned forwards and kissed her softly on the mouth. 'No trouble at all.' He smiled. 'When we get back … when all this is over, I want …' But she reached out and pressed her finger against his lips.

'There is no tomorrow, only today, only now.' Turning, she peered out of the *sala*, leaning against him as he put his arm around her. 'Soon the sun will rise and we shall go from here. It will be different.'

'Yita …' He went to kiss her but she drew back.

'You know about me, what I have been, how I have used my body in order to live.'

'You must forget –'

'And Kit Bailey? I cannot forget him. He was the first man I truly loved, the first man who truly loved me. I shall always keep a place for him in my heart.'

'Only if it's a very small place, Yita. Life is for the living.'

She smiled suddenly. 'I want to live now, today. This second. I want to make you happy. I must owe you that for what you did … those men …'

'You owe me nothing. Anyway, it makes us even, doesn't it?'

'When we were in the ruined temple … I started to look at the photographs but then something made me look at you. I watched your face as you studied each of the pictures and it was then that I knew you truly.'

'You obviously couldn't read my thoughts.'

'No, you are wrong. I could read your thoughts. There was grief in your eyes. And much anger. But I did not see hatred. And yet I know you have hatred for Shiba. I feel it but I cannot see it. You do hate him, don't you?'

Langford shrugged. 'I honestly don't know. In a way … yes, I could cheerfully kill the bastard with my bare hands but … I don't know. Perhaps there are too many things that I don't understand. They say the Japs …' He bit back the words and shook his head. 'I'm sorry, I didn't mean …'

'You must not worry.'

They kissed, slowly and gently, their arms around each other as they sat in the open-fronted *sala*, an island of flickering light in the purple darkness, serenaded by the throbbing cicadas. Then she pressed herself against him and he kissed her dark, scented hair, his hand softly caressing her neck, her shoulders.

'We ought to sleep,' he said. She didn't answer. Looking into her face, Langford saw that she was already sleeping, her lips set in a calm, contented smile.

She stirred only slightly as he got to his feet, cradling her in his arms and stepping carefully into the small room at the end of the *sala*, the floorboards creaking as he walked.

He laid her on the mattress and when he had slipped the shoes from her feet, covered her with the thin sheet. Then he kissed her again, gently brushing his lips against hers.

'Richard?' Her eyes fluttered open and she smiled up at him.

Then she sat up, taking hold of his hands. 'Will you love me? Now?'

'Yita, I ...'

'No, please. Never Yita again. You will call me Kimiko. Yes?'

Kneeling beside her, Langford pressed his hands against her cheek. 'Yes ... Kimiko ...'

'And you will love me?'

'Yes.'

2

The sun was low on the horizon when Langford came out of the *sala*, pulling on his shirt. Then he saw the monk. 'What time is it?' he demanded, seeing that his own wristwatch had stopped.

Heyashi looked up and smiled. 'The end of the day comes, Mister Langford. You are rested?'

'The end of the day?' Langford squinted up at the sun. 'A whole day wasted.'

His wizened face lit by a knowing smile, Heyashi stared back at him. 'Wasted? Surely you do not mean that?'

'How long have you been sitting here?'

'Does it matter? Come, there is fruit. And I thought you might need these.' He held out a pack of Thai cigarettes.

'Thank you, that's kind.' Langford lit up, inhaling deeply but the smoke tasted acrid and sharp so that he coughed before he could stop himself.

'Not as good as Virginia, I don't imagine,' remarked Heyashi, pouring a cup of water.

'No, they're fine.' Langford gulped at the cold water. 'How can we get back to Bangkok?'

'I have already made arrangements. There is a man in the village who will take you in his motor car. No, do not worry. You will be quite safe with him and he will take you direct to the airport.'

'Thanks,' said Langford, squatting down.

They sat in silence for a long time and then Heyashi started to rise, moving slowly and awkwardly, as if in pain, but he refused Langford's assistance.

'You will take the photographs from here and men will be punished.' It was a statement of fact. 'You will also stop to ask yourself about me. You will speculate as to the guilt or innocence of Soichi Heyashi, soldier, deserter, Buddhist monk and ... for a time, head of the *Wat* Keo.'

'It's not my problem,' said Langford.

'Perhaps not. But it is mine. Were I younger, Mister Langford, I would come with you and throw myself at the mercy of whatever authorities are thought competent to judge these things. But I am seventy-nine years of age. My health is not good and this worn, tired husk which is my body must soon cease to function. But I cannot die without easing my conscience.'

Langford frowned. 'Have you got anything on your conscience? Apart from the fact that you didn't protest?'

Heyashi produced an envelope from the folds of his robe, holding it for Langford to take. 'When you left me last night, I wrote down much of what I told you. And more. It's all there, all the evidence you need.'

Taking the envelope, Langford sighed. 'You're not sure, are you? Justice or unfair revenge, that's what you can't work out, isn't it?'

'You have wisdom beyond your years,' said Heyashi, leaning against one of the carved, wooden roof supports. 'What you say is true. I have had to live with this knowledge for so long that I no longer know what is right. For many years, I believed that if I could pass on the photographs and tell my story, it would be like shedding old and soiled clothes. But it is not so. The stains of the blood spilled in the name of Bushido cannot be washed away so easily.'

'You've mentioned Bushido before,' said Langford. 'Who was he?'

Heyashi smiled. 'What, Mister Langford. Not who. Bushido was ... perhaps still is, a code of ethics. It began in ancient Japan, with the Samurai. The code meant loyalty and duty, love and compassion. Strange how something so essentially good can be warped and twisted until it becomes inherently evil.'

Langford was about to speak when he heard Yita stirring within the little room. Heyashi also heard.

'Perhaps something good has come from all this. I shall bid you farewell, Mister Langford. The car will be here directly.' The old man made the *wai*, his gnarled hands trembling as he pressed them together. 'Go in peace ... and find peace wherever you go.'

Unable to frame a suitable reply, Langford merely nodded, watching the old monk walk slowly across the compound and pause at the *baisema* to remove his sandals before stepping into the shadowy entrance to the *bot*.

'Richard?'

He swung round and saw Yita framed in the doorway. 'What's the matter?'

'I am afraid. And I am sad.'

'Why?'

She shook her head. 'I am unhappy because I know that Heyashi-*san* will be unhappy until the day of his death. But I am afraid because ...' And she tried to smile, clasping and un-clasping her hands. 'I do not know why. I just am.'

'There's nothing for you to be afraid of,' he said, pulling her into his arms. Then he heard the sound of a car coming up to the *Wat* Keo.

3

Professor Whitaker stood on the starboard flying bridge and gazed into the gathering darkness as the six ocean-going tugs prepared to ease the *Shimada Maru* away from Pier 13. On Shiba's specific instructions, only essential personnel were admitted to the sealed-off portion of Kobe dockyard occupied by the Shimada Corporation. In so far as it was possible for a vessel the size of the *Shimada Maru* to be moved in secret, an amazing degree of secrecy had been achieved.

Whitaker was very much aware of Shiba's almost paranoiac concern with security. He was also deeply worried about the ship itself. Exactly what was troubling him the Professor had been unable to pin down. But at that moment, his passion for the sea and ships made him forget everything. He was totally absorbed in the task of getting the *Shimada Maru* away from Kobe, a task in which he had no active rôle to play but which he could enjoy as a leisured spectator.

Inside the bridge, Shiba and Samwashima stood together, watching in silence as Captain Umezu and his First Officer issued orders. There were no controls as such on the bridge itself, apart from radar and sonar repeaters, a bank of telephones and a digital repeater compass linked to the computerized navigation system. The ship's engines, steering, navigation systems — everything, including the complex instrumentation for the monitoring and management of the volatile cargo, was controlled from a large cabin far below. In theory, every manoeuvre could be accomplished without a living soul being on the bridge. The computer had been programmed to cope with every conceivable event and the officer of the watch could make use of full-colour closed-circuit television to maintain visual contact with almost every part of the ship. In practise, however, Captain Umezu preferred to see for himself.

In response to Umezu's command, the *Shimada Maru's* engines were started and Whitaker felt a sudden, tingling vibration as the massive turbine gathered speed. Then the Captain came out on to the flying bridge holding a compact transceiver with the aerial extended. If he noticed Whitaker at all, he gave no sign.

Umezu was the man responsible for putting the world's largest merchant ship to sea; he alone had custody of a vessel with a deadweight close on half a million tons, a man-made giant nearly a quarter of a mile long. He walked calmly across the deck, speaking into the walkie-talkie.

With tow-lines secured to three of the tugs, the heavy cables which had held the gigantic bows of the *Shimada Maru* against the pier were cast off. Slowly, almost imperceptibly, the gap between the bows and the pier widened as the tugs pulled, the sea boiling as their triple-sets of propellers bit into the water.

Whitaker could hardly see the tugs now. They were just tiny silhouettes flitting across the water and only their churning wake was clearly visible, white and luminescent in the darkness. As his hands gripped the guardrail, the Professor could not help experiencing a kind of elation at the sheer majesty of Shiba's creation.

The Captain snapped out more orders, the stern lines splashed down against the pier and two tugs, their stubby bows heavily fendered, pushed against the towering stern of the ship. The sixth tug stood away until the vessel was well clear of the pier, then it surged forward coming up to join the other tugs on the port side in the murky abyss between the *Shimada Maru* and the pier.

The string of lights running the length of Pier 13 were slowly slipping past but Whitaker had the sensation of the pier moving and not the *Shimada Maru*. Then, out of the corner of his eye, he saw Shiba come on to the flying bridge as Captain Umezu finally ordered slow ahead.

The tingling vibration increased as the tugs slipped their tow-lines and peeled away to take station, three on each side. There was a long, echoing blast from the ship's siren which left Whitaker momentarily deafened. He saw Toshiro Shiba smile, his lips moving as he spoke, but the Professor was unable to hear whatever it was that Shiba had said. Then a sudden gust of wind slapped against them as they moved into open water. The *Shimada Maru* was proceeding under her own power. The voyage to Kyomo had begun.

4

Richard Langford found it impossible to relax as they headed back to Bangkok in the low-slung American Ford. He was very conscious of Yita's presence in the back; conscious of the lingering sensation of pleasure in his loins. Above all, he was aware of a new feeling for her, an emotion which he could not define.

The driver was a chirpy little Thai who had obviously dressed up for the occasion and wore a shapeless suit of awful pale blue which almost matched the colour of the car. He seemed to have little knowledge of English but he drove well. And fast. There were moments when Langford was convinced that they would slew off the road but the Thai controlled the vehicle with a reckless skill which eventually compelled his admiration.

The journey was filled with recollections of Lim Mok and the ancient Volkswagen. After they had passed the shrine near where Langford had hidden the rifle, the car sped round the long, curving bends through the jungle and he tried to see where they had pushed the truck from the road. But there was nothing to be seen, no trace at all of the ambush which had cost Lim Mok his life. Then came the wooden bridge across the Mei Ping river, the Thai shooting over it around sixty miles an hour so that they scarcely felt the wheels jarring against the ribbed surface.

Once they were on the main road, the needle of the speedometer hovered consistently around eighty, even when they reached the ramshackle town of Tak. The Thai grinned as he laid on the two-tone horn and swerved to avoid a group of monks crossing the wide street with the kind of blind fatalism which Langford had come to associate with everything Oriental. Then, quite suddenly, it was pitch dark, an inky blackness penetrated by no less than six devastatingly bright lights which the Thai refused to dip so that on-coming vehicles passed them with their horns blaring.

They hurtled through the ruined town of Ayudhya, the Thai uttering shrill curses when the Ford splashed into pools of rain which flooded over the windscreen and caused clouds of steam to rise from the engine. And as they finally entered the outskirts of the capital, they met the rain, a wall of water which drummed on the roof of the car and somehow streamed in through the tightly-closed side windows. But neither the rain nor the chaotic traffic seemed to deter their driver who continued to keep his foot pressed to the floor, the horn blaring imperiously as he competed for passage.

It was well after midnight when they approached Bangkok's Don Muang airport. The rain had eased but the road was appalling and the Ford shuddered as it crashed over a succession of potholes. But Langford was concentrating on the next problem: getting back into Japan. That there might be any difficulty didn't seem to have crossed Yita's mind and Langford supposed that she wasn't thinking beyond Hong Kong. Then the Thai skidded the car to a halt outside the main entrance and smiled triumphantly.

'How much?' asked Langford, taking out his wallet. The man merely shook his head.

'No, no pay,' he yelled. 'No pay.'

Langford misunderstood and held up the bundle of notes. 'How much?'

'No. You no pay. Me make favour. See?'

It was Langford's turn to smile and pulling a couple of notes from the wad, pressed them into the driver's hand. 'Thanks,' he said, opening the door.

They stood for a moment in the hot, treacle-like air and watched the car speed away, the driver giving them a cheery wave and a farewell blast of the two-tone horn. Then they went into the airport building and Yita clutched nervously at his arm.

'We go to Hong Kong now, Richard?'

He didn't reply but led her towards the bar where he

339

bought coffee and American cigarettes. He also picked up a thick flight list and thumbed through it. Then he snapped the brochure closed and stood up. 'You stay put. I'll be right back.' Then he caught the look of apprehension in her eyes. 'Don't worry, I'm not going far.'

As he walked through the people milling around the airport building, Langford studied their faces, suddenly feeling exposed and vulnerable. On impulse, he swung round and felt his stomach turn. Yita had vanished.

He swore aloud as he started to retrace his steps, then twisted sharply when he felt someone tug at his arm.

'I was afraid. I am sorry.' As she stared up at him, her eyes wide, Langford felt a surge of relief.

'All right, stay close. And don't ever do the disappearing act again.'

The young man at the Air Siam desk was tired and disinterested but eventually Langford got what he wanted and handed over the return tickets to Hong Kong together with his American Express card. Yita stared vacantly as the Thai filled out seemingly endless forms, stamping them with a fatigued bitterness. When all the scribbling and thumping had been completed, he thrust the tickets across the counter with ill-concealed relief.

'What time does it leave?' demanded Langford.

'Nine a.m.'

As they walked away from the desk, Yita tugged at his arm. 'We have a long wait.'

'Can't be helped.' He glanced at her. 'We'd better buy a couple of cheap grips and some clothes. Airlines don't like people without luggage.'

'When we get to Hong Kong, I shall buy them. You will choose.' There was a sudden gleam in her eye.

Langford licked his lips. 'Yita, we're not going back to Hong Kong.'

She stopped and looked at him. 'But the American ... he said ...'

'I know what he said. Look, love, you must trust me. Just do as I ask and everything will work out fine.'

340

Langford led the way towards the small shops filled with overpriced junk, hoping he had sounded a good deal more confident than he felt.

5

As the congregation left St. Botolph's after the memorial service for James Maxwell, they quickly dispersed, many of them getting into chauffeur-driven limousines. A number of leading political figures had attended the service but the clutch of pressmen who had spent a cold hour waiting in the porch, seemed to photograph all who emerged from the church, including the two women, both dressed in black, who quickly hurried away before they could be canvassed by a young reporter.

'I do so hate being photographed,' said Miss Pym, unconsciously linking arms with Peggy Ashmore as they headed towards Aldgate.

Richard Langford's secretary shrugged and smoothed her coat against the wind. 'Where shall we go?'

'Certainly not the office.'

Peggy Ashmore agreed. 'Look, there's quite a nice little cafe along Minories. We'll go there. Unless you want a drink?'

'I think not,' said Miss Pym with quiet disapproval. 'A hot coffee will do splendidly.'

It was still a little before noon and there were few people in the small coffee bar so that they were able to sit at a table tucked away in the corner. When the two steaming cups had been placed before them, Miss Pym peered at the young woman who sat facing her. 'Well, tell me all.'

'I don't really know where to begin. But I'm awfully worried about Richard ... Mister Langford.'

'So you said.' Miss Pym's expression hardened. 'I confess to not liking him. I always found him a rather bumptious young man.'

Peggy smiled. 'That was just his way. He always ...'

341

Her smile gradually faded. 'Why did I say was? I should have ...'

'Start again, dear. You're obviously upset.'

'I was going to say that he's always like that when he's ill at ease. Did you know you scare him?'

'Me?' Miss Pym seemed genuinely shocked. 'You do surprise me. I never imagined that young man would have had the intelligence to be scared of anyone. He was often quite rude ... even to poor Mister Maxwell.' She sniffed and pretended to examine her nails for a moment.

'Mary, I ...' Peggy Ashmore leaned across the table. 'If you only knew what's been happening. Some of the telephone conversations I've overheard. Don't look so shocked. Hewens was saying the most horrible things. He even talked about murder.'

'Murder?' Miss Pym echoed the word incredulously. 'Mister Hewens? Murder? I think perhaps we ought to order something to eat. And you can start at the very beginning.'

The meal consisted of an anonymous lukewarm soup, a limp spaghetti and more coffee. As Peggy Ashmore lit a cigarette, the waiter thrust the bill on the table but neither of the women took any notice.

'I simply cannot ...' Miss Pym stopped and shook her head. 'I was going to say that I didn't believe you but ... well, if all you've said is true ...'

'It is true,' said Peggy Ashmore, vehemently. 'And I forgot about the letter.' She began rummaging in her handbag.

'What letter?'

'Richard sent a letter to the Hong Kong office. The manager there opened it and ... this was sent through to me on the telex.' She handed a folded sheet of paper across the table. 'Luckily the girl working the telex was a temp. If it had been anyone else and Mister Hewens had found out ...'

'Good Lord.' Miss Pym shook her head and let out a long sigh. 'The disgrace ... the scandal. I'm pleased that poor Mister Maxwell isn't here to see this. His reputation in the City was spotless. Utterly without blemish. And did you know …' She lowered her voice and glanced round. 'You know that he was going to be Lord Mayor? That would have meant a knighthood. He wanted that. Not that he ever said so, of course. But I knew.'

Peggy Ashmore nodded as she retrieved the piece of paper. 'Please, you've got to help me. I don't know what to do.'

'When Mister Maxwell was …'

'But he's dead, Mary. Please, I know you're upset but you must help me. They could kill Richard.'

'Yes, I'm sorry, I wasn't thinking.' She paused for a moment. 'You'll have to go to the police. There's nothing else you can do.'

6

The announcement came over the public address system in Thai, a distorted sing-song babble to which Langford listened intently, motioning Yita to remain silent as the call was repeated in English.

'*Air Siam announce the departure of their flight number AS131 for Los Angeles. All passengers should proceed to gate three where …*'

'We're on,' said Langford, standing up and stretching.

'Los Angeles?' Yita stared at him and frowned. 'But that is in America.'

'That's right. Come on.' He held out his hand.

'I don't understand.'

'Don't try. I know what I'm doing. Come on or we'll miss it.'

As they stepped into the coach which would take them out to the Boeing 747, Langford felt the bundle of photographs in his pocket and moistened his lips. His decision not to return to Hong Kong was a gamble. Even more of a gamble was his plan to leave the aircraft when it stopped to refuel at Tokyo.

343

FOURTEEN

1

Whitaker woke with a start. The sun was streaming into the cabin and when he had blinked his eyes into focus, he stared at his watch. Mildly surprised that it was almost a quarter past ten, he tried to remember what time he had got to bed. It must have been well past four. He sank down again into the warm pillows and watched the millions of minute specks of dust dancing in the shafts of sunlight. His eyes began to close, his tired body drugged by the warmth of the bed and lulled by the rhythmic throbbing of the engines as the *Shimada Maru* headed towards Kyomo on a glassy-calm sea.

Suddenly, Helen was there, standing beside him in the cockpit on some kind of yacht. But they weren't alone. Toshiro Shiba and the omnipresent Samwashima seemed to be crewing for them and both the Japanese were laughing. Then the water suddenly flooded over the gunwales. But it wasn't like the real water. It was a thick, viscous substance. And immensely heavy. Helen called out that they were sinking but before he could do anything, the deck seemed to collapse beneath Whitaker's feet. He caught a last glimpse of his wife standing inside the cabin. Then the yacht simply folded up like a house of cards, the treacle-like sea quickly closing over everything.

Instantly awake again he sat up, heart pounding, a film of perspiration glistening on his face. He looked at his watch again but the hands had scarcely moved. He swung himself from the bed, pulling on his dressing gown as he walked across to the makeshift desk littered with Doctor

Bailey's papers and began to rummage through the various plans and notes until he found what he wanted.

He sat for a long time just staring at the papers and stroking his unshaven face, conscious of the soft rasping. There was no instant revelation because Whitaker's ordered mind didn't work like that. He was an analyst, arriving at conclusions only after a carefully controlled process of calculation and elimination. But as the minutes ticked by, so the germ of the idea which had previously refused to develop finally took on a recognizable shape.

He didn't hear the soft knocking and only looked round when the cabin door swung open to reveal Samwashima. Whitaker stared open-mouthed, as if Shiba's deputy were some kind of ghost.

'Forgive me, Professor.' Samwashima entered, making a self-conscious half-bow and smiling. 'We had not seen you. It is late and Mister Shiba was concerned.'

Whitaker swallowed, a vain attempt at killing the sudden dryness in his mouth. 'I want to see Shiba,' he said, standing up, only then realizing that he was still wearing his pyjamas and dressing gown.

'I trust you slept well?'

'Yes, but I've just woken up.'

'Ah so.' Samwashima seemed faintly amused. 'We shall arrive at Kyomo soon. Mister Shiba wishes to speak with you about the necessary certification. You understand?'

Whitaker nodded. 'Now I do, yes. But you can tell your precious Mister Shiba that I'm not signing any certificates. It's madness. Sheer insanity.'

'I am sorry?' Samwashima had closed the cabin door and was lighting a cigarette. 'Is something wrong, Professor?'

'It is Shiba's intention to use the *Shimada Maru* as an underwater store for the irradiated waste, isn't it?' He paused for a moment. 'I am right in thinking that this ship will be sunk in deep water and that Bailey's work was geared solely to that end, aren't I?'

Samwashima's faced seemed to collapse as he pulled on

the cigarette. 'I think this is a matter about which you should speak to Mister Shiba himself.'

'That's exactly what I intend doing. But I am right, aren't I?'

The Japanese retreated to the door, his hand feeling for the handle. 'I … I am not competent to comment. But I will inform Mister Shiba.'

'Do that,' snapped Whitaker. 'Now if you'll excuse me, I'll get dressed.'

2

As the Boeing started its descent into Tokyo, Langford was beginning to realize the hopelessness of the situation. Throughout the flight from Bangkok, he had tried to convince Yita but either she failed to understand him or she was simply being stubborn. Whatever the truth, she remained adamant.

'I will not do it,' she said. 'I will not do it because you do not give me the reasons.'

Langford sighed. 'You must trust me. Just do as I say. Please?'

'I do trust you. It is others I cannot trust. If you are determined to go back, you will need me.'

'It could be dangerous,' he told her. 'You know what they're likely to do …'

'I do not care.' She shrugged her narrow shoulders. 'I only know that the American said we should return to Hong Kong.'

'I've already explained –'

'No, Richard, you have explained nothing. You will not tell me why you want to do this thing.'

'Because I choose, that's why. It's safer –'

'Then I shall come with you. I will not go to Los Angeles. And if you try to make me, I will …' She looked away, clasping her hands together. 'I will tell them … tell the airline people of your intention.'

Langford glared at her but there was more than just

defiance in her expression and his anger quickly melted. 'All right, we'll do it together.'

'You must tell me what I should do,' she said, smiling at him. 'I do not wish to fail you.'

'My worry is that I might just fail you.'

After a smooth landing, the airliner taxied to its parking place and the engines were shut off. People began to move around and as he watched them, Langford decided not to ask if they could leave the 'plane but simply to get up and go.

They edged their way into the aisle and headed slowly towards the nearest exit where a diminutive Thai stewardess was making the *wai* and smiling at the departing passengers. Watching her carefully, Langford thought the girl was tired, that she couldn't be paying much attention. He soon found out that he had misjudged her.

'Are you not flying on to Los Angeles?' she said, looking up at him.

Langford nodded. 'Yes but ...'

She smiled, a quick flash of even white teeth against her dusky complexion. 'Then you must go to the second bus.' She pointed down the steps at a pool of light. 'It will take you to the transit lounge. We should not be on the ground for longer than an hour.'

'Thanks,' said Langford, breathing again as he descended the steps and went towards the bus.

The transit lounge was quite full as he led Yita to a table in one of the bars, his eyes narrowed as he scanned the people around them. 'I'm going in there,' he said, pointing towards a men's cloakroom. 'When I come out ... when you see me, you know what to do?'

'Yes.' She nodded, emphatically. 'Please ... do not be long.'

'It won't be up to me. Just don't move, okay? When I come out, I expect you to be sitting right here.' He walked slowly across the carpeted lounge, glancing around as he entered the men's room.

The washroom was full of Japanese chattering furiously to each other. After a quick look inside one of the cubicles, Langford made his way to the row of basins, waiting until the one nearest the corner was free before removing his jacket and hanging it on the peg. Then he turned on the taps and began soaping his hands as he stared into the mirror.

The Japanese all left at once and he had the place to himself as he dried his hands on the roller towel and waited. The minutes ticked by. Then the door swung open and two more Japanese entered, one of them coming to the basins while the other disappeared into a cubicle, slamming the door behind him. Langford made a show of combing his hair. The two Japanese were talking, their shouted conversation echoing around the washroom. He wondered how long the man would remain in the lavatory, not that it mattered at that moment. Then the main door opened again and suddenly it mattered very much.

The man who came into the washroom looked vaguely Swedish. He was about Langford's height and build, with fair, curly hair and wore a garish blue uniform with two gold rings on each sleeve.

Langford nodded at him but before the newcomer could acknowledge the greeting of one European to another, the sound of the lavatory being flushed filled the room and the Japanese emerged from the cubicle, continuing the high-pitched conversation with his friend as he washed his hands.

The fair-haired man passed Langford and went into one of the cubicles. Then the two Japanese left the washroom. Langford paused, then darted towards the main door, taking the cigarette lighter from his pocket. Kneeling down, he eased the door open a fraction and then jammed the lighter underneath it with his foot. Whether the wedge would be effective was impossible to foresee but it had to be worth a try.

It seemed a long time before he heard the sound of running water and sharp click of the bolt being drawn back. As he started to move, Langford also became aware of another sound: someone was trying to come into the cloakroom.

The man emerged from the cubicle pulling on his jacket. He looked rather surprised as he caught a fleeting glimpse of Langford but it was no more than that because of the karate chop which slammed against his neck.

Catching the man as he sagged, Langford propelled him backwards into the cubicle and sat him on the lavatory before rushing out to retrieve his lighter. The very dapper Japanese gentlemen looked somewhat puzzled when the door with which he had been struggling suddenly flew open. And he was downright surprised when the tall European literally shoved him aside and charged into a cubicle, slamming the door.

It took Richard Langford seven and a half minutes to swap clothes with the fair-haired man, who turned out to be a Canadian. Using his discarded shirt, Langford tied him up as best he could and then gagged him. As he wedged the unconscious man against the lavatory, he judged that it would be some time before he was in any condition to make a noise, let alone get free. Then he heaved himself over the partition into the next cubicle.

Langford paused to check his appearance in the mirror. The clothes weren't a bad fit, except for the peaked cap which was far too large. Wedging the hat under one arm, he started to leave the washroom but hesitated when it suddenly struck him that the Canadian might easily have companions waiting for him.

He emerged from the men's room cautiously but then started purposefully towards the bar where he had left Yita. No one paid him any attention.

In spite of the time, there seemed to be even more people in the transit lounge, especially in the bar. Walking casually across the lounge, Langford felt a rising panic grip his stomach. Then he saw her, sitting demurely at the table where he had left her. She seemed to recognize him without difficulty and their eyes met for a brief moment. A flight call came over the public address system, the general buzz of conversation in the bar fading for a few seconds as people listened. Then Langford nodded at her.

Yita stood up, took two paces forwards and collapsed, sagging to the floor in a heap. Before anyone else could react, Langford was at her side, gathering her limp body into his arms. There was a murmur of concern from the people who quickly gathered round.

'Ambulance?' said Langford, loudly.

The crowd all seemed to speak at once, a confused Babel of sound. Then another uniformed figure appeared and for a brief moment, Langford thought the charade was going to come to an abrupt end.

'Passed out?' said the man in an anonymous, mid-Atlantic accent.

'Pregnant,' snapped Langford. 'She was on my flight. Can we get an ambulance?'

The man seemed to hesitate for a moment, then he nodded. 'Follow me,' he said, starting towards one of the exits.

People stared as Langford rushed after him, Yita's arms swinging limply from her inert body. The two Japanese policemen who stood by the exit saw them coming and held the doors open, standing aside as they passed.

They had emerged into a long, carpeted corridor lit by harsh, fluorescent lighting. It seemed endless, following a gentle curve. Then Langford felt a blast of cold air and a few seconds later saw that they were about to come out into a parking lot.

'There's usually an ambulance here,' said his guide, going ahead as the automatic doors slid open. 'Yes, there it is.'

The ambulance was very similar to the Continental variety, a kind of converted station-wagon. Two attendants quickly took charge of Yita, strapping her on to a stretcher.

'Thanks for your help,' said Langford, nodding at the

350

man who now stood watching, his face puckered by a deep frown.

'My pleasure, Mister ...?'

Before Langford could reply, the ambulancemen had started to close the door and he darted towards them. 'I'm coming with you,' he said, pushing himself into the back.

If the ambulancemen objected, they said nothing but as the vehicle began to move and the sound of the siren cut the air, Langford glanced out of the rear window. It was then he realized that the man who had helped him was wearing a uniform almost identical to the one he had taken from the Canadian.

There was no time to worry about it. As the ambulance sped into the maelstrom of traffic, he knelt over Yita and surreptitiously released the straps which held her to the stretcher. The attendant in the passenger seat seemed to sense that something was going on and started to speak. His words died as Langford's fist slammed into the side of his head.

When his companion slumped forwards, the driver reacted by stamping on the brakes and Yita shrieked as the ambulance skidded to stop in the middle of the busy street.

Making use of the momentum, Langford lurched forward, intending to repeat the tactic but the blow was clumsy and lacked the element of surprise. Yita shouted something in Japanese and the driver seemed to hesitate, giving Langford a vital second to regain his balance and grab him before he could open the door.

The siren continued its strident wailing as Langford struggled with the man in the cramped space. The Japanese was yelling now, his fists flailing wildly. And over the noise of the siren came the blast of horns as the traffic piled up behind.

The priority was to get the ambulance moving again. People were beginning to gather on the pavement and Langford knew that it couldn't be long before the police were on the scene. Using all his strength, he heaved the driver out of the seat so that Yita could scramble in. Langford shouted for her to hurry. The vehicle jerked forward. Then it stalled.

The sudden movement cost Richard Langford the slight advantage he had gained and as he pitched sideways, the driver rolled away from him.

Yita started the engine again, revving it fiercely and crashing through the gears before she finally succeeded in getting under way. Langford tried to regain the initiative but the ambulanceman snatched one of the drip-feed bottles from its rack and dived at him.

The ambulance was hurtling through the brightly-lit streets, its siren blaring as Yita drove with a reckless determination which Langford might have admired had he been given the opportunity. As it was, the wiry Japanese obviously knew just how to handle difficult patients and it was sheer luck which saved Langford from a blow which could have knocked him senseless.

Yita heard the sound of breaking glass as she flung the ambulance round a tight corner. The Japanese had struck at Langford with the bottle but instead of hitting his head, shattered it against the floor.

Richard Langford had had no wish to hurt the man, merely to immobilize him for a while. But his opponent had other ideas and was fighting with ruthless determination. He also had a new weapon: the jagged remains of the bottle. Langford knew that it had become a no-holds-barred contest.

With an immense effort, ne levered himself up but before he could make any headway, the Japanese lunged forward and Langford let out a gasp as he felt the pointed shards of glass slice into his chest. The actual pain was minimal but the shock of being cut and the warm, moist sensation of the blood running down his stomach made him lose his temper.

Seeing the ambulanceman poised to strike again, Langford jabbed his fingers into the man's eyes.

352

Screaming, the Japanese dropped the broken bottle and fell back. Then Langford kicked out with every ounce of strength he could muster and felt his heel grind against the man's face.

Rolling over, Langford's anger became a blind fury as he felt more fragments of glass pierce his body and by the time he had pinned the Japanese down, he had lost all his self-control.

Yita cried out as Langford smashed the man's head against the side of the ambulance, repeating the process over and over until the Japanese eventually slumped down, unconscious.

The siren continued its discordant screaming, the sound reverberating in Langford's ears as he jerked the driver's companion from the passenger seat.

'I think I am lost.'

'Just keep driving.' Langford was panting for breath as he struggled to lash the two men on to the stretcher, a task made doubly difficult by the swaying motion of the ambulance and his increasing awareness of the pain in his chest.

Once he had buckled the leather straps, he used lengths of bandage to gag the two men and covered them with a blanket before easing himself into the passenger seat alongside Yita.

'Where the hell are we?' He scanned the dashboard until he found the siren switch and flicked it off. The sudden silence swept over him as he stared down at his blood-soaked shirt.

'You are hurt, Richard?'

'Just keep driving.'

'I do not know where to go.'

'I thought you knew Tokyo?'

'Biggest city in the world.' She shook her head, her tense face suddenly lit by the glare of a massive neon display hanging over the street. 'Only know bits of it,' she muttered.

'Obviously the wrong bits.' And Langford held his

breath as she drove through a red light as if it didn't exist. An on-coming car swerved to avoid them, the driver laying on his horn. 'We'd better have this on again,' he said, flicking the siren switch.

'We must find the expressway.' Yita peered anxiously through the windscreen. 'I think I know this ...'

Swinging round in his seat, Langford winced with pain as he grabbed a first-aid box from behind him. Taking a wad of lint, he opened his shirt and pressed the makeshift dressing against his chest. He made an attempt to anchor the pad with lengths of sticky tape but it was hopeless and he gave up. Then Yita yelled.

'A sign for the expressway.' She jerked the wheel over. 'It will take us to Nagoya.'

'Where the hell's that?' He caught a brief glimpse of the car behind them having to brake and swerve as Yita cut into his lane.

'It is on the way to Kobe.'

Langford pulled on the cigarette. 'Okay, pull over and I'll drive.'

She turned and stared at him, narrowly missing a motorcycle. 'But you are hurt.'

'We'll be bloody well dead if you carry on.' He reached out and grabbed the steering wheel. 'How in God's name did you ever get a driving licence?'

'I do not have a driver's licence.' And she suddenly swerved into the side of the road, jamming on the brakes. A lorry sped past, its horn blaring.

'Jesus.'

It took less than a minute for them to change places and Langford felt a sudden glow of confidence as he settled himself behind the wheel and accelerated along the wide street, the siren continuing to shriek its warning.

The route leading to the expressway was clearly marked, the ambulance had an almost-full tank and unless the man at the airport took it into his head to make a report, they should have a clear run. Then the thought slowly filtered through his brain that someone might just begin to wonder what had happened to the ambulance and he began speculating about ditching it. Not only was it conspicuous but they also had two passengers and Langford's confidence began to evaporate. Then he knew they had a more immediate problem.

They were on the access road to the expressway. A brightly-lit overhead sign said *Kobe* in large letters. But across the road stretched a line of toll-booths, each with its own red light. Langford kept firmly in his lane and accelerated, holding his breath as he stared at the red light and listened to the screaming siren.

'We won't have to pay toll,' said Yita.

The red light changed to green and Langford let out a sigh as they sped on to the expressway. 'I didn't intend to.'

'We can go all the way to Kobe on this road,' said Yita.

'Then Kobe here we come.' And he grinned, concealing a growing fear that there were those who might have other ideas.

3

Captain Umezu stood in the centre of the stateroom, his portly figure erect, his arms smartly to his side. 'Shiba-*san*, I am a sailor, a man of the sea. It is an honourable profession and I will not do as you ask because I cannot.'

Samwashima went to speak but Shiba gestured for him to remain silent. 'There is no danger to you, Captain-*san*. You must take my word for that.'

'You do not understand. I have never lost a ship and what you propose is —'

'Have a care,' rasped Shiba. 'You were selected to command the *Shimada Maru* because of your record. You have been a loyal servant to me.'

'And is this how you reward me? It is fraud, Shiba-*san*. To scuttle one's ship would mean disgrace.'

'Fool. Do you imagine that the world will ever hear of

it?' Shiba stood up and went across to a tape recorder. 'I repeat that there is no danger to you, Captain-*san*. However, I have taken certain precautions which you would do well to mark.' He pressed a button on the recorder and the stateroom was suddenly filled with the sound of a woman's voice. She was speaking quickly and the noise of children could be heard in the background. Umezu continued to stand erect as he listened, but was shaking his head when the tape clicked into silence.

'You would not harm them,' he said, quietly. 'You have no reason to harm them.'

'None,' agreed Shiba, returning to his seat. 'But only so long as you co-operate. I am not a brutal man, Umezu. I do not harm women and innocent children ... unless my hand is forced.'

Nodding, Umezu said, 'I shall not force you. It will be as you wish, Shiba-*san*.'

'Good. And do not attempt any radio communications, Captain. Unlike you, the Wireless Officer is entirely loyal to me.'

'I will be loyal.'

Shiba's lips twitched to form a sardonic smile. 'Of course. Now leave us.' He waited until Umezu had bowed himself out of the stateroom before turning to Samwashima. 'You saw the message from Tokyo?'

'Yes, Shiba-*san*. But I did not think that –'

'The police have been informed. Hopefully, they will deal with Mister Langford and the woman until our affairs have been stabilized.'

Samwashima was sweating and licked his lips, nervously. 'About Whitaker?'

'Leave him to me.'

'But the certification of the ship ... the government will want –'

'I shall forget about it,' Shiba snapped.

'But they insisted, Shiba-san.'

'And they will continue to insist. But by the time they

356

demand to see their precious piece of paper, this vessel and its cargo will be safely at the bottom of the Marianas Trench.'

'But if Whitaker –'

'You will be silent, Norihiko. Your fatuous blabbering tires me. You have failed, time and again.'

'I was not responsible for what happened in Thailand,' retorted Samwashima, hotly.

'Not directly, no. But your stupidity created the situation which demanded such hasty, ill-advised action. I did not think they would dare to come back. Now ...' Shiba frowned, removing his glasses. 'We shall remain on board until the loading has been completed. Then we must return to Osaka. You will accompany me and we shall fly back to Tokyo.'

'What will Langford do now?'

'I am not gifted with second sight but I imagine he will attempt to return to Kobe. He is a predictable kind of man, I think.' He replaced his glasses. 'He is like you in many ways, Norihiko. Predictable, and stupid. You are like so much jelly. You tremble. Go, leave me. Creep into some hole and smoke your cigarettes. And tell them I will see Whitaker now.'

Samwashima opened his mouth to speak but thought better of it and bowed awkwardly before retreating from Shiba's presence.

Alone in the stateroom, Toshiro Shiba began pacing, his brow creased as he stared, preoccupied, at the floor. He was lost in his own thoughts when the door opened and Professor Whitaker was pushed into the spacious cabin by two Japanese crewmen.

'This is an outrage!'

Shiba started, his face suddenly taut as he stared at the Professor. 'Untie him,' he snapped and then shook his head, spreading his arms in a gesture which seemed to indicate hopeless despair. 'A thousand pardons, Whitaker-*san*. There has been a misunderstanding.' He glared at the two crewmen, speaking sharply in Japanese as they went out.

'Misunderstanding isn't the word I would have chosen,' growled Whitaker, massaging his wrists. 'Just who the hell do you think you are?'

'Clearly, there has been an awful mistake, Professor. I do assure you that –'

'You've made two big mistakes. The first was your plan to sink the *Shimada Maru*. The second was to try to use me. But it's not going to work, Shiba. When this ship ties up at Kyomo –'

'You will do nothing. Sit down.' Shiba's tone suddenly changed from one of apology to that of a man accustomed to unquestioning obedience. 'I do not make mistakes, Professor Whitaker. The arrangements for the disposal of the irradiated fuel rods from Kyomo have been sanctioned by the Japanese government in consultation with the United States. Doctor Bailey devised the project with –'

'I don't give a damn who sanctioned the project,' said Whitaker, raising his voice. 'It's madness.'

'You are saying that it will not work?' Shiba's expression softened. 'Please, do be seated, Professor, We are both educated, civilized men. We surely can discuss the matter?'

Biting back his anger, Whitaker sank down into a chair. 'I am saying two things to you. Firstly, the way I've been treated –'

'Professor, I give you my word that it was the result of a misunderstanding. There is no need for me to lie.'

After a long pause, Whitaker nodded. 'All right, we'll forget that for the time being. But you're playing with fire, Shiba. And a lot of people could get burnt besides you.'

'Bailey was a fool, but he was also a brilliant man. And he wasn't merely a scientist. He was an engineer, with the ability to work at a very high level on two planes: the theoretical and the practical. You must know this. And you must also have known that he had devoted many years to the problem of disposing of nuclear waste.'

'All over the world, scientists and technicians at universities and research centres are working towards a solution. But they haven't found one yet.'

'You are discounting the *Shimada Maru*,' said Shiba. 'It is a beautiful example of what can be achieved when the resources of an organisation like the Shimada Corporation are carefully harnessed. Insoluble problems can be solved, simply and expediently.'

'Look, Mister Shiba, I'm not saying that it won't work. Just that it might not work. There are two flaws in the scheme. To begin with, the waste from Kyomo hasn't been re-processed. Chemically speaking, it is still very active and highly dangerous.'

'That was taken into account in the design of the inner flasks,' said Shiba.

'All right. But what happens once you've sunk this ... this time-bomb? Because that's what it is. You open the stopcocks and the *Shimada Maru* sinks in deep water. What then? You don't know because you can't know. In Europe, a symposium of some of the world's leading physicists decided unanimously to reject a plan to dump active waste at sea even when the material had undergone a vitrification process. You know what I mean? The stuff is sealed in high-density glass so that you end up with something resembling a kingsize paperweight.'

'Timid little men,' rasped Shiba.

'Responsible men. For God's sake, the period of risk isn't just a matter of years or even a few decades. It's thousands of years. I won't deny Bailey his brilliance but perhaps if he'd been older ... perhaps he might have been more cautious.'

'I value caution as a virtue, Professor. But as I have tried to explain, this venture has the approval – in secret, of course – of all the major authorities. And you cannot stop it because my government no longer requires your certification.'

'I see.' Whitaker rose to his feet. 'In that case, we have nothing further to discuss. As soon as this ship reaches

Kyomo, I shall send a cable to Washington.' He started towards the door. 'I've devoted my life to science as you must have devoted yours to business. I sincerely believe that what you are about to attempt could result in catastrophe.'

'The sincerity of your beliefs is obvious, Professor.' Shiba also stood. 'However, I cannot permit you the opportunity to express your views. I am sorry.'

'What the hell do you mean?'

Shiba gave an apologetic shrug. 'Simply that your attitude ... your decision, leaves me no alternative. The Shimada Corporation is one of the world's richest companies. Measured in any currency, Professor, countless millions have been invested in this project. There is too much at stake.' He walked to the door and opening it, revealed the two crewmen waiting outside. 'I sincerely regret that your life is forfeit, Whitaker-*san*.'

'You're mad.'

'You may believe so, but you would be wrong.' Shiba gently pressed the tips of his fingers together. 'It is a mystery to me. You scientists are all alike. You dream your dreams and expound your theories and yet ... when it comes to the point and you are faced with reality, you retreat into the academic void.'

Whitaker shook his head and stared at the two crewmen. 'You're insane,' he muttered, trying to back away.

'Take him,' whispered Shiba.

As the two Japanese pinned back Whitaker's arms and began to drag him to the door, he broke free.

'You killed Bailey. Of course, I should have guessed. Bailey must have arrived at the same conclusion —' He gasped as Shiba's men went for him again.

'Guesswork never enters into my calculations, Professor. And you are wrong about Doctor Bailey. He believed in this project.'

'Then why kill him?'

'I did not.'

360

'Then you gave the orders. But if you kill me —'

'When, Professor, not if. Unless, of course, you are prepared to reconsider ... and act accordingly.'

'Listen, for God's sake ... if you sink this ship, you could be responsible for the end of the world.'

'Melodramatic nonsense, Professor. I remain convinced by Doctor Bailey's work even if you are not.'

'Then why did you have him killed?'

Shiba stared across the stateroom for a moment, slowly shaking his head. 'We disagreed ... about another matter.' And he turned away as the crewmen pulled Whitaker into the corridor.

4

It was shortly before dawn and Tokyo was a long way behind. Langford had switched off the siren and the illuminated ambulance sign but kept going at a steady eighty miles an hour. They had stopped briefly at Shimizu for petrol, which they bought in a large Jerry can, and were now approaching Nagoya. The two ambulancemen were still strapped on the stretcher and were both quiet, one because he was too scared and the other because he was dead.

As he drove along the almost deserted expressway, Richard Langford knew that he would have the man's death on his conscience for the rest of his days. With Shiba discredited, the killing of Oki could be defended, excused and perhaps even welcomed. But the ambulance attendant had merely been doing his duty. He had been the innocent bystander caught up in something he couldn't have been expected to understand. And he had died because Langford had taken the law into his own hands.

Yita had remained silent for most of the journey, staring impassively through the windscreen, and Langford had long since given up trying to fathom her mind. As the expressway curved around the glittering sea of light which was the city of Nagoya, his own thoughts were many thousands of miles distant.

The conditions were similar: just before dawn; a long stretch of wide road lit by harsh, yellow lights and virtually no other traffic apart from his own vehicle, an armoured Landrover. It had been a hunch, no more, no less. At least, that was the story he told at the official inquiry and they believed him. The man who had given the tip-off about the arms cache had proved himself to be reliable in the past. He also had a family and there was no way that Langford was going to put any of them in jeopardy. When the Landrover had pulled up, they all got out, Langford, a sergeant and two soldiers, youngsters fresh from basic training.

Up to that point, Richard Langford was perfectly clear about the sequence of events but from the moment they left the Landrover, it was impossible to be certain. Actions and reactions had been too swift. And so much was pure conjecture, possibility against probability. If one of them hadn't chosen to throw a stone, maybe nothing would have happened. But a large chunk of flint had been hurled down from the roof, clattering against the armoured Landrover. And when Langford had looked upwards, he caught a glimpse of them, two dark figures scurrying along the parapet, one of them holding what looked like a rifle. Barely aware of his own actions, Langford had literally shoved the two young soldiers out of the way, grabbed the rifle from his sergeant and fired. One of the figures stopped, staggered backwards and then tumbled from the roof to land in an obscene, broken heap almost at their feet.

At close range, it's difficult to mistake a thirteen year-old boy clutching a stick. But speed and distance had added another dimension. The child, a man; the stick, an Armourlite rifle.

At the official inquiry, Counsel for the boy's parents made a good case for a manslaughter prosecution but Langford was lucky. Everything was tidied up very neatly, including his own so-called resignation Later, another patrol found the arms cache but no one heard much about that. The reporters and the commentators were too busy exposing yet another example of British brutality in Ulster.

There was a fragment of time – Langford never knew whether it was measured in minutes or seconds – when he felt himself to be back in Belfast. He was on the way to another bomb alert. The police car was behind him, its siren piercing the air as they sped through the shabby, empty streets past the rows of houses with their windows bricked up. Then, quite suddenly, Yita was there, speaking to him, and it was a Japanese police car which was coming up fast in the outside lane.

Langford knew he had been stupid. The expressway had provided them with the means of covering a lot of ground in a short time, but he cursed himself for not having had the nous to escape from the high-speed trap while he had had the chance. Yita was gripping the dashboard, her face set. Langford had never heard her complain. She simply accepted everything and if it was the blind, Eastern brand of fatalism which he thought he so disliked, he now had reason to see at least some virtue in it.

Pressing the accelerator to the floor, he watched the speedo needle touch ninety. Reaching out, he flicked on the siren and the illuminated ambulance sign. The noise seemed curiously distant but the police car held its position and Langford decided that unless the driver was purposely holding back, the Japanese-built ambulance had a slight edge. But as they raced along the expressway, Langford was forced to consider the depressing certainty of other police cars being alerted by radio. It was as if an invisible net were being pulled tightly around them. Then he saw the sign.

It was impossible to read in any detail apart from one name: Gifu. Nor was there time to consult Yita. The slip-road from the expressway was rushing towards them and he had to decide quickly. Agonisingly, Langford weighed the possibilities. Dawn had hardly broken. The dusky light was deceptive. Then he knew that he had no option but to take a chance and pulled as far into the outside lane as he could.

The police car also shifted its position, trying to creep up on the inside. Langford obliged them by easing his foot off the accelerator so that the patrol car began to narrow the distance between them. The exit was coming up fast as he kept his eyes on the mirror. Tensing himself against the steering wheel, he waited until the front of the police car was level with the rear of the ambulance. Then he stamped on the accelerator and jerked the wheel hard over.

The police driver was obviously an expert with sharp reflexes but no amount of skill could have compensated sufficiently to outwit Langford's manoeuvre. The ambulance hurtled across the three-lane expressway at nearly ninety miles an hour. The police car braked, swerved and went into a lethal skid. Langford yelled for Yita to hang on as the ambulance missed the exit, jumping the hard shoulder before smashing down on the slip-road. As he stamped on the brakes and fought to bring the ambulance back under control, he caught a last glimpse of the police car crumpling against the crash barrier. Then Yita screamed.

The second car was parked at an angle across the road and a policeman was in the process of getting out when the ambulance sliced into it. But the ambulance was heavier, travelling at some seventy miles an hour and the jarring impact simply pushed the police car over. Langford did the only thing possible. He stamped on the accelerator and hoped for the best.

They headed into Gifu, a vicious, metallic scraping coming from the off-side front wheel.

'We need another car,' he said, glancing quickly at Yita.

'No good to steal one.' There was a tremor in her voice and she shook her head. 'Take a train. Better.'

'Train? For Christ's sake, we can't –'

364

'But we *can*, Richard. We can take the *Shinkansen* from here.' And she stared at him, wide-eyed. 'You know, the Bullet train?'

Frowning, Langford eventually nodded as he recalled having heard something about the hundred-mile-an-hour Japanese trains. 'How much further?'

Yita peered through the windscreen. It was nearly full-daylight now and there was more traffic as they neared the town. 'Maybe ten kilometres.'

'Maybe? All right, we'll give it a try. But we'll have to get rid of this quickly.'

Once they had located the railway station, Langford chose an un-manned underground car park and they left the ambulance in a far corner, shielded by a high trailer.

'What about them?' said Yita, pointing to the two men.

'Someone will find them ... later.' He pulled the blinds inside the windows. 'Come on, let's find that train.'

She hesitated, staring at him for a moment. 'Your shirt, Richard ...'

He looked down and saw that the white shirt front was now almost completely caked with blood. 'I'll have to buy something ... a raincoat.'

'You must wait here while I get the tickets.'

'But if there's a train ...'

Yita shook her head. 'We cannot travel like this. People will see.'

'Okay, go and get the tickets. And a timetable. I'll wait.'

Langford watched her go, her footsteps echoing in the underground car park long after she had disappeared from view. Standing by the ambulance, he lit a cigarette. His hand was shaking. Then he had an idea and unlocked the door, wincing as he leant inside and pulled at the sheet under the stretcher.

The dark eyes of the attendant were wide open and stared accusingly at Langford as he watched the sheet being torn. Langford was about to speak, but changed his mind. Slamming the door closed again, he locked it, pocketing the key before folding the torn piece of sheet. It was a coarse material but once he had wrapped it around his chest and buttoned up his jacket, the effect wasn't too bad. Then he noticed that the blood had begun to seep through the jacket as well. But he knew there was nothing he could do about it.

He kept staring at his watch as he waited by the ambulance. Time seemed to stand still. After about ten minutes, Yita reappeared, walking slowly. She seemed upset.

'No train?'

'One hour and twenty-five minutes to wait. We have just missed ...'

'Bound to happen.'

'That is better.' She reached out and raised the lapels of his uniform. 'There is a shop ... just near here. I looked inside. They have coats.'

'Okay, let's go buy one. We can't stay here.'

Langford felt conspicuous as they emerged into the watery sunlight. It had been raining and the pavements glistened. Yita had taken his arm and he walked with his head bowed, expecting to hear a shout or feel someone's hand on his shoulder at any moment. Then they reached the clothes store and went inside.

Yita did all the talking and a diminutive Japanese insisted on taking measurements before producing a selection of gaberdine macs. But Langford was determined to choose the right one first time. He had to. A mottled bloodstain was already showing through the piece of sheet. Yita saw it and reacted by diverting the assistant's attention while Langford quickly checked that the sleeve length was right. And while the man's back was turned, he pulled the coat on and stared at his reflection in the mirror.

All things considered, it wasn't a bad fit but the assistant thought otherwise and offered an alternative, chattering away to Yita in Japanese.

'Tell him this is fine,' snapped Langford, pulling a wad of notes from his pocket.

366

The man seemed upset and tried to argue but eventually gave way and took the money. It was all over. Or so Langford thought as he started towards the door. Then the man called out.

Both the shop assistant and Yita seemed to be talking at once but the Japanese was determined and lunged at Langford. He wanted the price tag which was still strung on the lapel.

'Don't do anything,' hissed Yita, watching as the man carefully removed the tag. Then they left, heading towards the station.

Langford breathed a sigh of relief. 'How long before the train …?'

'Ten minutes.'

'Let's hope it's running to time.'

'Japanese trains always on time.'

They approached the barrier and Yita presented the tickets. The man on the gate didn't give them a second glance and a few minutes later, they were on the platform, waiting.

'Richard?'

'What?'

'The man in the ambulance … he was dead, wasn't he?'

'Yes.'

'I am sorry.'

'You're sorry? How the hell do you think I feel?'

'When we get to Kobe –'

'We'll see Gunning. Look, I know this hasn't been easy but –' He stopped speaking as an announcement came over the public address sytem. 'What was that?'

'The train is coming, the *Shinkansen*. We must stand here.' And she pointed down at a pair of white lines.

'Just like the bloody Germans,' he muttered, glancing warily along the platform.

The train arrived dead on time and they boarded it gratefully, sinking down into the comfortable seats just as it pulled out. Langford felt unbearably tired. And hot. The heating in the carriage was so fierce that he was soon sweating from every pore. Other passengers had stripped off, many of them down to their shirts but Langford knew he daren't even unbutton the raincoat, let alone take it off.

'You are worried, Richard?'

Turning, he looked into her eyes and saw the gentle compassion he had noticed before. 'What do you think?' There seemed little point in pretending.

'Everything will be all right. You shall see.' And she smiled.

The smooth rhythm of the train as it sped towards Kobe was certainly conducive to sleep and most of the other passengers were taking full advantage of it. But there was no way Langford could sleep. Apart from the throbbing pain in his chest, he felt a nagging uncertainty which he hadn't confided to Yita. When they reached Kobe, they would go to the American Consulate because there was nowhere else but Langford was far from happy about it.

Feeling the bulging pack of photographs in his pocket, he remembered the *Wat* Keo, Soichi Heyashi in the ruined temple lit by the oil lamps. And he remembered Lim Mok slumped in the Volkswagen, half his head shot away.

Langford moistened his lips and stared out of the window. The train appeared to be slowing down and he felt his pulse thudding. 'Why are we stopping?'

Yita shrugged and looked at the tickets. 'The train stops ... this will be Maibura. Then there is Kyoto, Osaka and Kobe.'

'I thought this was a non-stop express?'

'No ... but it is very fast.'

Langford took a deep breath. He was running scared. And knowing scared men make wrong judgements, he was worried. Every stop posed a threat and as the train pulled into Maibura, he peered anxiously from the window. Then he felt Yita take his hand.

'You must not worry, Richard. If it is written ...'

'So you keep saying.'

Four seemingly endless minutes elapsed before the *Shinkansen* pulled away again, quickly accelerating.

Langford began to relax, reasoning that if the Japanese police knew they were on the train, they would have been waiting. The problem was knowing where.

When they stopped at Kyoto, he was on edge again, his eyes narrowed as he scanned the platform.

Another four minutes passed, the sweep-hand of his watch jerking round the dial so that each second seemed like a minute. Then the train moved out.

Langford eventually managed to extract a handkerchief from an inner pocket. The effort cost him a lot of pain and he could feel the cuts on his chest as he mopped his perspiring face. Yita remained silent, staring vacantly into space, her eyes open but suddenly expressionless. He wanted to talk to her but he knew that even if he could have found the right words, the presence of the other people in the carriage would have inhibited him into silence.

When the train pulled into Osaka, there was a general exodus, most of the passengers in their carriage getting out. Langford was still uneasy but there was no sign of any police activity and he began to breathe again as the seconds ticked away. Four minutes passed.

'What's holding us up?'

Yita shrugged. 'Maybe ...' But she didn't finish the sentence and knowing that Osaka was within reasonable driving distance of Kobe, Langford speculated about leaving the train there and going by road.

'If we hired a car from here ...'

'Better to wait,' said Yita.

Langford opened his mouth to speak but the train suddenly jerked into motion. 'Next stop Kobe,' he muttered, feeling that steam should have been rising from his over-heated body.

Twenty minutes later, the *Shinkansen* began to slow down as it approached Kobe. Langford went to move but Yita cautioned him to remain seated. And as they pulled into the station, Langford was glad he had taken her advice. The platform was swarming with police.

Apart from the uniformed men – and women – it wasn't difficult to spot the plain-clothes detectives. It was a show of force which surprised Langford as he gazed from the carriage. Then he remembered the man in the ambulance. And the Canadian at the airport. If he had died too …

'We've had it,' said Langford, dully. 'Damn.'

The serried ranks of police seemed content to let other passengers disembark and Yita took his hand. 'Come. We shall go now.'

'Might as well.' He stood up slowly, wincing as the muscles in his chest sent shafts of pain through his body.

As they left the carriage, two policemen confronted them in the doorway and Langford smiled, ruefully. Then Yita said something in Japanese and the police simply stood aside, bowing politely as she and Langford stepped past them on to the platform.

'What the hell's going on?'

Yita shook her head and smiled. 'They are just taking the train. I had a feeling. They did not look like men on duty.'

'Jesus.' Langford glanced back but all the policemen had got on to the train and before they had reached the steps leading down to the exit, the *Shinkansen* had started to move.

'Maybe there has been a big police meeting,' said Yita, handing over the ticket stubs at the barrier.

Langford was in no mood to guess at probabilities. There were more police standing around the main booking hall and unlike the men who had boarded the train, they seemed to be rather more alert.

It took less than three minutes to reach the main exit where a line of cabs stood waiting. Only one set of doors seemed to be in use and there were more police waiting outside who appeared to scrutinize them as they emerged into the watery sunlight. Langford could feel his pulse racing as they approached the leading taxi. Then it was over.

Sweating, Langford pushed her into the cab and they

370

set off for the American Consulate. 'So far so good,' he said, unable to stop himself glancing quickly out of the rear window.

'We shall see Gunning?' said Yita, quietly. He nodded.

'And then you're going to get the hell out of it.'

'What about you, Richard?'

'Never mind about me. This time ... this time, you'll do as I say.' She didn't answer and he grabbed her arm, almost fiercely. 'I mean it, Yita. They won't take that American passport back. You can go on to the States now. I'll give you some addresses ... people who know me. Later, when I've sorted a few things out, we'll make a new start.' But she shook her head, staring out of the windows.

The journey from the Shin-Kobe station took almost as long as the train had taken to cover more than twenty times the distance, the cab often reduced to a slow, jerking crawl through the rush-hour traffic.

'I will not leave you in Japan, Richard. Whatever you say.'

He was about to say a great deal but they finally pulled up outside the Consulate.

As they stood waiting in the foyer of the modern building overlooking Higashimachi Street, Richard Langford felt a sensation of at least partial security. He was on American territory and safe from arrest, if only for a short time. Then Gunning appeared, his expression one of unconcealed hostility.

'I might have known,' he rasped, taking Langford by the arm and leading him quickly into a windowless interview room. 'Why in God's name did you come back? I gave you explicit instructions ...'

'I had my reasons. Mind if we sit? We've had a rather difficult journey.'

'I bet you have. But you can't stay here.'

'I have to talk to you. About the photographs.'

Gunning held out his hand. 'Let me have them.'

'In a moment. First –'

'You don't have many moments left, Langford. Almost

every cop in Japan will have got your number by now. And hers.' He jerked his thumb at Yita. 'Give me the pictures and I'll arrange transportation ... if I can.'

'Where to?'

'Wherever they can get you, you jerk. Is it true you knocked off some guy in Tokyo?'

Langford sighed. 'It wasn't intentional. And right this minute, I'm too damned tired to care either way.'

'Is that so?' Gunning snatched at the khaki bundle containing Heyashi's photographs. 'You fool. You Goddamn fool. If you hadn't come back I could have saved you.'

'It's a bit late to talk about saving me.'

'But I warned you ... told you that —'

'You told me nothing,' snapped Langford. 'But there's a whole lot I'm going to tell you.'

'Some other time. I have to make a call and get you off the premises. If the Consul found out that I was harbouring a wanted criminal ...'

'What are you going to do? Turn us in?'

'If I had any sense, yes. As it is, I'll do what I can to help.' And he left the room, slamming the door behind him.

'Why is he so angry? You got the photographs. He should be grateful to you.'

'Don't expect any thanks from him.'

'I do not think he likes us, Richard.'

'It's mutual.' He lit a cigarette and they sat in silence until Gunning returned.

'I've got a call in to one of my contacts. Hopefully, we can set up the same sort of deal as before. Except this time, you don't come back.'

'Look, Gunning, I want —'

'What you want doesn't matter any more. Just hear me and hear me good, Langford. The Jap police want you and the broad and there's no way that the U.S. Foreign Service can become involved. Frankly, I don't give a shit if you slaughter every Jap on the islands but my people in

372

Washington are rather sensitive.'

Langford stood up and pulled off the raincoat. 'I need clothes,' he muttered and carefully removed the length of sheet from his chest.

'God in heaven.' Gunning stared at him for a moment. 'Shot?'

'Glass. Is there a doctor?'

'What the hell do you think this place is, a welfare centre?'

Langford's arm shot out and he grabbed Gunning's jacket. 'We've been through hell to get your bloody photographs. Now I want some attention. And unless you co-operate, I'll raise Cain.' He shoved the American towards the door. 'I mean it. I've had just about enough of your double-dealing.'

'What double-dealing?' Gunning eyed him suspiciously.

'You know perfectly well.' He started to take off the blood-stained jacket. 'Okay, a doctor and clothes. And some food, too.'

'See here, Langford, we may have a pretty tight schedule.'

'Stuff it. Unless you want one very colourful diplomatic incident. I've got nothing to lose now. Remember?'

'Okay, cool it, I'll see what I can do.' He started towards the door.

'One more thing,' said Langford. 'Your Vietnamese chum, Lim Mok.'

'Yeah, I heard.'

'Good. You can use some of your unaccounted-for budget to help his family.'

Gunning nodded. 'You think of everything, don't you?'

'No, unfortunately I don't. I made several mistakes. But from here on, I'll be more careful. So don't try setting me up again or by Christ, I'll add you to my list.'

The American stared at him for a long moment. 'Don't try to hustle me, Langford. You need my help. Okay, I'll do the best I can. But not because you're holding a pistol

373

to my head. I've got to keep the lid down tight or the pot's going to boil over. You understand me?'

'Yes, I think I do. But as far as threats go, you're the one who should be worried.'

'Yeah, that makes two of us.' He opened the door. 'You stay here. And in case you get any funny ideas, there's a pair of Marines outside with orders to restrain you. They're not very gentle.'

After the door had closed behind him, Yita went to Langford and helped him undo the shirt.

'Will we go on the boat again, Richard?'

'I don't know.' He shook his head. 'Look, I want to explain something, the reason why I had to come back to Japan ... and why I have to stay.'

'But Gunning said—'

'Never mind him. Just listen and pay attention. I don't want you to get hurt, Yita. The important thing is for you to get out of Japan. If there is another boat to Hong Kong, you can go to the office there ... I'll write down the name of the man. He's a friend. But there's something you must know, just in case something happens to me.'

'You are going to leave me?'

'I may have to ... just for a bit. So listen carefully because what I have to tell you is important.

5

The air inside the Minister's office was thick with smoke. Because it faced onto a large courtyard some way back from the street, the office was very quiet. But instead of the calm tranquility to which the Minister was accustomed, the silence was heavy and tense.

From his seat in the corner of the room, DuCros glowered at Bouscat. 'You have exceeded your authority, Inspector.'

'I think not, *M'sieu*.' Bouscat sucked at his cigarette. 'Besides, my department is not responsible to SDECE.'

'But I ordered you to —'

'Enough.' And the Minister rapped the desk with his knuckles. 'You will kindly stop this childish bickering.' He swung round and faced DuCros. 'The Inspector has done no more than his duty. As a result of his investigations —'

'We are no nearer to finding Picot,' DuCros interjected.

The Minister fixed DuCros with a piercing stare. 'Perhaps, *mon Colonel*, you will do me the courtesy of remaining silent whilst I am speaking?' He paused and for all its blatant theatricality, the performance was devastatingly effective. 'As I was saying. Bouscat seems to have uncovered what may be some kind of plot ... conspiracy, even. Of course, there may be a very simple explanation. Pure coincidence cannot be ruled out. But we still have to decide what action to take.'

After a moment's hesitation, DuCros said, 'There is too much supposition for my liking. Had my department been consulted ...'

'Please, Colonel, this futile wrangling must cease.' The Minister picked up his pipe and began to fill it. 'Inspector, I have to be certain. You are sure of your facts?'

Bouscat nodded, gravely. 'We have learned from our colleagues in Bonn that Doctor Bailey left Germany before his contract with the Bayer Group expired. We also know that he went to Japan, where he was killed.'

'But you say in your report that Bailey's death was accidental,' snapped DuCross.

'I think it is less important for us to worry about how Doctor Bailey died,' explained Bouscat. 'It is the fact of his death which concerns me because seen in the context of Picot's disappearance, his flight to Tokyo —'

'And the American,' said the Minister, thoughtfully. 'The American Professor.'

'Whitaker is English. He merely happens to live in the United States. As I have said in my report, American FBI people visited his home and spoke with Whitaker's wife.'

The Minister nodded. 'So this Professor Whitaker also

goes to Japan to work for the Shimada Corporation, an organisation with which our American friend, Hewens, has connexions. Is that correct?'

'Exactly so, *M'sieu le Ministre*.' Bouscat stubbed out his cigarette and stared briefly at DuCros, noting the Colonel's sour, almost hurt expression. 'I have suggested in my report that we now liaise officially with Washington and Tokyo. I do not believe that there is any more we can do here.'

The tense silence returned until DuCros cleared his throat and stood up, his shoulders hunched as he walked to the window. 'If I know anything about the Americans, they will have already begun to make inquiries on the basis of your so-called unofficial telephone conversations. You may find that you have stirred up a hornets' nest, Inspector. We can only hope that you are not too badly stung.'

The Minister leaned back in his chair and sighed. 'At least Bouscat discovered the nest, Colonel. And if your own department had acted more decisively when you found out that Picot was a homosexual ...'

DuCross started, his lean face like stretched parchment as he fought to contain his anger. Then his expression changed to one of surprise as Bouscat intervened.

'I am fairly confident the Colonel could not have done more. I have checked the files and they show that Section Nine compiled a very full dossier on Claude Picot which your predecessor chose to ignore.'

The Minister countered by lighting his pipe. And when he finally opened his mouth to speak, they were interrupted.

'*Mes regrets, M'sieu le Ministre*.' The clerk bowed and glanced towards Bouscat. 'There is an urgent communication for the Inspector. It has just arrived.' He handed a long envelope to Bouscat and then withdrew.

After a short pause, Henri Bouscat stood up and placed the contents of the envelope on the desk. 'There has been a formal complaint,' he said. 'Someone in London has gone to the British police about Meyrick Hewens. The Scotland Yard people have officially requested our co-operation.'

The pipe clenched firmly between his teeth, the Minister stared at the sheet of paper before handing it on to DuCros. 'The solution to our problems, gentlemen. You will reply immediately, Inspector. You may inform the British that we shall co-operate to the full.'

DuCros had recovered his composure. 'But there can be no official co-operation with Washington,' he said. 'Government policy –'

'I have just said that we shall co-operate to the full, Colonel. If that requires liaison with Washington, so be it. You have my authority.'

'In writing?' said DuCros, smiling slightly.

'Of course not.'

DuCross shook his head. 'In that case ...'

'You will obey orders, Colonel,' snapped the Minister, his tone defying any argument. 'You will act in concert with Inspector Bouscat. Go to London if necessary. Anything. Just remember that our priority is to find Picot without there being any scandal.'

'Very well.' DuCros almost jumped to his feet. 'If you will excuse me, I shall begin by collating all the information we can on the Shimada Corporation.'

'I've already done that,' said Bouscat. 'The file is in my office. It operates world-wide and has offices here in Paris, in the Rue Oudinot. It also has two electronics factories just outside Limoges.'

'You are thorough, Inspector,' said the Minister, appreciatively. 'Very well, gentlemen, proceed. And keep me informed of developments.'

As they descended the long, curving stairway to the main hall, Bouscat touched DuCros' arm.

'I have an apology to make to you, *M'sieu le Colonel.*'

'Several, I would have thought.'

'Only one that I know of,' retorted Bouscat. 'It concerns

Rueff. We now know who killed him ... or near enough. It was a gang contract. The word was put out that he'd turned informer.'

'Dog eats dog, Bouscat,' said DuCros, acidly. 'You of all people should know that.'

'And some dogs get eaten by other beasts, Colonel. You should know that.'

The two men stood at the bottom of the stairs and faced each other in hostile silence. Then DuCros spoke again.

'Don't let the Minister's effusive praise swell your head, my friend. He is a political bird sitting on an unsteady perch. He is also young and still not quite sure of his wings. You would do well to reflect on that. And the reason that we in SDECE dislike co-operation with Washington is because in the final analysis, it means working with the CIA, and they have proved to be unreliable.'

Bouscat shrugged. 'These matters are beyond me. But it is the Minister's wish that you and I work together.'

'I see no problems,' replied DuCros, tartly. 'Do you?'

'Always, *M'sieu*. But I do my best to avoid them.'

6

Yita's placid expression had disappeared and her eyes were downcast. 'I find it difficult to understand what you say, Richard.'

'Don't try to. But now you know the truth, we'll do things my way. Okay?'

She stared at him for a moment and then nodded. 'I have made trouble for you. I can see that now. I should have stayed on the 'plane and gone to Los Angeles.'

'No, you did the right thing. If it hadn't been for you, I probably wouldn't have got out of the airport.'

'That might have been better ... the man ...'

'Sure. But what's done is done.' He glanced round as the door swung open.

'Those clothes aren't a bad fit,' said Gunning. 'The Doc patch you up okay?'

'Yes. What happens now?'

'Don't I even get a word of thanks?'

'Thanks? If it hadn't been for you –'

'All right, Langford, knock it off. By the way, the photographs ... you did a great job. They're dynamite. If you hadn't come back to Japan ... Aw, what the hell, it's too late now. We've made some inquiries and the Jap cops have got official warrants out for the both of you. Anyways, I've done what I can. There's a truck waiting out the back.'

'Another sea-trip to Hong Kong?' said Langford. 'I don't think your chum on the freighter will welcome us with open arms.'

'This doesn't involve him. You just do as you're told – right down the line. It's the last time I'm putting my neck at risk for you.'

'That's rich. I seem to recall that the whole thing was your idea. We were supposed to have a mutual interest. Wasn't that what you said?'

'Our interests ceased to be mutual when you decided to go and do your own thing.'

Langford shook his head. 'No, that's not true. You needed someone expendable to do your dirty work. Now you've got what you wanted, I'm just a liability.'

'I won't deny that.' Gunning held open the door. 'Come on, I'll take you out.'

They followed the American through the Consulate and into the garden where a group of children were playing a kind of rudimentary baseball. Langford grinned at them as they walked past but none of the kids seemed to take any notice. Then they reached the back entrance, a very solid looking door set in a high brick wall and Gunning paused, his hand resting on the security combination lock.

'Look, Langford, I just want to say ... well, you did a good job. We're grateful.'

'Handing out medals, are we?'

Gunning scowled. 'I just wanted you to know, that's all. If you hadn't come back … if you'd stuck to orders, things would have been a whole lot easier. As it turned out …'

'What about her?'

'She'll be okay. She can keep the passport.' Gunning gave Yita a quick smile. 'You're an American citizen … Mrs Langford.'

'That's not what I meant and you know it. Let her go. Get her to Hong Kong. I'll stay and take my chances.'

'Sorry, Langford, no can do.'

'Why not? There are still a lot of loose ends … about the photographs … what happened in Thailand …'

'Some other time.' Gunning eased the door open and peered out. 'Okay, they're waiting.' He stood to one side so that Langford could see out into the street. A small, grey truck like a miniature pantechnicon was parked about ten yards distant. Two Japanese were standing by the rear doors, waiting.

'Who are they?' asked Langford, warily.

'You should know better than to ask, friend. For Chrissakes, you're hot now. What do you expect, a Cadillac with outriders?' Gunning stepped out into the street and nodded at the two Japanese who began opening the rear doors of the truck. 'Okay, away you go now. Just walk straight in.'

Taking Yita's arm, Langford went out. 'You haven't finished with me, Gunning.'

'Save it, Langford. And have a good trip.'

As they walked towards the truck, one of the doors swung open and Langford stiffened as he caught sight of the shadowy figures inside. He paused in mid-stride, gripping Yita's arm as he made a split-second decision based on nothing more substantial than a sudden, inarticulate fear.

'Run,' he hissed, almost jerking Yita off her feet. But before he had gone two paces, they came at him.

Letting go of Yita, Langford threw a punch which caught the first man squarely on the jaw and as he went down, Langford pivotted round in time to fend off another attacker, kicking him hard in the shins before delivering a powerful chop against the side of his head. Turning, he saw the American still framed in the doorway, his swarthy features compressed into a hard frown. Then Yita screamed.

More men jumped from the back of the truck and Langford knew he was hopelessly outnumbered. He was also in pain from the wounds on his chest.

His decision to cut and run came too late. His hesitation had lasted no more than two seconds but that was just long enough for the Japanese to close the gap which Langford had chosen as the way out.

The first of the heavily-built men who tried to stop him came to grief. Dodging the man's punch, Langford hit him so far below the belt that the blow almost went between his legs. The Jap folded to the ground, gasping and vomiting. Then Langford staggered under the impact of a sharp stab of pain in his kidneys and wheeling round, he just managed one last flailing punch before they closed in.

He would have given up there and then, bowing to the inevitable. The new dressing had come away from his chest and the clothes supplied by Gunning were quickly becoming stained with blood. But as he backed away, about to raise his arms in a gesture of surrender, he heard a yelp of pain from inside the truck which was quickly followed by another ear-splitting cry from Yita.

Once again, blind anger overcame any feeling of pain and he lashed out in all directions, taking at least two of the Japanese by surprise. Butting, kicking and punching his way through the men, Langford fought his way to the truck.

Leaping on to the tailboard, he kicked the nearest man in the crotch and then grabbed at the door, swinging it round so that it caught another of the Japanese in the face and sent him flying. Langford shouted for Yita and heard her muffled attempt to answer. Then he knew he had made a fatal mistake. Outnumbered, tired and with his chest feeling as if someone were peeling the skin off with a blunt knife, Richard Langford knew the odds were stacked heavily against him.

Seeing the man with the cosh come from inside the truck, he heard Yita whimper and got one last look at Gunning before his head exploded.

7

Muga Tasaki stared from the window which overlooked the tiny harbour. He was smiling. Hearing the door click open, he turned as Komai entered.

'All is well?'

Komai nodded and went to the fire. 'Everything has gone according to plan.'

'Good.' Tasaki gave a low chuckle. 'I have a strange sadness for Toshiro Shiba. He is like the decaying body of a giant animal which plays host to the maggots which must inevitably destroy him.'

'You suppose he is unaware of the extent to which we have infiltrated his organization?'

Tasaki shook his head, slowly. 'No-o, he is not a fool and it would be wrong to underestimate him. But it is a measure of his predicament, I think, that he has thus far been unable to move against us.'

'The *Shimada Maru* sailed sooner than we had anticipated,' said Komai.

'That was not Shiba's doing. The technicians at Kyomo were getting desperate and put a lot of pressure on the government. I do not mind. We are ready, which is all that matters.'

'What will happen afterwards, Tasaki-*san*? What shall be done with the ship?'

'Nothing ... immediately. But once our affairs are certain, we shall create our own reprocessing industry. Then, my friend, we shall have plutonium.'

Komai started. 'You would support the development of

nuclear weapons by Japan?'

'Secretly, yes. Our neighbours have them. Why should China and the USSR possess such power without there being a counter-balance?'

'What about the treaties?'

'The new government will abrogate the treaties. And remember that both the United States of America and Russia have found it convenient to use such pacts for their own ends. Non-proliferation of nuclear weapons has had the advantage of concentrating power among a few nations, each seeking to dominate a certain region. I see no reason why the new Japan should not do the same.'

'Politically, there could be great risk in such developments,' said Komai. 'The people – '

'The people have become apathetic and degenerate. All the beauty, the perfection, the morality so revered by our forefathers, all this has been abused. Japan ... the Japan of Bushido has been smothered by the excrement of Western materialism. But it lives on in all our hearts, like a seed which lies dormant throughout the longest winter ...'

The shrill ringing of the telephone echoed in the room. Tasaki went to it and lifted the receiver to his ear.

'*Hei*?' He glanced at Komai as he listened, his lined face slowly creasing into a smile. '*Hei. Hei.*' Dropping the receiver back into its cradle, he came towards Komai, his arms outstretched. 'We are within hours of our goal, my friend. Soon, the destiny of Japan will lie in our hands. The *Shimada Maru* sails from Kyomo at noon tomorrow.'.

FIFTEEN

1

A doctor could have told Richard Langford that he was suffering from a severe contusion in the occipital region of the skull, caused by a blunt instrument which resulted in temporary loss of consciousness. The same doctor might have prescribed a short course of pain-killing drugs, rest and possibly an x-ray to establish that there was no physiological damage. But there was no doctor and all Langford knew was the blinding pain in the back of his head, an excruciating torment which also possessed an acoustic quality, so that he could actually hear the pain as well as feel it. It was a strangely familiar sound, a muffled kind of thudding which ebbed and flowed.

When he opened his eyes, he saw Yita bending over him in the gloomy half-light. Sitting up, he felt dizzy and sick. Then she reached out and gently eased him down again.

'You rest,' she said, her voice echoing.

'It's cold.' He stared at her, screwing up his eyes in a vain attempt to rid himself of the pain and the incessant throbbing. 'Where are we?'

'You must rest, Richard.'

'Noise,' he murmured, closing his eyes again. 'I can hear my head.'

'No, you hear the helicopters.'

Langford blinked open his eyes and gazed at her. The word meant nothing, just a meaningless jumble of sounds. Then his mind suddenly cleared and he jumped up, moving too quickly so that he almost fell. 'Choppers. Of course. But where are we?'

'I am not sure.' Yita was watching him carefully and he saw the livid bruise under her right eye.

'They hurt you,' he said. 'What happened?'

Yita shrugged as she helped him light a cigarette. 'I thought you were dead when they brought you into the truck. We seemed to drive for a long time. I'm not sure where except that it was a deserted place by the sea. There was a boat and we were brought here.'

'Where's here?'

'I think we are on one of the islands.'

'And the helicopters?' said Langford, trying to estimate from the noise how many machines there were.

'I saw them ... and men in uniform.'

'Is it an air-base?'

'No, I do not think so. But all the men have guns.'

Moving his head cautiously, Langford stared up at the small, barred window through which a thin shaft of sunlight came. They seemed to be in a kind of cellar or dungeon with walls constructed of massive granite blocks. The atmosphere was chill and dank.

'Does it hurt much?' said Yita, watching as he probed the back of his head.

'Yes, a bit.' He closed his eyes, wincing as his fingers came into contact with a lump the size of an egg. Then the thudding of the helicopters stopped abruptly.

'They have gone?'

'No,' said Langford, slowly getting to his feet. 'They were obviously just running the engines. If I could get at that window ...' But he staggered, dropping his cigarette and ended up leaning against the wall. It was wet and very slippery.

'You should stay lying down.'

'Maybe.' Taking his lighter from his pocket, he flicked it into life and held the flame against the wall. 'This place floods,' he muttered, staring at the dark strands of weed hanging from the granite. Then he slowly raised the lighter until he could clearly discern the high-water mark.

'What does it mean?'

He pocketed the lighter. 'When we arrived here, what was the state of the sea? Do you remember if it was high tide?'

She shook her head. 'I do not know.'

'All right. How long …' He stared at his watch. It was nearly three o'clock. 'What did you see when they brought us here?'

'Not very much. There is a small harbour. They carried you into a house. There was an old man there who laughed …'

'Shiba?'

'No, I have met Shiba. It was not him.'

Langford went slowly to the flight of stone steps which led up to a rusting iron door. The steps were covered with the slimy green Throng weed and he had to go on all-fours to climb up. The iron door was locked solid and there wasn't even a handle on the inside. Then he turned and discovered that he had gained at least a partial view through the barred window. He could see the grey, slate-like sea. And now that the helicopters were silent, he became aware of the rush and hiss of the breakers.

'How long have we been here?' he said, slowly descending the stone steps.

'Not long. An hour, maybe.'

Langford sat down again. The pain in his head was like a continuous rain of hammer-blows and it took all his powers of concentration to make his brain work.

'This place must flood at every high tide,' he murmured, thinking aloud. 'If we assume it was low water when they put us in here, we could have ten or eleven hours.' He sighed. 'Or maybe rather less than that.' Then he started up the steps again.

'You should not move about so much,' said Yita. 'It will be bad for your head.'

'My head won't matter unless we can get out of here before the water comes in again.'

'You think … you think they will leave us to …?'

'They certainly haven't put us here for the benefit of our health.' He stared out at the sea, craning his neck to gain as much height as possible. It was no use. He could see nothing except the water and he turned, examining the door again before he stepped down, almost losing his foothold as his shoes slipped on the weed. 'Did you notice if the choppers – the helicopters – if they had any markings?'

'No ... they were just there.'

'How many?'

'Four?' she shook her head. 'I did not count them.'

'Doesn't matter.' He sank down and took out his handkerchief. 'Here, fill this with weed. As wet as you can.'

She obeyed without question and he held the makeshift ice-pack against the back of his head. It seemed to help except for the trickle of icy-cold water which ran down the back of his neck. He shuddered.

'What are we going to do, Richard?'

'I'm thinking about it.' He looked at her, saw his own fear reflected in her eyes. 'If it's any comfort, you were right about Gunning. I imagine that had we gone back to Hong Kong, his friends would have ...' He left the sentence unfinished. 'Listen ...'

There was the muffled sound of footsteps outside the door, followed by a metallic scraping.

Looking up, Langford saw that a small grille had opened in the door, behind which a light glowed.

'So you are the Englishman?'

The voice had a cracked timbre and each word was enunciated with tremendous care.

'Who the hell are you?' Langford went towards the steps, peering up at the shadowy face.

'You have meddled in matters beyond your understanding, Mister Langford. That was foolish.'

'Shiba?' Langford moved closer to the door. 'You bastard ...'

387

'I am not Toshiro Shiba,' he said, laughing. And as Langford came close to the grille, the man backed away, standing under a light.

'No,' muttered Langford. 'I can see that. Major-General Tasaki, isn't it? You haven't changed much.'

Tasaki gave a slight bow so that his white hair flashed in the glare of the overhead light. 'I must bid you welcome to my island home, Mister Langford. You will not have long to wait. And you have a pleasant companion to while away your last hours, no?'

'Why?' said Langford, staring through into the corridor. 'Your pal Gunning has got the photographs ... what more do you want?'

'The photographs are of no consequence to me, Mister Langford. Not now. It is already too late to worry about petty history.'

'That doesn't answer my question.'

'I have to dispose of you and this seems as effective a method as any. You will not see the next sunrise, Mister Langford. Perhaps that is a pity because it will be ... memorable, in many ways.'

'I don't understand.'

'Of course not. I would not expect you to ... unless Toshiro Shiba ... but no, I can see in your face the look of the dumb animal.'

'I take it you intend leaving us here to drown?'

'Perceptive of you, Mister Langford. Yes. I am not certain of the timing but the tides are running high ... something to do with the season, no doubt.' He began to approach the door again. 'I must close the grille,' he said, moving cautiously, his eyes fixed on Langford's face. 'The water, you see. I would not want a flood here.'

'Soichi Heyashi sent his regards,' said Langford. 'And a few other things. You're sold out, Tasaki. The evidence against you – '

'Heads of State are difficult men to impeach, Mister Langford. The gossip of demented Buddhist monks will not affect me. By this time tomorrow, the world will be faced with a different kind of Japan.'

'Are you all mad or are there only a few like you?'

'There are a few men of vision, men prepared to seize the opportunity which I shall provide. As for the rest ... they are so much apathetic trash. But I keep you from your pleasures.' He started to close the grille.

'Let her go,' said Langford, quickly. 'I'll stay ...'

'Goodbye, Mister Langford. They say drowning is a pleasant death. Certainly it is preferable to dying slowly of radiation sickness.'

'Please, I ...' Langford clenched his fists and pounded against the door as the grille slammed shut. He began to yell, his cries echoing round the dungeon. Then he slowly sank down and stared hopelessly at the barred window.

'What did he mean, Richard?'

'I'm not sure.' Langford lit another cigarette, Tasaki's slowly spoken words hammering in his brain, meaningless words that somehow meant so much. 'Was that the man you saw?'

Yita shook her head. 'No, I do not think so. The other man ... the voice ... it was different.'

'Well, at least we know. Not that it's much comfort.' He descended the steps slowly, the pain in his head throbbing with an intensity which almost made him lose his balance. 'I'm sorry. I didn't know ...'

She came to him and took his hand. 'Please, Richard, you must not blame yourself. We have to accept what happens.'

'Do we hell.'

'But we do. Truly. No one can be blamed.'

'I blame myself,' growled Langford, staring up at the barred window and hearing the noise of the sea. The thin shaft of light had paled and he was beginning to feel the cold seeping into his body, sharpening the pain so that even the smallest movement became an agonising torture. But he knew that somehow he had to make an effort.

After taking one last pull on the cigarette, he dropped

389

the butt. There was a barely perceptible hiss as the lighted end hit the floor and bending down, Langford saw the water coming in under the wall. Closer examination revealed a series of holes, obviously intended for drainage.

'What are you doing?'

'Looking for a way out of here,' he said, his voice absolutely calm. 'I want you to take a look out of the window, okay? I'll give you a leg-up and you can stand on my shoulders. Think you can do it?'

She glanced apprehensively at the square of light and then nodded. 'I will try.'

'Good girl.' Yita was light but it still required a lot of effort to get her up on to his shoulders. But once she was balanced, Yita was able to grasp the bars for support.

'Tell me what you can see,' he said, gripping her legs.

'Just the water.'

'Nothing else?'

'No. Even ... even pressing my face against the bars ... nothing but the water. And it is right below us.'

'Yes, I rather suspected it might be. Okay, start to get ...' But he was interrupted by a sharp scraping sound and Yita shrieked as she nearly fell. 'Steady, I've got you.'

When he had lowered her to the floor, he saw the blood on her hand. 'How ...?' But the question died on his lips as he stared up at the window.

'The bar ... it cut me.' He could feel her shaking. 'Richard, I am very afraid.'

'Don't be. You've just found the way out. Those bars are shot, rusted through.' The bar on which Yita had pulled was already bent inwards and looked as though it might break, assuming he could get at it. 'If you knelt down ...'

'I think I could take your weight ... just for a little.'

'Good.' He watched her kneel, noting that the water had risen some four inches.

As he stepped up, he could feel her body trembling under his weight. The pain also tore at his chest but he forced himself by an effort of will to ignore it as he reached out to grasp the rusty bars. Exerting all his strength, he slowly pulled himself up.

'Get out of the way,' he yelled, and letting his arms straighten, hung there, fervently hoping that his weight would be sufficient. Then he heard the helicopters again.

They started up one by one, the engines coughing into life, the rotor blades thudding against the air. Langford counted at least three before the total volume of noise made it impossible to distinguish individual machines. Yita said something but her words were lost in the roar as the helicopters took off. Heaving himself up, he was able to see them, five dark shapes swooping low over the sea as they headed away.

His concentration on the helicopters was total. He had managed to overcome the pain and didn't even feel the strain in his arms. His hands were numb with cold and it was Yita who alerted him to the fact that one of the bars was slowly coming away from the stone lintel over the window.

Quickly changing his grip, Langford's entire weight was pitted against the one bar. It came free suddenly, sending a shower of stone fragments into his face. But the bar had been well bedded-in so that it bent backwards under the pressure. As soon as it was just below the horizontal, Langford let go and dropped down, his feet splashing into the water.

All the pain returned with a rush as he sat on the raised stone and discovered that the water was now more than a foot deep. When he had rubbed his hands together to restore the circulation, he began feeling around under the water at the base of the wall.

'The tide's rising fast,' he said. 'It's coming in under pressure.'

Yita was sitting behind him on the raised stone, her legs tucked up under her chin. 'We will drown,' she murmured.

'No way.' And he grinned at her. 'Come on, we've got three more bars, as the actress said to the bishop.'

'Please, it is no use.'

'We've got to try, love. If we can make a big enough gap ...'

'No.' She shook her head, her lips swelling as she fought to control her tears. 'I cannot swim.'

Langford carefully probed the lump on his head. It was throbbing, violently. The water now felt like so much melted ice as it splashed around his legs, and he wondered just how long they could last, even if they did manage to break out of the dungeon.

2

The Mercedes was travelling fast along the main road, Samwashima silently calculating the number of hours before he could escape from Shiba and have a cigarette. Then the car began to slow.

'We are stopping?' he said, hopefully.

'For a moment, yes.'

Samwashima frowned as the car swung off the road and into a narrow lane which quickly became little more than a rough track through sparse woodland. 'Where are we going?'

Shiba smiled. 'You shall see, my friend. I have one last item of business to conclude before I can return to Tokyo.'

'Ah so.' Samwashima grinned. 'The photographs.'

Shiba didn't reply, contenting himself with another sly smile as the car finally came to a halt and the driver got out to open the doors.

'Come with me, Norihiko.'

Samwashima got out of the car, buttoning his coat against the cold and staring through the trees. 'We are meeting someone?'

'Please, smoke if you wish.'

As his hands went automatically to his pockets, Samwashima was worried. Even in the open air, Toshiro Shiba had been known to abuse people who smoked anywhere near him. 'Who are we meeting?' His hands trembled as he lit the cigarette. 'Are they late?' There was no answer. He drew the smoke into his lungs. 'I wish I could rid myself of this vice,' he said, smiling uneasily.

'You are a weak man, Norihiko. Weak men cannot rid themselves of vices. Smoking, drinking, women ... ambition. Or perhaps avarice would be a better word.'

Samwashima experienced a curious hollowness in the pit of his belly, a faint stirring of fear which was mirrored in his eyes. 'I work only to serve you, Shiba-*san*. You know that.'

'Do I?' Toshiro Shiba's expression froze. 'I know you attempted to betray me.'

There was a choking dryness in Samwashima's throat and when he raised his shaking hand to remove the cigarette from his mouth, the tip stuck fast to his lips so that his fingers slid over the cigarette, dislodging the lighted end and burning his fingers.

'Go ahead,' said Shiba. 'Light another one.' Samwashima obeyed without comment. 'You betrayed my trust, Norihiko. It was a stupid mistake.'

'No, Shiba-*san*. I would not ...'

'Please, do not compound your stupidity with lies. You attempted to sell me to Muga Tasaki so that you could take over the Shimada Corporation.' He shook his head and then shrugged. 'I have kept you for many years now, out of compassion. I believed that you were an honourable man. I knew your weaknesses, of course. But I chose to overlook them because I considered you to be someone on whose devotion I could always depend. Whilst I knew that you did not have the flair, the capability for great things, it did not matter because you were loyal. Or so I thought. You were like a pet dog, Norihiko. I was fond of you but now, my sense of compassion ...'

Samwashima took a pace backwards as he stared hopelessly at Shiba. Then he noticed the driver of the car standing a few feet away. 'What ... what do you intend, Shiba-*san*?'

'To be rid of you.'

'Please, Shiba-*san*. I had no intention of betraying you. My purpose was to stop Tasaki from destroying you. He has political ambitions ... he seeks – '

'I am fully aware of what Tasaki seeks,' said Shiba, scornfully. 'But he will fail because although more intelligent, he is like you in that he is essentially an opportunist. And opportunism is the wisdom of fools. Your pledge to Muga Tasaki gave him what he needed most: an ally who could be sacrificed without a second thought. You did not betray me. You betrayed yourself. *Sayo nara*, Norihiko.' Shiba made a deep bow then nodded to the driver.

Samwashima opened his mouth to speak as the man carefully aimed the silenced pistol. He actually heard the dull plop of the first shot and felt a strange, sharp warmth in his stomach. But he didn't hear the report of the second bullet which smashed into his brain.

3

'Have they arrested him?' said Miss Pym, pouring the tea with precision.

'I suppose so.' Peggy Ashmore lit a cigarette and shrugged. 'He was absolutely white as a sheet. And as for her ...'

Miss Pym passed over a cup. 'And no news about Mister Langford?'

'No, none.'

'I expect he'll survive. That type always does.'

'He's not all bad, you know,' said Peggy Ashmore, defensively. 'There's a rumour going round the office ... about Mister Maxwell's Will.'

'Yes, so I gather.'

'It is true then?'

'That depends on what they're saying.' Miss Pym shuddered.

'I heard that he ... Mister Maxwell had left everything to you.'

'That's complete nonsense.'

'And Richard? Mister Langford? They're saying –'

'Why can't they mind their own business?' snapped Miss Pym, sighing. 'The bulk of Mister Maxwell's estate went to his wife, of course. He did leave me a little money and ... well, Mister Langford was mentioned in the Will but I won't say any more than that. As for the firm ... that already belongs to Mister Hewens.'

'Yes, that's caused some surprise in the office, especially in view of what's happened.'

'Do you know where he is? Mister Hewens, I mean.'

'Scotland Yard. Helping the police with their inquiries, whatever that means.'

'You know perfectly well what it means. The man's obviously a crook. I never liked him ... never trusted him. If he ends up in prison for life I shouldn't be at all surprised. Of course, the publicity will destroy the firm ... all our clients ... your clients, they won't take kindly to dealing with a gaolbird.'

'He isn't there yet,' said Peggy Ashmore. 'His kind always get away with murder. Anyway, I'm more concerned about Richard.'

Miss Pym stared at the girl for a time, her eyes narrowing. 'You're very fond of him, aren't you?'

'Yes ... yes, I suppose I am.'

Miss Pym suddenly reached out and took hold of Peggy's hand. 'You will let me know what happens, won't you?'

'Yes, I will.'

'If you were to play your cards right, you could catch that young man. Don't make my mistake, dear. I waited for James Maxwell ...'

Peggy Ashmore was startled. 'I never knew ... no one ever spoke about it.'

'I sincerely hope no one ever will. When his wife left

395

him, there was talk of a divorce but it never happened. I always somehow thought that it would, but I never said anything, do you see? I just waited.'

'Were you and Maxwell …?'

'No, nothing like that. I missed my chance. Don't you miss yours. As soon as that young man comes back, you pounce on him.' And she grinned until she saw the moisture brimming in Peggy Ashmore's eyes. 'What is it? What's the matter?'

Gathering up her things, Peggy shook her head. 'It's just … I don't think he ever will come back.' And she quickly left the restaurant.

4

The launch was travelling at speed, the bows rising clear of the water. Sitting wedged in the corner of the cockpit, Gunning stared morosely at the turbulent wake as the light faded and the sea took on a chill, grey hue. Then he turned, switching his gaze to Toshiro Shiba.

'Be dark soon. We have to make it before sunset.'

'There is ample time, at least another hour of daylight.'

'If you hadn't kept me waiting …'

'I have already explained that I was otherwise occupied,' retorted Shiba. 'I should also tell you that I take exception at your attempt to commandeer this boat and give orders to my crew.'

Gunning shrugged. 'Too bad.'

'I am cold.' Shiba steadied himself as he rose. 'Let us go into the cabin.'

When he had closed the door behind them, Gunning lit a cigarette, hoping that Shiba would comment. He didn't and the American sank down into one of the well-padded seats. 'So much for your assurances that everything was under control.'

'I could not know that Tasaki would want to abduct the Englishman. There was no reason.'

'We-ell, he obviously had one. But what happened to your people, for Chrissakes?'

'Dead,' muttered Shiba, removing his horn-rimmed glasses and polishing the lenses with a silk handkerchief. 'And Tasaki has now over-reached himself. As he shall soon discover.'

'Too damn right.'

The Japanese stared across the cabin, reaching out for the handrail as the launch hit a patch of swell and bucked, violently. 'What do you mean?'

'You may as well know that I've already sent in three of my guys.'

'Three?' Shiba replaced his glasses. 'Three men against –'

'They're experts and they're armed. By the time we get there, Tasaki should be nicely trussed up, just like a Thanksgiving turkey.'

Shiba shook his head. 'You fool. You stupid, naive fool.'

'Watch your Goddamn tongue ... *Mister* Shiba. I've had just about enough.'

'You do not understand. Tasaki has a well-trained team of men at his disposal, almost a para-military force.'

Gunning started. 'You never said ... you knew about that and you said nothing. Why?'

'There was never any reason why I should.' Shiba made a fanning gesture with his hand, wrinkling his nose as a skein of smoke from Gunning's cigarette curled around him. 'It makes no difference. The plan for the Englishman was –'

'It could make one hell of a difference. Suppose Tasaki decides to interrogate Langford? Then what?'

'What could he tell him?'

'Our involvement with you.'

'Muga Tasaki will already be aware of that. And as for sending in your men, it can only serve to make our negotiations more difficult.'

'We're not negotiating with that sonafabitch. No way

397

Hopefully, he may have put up some resistance, in which case – '

'Your three men will probably be dead. Like the Englishman.'

Gunning pulled on the cigarette and sighed. 'Look, I don't give a shit about Langford. But I do care about my own people. And if anything has happened ...' He stopped as the cabin door suddenly flew open and one of the two crewmen entered, speaking quickly in Japanese. Shiba tried to silence him but it was Gunning who snatched the sheet of paper from the man's hand. 'Holy Christ.' He tossed the paper at Shiba. 'So much for your promises.'

After staring at the paper for a moment, Shiba motioned the crewman to leave. 'It would appear that Tasaki has made his move,' he said, his voice very quiet.

'Some move.' Gunning slowly stubbed out the cigarette and immediately lit another. 'This has to be a bluff.'

Shiba remained silent for a long time. Then he shook his head. 'No, he is not a man to issue an empty threat.'

'Dear God.'

Shiba stared at his watch. 'The authorities have until dawn. Then ...'

'You realize what this could mean?'

'Of course. I did not imagine that he would countenance such a tactic.'

'Your radio ... can it transmit?'

'Yes, but – '

'No buts.' Gunning stood up. 'Come on, I need to get a call through to Tokyo.' But Shiba remained seated.

'First I must speak ... I must know how the government intend to react. If they mean to oppose him ...'

'End of story,' said Gunning.

'I imagine that Tasaki has in mind a new beginning.'

'You knew.' Gunning braced himself against the door. 'You've already made a deal with Tasaki, haven't you?' Shiba didn't answer. 'You sold out, didn't you?' Gunning's shout echoed within the small cabin.

'We reached an understanding but I was misled. And Samwashima must have told him everything.'

'Never mind about Sam. We'll take care of him later.'

'I already have.' Shiba started to rise but fell back as the boat gave a sudden lurch. Then he clasped his hands together and frowned, little beads of perspiration standing out on his face. 'Never for one moment did I dream that such a thing could happen.'

'This isn't a dream, Shiba. It's pure nightmare. Even Tasaki may not know it but as of now, he has the world by its balls.'

5

The daylight had almost gone and the water had risen to a depth of nearly four feet. Perched on the top step by the iron door, Yita watched as Langford pulled against the third bar. Although it was icy-cold, the water had actually helped, enabling him to reach the window by swimming. If he could wrench the third bar free, the gap would be just big enough for them to squeeze through. Getting Yita into the water which so terrified her would be difficult but Langford knew himself well enough. If it came to it, he would knock her out, not cold-bloodedly but in the fierce temper to which the lack of an alternative would drive him. The problem was the third bar. For reasons he could only guess at, it was in better shape than the others. Although heavily encrusted with flakes of rust, it showed no inclination to give under his weight as the other two had.

Because of the water-level, Langford was able to get the maximum benefit from his own weight, gripping the bar with both hands and pushing against the wall with his feet. But the cold, the pain and massive fatigue had taken their toll. Every fibre of his being ached abominably and if the chill water had initially numbed him, the numbness itself was beginning to cause pain too. Then the first breaker splashed over the window ledge.

It was sheer surprise which made him let go of the bar and fall backwards into the water. Kicking out, he reached the steps leading up to the iron door and Yita helped him out. He was shivering, his whole body shaking uncontrollably.

'It is no use, Richard.'

Another breaker smashed against the window sending plumes of foam into the dungeon.

From the top of the stone steps, Langford looked out of the window, past the two tantalizingly bent oars and along the surface of the sea. He compared the level of the water outside with the depth inside and knew it was only a matter of time.

'I'll have another go at the bar,' he said, easing his tired body into the water. But even as he started to swim, he knew he had no further reserves of strength on which to draw and when he gripped the bar, he was unable to pull himself up.

The sea finally boiled over the stone ledge and poured into the dungeon. Langford began cursing as the water levels equalized but as he changed his grip, he felt movement in one of the bars he had already bent. Suddenly there was a new spark of hope and he pulled, working the bar backwards and forwards until it eventually came free. His intention was to use it as a lever against the middle bar but before he could put theory into practice, his trained ears picked up the unmistakable chatter of small-arms fire echoing over the noise of the sea.

Once he had identified the sound, he concentrated on it, listening carefully and deciding that there was a running battle in progress. And fairly close.

Taking the bar, he kicked out and rejoined Yita on the steps. Because of his shivering, simply holding the rusty length of iron was difficult enough, let alone trying to jam it into the edge of the door. He paused, staring at the hinges, just visible in the deepening gloom. Then he began to hammer desperately at the top one.

Each ringing blow reverberated in his ears and sent

spurts of pain through his head. It was virtually impossible to see what effect he was having but if the dull clanging of iron against iron was anything to go by, he guessed that he might as well have been using his fists against the granite walls. Stopping, he leaned against the door, his breathing reduced to short, laboured gasps.

'Maybe if we called out?' Yita said. 'And banged on the door with the bar?'

Langford shrugged, suddenly remembering the many times he had come close to death as a soldier. He remembered the sniper's bullet which had actually passed through the top of his cap, a car-bomb which had exploded less than a minute after he had left the vehicle, a NATO exercise in Norway when some clown had put fifty live rounds through the jeep in which he had been travelling. But there had never been anything like this before, a slow, certain death.

As the water crested the top step and splashed around his legs, he began hammering against the iron door and shouting. Yita joined in, her shrill screaming somehow muffled in the fast-diminishing space between the surface of the water and the roof of the dungeon.

Deafened by the volume of noise, aching with fatigue and chilled to the marrow, Langford's frantic hammering and yelling slowly died away. Then his ears picked up another sound, a kind of scraping. Without being wholly aware of his actions, he banged at the door again, shouting for all he was worth until the bar fell from his numbed fingers and his voice became little more than a harsh croak.

'Pull. Pull.'

For what seemed like an eternity, he stood absolutely still until his brain finally grasped the fact that someone was trying to push the door open from the other side.

Because of the water, it was like trying to move a deadweight. But very slowly, the door began to open and as soon as the gap was wide enough, he pushed Yita out, the water bubbling around them.

Momentarily blinded by the light, Langford stumbled as his feet came into contact with a stone barrier across the passage, obviously constructed as a dam against the water now lapping coldly around his legs.

'Richard!'

Yita's shout made him look up and he stared in disbelief at the dark figure. 'Changed your mind?' he growled, stepping clear of the water.

'You all right?'

'We survived ... just.' He leaned against the wall and fought to control his shivering. 'Why don't you pull the trigger and have done with it?'

Gunning flicked the safety catch on the Smith & Wesson automatic but continued to hold the gun in his hand, the muzzle pointing upwards. 'You come this way ... nice and easy, okay?'

Langford didn't move. 'Just whose side are you on, damn you?'

'Mine.'

'That I can believe.'

'There are dry clothes up here.'

'Tasaki's here ... but you'd know that, of course.'

'Was here.' Gunning shook his head. 'The bird's flown.' He started backing along the passage. 'Come on, I need you alive, not dying of pneumonia.'

'You should have thought of that at the Consulate.'

'There was a mistake.'

'You're telling me.' He glanced round at Yita and saw her shivering, her face pinched and drawn. 'Okay, where are the clothes?'

'Right this way.' He continued moving backwards, the automatic still ready in his hand. 'Far enough. That door.' And he pointed.

Opening the door, Langford found himself facing into what was obviously a storeroom. The walls were lined with shelves piled with uniforms.

'Help yourself,' drawled Gunning. 'But make it quick. We don't have that much time.'

'When did we ever?' Langford pushed Yita inside. 'Strip,' he said, wincing as he began peeling off his own clothes. 'Are you going to explain just what's going on or do I have to guess?'

Gunning was standing by the door, his dark eyes resting briefly on Yita's naked body as she rubbed herself down. 'You saw Tasaki?'

'Yes.' Langford paused, trying to remember just what it was the Japanese had said, but his memory seemed to have seized up. Then he knew. 'It's you ... you and Shiba, isn't it?'

'In a way, yes. But right now, we have a problem.'

'By the time I'm through, you'll have a number of problems.'

'Just get dressed.' Gunning fingered the safety catch on the automatic and folded his arms so that the barrel of the gun rested lightly in the crook of his elbow. 'You're in no position to make threats. Besides, you're about to become an employee of the U.S. government.'

'Like hell.' Langford sorted through a pile of trousers until he eventually found a pair about his size. He pulled them on and then picked up his sodden jacket, carefully removing his wallet and lighter. The pack of cigarettes was still dripping and he threw them down as he turned to Yita. 'You okay, love?'

She nodded. 'I am cold.'

'All right, Gunning, what happens now?'

'You come with me. Like I say, I need you.'

'Why?'

'You'll see.'

Langford slowly sank down on to a bench. 'Why?'

'On your feet, Langford.' He levelled the gun. 'Come on, move it.'

'If you need me, you're not going to pull the trigger, are you? I think it's time we had what they call a full and frank discussion.' He held out his hand. 'Do you have a cigarette?'

Gunning tossed a pack across to him. 'Muga Tasaki has

taken over the *Shimada Maru*.'

'So what?' Langford lit up, gratefully inhaling the smoke.

'So it's sailed from Kyomo, loaded to the gunwales with active nuclear waste. Tasaki is using it as a bargaining counter. You know what that means.'

Langford nodded, his tired mind realizing that he should have known this all along. 'It's a bit beyond my scope, I'm afraid.'

Gunning came towards him. 'Out there ...' He jerked his thumb over his shoulder. 'There's a helicopter. I need a pilot.'

'Find someone else.'

'There isn't anyone else and there isn't any time to start looking.'

'Hard luck.'

'You're going to do it, Langford. Whether you like it or not.'

'No.' Yita came forward. 'You cannot ask this of him. He is –'

Before she could complete the sentence Gunning had darted between them. Grabbing Yita, he spun her round and jabbed the muzzle of the Smith & Wesson against the side of her head.

'Okay, Langford, just listen. Tasaki has the *Shimada Maru* and threatens to blow it out of the water unless the Tokyo government resigns. If that ship blows ... hell, you know what the result would be. Now either you co-operate with me or I'm going to give you a close-up view of Madam Butterfly's brains. What's it to be?'

'You really mean it, don't you?'

'Sure as God I mean it. All I'm asking is that you fly me out to the ship. From then on ...' He pushed Yita into a sitting position and keeping the gun pressed to her head, took a flask from his pocket. 'Here,' he said, sliding it across the floor. 'Take a shot of that and then push it back ... nice and slow.'

After a moment's hesitation, Langford complied. The

404

spirit seared his throat and seemed to burn his insides but it generated a welcome warmth and he flexed his hands.

'Don't even consider it, Langford. I don't want to hurt her but I will if you make me. Her life ... our lives aren't going to be worth a row of beans unless we can stop that ship.'

'We heard shooting,' said Langford, carefully sliding the flask back across the stone floor after he had taken a second swig.

'Yeah, I guess you would have. You heard my guys but they arrived too late for Tasaki.'

'Where is the ship?'

'At sea. We have a course and estimated position but they could deviate which is why we don't have that much time. Are you ready?'

Shrugging, Langford almost smiled. 'I don't seem to have much choice, do I?'

'No.'

'All right.' He stepped back. 'After you.'

'No thanks. You go first. And remember that I'm right behind you.'

Langford nodded and went slowly into the passageway. 'What is this place?'

'Tasaki's HQ. It's a kind of Japanese *Führer-bunker*, I guess. There are workshops, laboratories, stores, armouries ... you name it, he's got it.' Seeing Langford hesitate, he called out, his words echoing. 'Just keep it moving. There's a flight of steps at the end. We go straight out and you'll see the helicopter over to your right.'

'I may not be able to handle it.'

'You can try.'

'Oh yes, I can certainly do that. I could even fail. Your problem is going to be how to know when ... Jesus.' He stopped in his tracks at the bottom of the steps.

'It's all under control,' shouted Gunning. 'Did you do as I asked?'

Before the stocky figure at the top of the steps could reply, Langford swung round. 'These bastards certainly wear well, don't they? He should have hanged.'

Gunning ignored the remark. 'You beat it.'

'Will he fly the machine?'

'He'll fly it.'

Langford had started up the steps, his eyes fixed on the fleshy face. 'The pictures ... the photographs were very good.' And he smiled as Shiba backed out into the darkness. 'Quite a little protection racket.'

'Keep going, Langford.'

'What about him?'

'Nothing for you to worry about.'

There was a sudden coldness in the air and looking around as he emerged from the bunker, Langford saw the helicopter, a dark, predatory shape standing on the tarmac apron. There were two men lying some distance away, shot down as they had tried to run.

Langford heard Gunning's footsteps behind him and the scuffing sound of Yita being dragged along. The sight of Toshiro Shiba, the helicopter and the sudden thought that there could be no more opportunities, all combined to make him risk everything on one last throw.

'Get moving.'

Hearing Gunning's voice, Langford nodded and took a pace forward. Then he swung round, diving headlong at Shiba. The Japanese collapsed under the impact and a split-second later, Langford was half-kneeling, holding Shiba in a powerful arm-lock which could only have one outcome.

'I can break his neck,' said Langford, quietly. 'Let her go.'

The American hesitated for a moment. Then he nodded and Langford caught the sound of the safety catch.

'And I can blow her brains out. What's it to be, Langford? It's your choice but before you make it, just consider the sequence of events. You kill him. Okay, maybe he deserves it. But I have the gun and the broad gets her head blown off. After that ... hell, the odds have to be in my favour. Then what? The authorities in Tokyo are

406

going to call Tasaki's bluff. Come dawn, the *Shimada Maru* gets blown to pieces and then ... goodbye world.'

Langford could feel Shiba's body trembling against him. 'What he did – '

'Doesn't matter any more. Nothing will matter unless you come to your senses.'

'And Tasaki?'

'On his way to Tokyo. Goddammit, he can afford to stroll down the Ginza and no one dare touch him.' Gunning paused as if to check that the muzzle of the automatic was still pressed against Yita's temple. 'Your move, friend. I've done all I can.'

Even in the darkness, Langford could see the perspiration streaming from Shiba's face. He hadn't relaxed his grip on the Japanese but he suddenly doubted if he had either the strength or the will to kill the man in cold blood.

'I'm going to count up to five, Langford.'

Very slowly, Langford released the man, watching as he tumbled on to the grass and the horn-rimmed spectacles fell from his face. Seeing the Japanese grope for them, Langford stamped them into the dirt, wishing that it could have been Shiba's own eyes which he was grinding to fragments with his heel.

'One day ... one day, you'll pay for what you did.'

Shiba began to struggle to his feet. 'I have already paid, many times.'

'You bastard.'

'That's enough. Now get over to the chopper.'

Leaving Shiba to stare sightlessly after him, Langford went across to the tarmac apron and stood by the helicopter.

'Can you handle it?'

'Yes.' There seemed little point in holding out. He began to climb aboard but Gunning stopped him.

'We'll go first.'

'She stays.'

'Oh no, she's my guarantee of your continued co-operation.' And he pushed Yita into the cabin, quickly following her. 'Okay, let's get moving.'

Langford pulled himself slowly into the cabin. Staring through the plexi-glass, he could see Toshiro Shiba standing like a statue, his arms hanging limply at his side. 'If we get back, I want him.'

'If we get back, you can have him. Just get flying, Langford. Now.'

Once he had settled himself in the pilot's seat, Langford strapped himself in without a second thought. Then he began tearing at the inner recesses of his mind as he studied the instrumentation and felt for the controls. The helicopter was a Westland Gazelle, a model with which he had been reasonably familiar. It was an Anglo-French machine built by Westland in co-operation with Aerospatiale; powered by a Turbomeca Astazou-3 gas turbine engine with a maximum continuous rating of 600shp; all-up weight 1800 kilograms; maximum speed one-six-seven knots; range with maximum payload one-seven-zero nautical miles ...

Even as the basic information filtered through his brain, Langford started the engine. It was a smooth start and as the rotors slowly gathered momentum, he mentally complimented whoever had had charge of servicing the machine.

He eased the throttle forward and the Gazelle lifted off the ground. But Langford's technique was rusty and the helicopter suddenly pitched forward, tipping sideways and threatening to clip the trees alongside the perimeter fence.

Yita's cry echoed above the roar of the engine and Gunning shouted a torrent of obscene blasphemies as Langford struggled to gain height. Then they were clear and heading out over the sea.

Gunning thrust a chart at him. 'Your course,' he yelled. 'The mark represents the *Shimada Maru*'s estimated position at 1800 hours.'

Langford nodded and glanced quickly at the chart.

'Okay, but if she isn't where you think she is, we won't be able to hang around.' Then he stared at the fuel gauge and grimaced. His statement had been based on the assumption of a light pay-load and full tanks. The combined weight of himself, Gunning and Yita was far below the maximum loading. But the fuel tanks were barely half full.

6

Colonel DuCros was almost asleep in the chair when the Minister came into the office and he jumped up, startled.

'My apologies for dragging you here so late, Colonel.' The Minister went to his desk and sat down. 'Please, be seated.'

'What has happened?'

'I have just come from the Elysée.' He paused, flicking open the catches on his attaché case and removing a sheet of paper. 'A little over two hours ago, this signal was received from our embassy in Tokyo.' He handed the paper across the desk.

'About Picot?'

'Read it,' snapped the Minister.

DuCros obeyed, his lean face tightening as he scanned the decoded signal. He shook his head. 'Has this been verified?'

'Yes, insofar as it is possible to do so.' He reached out, took the paper back, then fed it into the shredding machine. He contemplated his unlit pipe for a moment. 'I have to tell you that the President ... and his advisers at the Quai D'Orsay, are of the opinion that this ... this event is a direct consequence of your Section's carelessness concerning Claude Picot.'

DuCros blanched. 'That's nonsense and you know it.'

'Of course I know it.' The Minister began tapping his pipe against the ashtray. 'However, the President ... and the Quai D'Orsay, of course, do not. Now I have to consider what action should be taken.'

DuCros spread his hands in a gesture of despair. 'But there is nothing we can do. The Far East? It is for the Japanese ... and the Americans to sort out.'

'No, you misunderstand me, Colonel. I am very sorry, but in the circumstances, I have no other course open but to ask for your resignation.'

DuCros rose slowly to his feet. 'Then I shall not give it. You are making use of this incident ...'

'This incident, as you call it, could develop into a catastrophe of unimaginable proportions. We, France, must be seen not to be involved in any way. It has therefore been agreed that you should resign – for health reasons.'

'Agreed? Agreed by whom? I have not agreed. I shall not agree.'

'I am not deaf, Colonel. You will submit your resignation.'

'And if I refuse?'

The Minister hesitated, staring into the empty bowl of his pipe for a moment and then starting to fill it. 'You are a soldier and you have first-hand experience of SDECE. You should not need me to tell you.'

'I am being used as a scapegoat.'

'Perhaps. I shall expect your letter of resignation in the morning.'

The Colonel stiffened. 'I am still a serving officer, *M'sieu le Ministre.* I shall offer my resignation – in writing – to the Commander-in-Chief, as is my right. And I do assure you, *M'sieu*, that my explanation will omit nothing.'

•

SIXTEEN

1

They were flying at an altitude of four hundred feet. It was a clear night. There was no moon, but with little cloud, visibility was good. The tension inside the noisy cabin was almost palpable and every time the lights of a big ship were seen, they all peered down, anxiously. But there was no sign of the *Shimada Maru*.

With conversation limited by the engine noise to an occasional shout and hand signals, Richard Langford should have been able to concentrate on flying but his mind kept wandering. Having got over the initial elation at being airborne again, he was plagued by questions which he knew Gunning would be reluctant to answer. He was also apprehensive, fearing as much for his own safety as for Yita. And as his eyes maintained a flickering contact with the fuel gauge, there was another worry gnawing at his tired brain, something he knew he should have remembered but couldn't.

Feeling the American touch his arm, Langford peered out, squinting as he saw the lights. He eased the Gazelle down to three hundred feet. The ship turned out to be a container vessel and as they levelled out, Langford pointed towards the fuel gauge.

'Thirty minutes,' shouted Langford. 'Forty at the outside.'

'Forget about the return trip. That should give us another hour.'

Langford shook his head. 'I already have,' he yelled. 'In about half an hour this machine is going to stop, whether we like it or not.'

411

'It must be here somewhere,' Gunning bellowed.

'Are you certain about course and position?'

'Yes. I pulled out two fingernails to make sure.'

'Charming. How many people on board?'

'That I'm not certain about. But Tasaki and most of his hoods were supposed to fly on to Tokyo once they had secured the ship. With luck, there shouldn't be too much opposition because they won't be expecting any.'

'With luck, we may not even find the bloody ship.'

Gunning leaned across and shouted into Langford's ear. 'If we don't find the *Shimada Maru*, everyone's luck will have run out.'

The small flotilla of fishing boats lay on the water, their trawling lights reflecting on the calm surface like so many stars. Langford stared down at them for a time, thinking peaceful thoughts until his pilot's training reimposed its discipline. The fuel gauge was almost on red and he knew that he had to make a decision. He had been flying with extreme caution, maintaining just the right combination of speed and altitude for optimum use of what fuel remained. His problem was just when to go down. Either he used that much more fuel by going low over the sea so that they could ditch with reasonable safety. Or he could hang on between three and four hundred feet, the ideal height for spotting the *Shimada Maru*, assuming the ship was there to be spotted. But there was really no choice. If the helicopter lost power at that altitude, it would simply drop out of the sky.

Easing the throttle back, he lost height quickly and the Gazelle was soon skimming along just a few feet above the water. Gunning tried to protest but Langford refused to argue, concentrating on flying. There was no longer any point in checking the fuel gauge or any of the other instruments. He was wave-hopping, except that there were no waves to speak of. The sea was beautifully calm and if he had ever felt gratitude for anything, Langford was more than grateful for that.

Nudging the American, he pointed towards the self-inflating dinghy and the life-jackets. 'Any minute,' he shouted. Gunning nodded and began to prepare.

Richard Langford's nerves were stretched to a point at which pain, fatigue or fear held no sway. His eyes were fixed on the water, his ears tuned to the noise of the engine, ready to react to the slightest change of pitch. Gunning's threats and the *Shimada Maru* were no longer important. All Langford's training, all his experience, every fibre of his being was concentrated on one objective: survival.

He responded angrily when Gunning suddenly shouted and jabbed at him. Until he looked away to starboard. Even at that distance, the mammoth vessel was an incredible sight, a great slab of blackness rising like a cliff out of the water.

'Up!'

Even before Gunning shouted, Langford had started to gain height, turning towards the *Shimada Maru*.

'We'll do a pass first.'

Langford shook his head as the engine coughed. 'We're going straight in ... if we're lucky.'

Langford had never landed on a ship before and he knew that had the sea been rough, he wouldn't have had a hope in hell. Even in the flat calm, putting the chopper down was going to be difficult.

The engine coughing and missing as the petrol flow became erratic, Langford hovered at about a hundred feet just alongside the vessel, in an attempt to judge its speed. Very slowly, he edged the Gazelle over the vast expanse of deck. But just as he was about to go down, he saw the towering superstructure at the stern. As it rushed towards them Langford peeled off for a second approach.

This time he came in at deck-level. The engine was within seconds of cutting out completely and fearing that he was too low, he slammed the throttle forward, climbing steeply. Then he hovered again until he was absolutely certain of his position before starting to go down.

The Gazelle had about twenty feet to go when the

engine finally died. The spinning rotors slowed their descent but not enough to stop the helicopter from hitting the steel deck with a jarring crash which fractured the plexi-glass bubble.

There was an uncanny silence until Langford unclasped his straps and kicked open the cabin door. 'What happens now?' But the American was too stunned to reply. 'You'd better wake up,' snapped Langford. 'We've got company.'

There were four men running along the deck towards the helicopter. Each of them was armed with a sub-machine gun.

Gunning began to move. 'Hopefully, they'll be thinking it's some of their own guys come back,' he muttered, checking the magazine of the Smith & Wesson.

'No.' Langford had started to ease himself out of the cabin. 'I should have remembered. I knew there was something wrong. They would have seen us coming on their radar.'

'So what?'

'The radio.' Langford yelled. 'This chopper was left behind because the radio must be *kaput*. If it had been working, we'd have heard them trying to call us up ...'

A shout echoed across the deck as the four Japanese came closer.

'Here.' Gunning was holding a 9mm Ingram sub-machine gun. 'And three spare magazines.'

'Where the hell did you get this?'

'Borrowed from Tasaki's own armoury. I had Shiba put 'em aboard.'

'You knew, didn't you?' growled Langford, jamming the spare 32-round magazines into his pockets.

'Let's say I had a sneaking suspicion.'

'Down!'

Langford's shout had scarcely left his lips before he dived out of the helicopter, working the bolt of the Ingram and firing at precisely the same moment as the Japanese. Two of the attackers went down immediately, one of them screaming. From the other side of the helicopter,

414

Gunning's Smith & Wesson spat flame and the air was filled with the hideous whine of bullets richocheting off the steel-plated deck.

When Langford fired another burst, almost cutting the third man in half, the last of the Japanese rushed forward, spraying the Gazelle with a fusilade of nine millimetre ammunition which drilled the cabin full of holes

Without thinking, Langford raised the gun and went to fire, cursing as the trigger clicked uselessly.

Changing the magazine was easy. It was almost a reflex action but Langford fumbled it when he caught sight of Gunning. The American was slumped awkwardly in his seat. But there was no time to do anything. The fourth Japanese was almost on them, changing his own magazine as he ran across the deck.

It was a race against time but Langford had had a split-second start and just as his opponent was about to fire, Langford stopped him dead in his tracks, splitting his chest apart with a murderous burst which emptied yet another magazine.

Climbing back inside the Gazelle, Langford watched Yita open the basic first-aid kit and then helped her ease Gunning back in his seat.

'Where's he hit?'

'Chest.' It was Gunning who answered, his voice hoarse, his breathing reduced to short and painful gasps.

Langford bent over him and tore at his shirt until he could see the pattern of bloody holes running from the top of his shoulder to a point just below his throat. 'Okay, take it easy.'

'Stop them, Langford … for Christ's sake …'

'I'll deal with it. Just save your breath.'

Gunning coughed. 'I was figuring on using it while I still have some to use.'

Yita was holding a pack of dressings and glanced at Langford.

'Stop the bleeding and then see if you can strap him up … as tight as you can.'

'It is bad?'

Langford shrugged. 'I'm no doctor,' he muttered.

'You are going?'

'Yes ... but I'll be back. Stay here and do what you can for him. If anyone comes ...' He hesitated and then picked up Gunning's automatic. 'Use this, okay?'

She took the gun. 'Be careful.'

'Yes.' He stared at the American for a moment. 'You stay put.'

It was a strange sensation, making his way along the deck. He recalled the first time he had stood there with Samwashima, staring down into the steel cavern in which Bailey had met his death. For some reason, that was the most vivid memory and his private, nocturnal visit was just a series of blurred images in his mind.

Apart from its navigation lights, the *Shimada Maru* was in darkness. It was altogether different. Tied up alongside the pier at Kobe, the ship had been dead, just so many slabs of riveted steel. Now, driving through the water, it was very much alive.

He kept his eyes on the white-painted superstructure as he made his way aft. In addition to the gun which the American had given him, he had retrieved the weapon discarded by the Japanese, carrying it wedged under his arm, his own gun held at the ready.

There was no sign of life and Richard Langford had the feeling of being utterly alone. He thought about Toshiro Shiba standing on the tarmac apron; of Tasaki taunting him through the grille as the water swirled into the dungeon; of Gunning, badly wounded, and of Heyashi, an old man whose soul was in torment. Then he thought about Yita and began speculating about the future – if there was a future.

The crack of the rifle was somehow muted and unreal but there was nothing unreal about the bullet which whipped past Langford's head.

Flinging himself down, he crawled quickly to the relative cover provided by the coaming of a small

416

hatchway. Another bullet richocheted off the deck and whined away over the sea.

Very slowly, Langford raised his head and peered upwards, searching for the sniper. Then the man fired again and he saw the tell-tale flash.

Langford raised the Ingram and fired a long burst. Most of the shots bounced harmlessly off the steel plating but the sight of an arm protruding limply from the window told him that he had found his target.

Discarding the empty gun, Langford waited for a few seconds before dashing for the next cover, a cluster of winches. He had almost reached them when two shots came in quick succession. Throwing himself down again, he began to crawl the last few feet. Then another shot rang out and he felt a warm, stabbing sensation in his thigh.

As he rolled over the sub-machine gun slipped from his grasp, sliding away across the deck, out of reach. More shots clanged against the winches and Langford shuddered. He waited some time before he looked up again and saw the dark silhouette on the flying bridge.

Pressing himself down against the cold steel deck, he waited, scarcely able to breathe. He was a sitting target now. All the man had to do was aim in his direction and so far he had shown some skill. Then the air was filled with the staccato chatter of automatic fire and Langford lay as still as death, every nerve and muscle tensed as he waited for the bullets to smash into his body. But he felt nothing. Until Yita flung herself down beside him.

'What the hell …?' He stared at the sub-machine gun and could almost taste the reek of cordite rising from the muzzle. Glancing up, he saw that the dark shape had vanished. 'I told you to stay put,' he growled.

'He is dead, Richard.'

'Yes. Good shooting.'

'No … Gunning. He died.'

'Ah.' Starting to move, Langford felt the tearing pain in his leg and swore. 'Give me the gun,' he said, snatching the weapon from her and ramming in his last magazine.

'Okay, that doorway over there. You go first and I'll cover you. And run.'

She went quickly, moving like a cat across the open space, but when Langford rose to follow her, he soon knew that running was out of the question. He limped, painfully, but kept his eyes fixed on the bridge for as long as possible until he reached the shelter of the doorway.

'You must bind your leg,' said Yita.

'Later. We've got to get to the bridge.'

He pushed open the door and they found themselves in a lighted corridor.

Apart from the remote throbbing of the engines, the interior of the *Shimada Maru* seemed curiously silent as they made their way along the corridor and up a flight of stairs. As he neared the top, Langford heard footsteps and hesitated, gun at the ready. Then a door slammed somewhere below. He swung round, wincing as he twisted his leg.

He pressed his hand against the wound so that the blood welled up between his fingers. Then he continued up the last of the stairs, halting as he gazed incredulously along the corridor. Yita came forward and clutched at his arm.

'Jesus.'

The walls and the ceiling of the corridor were torn and splintered with jagged lines of bullet holes and Langford counted at least six bodies, many with their faces and chests shot away. They must have come running from the door at the far end of the corridor and been mown down.

"You stay here," he said.

Then he saw the door begin to open. "Come out with your hands up," he yelled and fired a short burst into the ceiling.

'Do not shoot. Please ... do not shoot.'

The shouted plea mingled eerily with the ringing reports and Langford waited for his hearing to return to normal.

'Do not shoot.'

418

'Okay ... just come out with your hands on your head.'

The seconds ticked away. Then the door slowly opened to reveal a short, portly figure in a dark blue uniform, the man gripping the top of his head as if it might fall apart. He was scared rigid.

'That's far enough,' barked Langford. 'Who the hell are you?'

'My name is Umezu. I am the Master of the *Shimada Maru*.' He seemed to sway slightly. 'Did Shiba-*san* send you?'

Langford didn't reply but advanced slowly along the corridor. 'Back off,' he snapped.

Umezu obeyed, stepping cautiously backwards until he stood in the centre of the bridge.

Langford stared around the empty space. 'Where is everyone?'

Umezu's lips quivered but there was a long pause before he actually spoke. 'I think ... I think I am the only one left.'

'But someone's got to be running the ship. It is moving, isn't it?' Langford peered out into the darkness.

'Yes.' Umezu nodded. 'The *Shimada Maru* is under power. I should be down in the control room ... there is no one else. But if you are not from Shiba ...?'

'Never mind me. Can you stop the ship?'

'It can be done, yes. It means someone going up to the bows and letting go the anchor.'

'Then do it.'

Umezu stared at them, his eyes wide. 'Please ... what you going to do?'

'Never mind. Just stop the ship or you'll end up like your friend out there.' And Langford limped past the Japanese and stared at the corpse lying on the flying bridge.

'He was not my friend,' said Umezu, his hands still firmly on his head.

'Richard, it is the man who was on the island ... the one who hit me.'

'His name is Komai.'

Langford came back towards her. 'What the hell's going on?'

'The ship is being operated by the automatic navigation system ... the computer ... and there is a bomb ...'

'What kind of bomb?'

'A time-bomb.' Umezu moistened his lips. 'Tasaki said –'

'Tasaki? Is Tasaki on board?'

'He was, yes. Now ... I do not know ... the shooting ...'

'When's the bomb set to go off?'

'At sunrise.'

Langford stared at his watch. 'When is that?'

'I have already checked. According to the ship's chronometers, the sun will rise at zero-six-thirty-four. But their timing may not be as accurate.' Umezu was sweating. 'If they made a mistake –'

'Where is it?' snapped Langford, feeling sick and dizzy again.

'I do not know.'

'Jesus.' Langford sank down on to one of the bridge stools. 'All right, stop the ship.' His eyes became glassy as Umezu walked from the bridge. 'My Leg ...'

Yita came to him. 'There is a first aid kit,' she said, crossing to the far corner and taking the metal container marked with a red cross from the wall.

Langford never knew at what point he lost consciousness. But he remembered Yita being there, her hands on his thigh as she cut away the trouser-leg and applied the bandage. And he had a vague memory of a distant rumbling, like a small explosion. Then he was lying on the bridge, staring up at them.

'What happened? Where's Gunning?'

'Gunning is dead, Richard. You knew that. I told you.'

'But the bomb ... I heard the bomb.' He started to sit up his head swimming.

'You heard the anchor chain,' explained Umezu. 'I have stopped the ship. But we must hurry ...'

'Yes.' Langford gritted his teeth as he struggled to his feet. The pain was crippling and for a moment or so, he thought he would vomit. Then after several deep breaths, the wave of nausea subsided. 'The bomb. We have to find it.' He leaned against a bulkhead. 'You have no idea where it could be?'

'I was told to remain here. I do not know.'

'Then we search.'

'There is something else,' said Umezu. 'I have looked among the dead men ... Tasaki is not among them.'

'Then we can't take any chances.'

Progress was slow and wickedly painful. Langford knew they should have split up but he needed Yita's support and couldn't bring himself to trust Umezu.

Working their way down from the bridge, they checked every cabin, storage room and locker until they reached the second poop deck and found the stateroom which had been occupied by Toshiro Shiba. It seemed to Langford a likely spot but a minute search revealed nothing.

Leaving the stateroom, they went along the corridor, opening every door, without success. Then they came to a cabin which was locked.

'What's in here?'

Umezu shook his head, his mouth opening and closing soundlessly.

'Stand back.' Langford levelled the sub-machine gun and fired a short burst at the lock. The door shattered, sending splinters of wood flying across the deck. Then it swung open and Langford went in.

'Christ.' He peered down at the body of a European whose hairless head was caked with dried blood. 'Who the hell's that?'

'His name was Whitaker. He was a scientist. He worked for Toshiro Shiba.'

'No one can say that bastard isn't consistent.' After another search, he limped back into the corridor and leaned heavily against the wall.

'You should rest,' said Yita.

'No time.' He stared at his watch. 'If only we had a clue ... something which would tell us ...' He stopped speaking and listened for a moment.

'It is the automatic pumps you hear.'

'Shut up.' Langford glared at the Captain. He could hear a mechanical sound, a dull, resonant humming. But there was something else, a kind of scuffling. He looked round and saw another door set in a recess, almost concealed from sight.

'It is the entrance to the pump room.'

Once again, Langford cautioned Umezu to stay silent as he gently eased the door open. Looking down, he saw that the door led on to a narrow flight of steps. He could still hear the persistent humming but nothing else. Getting down the steps would be difficult and Langford had almost decided to let Umezu check it out when his ears picked up the scuffling noise again.

Gesturing the other two to stay put, he eased himself on to the stairs. It was the least painful method. And the quietest.

The effort of the descent was punishing and once he had reached the bottom, he paused, striving to silence his own breathing as he gazed at the rows of electric motors, each linked to a pumping mechanism. One of the pumps was working but even as he watched, it cut out and the humming sound slowly died away to leave an eerie silence.

Turning, he caught sight of Umezu at the top of the stairs and was about to speak when another of the pumps started up, the electric motor whining into life. Langford swung round just as the motor reached the number of revolutions required to set the pump in motion.

He saw the pump start, a sudden, flashing movement of the fly-wheel. Then an armed Japanese came out fast from behind the machinery and rolled, firing as he came up. Langford felt as though he was swimming through treacle. Groping wildly for the trigger, he loosed off a burst which smashed the man's head into bloody fragments. Then another Japanese appeared.

Hatred, fury, revenge, each played a part in driving Langford forward. He felt no pain as he charged at the Japanese and before the man had time to react, the hot muzzle of the sub-machine gun was jammed so hard against his neck that the flesh had turned the colour of polished ivory.

'It is Tasaki,' said the Captain, coming up behind him.

'We've already met.' Langford gasped as the pain reasserted itself. 'The bomb, you bastard. Where is it?'

Tasaki gaped up at him, his rheumy eyes somehow glazed with a film of disbelief. 'You? It is you?'

'Where's the bomb?' And he jabbed the gun even harder into the old man's neck.

'You are too late.'

'You'll tell me.' He stepped back and nodded at Umezu. 'Tie him up. And make a good job of it.'

'Richard, what are you going to do?'

Langford took out his cigarette lighter. 'Make him talk. I won't match his expertise, but I've not had his experience.' He snapped the lighter, his hand shaking as he held the flame under Tasaki's chin until the man gave a sudden gasp and jerked his head away.

'What you are doing is evil,' said Yita.

'Get out. You don't have to watch.' Langford worked himself into a more comfortable sitting position and lit a cigarette. Then he grabbed at the shock of silvery-white hair. 'You ... are going to tell me ... where's the bomb? *Come on!*'

The Japanese remained silent, his eyes fixed on Langford as the lighted end of the cigarette was pressed slowly against his face. Then he began to laugh. 'I will never tell you. Never.'

His hand shaking, Langford ground the cigarette into Tasaki's cheek. He knew what he had to do. He also knew that he was incapable of doing it. Perhaps if he had not been hurt, it might have been different. But tiredness, loss of blood, everything was against him. Then his temper snapped and he drove his fist into Tasaki's face. Blood was pouring from the old man's nose as he lolled forward, sobbing or chuckling, Langford couldn't decide which.

'Please.' Umezu stepped closer. 'Leave me with him. He will tell me.'

'No way. This is going to be my trick.'

'You cannot do it.' Umezu looked down at him. 'I have the strength. The ship must be saved. Shiba has my wife, my children ... I have nothing more to lose. Please?' He bent down and helped Langford to his feet. 'Take him,' he said, turning to Yita. 'Take him out of here.'

Richard Langford had passed the crisis point. Mentally and physically exhausted, he made no protest as Yita helped him up the narrow steps and out into the corridor. But he would go no further and sank down, lying crookedly on the floor. A few minutes later, he wished he had gone a great deal further.

The first scream which echoed up from the pump room tore at Langford's shredded nerves. But it was only the prelude to a vicious symphony of suffering. He tried to shut the noise out but it was impossible. Gradually, the screaming became high-pitched, a remorseless threnody of pain culminating in an ear-splitting crescendo of pure agony far beyond the range of any human voice. Then there was silence and Umezu stood before him, his hands flecked with blood.

'Is he dead?'

'No.' The Captain shook his head. 'The device is located in one of the for'ard inspection chambers. It may be difficult to remove but ... if you can walk?'

Langford slowly pulled himself up, staring at Umezu with an uneasy mixture of admiration and revulsion. 'I'll manage.'

2

Nearly an hour had passed before Langford and Umezu were crouched uncomfortably in the inspection chamber. While the Japanese Captain had rigged up lighting, Yita had put new dressings on Langford's wounds and fetched the hip-flask from Gunning's lifeless body. Several shots of the whisky and four pain-killing tablets gave him some relief but he knew he was working on borrowed time. He felt light-headed and it was only by a supreme effort that he succeeded in co-ordinating his movements.

'They must have used the derrick to lower it down here.' Langford examined the casing carefully, his words echoing around them. When he saw Umezu reaching towards the bomb, he grabbed at his hand. 'Don't touch it.'

'I was going to lift the flap –'

'Wait.' And Langford pressed his ear against the casing. 'It's ticking. How much longer?'

Umezu studied his watch. 'Two hours ... perhaps a little less.'

'You get out of here. I'll lift the flap.'

'If it explodes, it will not matter whether I am here.'

'No, I suppose you're right.' Langford rubbed his hands together and then started to lift the flap. Nothing happened. He stared at the row of buttons and the dark display panel. 'A combination. Press out the numbers and it stops ... assuming you have the right numbers ...'

'Tasaki will give me the combination.'

'Yes, I'm sure he will.'

'There is no need for you to accompany me,' said Umezu.

'No. But I will.'

The climb from the hatchway and the walk back along the deck bit deeply into what little was left of his failing strength. He could have stayed put but he felt a strange compulsion to be there, to see for himself.

'The bomb is safe?' said Yita, coming from the entrance where Langford had ordered her to wait.

'Not yet. You stay here. We need Tasaki's help.'

Yita stared at him, a look of horror spreading across her face. 'Please –'

'Just stay put.' Langford stumbled towards the steps

425

leading down to the pump room but Umezu was already on his way up again.

'We are too late.'

Langford glared at him. 'What do you mean, too late?'

'He is dead.'

'Damn. If you hadn't been so heavy-handed ...'

'See for yourself,' retorted Umezu, backing down to let Langford pass. 'I should have known he would carry a knife.'

Gripping the handrail for support, Langford went slowly into the pump room and stared at Muga Tasaki. 'Jesus wept.' Then he turned away and threw up.

'*Seppuku*,' said the Captain. 'You would call it *harikiri* but that is not ... is not the polite term.'

Langford coughed and spat before steeling himself for another look. 'Polite? Jesus Christ, how could anyone do that to themselves?'

Umezu seemed faintly surprised. 'It is a matter of belief and will-power. I am told that it is relatively painless once the knife has been inserted into the belly. Then it is simply a matter of continuing to cut upwards, a circular motion ... he has done it well. It is as it should be, an honourable death.'

'Honourable?' Langford was shaking with rage as he turned on the Japanese. 'You're a bunch of fucking savages.' He staggered past the Captain, hauling himself up the narrow steps into the corridor where Yita was waiting.

'Richard –'

He ignored her and leaned against the wall as Umezu emerged from the pump room. 'The only thing now ...' He hesitated, screwing up his eyes in a vain attempt to quell the pain. 'Is there any cutting gear on board? An oxy-acetylene torch?'

'Yes. I will bring it.'

'Do that. We can't risk touching the bomb but we can cut the steel strut they've fixed it to.'

'It will take much time,' said Umezu.

'Then get a bloody move on. If we can get the damn thing up, we can tip it over the side.' As the Captain disappeared towards the main storage rooms, Langford stared at Yita. 'You'll have to help me.'

'I will help you, Richard.' She came to him and held his arm. 'But please ... there is something I must tell you ...'

'Not now. Come on, you're going to learn how to work that derrick.'

The *Shimada Maru* lay motionless on the sea, silent, no longer alive. As they walked slowly along the vast main deck, Langford was again reminded of a desert, a wasteland of cold, unyielding steel. Then he heard an eerie squeaking sound and when he turned, saw Umezu pulling a small trolley bearing the oxy-acetylene cutting equipment.

'This isn't going to be easy,' he said, donning the protective visor.

'The heat ...' Umezu shook his head. 'The bomb might react to the heat ...'

'It might. But it's a risk against a certainty.' Using his lighter, he ignited the cutting torch and waited while Umezu worked the valves on the cylinders to correct the mixture. 'Okay, I'll go down now. You lower the torch.'

Working in the confined space was difficult. Langford had no experience of cutting through steel and for a long time, the torch seemed to be having no effect on the strut to which the bomb had been attached. And he was often forced back by the endless showers of sparks which spattered around him, burning his clothes and his flesh.

Langford's hands suffered most, the skin becoming raw and pock-marked with dozens of tiny burns. Twice he had to stop, painfully levering himself out to get some fresh air into his scorched lungs.

'We have less than an hour,' said Umezu, tonelessly.

Wiping the sweat from his face, Langford peered up at the fading stars. 'We're going to need every second.'

'If we can just succeed in getting the bomb away from here ... away from the waste ...'

'Get the derrick ready. We'll need a cable ... and two

427

shackles.' Langford carefully lowered himself down again and resumed his cutting. The temperature inside the chamber was rising fast. He was sweating profusely and even with his burnt, desensitized hands, he was able to feel the increasing warmth of the metal casing.

It was necessary to cut the steel strut in two places so that the bomb could be pulled clear, the remains of the strut still hanging from the curved bar which was an integral part of the device itself.

'Thirty minutes left.'

Umezu's warning echoed inside the chamber as Langford worked. Then the pressure on the torch suddenly faltered.

'Open the valves!'

The words had scarcely left his lips before the cutting torch spouted more flame but the cylinders were almost spent.

Langford prayed, not an orthodox plea to a merciful God but a silent, fiercely blasphemous prayer to any power – good or evil. And as the section of the steel strut finally fell away, the torch sputtered and the hissing blue flame quickly died.

Langford waited on deck while Umezu secured the steel cable around the bomb. Then the derrick was set in motion, the cable slowly tightening as it took the strain. And as the rectangular device was raised above the deck, Langford noted the faint glow on the eastern horizon.

'Swing it over the side,' he bellowed.

'No good.' Umezu stared at him. 'The jib will not reach that far. It is only for lifting the main hatches.'

'Jesus.' Langford glanced around, his brain racing. Then he spotted the trolley for the oxy-acetylene equipment. 'Help me get rid of this lot.'

The cylinders crashed on to the steel deck and rolled away as Langford manoeuvred the trolley and Umezu began to lower the bomb. It was an awkward fit and once they had unshackled the cable, the trolley threatened to tip over. But they managed to hold it steady and started pulling it aft.

'Ten minutes,' hissed Umezu. 'It would be better to put it into one of the launches.' The air was filled with the metallic squeaking of the wheels as they struggled along the deck. 'If it were to explode just below the ship ... I do not know the depth here ...'

'Okay, one of the launches,' snapped Langford.

The *Shimada Maru* carried two motorized launches, one to port, the other to starboard. They hung from davits above the second poop deck and it was Umezu who ran up and loosed the davits so that the starboard launch hung out over the water, level with the main deck. The problem was how to get the bomb into the launch.

The stars had almost gone and the inky darkness was turning grey as the glow in the east brightened inexorably.

Umezu returned to the main deck and using the trolley, the three of them managed to lever the bomb up until it was balanced on the guardrail. Fighting off the throbbing pain in his leg, Langford heaved himself into the launch, knowing instinctively that if the device fell into the boat unchecked, it would go straight through the bottom.

'Okay ... easy does it,' said Langford, steadying himself.

In response to Langford's orders, Umezu and Yita pushed with all their strength and the bomb began to move.

Slowly tipping forward, it began to over balance. Seeing that it was going to slide sideways, Langford called out for them to hold back while he struggled to take the weight.

Pushing Yita aside, Umezu grabbed at the bomb, wrapping his arms around the casing as it slid down into the launch. Then he screamed as the jagged section of cut steel sliced through his hands, crushing them against the guardrail.

The launch gave a shuddering lurch, the falls creaking ominously as they tightened against the blocks in the

429

davits. But the bomb was safely aboard and Langford set about starting the engine.

'Lower away,' he shouted, jerking the pull-start. The engine refused to fire. It took six more attempts before it finally sputtered into life. But the launch was still hanging from the davits.

'Lower the bloody boat!'

'I cannot do it, Langford-*san*.'

Yita's plaintive cry was barely audible above the clamour of the two-stroke engine which Langford was reluctant to leave in case it stalled. But a quick glance on the deck of the *Shimada Maru* made him change his mind.

Umezu was kneeling awkwardly and moaning as he stared in disbelief at his crushed hands.

'I do not know how to lower the boat,' said Yita.

Nor did Langford. Once he had pulled himself over the rail, he stared up at the davits. 'What do we have to do?' he shouted, looking round at Umezu.

The Japanese started to rise, blood dripping on to the deck. He was muttering incoherently and nodded towards the set of levers. There was clearly no way he could do anything now and he stared at Langford with the eyes of an animal unable to communicate its pain.

The creamy-white glow in the east was tinged with a fiery red as Langford reached out and tried to pull the lever. It seemed to be locked solid and knowing that every second was vital, Langford swung round and pushed against the lever with all his weight. He was utterly beyond pain now. There was nothing left but the imminent certainty of sunrise. And death.

It all happened too quickly. The release lever jerked free with a jarring suddenness, pitching Langford forward as the launch dropped away, the falls rattling through the davits in a curious harmony with the sputtering two-stroke engine.

Then the launch splashed heavily into the water and pulling himself to the guardrail, Langford peered down.

The sight of Yita struggling to cast off the falls shocked

430

him into silence. And by the time he found his voice and was able to shout, it was too late. The launch was already moving, running parallel with the ship's side until Yita finally mastered the tiller. Then the boat swerved away from the *Shimada Maru* at a right-angle, heading towards the rising sun.

Langford was dimly aware of the movement behind him but he didn't look round. Then Umezu staggered up to the guardrail, carefully holding his shattered hands against his chest.

'She asked me to tell you,' he said, his voice hoarse and somehow distant. 'She wanted you to know that it was she who gave Tasaki the knife.'

But Langford no longer cared. Nothing seemed to matter any more as he watched the launch speeding away.

Then the sun peeped over the horizon, carpeting the sea with a new, fresh brilliance so that the wake created by the launch sparkled like a huge, jewelled arrow.

His lips moving soundlessly, Langford willed her to jump clear. She still had a chance but even as the thought filtered through his tired brain, he knew with sickening certainty that she wouldn't take it.

The ball of fire mushroomed upwards and for two or three seconds, the rising sun was almost completely blotted out, the smooth sea becoming leaden and grey. The launch had vanished. All that remained was a dark pall of smoke hanging in the air and the last glittering ripples of the wake on the water which Yita had so feared.

Langford could feel the painful stinging behind his eyes as the sharp crack of the explosion echoed back over the sea. Then the tears came, blurring his vision so that he didn't see the destroyer bearing down on the *Shimada Maru*.

3

The Minister leaned back in his chair and surveyed the bundle of papers which Henri Bouscat had placed before him. 'And you are certain everything is here? There are no copies ... missing?'

'Everything is there.' Bouscat closed his briefcase and waited.

'I know what you want,' said the Minister, tapping out his pipe. 'I regret that I can tell you nothing.'

'You could if you chose to.'

The Minister shrugged. 'The American State Department deny that there was ever anything amiss. The authorities in Tokyo and London are similarly reticent.'

'Reticent is not the word I should have used.'

'Sit down, Inspector ' The Minister gestured towards a chair and began to fill his pipe. 'There is a question I must ask you.'

'*M'sieu?*'

'You attended the funeral of Colonel DuCros. Why?'

Bouscat hesitated. 'I was invited to attend ... invited at my own request, if you understand.'

'By whom?'

'DuCros' widow.'

'Yes, that is what I gathered. However, when you called on her yesterday, she –'

'I did not see her because she sent word that my presence was no longer required.' Bouscat's eyes narrowed. 'Why ask me what you already know?'

'Colonel DuCros died of heart failure. And there were complications due to a gastric ulcer, I believe.' The Minister paused. 'Bouscat, I am looking for someone ... a certain kind of person to run Section Nine. I think you could be the man I seek.'

'Me? *Non, M'sieu.* I am a policeman, not a spy. Besides, I would be worried by ... what shall we say? Job security, perhaps?'

'Meaning?'

'Simply that Colonel DuCros' death ...' He shrugged. 'It no longer matters. I thank you for your confidence, *M'sieu le Ministre.*'

'I would ask you to reconsider the offer, Bouscat.'

'There is no point. I wouldn't touch it with a bargepole.'

The Minister grinned. 'At least you are frank. So, *au revoir*, Inspector. I thank you for your help. It will not be forgotten.'

Bouscat rose and they shook hands. 'Indeed it will not, *M'sieu*.' He stared for a moment at the bundle of papers. 'You may destroy all the evidence but one day, someone ... somewhere, will reveal the truth.' He started towards the door, shaking his head. 'Whatever it may be.'

EPILOGUE

1

A thick, dank mist pressed down on the landscape, shrouding the leafless trees which surrounded the house and creating a stillness through which the slightest sound seemed to echo. It was very cold but inside was a relaxing warmth undreamt of by the men who had used their skills to build the house nearly three centuries earlier.

The housekeeper, a rotund woman with a jolly face, greeted Langford with sympathetic caution, taking his coat and speculating about the stick on which he leaned quite heavily.

'I'm Mrs Timothy,' she said, studying him.

'Ah.' Langford nodded and lit a cigarette.

'Everything's just as Mister Maxwell left it. But I expect you'll want to make some changes.'

'No,' replied Langford, detecting the anxiety in her voice as he stared round the panelled hall. 'No, I don't think so. What have you done with – ?'

'I put the American gentleman in the library, sir.' And she pointed towards one of the doors leading off the hall. 'Shall I bring coffee?'

'No, he won't be staying long. I'll attend to him and then you can show me round.'

The library was exactly the kind of room Langford had expected it to be, a gentle, peaceful harmony of leather-bound books, deep winged chairs and a crackling fire. It was absolutely perfect until his senses took in the only jarring note: Meyrick Hewens sprawled in an extra-large chair which Langford somehow knew had been Maxwell's favourite.

'Are you fit again?' drawled Hewens, not bothering to move.

Langford walked slowly across to the fire. 'I'm mending, no thanks to you.'

'You had a rough time. I'm sorry.'

'Are you?' He sat down opposite the American. 'You don't give a damn and you know it.'

'Look, Langford, I'm kinda busy. Maxwell's attorney said —'

'Solicitor. We don't have attorneys in this country.'

'Okay, his solicitor said that I had to come down here and sort out something to do with Maxwell's affairs. I thought everything was tidied up.'

'Oh no, far from it. There's the small question of my position, amongst other things.'

'Your position? You've done very nicely. Being left a place like this …'

'I was referring to my job.'

'You don't have one, Langford. I've arranged for you to receive three months' money.'

'That's very generous.'

'I thought so. Maxwell only kept you on as a favour. Now … well, things are going to be different. I have planned certain changes.'

'Things are certainly going to be different. You imagined that you'd got away with it, didn't you?'

Hewens hesitated. 'Okay, between these four walls … yes. In the event, things didn't work out too bad. I've no complaints about the way you handled your end of it.'

'You crawling little bastard.'

'Knock it off, Langford. Just remember that I can still make a lot of trouble for you.'

'Not half as much as I could make for you. I was set up — but I discovered that fairly early on. You, Gunning and Shiba, all playing at not rocking the boat. It stinks. Shiba

435

should have hanged along with the others ... what he did ...'

'Okay, I know you had it rough ... '

'Not half as rough as those poor devils at Ba Wan. But then, you know all about that too, don't you?'

The room was filled with a sudden, heavy silence. Then the mahogany bracket clock over the fireplace struck the quarter in clear, silvery chimes.

'Just what are you getting at?' said Hewens, watching him carefully.

'You were at Ba Wan,' said Langford, tossing his cigarette butt into the fire. 'I feel sorry for you in many ways. Having your balls chopped off with a penknife can't be much fun.'

Hewens jumped up, the colour slowly draining from his face. 'How did you find out?'

'I talked to one of the men who did it. He didn't tell me but he wrote it down. It was ... it was a sort of confession, I suppose.' Langford lit another cigarette, staring blankly as the smoke was drawn into the fire. 'When I saw the photographs –'

'I wasn't in any of those pictures. Gunning told Shiba that I wasn't in them.'

'You weren't ... at least, not in the ones I gave to Gunning. But I kept three for myself.' He took a manilla envelope from his inside pocket. 'Here, these are copies. They're not very good because the originals were old and got a bit wet. But they're good enough. You haven't changed all that much. Neither had the others.'

Hewens studied the pictures, his hands trembling. 'Okay, so I was there. What difference does it make?'

'Difficult to know. From what Heyashi told me, probably about two hundred and sixty lives at a conservative estimate, not to mention a few others who've died rather more recently.'

'Jesus Christ, you can't blame me for what the Japs did.'

'I don't,' replied Langford, quietly. 'But I do blame you for betraying Captain Becker's escape plan ... and for vouching for Shiba's good behaviour when you finally made contact with the advancing Allies. What was it worth, a bag of un-cut rubies then and a percentage of the Shimada profits later?'

'You don't know ...' Hewens slowly sank back into the chair, his face the colour of moist chalk. 'You can't imagine what it was like ... what they did to us ... the things ...'

'That's where you're wrong. And I don't need to use my imagination, not now.'

There was a long silence before Hewens nodded. 'Okay, name your price.'

'Not money ... not in the way you mean. I've arranged for Maxwell's solicitor to call at the office in the morning. He'll be acting for me. All you have to do is sign the papers he's drawn up. It's just a simple transfer of ownership. You're going to give me the firm you bought from James Maxwell.'

'What? You must be out of your mind ...'

'I was never more sane, Hewens. The originals of those pictures are in a bank, together with Heyashi's statement and a few words of my own. But as I said, I feel sorry for you in some ways, so you can keep your New York business. Just forget London because I'm taking over.'

'You? You couldn't run it. You're just a two-bit hustler, Langford.'

'Maybe. But I don't intend running it. In fact, I don't intend even working any more.'

'What if I refuse?'

'I'll destroy you. The story would be sold to a newspaper ... probably in Europe. Then ... well, you can imagine what would happen.'

Hewens stood up. 'What guarantee do I have?'

'None. You'll have to sweat. Now get out before I change my mind.'

'My husband looks after the gardens,' explained Mrs Timothy as they stood on the terrace. 'When the fog clears, you can see the Downs ... and the village, of course. It's lovely in summer, sir. Really lovely. I do hope you'll be happy here.'

'I'm sure I will,' said Langford. 'If you and your husband can stay on to look after – ' The words died on his lips as the air was filled with a strange, discordant ringing which sent a cold shiver down his spine. 'What the hell's that?'

'Why, it's the church bell, sir,' replied the housekeeper. 'There's a funeral this morning.'

Langford shivered as the sombre knell echoed through the mist and suddenly Yita was there beside him in the *sala*, the rain drumming on the gaudy tiles and the throbbing rhythm of the great bell of the *Wat* Keo hammering inside his head ...

'Are you all right, sir?'

Langford spun round and stared at the woman. 'That bell, it's ...' But his voice was choked into silence.

'It's cracked, sir,' said Mrs Timothy, her round face puckered by a deep frown. 'The Vicar's trying to raise money for a new one but – '

'How much do they need?'

'I'm not sure, sir. I think it's about five hundred pounds.'

'Telephone the Vicar and tell him he can have it.' Then Langford limped slowly back into the house, slamming the library door behind him.

THE CHINESE ASSASSIN

Anthony Grey

On the night of 12 September 1971, a Trident airliner flying secretly towards Russia from China crashed in flames in Mongolia. Nine bodies charred beyond recognition were later found in the wreckage. Nearly a year passed before China's leaders announced that Lin Piao, Mao Tse-tung's Defence Minister and chosen successor, had died in the crash while fleeing to the Soviet Union after failing to assassinate Mao and seize power. The statement only served to deepen the intrigue surrounding perhaps the greatest political mystery of modern times.

Suddenly, five years later, a chinese defector named Yang surfaces in London to make a sensational claim – that he survived the mysterious Mongolian air crash. Moreover, the defector presents dramatic new evidence that Lin Piao was murdered – and that the same radical faction is now planning to assassinate Mao. An English sinologist, Richard Scholefield, is drawn into the web of intrigue as the intelligence services of China, the Soviet Union and the United States become locked in a lethal struggle for the possession of this dangerous defector.

Page-turning Suspense from
CHARTER BOOKS

CHARTER MYSTERIES

Stunning Thrillers You
Won't Want to Miss

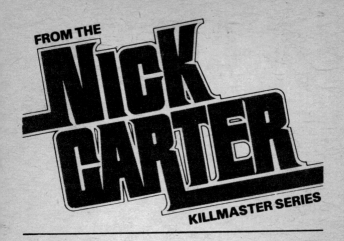

FROM THE NICK CARTER

KILLMASTER SERIES

☐ **TEMPLE OF FEAR**	80215-X	$1.75
☐ **THE NICHOVEV PLOT**	57435-1	$1.75
☐ **TIME CLOCK OF DEATH**	81025-X	$1.75
☐ **UNDER THE WALL**	84499-6	$1.75
☐ **THE PEMEX CHART**	65858-X	$1.95
☐ **SIGN OF THE PRAYER SHAWL**	76355-3	$1.75
☐ **THUNDERSTRUCK IN SYRIA**	80860-3	$1.95
☐ **THE MAN WHO SOLD DEATH**	51921-0	$1.75
☐ **THE SUICIDE SEAT**	79077-1	$2.25
☐ **SAFARI OF SPIES**	75330-2	$1.95
☐ **TURKISH BLOODBATH**	82726-8	$2.25
☐ **WAR FROM THE CLOUDS**	87192-5	$2.25
☐ **THE JUDAS SPY**	41295-5	$1.75

 ACE CHARTER BOOKS
P.O. Box 400, Kirkwood, N.Y. 13795

N-01

Please send me the titles checked above. I enclose _____.
Include 75¢ for postage and handling if one book is ordered; 50¢ per book for two to five. If six or more are ordered, postage is free. California, Illinois, New York and Tennessee residents please add sales tax.

NAME_____

ADDRESS_____

CITY_____STATE_____ZIP_____

HEALTH AND BEAUTY—ADVICE FROM THE EXPERTS